TOXIC
Creek

BY

KC KEAN

Toxic Creek

The Allstars Series #1

Copyright © 2021 KC Kean

This book is licensed for your personal enjoyment only. This book may not be re-sold or given away to other people. If you would like to share this book with another person, please purchase an additional copy for each recipient. If you're reading this book and did not purchase it, or it wasn't purchased for your use only, then please return to your favourite book retailer and purchase your own copy. Thank you for respecting the hard work of this author.

All rights reserved.

This is a work of fiction. Names, characters, places, brands, media, and incidents are either the product of the authors imagination or are used fictitiously. The author acknowledges the trademark status and trademark owners of various products referred to in this work of fiction, which have been used without permission. The publication/use of these trademarks is not authorised, associated with, or sponsored by the trademark owners.

Cover Designer: Bellaluna Designs

Content Editor: Valerie Victoria

Proofreader: Bookish Dreams Editing

Toxic Creek/KC Kean – 2nd ed.

ISBN-13 -

To Nan,

My best friend.

Thank you for supporting me without actually having a clue what's going on.

Thank you for letting me overhaul your house with signed paperbacks while providing the perfect cup of tea to get me through it.

Here's to eventually being able to people watch with a coffee again soon. Maybe even in a foreign country!

It's gonna be boot-iful

One thing I've learned in Knight's Creek, is that you don't question shit the adults say because you never get the truth. There's always some form of ulterior motive in play.
- Eden Grady, Toxic Creek

KC KEAN

PROLOGUE

"No!" she screams down the phone, the sound of her fist slamming against a nearby surface following soon after. "You fucking listen to me…"

"I'm done listening to you. I've had to spend all my life listening to the shit that comes out of your mouth. You gave your word that we would be out from under your thumb if we split up and the two of us never looked back, yet you somehow still seem to be dictating my life. No more. Not when it comes to Eden."

The familiar fear that trickles through my veins ignites as she cackles, the sound vibrating around me, but she comes first. Eden will always come first.

"Carl, you should have gone with option A when we were kids."

"Option A was a direct ticket to hell. I will always be

thankful I passed."

Pulling up outside of our family home, I hold in my sigh, knowing she'll hear it and it'll only add to her satisfaction.

"You do as I say, Carl, or I'll have no choice but to force your hand."

"I'm not repeating myself. The whole agreement to begin with was so we kept them safe."

"Hmm, well it's not enough for me anymore, and I'm bored of talking about it. So, what'll it be—Eden or your life?"

"My life is nothing without her."

Ending the call, I know she's never full of meaningless threats, but she's going too far and I won't stand by and let her destroy more lives.

Making my way inside the house, I try to plaster on my normal smile, but one glance from Jennifer and she sees right through me, while Eden doesn't.

Glancing up at me, her blonde hair pulled back from her face as she paints her nails on the dining table, she offers me her most perfect smile. My feet move towards hers of their own accord, and I'm leaning down to kiss her forehead before I even realize what I'm doing.

"I love you, honey," I whisper, and she sighs.

"You're being all cheesy again, Dad. But I love you too. I'll love you even more if you tell Mom we should have tacos for dinner so we can get started on the new game pass that was released today."

She knows I'm going to agree with her. I don't think there is ever a time I don't, if I'm honest. She's my girl, my world. And if that costs me my life, then so be it. She's worth it. She will *always* be worth it.

KC KEAN

ONE
Eden

The music blasts through the speakers as sweat drips down my body. My hips sway in time with Lou-Lou's as she grinds behind me, and we get lost to the rhythm. "Girl Like Me" by the Black Eyed Peas and Shakira plays as the cheap, green strobe lighting colors the room in lines and dots, which is filled to the brim with bodies.

If there is one thing I love to do, it's dancing, especially at grungy parties across the river.

Living on the west side of White River means everyone is so stuck up their own fucking asses, there ends up being no room to breathe. Even their parties are pretentious as shit. The east side might not have the money, but they sure have the resources for a good time.

The east side offers much more fun. Hotter guys with bigger dicks. The girls like to wear skimpier outfits with more skin on display, and that's exactly what I need in the midsummer heat in Arizona.

It might be close to midnight, but the temperature doesn't feel like it's eased off at all since lunch. Still hovering above ninety degrees even now.

So here I am, surrounded by drugs and alcohol, searching for a good time. Lou-Lou and I chilled for most of the day, relaxing by my pool on the west side, soaking up the sun, and now I was almost desperate to get sweaty for completely different reasons.

"Eden. Shots," Lou-Lou hollers in my ear, and I nod in agreement.

Slipping my hand in hers, I let her pull me towards the kitchen. The cheap disco lights flashing around the small room blur my vision. The kitchen is much quieter as we squeeze through the bodies, heading straight for the back door.

No air conditioning inside is the main downfall of these parties, especially when stepping outside into the backyard offers no comfort either. Releasing Lou-Lou's hand, I swipe my blonde, wavy hair away from my face and wipe the sweat down my short, black, ribbed dress.

Straightening the spaghetti straps at my shoulder, I spot an empty bench near the makeshift drink table and quickly grab Lou-Lou's hand again. My feet are killing me in these five-inch studded heels, and I need a quick break before we dance again.

Dropping down onto the seat, Lou-Lou laughs at nothing in her tipsy state. "Girl, I'll get the shots."

Her blonde hair is already up in a messy bun, a few loose tendrils framing her face. Her freckles are on full display as she flutters her lashes at me.

"And a water," I call back, and she waves over her shoulder in acknowledgment, her pink dress rising as she does.

Relaxing back in my seat, I glance around the yard. The space is so small in comparison to my neighborhood. Apart from a tattered wooden fence lining the perimeter and dried out grass beneath our feet, there is very little else out here. A few benches and the all-important drinks table, and the rest of the space is filled with bodies.

I can't remember whose party this is, but I'm having a good time and that's what matters.

I recognize a few faces from the parties I've been to before, a few offering a smile in greeting, but my mind is focused on the gazes caressing my skin.

I wasn't joking when I said they have better dick over here, and that's the main goal of the evening. But I'd rather not sample the same meat twice, and the guys I can see from here would mean a repeat.

Live. Love. Laugh. That's my mantra. Everything happens for a reason is my other. And the two go hand in hand with my life.

Hearing Lou-Lou cackle by the drinks table, I turn my gaze

in her direction. She lives two doors down from here and is always willing to pacify the spoiled rich kid.

I don't do close friends. I function better in groups, so I can disappear and be a loner whenever my heart desires. But if I did, Lou-Lou Carter would be close to best friend status.

"Hey, Eden." I hear murmuring coming from behind me, and I sigh, knowing the voice instantly.

"No repeats, Bobby. Remember?" I state, not even bothering to turn around and face him. I feel the bench shake as he pats the seat back and swiftly moves along.

Admittedly, he was the first piece of east side cock I'd tasted and has since had me addicted to their specialty. But even knowing the rules, he still approaches me every time.

"Girl, you're never getting rid of that one," Lou-Lou says with a smirk, nodding in the direction I assume Bobby went. "Drink up so we can get our dance on again," she squeals as she hands me my shot and bottle of water. Listening to her count us down, I lift the shot glass to my lips, letting the liquor burn down my throat.

Fuck.

Their parties may consist of the sweaty grinding I love so much, but their quality of tequila is questionable.

The backyard is thrumming, just as it was inside, the same music pumping through the wireless speakers, but there is a little more space out here compared to inside.

Perfect.

Swiping the back of my hand across my mouth, I'm pulled to my feet as Lou-Lou encourages us to join them, and I can't bring myself to say no, even if my feet are screaming for a longer break.

The song switches to "God is a Woman" by Ariana Grande, and our hands instantly lift above our heads as we slip between the bodies, taking the center spot of the makeshift dance space. This song always hits me differently, and my body moves of its own accord.

Lost in the music, the thought of the summer ending plays on my mind. Senior year. I'm so ready for it. Turning eighteen in six weeks, my mom is already planning the birthday party of her life, and my dad already gifted me my brand-new matte black Mercedes G-Wagon.

I wear designer clothes on the daily, but it doesn't excite me. Not like my G-Wagon does. The sense of freedom and all its high-tech fittings gives me tingles.

I think this is the longest we have ever stayed in one spot. We move *all* the time. Hopping from state to state, covering every inch of the US. I wish I could say it was because I was an army brat or something, but I have no idea why. By the time we have been somewhere for two years, we're suddenly packing up and moving again.

I'm not saying I now have issues forming a connection with people, but I'm not *not* saying that either. So I hold everyone at a distance, taking the pleasure I want from them before we move along.

I do, however, love how there is never any expectation from me. I have parents loving me for me. Even if that means I'm a quirky-ass bitch, who loves curling up to watch an old movie one moment, challenging my dad to a game-a-thon on the Xbox, or grinding to the top hits the next.

A stroke of a palm across my ass stalls my movement. Fingers splay out across the material of my dress as they make their way around to my stomach, pulling my back into a hard chest.

Glancing over my shoulder, I come face-to-face with a guy I haven't seen before.

Excellent.

He's taller than my five-foot-eight height, plus heels. The grin on his lips as he looks down at my chest doesn't leave me filled with desire, but he looks pretty enough to find ecstasy with. In a pair of shorts and a loose dark tee, he looks completely in his element.

Reaching my hand above my head, I run my fingers through his hair as I continue to dance, letting him grind up against me. The second I feel his length pressed up against my ass, I know where this is heading.

Exactly where I want it to.

"I haven't seen you around here before," he murmurs in my ear, his husky voice sexier than I expected, and I shiver uncontrollably.

"Clearly, you weren't looking hard enough," I tease, tilting my head back to look at him. As if on cue, his hand grips my waist. Guys love feeling big and strong, and looking back at them like this gives the illusion, at least.

"What's your name, sweet cheeks?" he drawls, and I bite my lip.

"Does it really matter?" I ask, internally cringing at his attempt at a nickname, hoping he catches my drift, and in response, his lips trail down my neck.

"Have a good night, girl. Call me if you need me," Lou-Lou interrupts, squeezing my arm as I tilt my gaze to offer her a wink. This is usual practice for us.

Dance. Drink. Fuck.

"Want to take this somewhere a little more private?"

"Yes," I breathe out in response as my little black clutch vibrates under my arm, the strap over my shoulder holding it in place. Fuck. Not now. Letting the hot guy lace his fingers with mine, I follow his lead inside the house. He guides me through the crowd of bodies as I ignore the continued vibrations from my purse.

As we take the stairs, my phone stops and starts vibrating again for the third time, and I sigh. Apparently, somebody wants my attention, and they better believe they're going to get a whole lot of fucking snark when I answer.

Extracting my fingers from his, I pause mid step on the stairs, ignoring everyone trying to get past.

Twirling my phone in my hand, *Mom* flashes across the screen.

Mom? Why would she be calling right now? She never calls when I'm out. Not unless something bad has happened, or worse, we have to move again.

My thumb hits the green answer button automatically, and I lift the phone to my ear.

"Hey, Mom, is everything—"

I can tell she is frantically screaming down the phone, but the music around me is drowning out every word. My gut clenches, the panic in her voice instantly setting me on edge.

Racing back down the stairs, attempting two steps at a time in these damn heels, I hear the hot guy trying to get my attention, but I'm too busy trying to get out the front door to offer him a response.

"Mom? Mom!" I call out over the music, pushing through the crowd blocking my exit. As soon as I pass one person, there's suddenly another three in the way.

Finally stepping out of the front door, I hear my mom respond.

"Eden, can you hear me? Eden!"

Whirling around in the front yard, there are a few stragglers out here, but I pay them no mind as I try to focus on my mom's voice.

"Eden, I need you to come home. As quickly as you can."

"Mom, calm down. Talk to me. Tell me what's going on," I

plead, trying to keep the fear from my own voice as I do my best to calm her frantic shouts.

"Eden, there's no time," she sobs, my heart breaking at the sound of hers doing the same. "He's gone, Eden. Gone. And I need you to get here quickly. Please, Eden. Please," she repeats, and my blood runs cold.

Frozen in place, there is only one man, one *he*, in my life. My voice is barely above a whisper as I ask the one question I know the answer to but never want to hear.

"Who's gone, Mom?"

"Dad," she wails, and I can almost feel her drop to her knees in despair as I stumble. "Your dad is gone. He's gone, and I'm going to lose you too."

My phone slips from my hand, and I watch as it hits the concrete path, the screen shattering into a dozen pieces, just like my heart.

I try to process her words, but the pain ricocheting through my bones tells me all I need to know.

No way. It can't be true. My dad was sitting in his little man cave before I left, tapping away on his Xbox controller like he always does. It's impossible to die from that.

Right?

KC KEAN

TWO
Eden

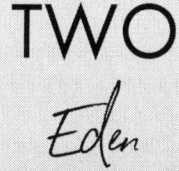

Dead.

My father, the only man in my life, my best friend, is dead.

I feel broken beyond repair, and the one person who might have been able to piece me back together again is the reason for the pain.

I stood at the wake yesterday and cried over my dad lying peacefully before me in his solid oak casket. He was so cold to the touch, the crow's feet wrinkles around his eyes from constantly laughing were suddenly gone, and I was heartbroken. The room was filled with white and blue flowers, his favorite colors, and I regret not taking one for myself.

I was too focused on my dad to even register who else was

in attendance, except for my mom. Going through the motions as people approached me repeatedly, offering their condolences.

I want answers, but as much as my mom manages to meet my gaze, she can't seem to find her tongue. There is something going on here, something I'm clearly not clued in on, and it's driving me crazy.

On Saturday night, I arrived home in an Uber to find paramedics and police cars lining the street outside our house. My dad was pronounced dead on arrival. A bullet hole between his eyes, apparently, but there are no fucking suspects.

None.

It's bullshit. I know it, and my mom knows it too. I can see it in the strain in her eyes when she has to tell her lie, wringing her hands in front of her as she fumbles to cover up this mess.

They'd already carted my father's lifeless body away before I arrived, and my mom hadn't called until the fucking forensics team had come and gone too. In my disheveled state, I was questioned by some random officers about whether I knew of any criminal activity my father could be a part of.

Even in my disoriented condition, I laughed in their face. Never. My dad is...*was* the most wholesome guy that ever existed. He loved me, my mother, and was the perfect citizen. Yet he wound up dead.

The authorities didn't seem to care that we were numb with grief, shaken to the core with pain. All they wanted were answers to questions I didn't understand.

My mom was a shell of her usual self, sleeping beside me the past three nights since our lives crumbled around us. Refusing to let me out of her sight for even a moment. I don't know if she's waiting for me to break down, but my eyes burn from the constant tears, and I don't know what else she's watching for.

And if one more fucking person tells me, "God only takes the good ones," I won't be liable for my actions. There is no plausible reason for my dad to have been taken away from me. Not now, not ever. Especially not like this. And definitely not because of an open and closed case with no conviction.

No one will give me a straight answer as to why they can do that, and there's a thought at the back of my mind telling me there is something bigger at play here, even involving the local sheriff.

The pastor clears his throat, pulling me from my thoughts, and I stroke a hand down the front of my black pencil skirt. I'm dressed head to toe in black, and I feel like the color has seeped into my heart and soul, complete numbness coating every inch of my body.

The heat is unbearable, sweat dripping down my back as I focus on the grass beneath my feet. Silent cries echo around me as the pastor mutters his shit.

Standing around my father's grave, my chest squeezes tight as my mother steps from my side and drops her red rose into the hole. A fucking hole. I watch as she sobs, cupping a hand over her mouth, and blindly walks back to me.

I feel everyone's eyes trail to me, waiting for me to do the same. Did any of these people even know Carl Grady? Sure, they were our neighbors, but we kept to ourselves, the constant moving from state to state making it inconvenient to make friends.

A part of me appreciates the respect they're here to offer, but deep down, I want to scream at them all to fuck off.

Squeezing the stem of my white rose tightly in my fist, I take slow, steady steps to where my father now lies. Thankful for the blacked-out glasses covering my eyes, I let the tears track down my face.

My hand hovers over the gaping hole in the ground, but I can't bring myself to release my hold on the flower. The second I drop it makes his death even more real.

If I release my grip and drop the rose, it will take a piece of my soul with it, and half of my heart already lies with my dad.

Eden Grady, you are my badass, number one girl. We survive through everything. No matter what happens in life, just know I love you with every inch of my heart. Everything happens for a reason. You were meant to be my daughter because we can weather any storm together.

My father's classic words replay through my mind. Whenever I had a difficult time with life, like having to move again or feeling the harsh reality of bitchy girls as a kid, he would say those words to me. Trying to take strength from them, I watch as my white rose falls beside my mom's red rose.

I'm done. This is too much.

I smell my mom's perfume as she pulls me into her side, wrapping her arms around me tightly. I have no idea how long we stand there, consoling each other and finally letting the weight of the whole situation wash over us.

I don't know how we will ever get past this. I have so many unanswered questions about what happened that night, questions my mom has yet to answer.

But one thing I do know for sure is I'm ready to move on from this town. I've never said that before, always wanting to settle down in every town. Just not this one. I don't want to see my dad leaning against my door as he tells me goodnight, and I don't want to step anywhere near his man cave. Ever.

It's time for us to go. I just need to convince my mom. I'm sure it won't take much. We're used to it.

I'm so ready for these people to get the fuck out of our house.

I don't even understand why my mom felt it was necessary for us to hold a reception after the service. Admittedly, I'd never been to a funeral before, so I didn't know the actual process. Still, my skin was crawling with anxiety the longer we sat here thanking people for attending.

Little old Judith from across the street keeps randomly patting my cheek and reciting the Bible to me, and as sweet as she is, it feels like my cheeks are close to bruising and it's getting on my fucking nerves.

Squished between her and the arm of the sofa, sitting in front of the window in the living room, my gaze keeps flitting around the room. Watching to see if any of these fuckers act suspiciously because one of these people could have pulled the trigger and murdered my dad.

My mother is perched on the other sofa across from me, tapping her nails on the champagne glass in her hand nervously. It's no celebration, but I think she needs the alcohol to take the edge off. She looks as lost as I feel, but I've never felt so distant from her. My dad was clearly the glue holding us all together.

I want everyone to leave so my underage ass can join her. I need to get lost too. Forget. And I know a little glass of bubbles or two will help me find what I'm looking for. It can be our bonding session.

My phone vibrates in my purse on my lap, but I ignore it. The day after my phone shattered from my hands, my mom replaced it, and I already regret it. I don't want the outside world to reach me right now.

I've had messages from half my damn school offering their condolences, and Lou-Lou has been blowing my phone up ever since she got wind of the news. But it's better just to cut ties now. Tomorrow, I'm going to work on convincing my mom to leave.

I spy the door to my dad's man cave through the open living

room door, and my breath falters as beads of sweat gather on my brow. Clenching my hands tightly in my lap, I feel my acrylic nails biting into my skin, but I don't care.

If anything, the pain seems to calm me.

"Eden, you should eat," my mom murmurs as she crosses the room to me, but I can't pretend to have an appetite right now. She looks on edge, paranoid.

"I'm fine, Mom. I'll eat when everyone has left."

She sighs as she stands before me, fidgeting with her wedding band as she glances out the window, struggling to know what to say to me. I watch her eyes well with tears, and she rapidly tries to blink them away. We're becoming masters at it, tamping down our feelings and emotions. Not on purpose. We just don't know how to fucking handle the vulnerability.

I'm scared I'm going to turn into some cold-hearted ice queen, completely numb to the core, but I can't control it. It seems my instinctive reaction is to feel every inch of my emotions without showing them to the world, just like my mom.

It's a trait my dad could never really get us to shake, no matter how much we knew he loved us.

Suddenly, her jaw falls open, and her spine goes stiff as she gapes at something out of the window. Trying to stand to see what exactly has her reacting like that, I'm surprised when she clamps her hand down on my shoulder and forces me to stay exactly where I am.

"No. Oh, hell no. She promised not today," she growls out,

her fists clenching as her face heats with anger, and I frown in confusion.

"Mom, what's—"

Her eyes fly down to meet my gaze, her lips in a thin line. "Do not move from this spot. I mean it, Eden. Not an inch." She gives me a pointed look before flying out of the living room.

My nose crinkles as I try to process what she just said. *She promised not today.* Who promised? And what exactly was agreed? Fuck this. I'm not a five-year-old. I deserve answers.

Judith says nothing as I rise from the sofa, likely having heard my mom's order but not stopping me from going against it.

Snooping through the window, I can see my mom standing toe-to-toe with some dark-haired woman. My mom's blonde hair falls loose from the tight bun she had wrapped it in earlier. She looks like she's half crying, half growling, while this woman stands there all cool and collected, and I can tell from here she doesn't want to pay her respects.

No. Fuck this. Nobody pulls such a reaction from my mother while acting unaffected by it. Who is this woman?

Nobody pays me any attention as I rush through the living room and head for the front door. They're the only people out here, likely because it's so hot and the air conditioning is on inside. Not that I would care, but whatever is going on right now isn't for everyone to see.

"What's going on?" I shout, marching down the stone steps

from our porch, and my mom whirls around to give me her solid death glare.

I don't know why she has to act so surprised. Me not listening to her is nothing new.

"Go back inside, Eden."

I look past her to the dark-haired woman, who now stands with her hands crossed firmly over her chest and a grin on her face as she takes me in. Running her tongue over her teeth, she turns her gaze back to my mom.

She is stunning, but there is a cruel glint in her eyes. Wealth seeps from her pores as she stands tall in her flared black trousers and black, see-through blouse. I've definitely never seen this woman before.

"You have forty-eight hours to get her there of her own free will, or I take matters into my own hands." Spinning on her heel, the mystery woman climbs into the backseat of a nearby SUV with blacked-out windows.

"Mom?" I ask, moving slowly towards her as she stares at the SUV until it can no longer be seen, turning the corner at the end of the road. "Who was that?"

Standing beside her, I place my hand on her shoulder, and I instantly feel her shaking beneath my touch. A mixture of fear and anger swirls in her eyes before she finally meets my gaze.

"Please, Eden. Let's just get through today. Take this time together to grieve, and I will explain everything else tomorrow."

"I don't understand what there is to explain," I murmur

back, raking my fingers through my hair.

"Tomorrow, Eden. Please give me that," she whispers, tears streaming down her face as she pulls me in close.

Seeing how much pain this is causing her on top of today, I reluctantly drop the issue. She's definitely got some explaining to do, but I can't add any more pressure right now. Nothing can turn our world anymore upside down than it already is, so whatever it is can wait.

TOXIC CREEK

THREE
Eden

My face scrunches in disgust as the sun glares through my bedroom window, letting me know it's time to wake up, but I'm just not feeling it.

Throwing my arm over my face to block the sun from my eyes, I peek at my alarm clock to see it's a little after eight a.m., and I groan. It was five in the morning before I actually managed to fall asleep, the weight of yesterday lying heavy on my heart as I stared up at my ceiling. No amount of relaxing music or effort pushed me into a deep sleep.

As much as I want to lie here and wallow in my misery, yesterday, my mom said she would explain what was going on with that woman, and my curiosity outweighs my ability to fall back asleep.

It seems like insomnia has made me its bitch.

I had hoped the half a bottle of champagne I drank last night would have helped, but that was a waste of time too. Now I just have a damn headache.

Redoing my messy bun as I swing my legs over the side of the bed, I sigh. My fingers feel raw since I pulled off my acrylic nails last night in my tipsy state. I'm already not feeling the day, but I reluctantly head for a shower.

Feeling a little fresher but still groggy, I moisturize my skin with my favorite coconut body butter before a knock sounds at my door.

"It's open," I call out as I open my closet to find it empty.

What the fuck?

"Morning," my mom murmurs from the door, and I turn quickly to see guilt written all over her face before she tips her head down. She looks small in her yoga pants and loose-fitted tee. Swiping a hand through her hair, she has no makeup on, and the bags under her eyes makes it look like she hasn't slept.

"Mom, where are all my clothes?" I ask, gripping my towel tighter around my chest.

Clearing her throat, she points to the cushioned bench at my vanity, where my favorite black oversized lounge set is folded up neatly with underwear to go with it.

"Where are the rest of my clothes?" I ask again, my heart pounding in my chest as I scramble to understand what the hell is going on. My mom hasn't pulled an outfit out for me since I was ten years old.

"Get dressed, Eden. We don't have much time, and I'll explain what I can, okay?" Her voice is barely a croak as she forces herself to meet my gaze. The pain in her eyes causes me to hold my tongue.

I want to bitch her out and demand answers right now, but I simply nod. "I'll be two minutes."

Clicking the door shut behind her, I rush to put my outfit on, but I can't unsee my empty closet. Does this mean we're leaving? I fucking hope so.

Glancing around the room, I notice all my photos have been taken down, and my memory board has gone. All that really remains is the bare bones of the room with the bulky furniture.

Stepping into my white sneakers, which my mom also placed by my clothes, I make my way downstairs. My heart jolts as I expect to hear my father singing in the kitchen, but all I'm met with is silence. Not a hint of his morning rendition of indie rock music as he cooks breakfast.

The house is a perfect frame for a home, with a cozy lounge, open kitchen, three bedrooms, two and a half baths, and a pool out in the backyard. But I learned never to get attached to the homes we live in. I just miss the memories we make in each place. Here will only be the same. Except it's the last place I'll have ever seen my dad alive.

My chest aches with the fresh wave of loss. Clearing my throat, I blink back the tears. Finding the front door wide open, I step outside to see my mom sitting in my dad's favorite spot on the wrap-around porch, looking up at the clear sky.

"What's going on, Mom? Are we leaving?" I ask, sitting on the cushioned wicker chair beside her, looking around for all the luggage, or at least some sign that things are packed, but I don't see anything.

"Yes and no," she mumbles, and as much as I love the woman, her cryptic and short answers are starting to get on my nerves.

"Mom—"

"There is a lot you do not know, Eden." She almost snickers to herself, her eyes squeezing shut before she meets my gaze. "More than I can say if I want us to live."

What?

Before I can ask what she means, she cuts me off with a shake of her head. "I need you to do as I say, Eden. You will have questions, I'm sure, but ultimately, you will have to do it anyway. We both will."

Rubbing my arms, I continue to stare at her nervously, already feeling this heading in a bad direction.

"That depends on what it is you expect me to do," I answer honestly, releasing a shaky breath. I watch her eyes get more and more bloodshot as she holds back tears.

She looks even worse than I do, which makes sense if she managed to invade my room and clear all my clothes while I was sleeping, resulting in little to no sleep for herself.

Rubbing her hands down her yoga pants, she looks at me with a new sense of resolution in her eyes.

"You are going to go to Knight's Creek. Today." My head tilts as I stare at her and take in her words.

"Wait, we're going to Knight's Creek, as in where you and Dad grew up?" I ask, remembering the town pop up a few times when they decided to take a trip down memory lane.

"Yes, but, uhh, not we...*you*." Guilt is scrawled across her face, in the tightness of her eyes and her lips thinning.

My back stiffens as I sit upright in my chair, my fingers digging into the armrests as I glare at her. "What the fuck does that mean?"

"Eden," she snaps, used to me swearing, but not actually at her, but I don't apologize.

"What is with all this mysterious shit? You need to explain why you think I'm going to go to your childhood town without you. Why aren't you coming with me? Where am I supposed to stay? And why? Just why?" I ramble, throwing every question at her as it comes to mind, my brain overloading.

Is she purposely trying to scar my heart and soul?

Swiping the tears from her cheek, she looks at me with pleading eyes. "I can't tell you much because that'll only make things worse or put you at risk," she whimpers.

Unable to contain the anger building inside of me, I slam my fist down on the armrest, but before I can shout any protest, she continues.

"You were right, Eden. Your father's death wasn't an accident, but people in high places with a lot of power can have a case closed in an instant if they see fit," she offers, still just as cryptic. My palms begin to sweat, and my ears ring with white noise as I let her words settle in.

"Carry on," I whisper, trying to control my breathing as pain sears through my body, scrambling to understand who would want to hurt my dad.

"We left Knight's Creek on an understanding, but we should have known it would never have been that easy. So when we later learned the bigger picture, we knew there was no turning back, and that's why we continued to move around the country."

My eyes widen as I listen to another truth fall from her lips so casually, and it hurts to know I've been kept in the dark. Unable to form any kind of response, I just continue to watch her, waiting for her to drip feed me more vital information.

"We knew we had overstayed here, but we had finally found somewhere that we all settled. Your father and I agreed we would let you finish your senior year in the same place, and we would move when it came time for college." Brushing her loose blonde hair back off her face, I can see the regret in her grey eyes at thinking they could offer me that luxury. "They found us on Saturday night, Eden. And now we do as they say, or we face the same fate as him."

Him being my father, I assume as I stare out at the street, in utter shock at the whole fucked-up situation.

Swiping a hand down my face, I try to calm my racing heart, but it's no use.

"So, why do I have to go to Knight's Creek?"

Standing, she braces her hands on the wooden railing that surrounds the porch. With a heavy sigh, she looks out across the garden. "Because it's what they want, and they *always* get what they want. As much as I don't want to give into them, I also want to see you alive and breathing, Eden. They've already taken enough from us, and I refuse to let them take anymore."

Frowning at her back, I can't stop my voice from rising. "You expect me to just give into them? To live in a town where I *know* someone played a part in killing my dad? Are you crazy? Let's go, let's run again."

"We have no other option, Eden. They're sitting in the SUV parked across the street, waiting for you to climb into your G-Wagon, or to force you into their vehicle if you don't. But the latter option comes with a bullet between my eyes too." Her voice cracks, and my heart all but stops as I frantically search the road, spotting the SUV just like she said.

Bolting from my seat, my mom grabs my arm before I can step off the porch. "Let go, Mom. I'm going to show these assholes they can't just go around doing as they please," I growl out, but her grip on me only tightens.

"Eden, we can't act rashly. Did you forget the part where I said they killed your father and had the case closed before it even began?" she pleads, and I stop trying to pull away.

Glaring back at the SUV, I feel like I'm drowning. "We can't do nothing, Mom," I state, refusing to let these people destroy my family.

"I know, Eden. I'm not saying we will, but we need to let them think they're winning, and to do that, we must play by their rules. For now." Rubbing my arm in comfort, I turn my gaze to my mom.

"Do you have some secret life I don't know about where you're a secret agent or a damn ninja? Because I don't see how we are going to play them at their own game and come out alive if they're as bad as you say."

"We'll figure this out. We always do," she responds, ignoring my sarcasm as her gaze flickers back to the SUV.

"So, you want me to go to Knight's Creek and do what exactly?"

She visibly swallows, blinking back tears as she answers. "They want you to stay at the Freemont house and attend Asheville High for your senior year."

Squeezing the bridge of my nose, I try to calm myself. "*They* must want more than that, Mom."

"I'm sure of it too." She nods in agreement. "But they haven't given me anything else."

"And where will you be while I'm sent to live in the snake's den?" I try to ask calmly, but there's a harshness to my tone I can't shift.

"Wherever they want me to be," she answers back solemnly,

and I squeeze my fists at my side, feeling my fingernails mark my palms.

"This is a lot of bullshit, Mom. Please, just please get in the car with me. The G-Wagon is fast as hell. I'll be able to put some distance between us," I beg, feeling my body tremble as fear begins to coat my skin.

The passenger door on the SUV swings open, and I instantly feel the panic from my mom as she suddenly starts pushing me down the steps of the porch, and I stumble over my own feet.

"What the fuck," I grunt, pulling on my mom's arm to turn her around, but the tears streaming down my mother's face makes my anger waiver.

"Get in the car, Eden," she pleads, continuing to push me over to my black G-Wagon parked on the driveway. "I've packed all your clothes and restocked all your cosmetics. You have everything you need ready for school too. It's all in the trunk."

Reaching my car, she pulls my keys from her pocket, fumbling with them as she tries to unlock it.

"Mom, calm down."

"I can't calm down, Eden," she cries. "If you don't get in the car now, they're either going to start shooting or take you kicking and screaming anyway. And I raised you to keep your head held high. I refuse to let them have the satisfaction of taking you against your will."

"Who the hell are *they*? And why the fuck isn't your head

held high? We're giving in to them. That doesn't show any backbone, does it?" I yell back, my heart in my chest as I feel my mother pushing me away.

"Get in the car, Eden!" she screams, opening the door and trying to push me into the driver's seat. A part of me registers that her actions are out of fear, and I hold onto that as I step up into my seat and watch as she quickly slams the door shut behind me.

Putting my key in the ignition, I lower my window. "Mom—"

"She's going. She's going," she shrieks, her back against the door as she talks to whoever is sitting in the SUV with her arms waving in the air, but the driver's side door opens too. "Please, Eden. Please," my mom begs, whirling around to face me, her hands sneaking in through the window to cup my cheeks. "I've put the address into the GPS for you. Please, just go."

My heart feels like it's about to pound out of my chest. I don't want to give in to these psychotic assholes, but the pain in my mom's eyes encourages me to start the car.

"Who are these people?"

"It doesn't matter. As long as you stay at the Freemont house and finish school in Knight's Creek, they'll leave you alone," she sobs, pulling my face closer to hers so she can bring our foreheads together.

"You can't know that, Mom," I whimper, feeling the emotions wash over me.

"I know, I know, but I have to hold on to that hope. Now go," she orders, kissing my forehead and stepping back from the G-Wagon. "Just know I always loved you, with all of my heart. We both did."

Tears stream down my face as I glance over at the SUV, another door opening and adding to their threat.

Fuck.

Nodding at my mom, my family, my life, I reverse out of the driveway.

I want to ram my fucking car straight into the SUV and send us all to hell, but I know that wouldn't work.

Watching as my mother sobs, her hand on her chest as she encourages me to go, I turn on to the road. A quick glance in my rearview mirror shows the SUV doors shut as I move farther away from the house. My heart burns as I see my mother sag to the ground.

I will fix this. I will figure this shit out, right under their noses, and make them regret the pain they've rained down on my family.

KC KEAN

FOUR
Eden

The navigation system tells me I'm twenty minutes out from the address my mom put into the system, so I pull into the gas station up ahead to give myself a minute.

Five hours. I've been driving for five hours, my heart breaking with every mile I cover. I'm so confused right now. What the fuck is my life, and why the hell is any of this happening to me?

I've tried calling my mom so many times, getting more panicked each time the line went to voicemail. Until she finally sent me a text letting me know she was okay but couldn't talk.

Couldn't talk? I was crossing states against my will to travel to a town I didn't want to be in because suddenly, our lives are in danger.

From the hints of truths she spilled, maybe we have always been in danger and I've just been sheltered from it. It kind of justifies why we have never stayed in the same place for very long—we were on the run. Yet I still don't know from who.

Filling the G-Wagon up with gas, I grab my favorite bag of Swedish Fish and a bottle of peach iced tea. Sitting in silence, I contemplate my life. Less than a week ago, I was living my life, partying with Lou-Lou, and relaxing in the sun. Now I'm almost four hundred miles away from where I last called home. Alone. I hope my black Amex continues to work, otherwise I have no idea how I'll get by.

My eyes scan the backseat of my SUV, which is piled high with suitcases and boxes. I still can't believe my mom packed everything I own while I slept.

With a sigh, I put the car into drive and continue to follow the directions. My eyes have flickered in my rearview mirror the whole way, watching to see if I'm being followed. But I was fucking stupid and didn't glance at their license plate, and there are black SUVs everywhere.

I don't have the energy to connect my music account up, so I opt to listen to the radio instead. "Fairytale" by Livingston begins to thrum through the speakers, and my heart almost stops. This probably isn't the right time to hear these lyrics, but it's fucking ironic and I can't seem to turn it off.

I've come to the realization that I need to learn what the hell is going on, why my parents were forced to hide with me, and then I can figure a way out of this mess.

No more being the naïve Eden I have been. I need to wear my resting bitch face like a mask. I don't need any attachments or connections with people here. I just need to dig all of this shit up and find a solution. Why are we being threatened and murdered?

Clearly, there is more to my own mom and dad than I've ever been aware of, and as much as I don't always see eye to eye with my mom, I'd rather be with her than in some town with complete strangers.

Driving down a quiet road lined with nothing but palm trees, I spot a sign up ahead.

Welcome to Knight's Creek

Where the sun shines bright, and the waves crash hard.

A shiver runs down my spine. Hopefully, it's not a metaphor for anything. But my gut tells me my simple life is gone forever.

Following the directions, the scenery slowly starts to change as the town center comes into view. Shops, bars, restaurants, it has everything. A lot seem to be small businesses, but there is the occasional designer label dotted around as well.

I don't miss the In-N-Out Burger drive-through, and I make a mental note to visit there as soon as I can. I'll be able to research better with a burger in hand.

My speed slows as I notice the most stunning view up ahead—the ocean. Tingles zing up my arms at the sight. It's been so long since I've been able to see the ocean, feel the waves crash on my legs and my toes dig into the sand.

What on earth ever made my mom and dad leave this place? Because right now, I can't seem to see a single reason. Knight's Creek is stunning.

With each turn I take, I find myself heading closer and closer to the water, and even under these extreme circumstances, I'm excited at the prospect of being so close. My excitement is instantly cut short with guilt. Guilt for being so damn selfish. But if I have to be here, I at least deserve something to make me smile, I think.

The houses are getting bigger, and as big as my house was back in Arizona, these are seriously next level. They all have direct access to the beach.

"Six hundred feet on your left, and you have reached your destination."

My excitement instantly fizzles out as I remember why I'm here and the unknown world that waits for me at this house.

Pulling to a stop a few houses away, I stare at the Freemont house. Why would I have to stay here? What significance does this hold?

Dammit. I have so many questions and nowhere near enough answers, but the only way I'll get them is if I grow some big ass ovaries and find out.

My phone vibrates on the dashboard, pulling my attention from the house. I pray it's my mom, but it's Lou-Lou's name that flashes across the front.

I haven't spoken to her since the night of the party. I've sent quick one-worded responses via text, but that's it. I've been too busy mourning my father's death and sinking in self-pity to offer anything more.

Right now, though, I could use some of her sass to fire me up.

Swiping the screen, I answer her call and place her on speakerphone all at once.

"Hey, Lou," I murmur, and I hear her gasp in surprise that I've answered.

"Don't 'hey, Lou' me like you haven't been avoiding my calls," she grouches, and I shake my head.

"Would you rather I said, what the fuck do you want, Lou? My dad's dead, and I'm suddenly sitting on the coast of California with my life literally flipped upside down?"

My snark is greeted with pure silence, and I instantly feel like a bitch.

"I've tried to call and support you about your dad, Eden, and it's because of that I'll let your attitude slide. But what the fuck are you doing in California? I thought you might appreciate a party and some alcohol. Help forget all your worries for a minute, but I can't offer that if you're so far away."

Pulling invisible lint from my hoodie, I regret my mother's choice of clothing this morning, wishing for nothing more than being able to do just that with her.

"I don't even know myself, to be honest, Lou. It seems there is a lot about my life I'm unaware of," I mutter, finding no relief in talking to someone.

"Well, can you not come back home?" she asks, and I can hear laughter in the background. Likely her brother and his gang causing a riot again, their usual banter filtering through the phone.

"I don't think White River ever really was my home," I admit, leaning my head back against the headrest and taking a deep breath. Lou-Lou has lived in the same house since she was born. She doesn't understand the normalcy of moving homes, restarting life. I do. "And now I'm apparently at my new temporary home for the foreseeable future."

"What in the motherfucking hell has happened, Eden?" Her choice of curse words almost brings a smile to my lips, but the sight of someone opening the front door of my *new home* draws my attention.

"I don't know, Lou, but I'll try to keep you up to date. I'll call soon."

Ending the call, I watch as an older guy, around my parent's age, walks to the end of the driveway and looks directly at my SUV. Hands on his hips, he glances down at his feet as if composing himself, swipes at his face before nodding his head. With one quick sweep, he waves his hand in my direction, encouraging me forward.

How the hell does he know I'm here? Or who I am?

I can see the strain on his face from here, and it's that look that has me crawling forward and pulling into the driveway, as he indicates.

My heart pounds in my chest, and my palms sweat as I feel his eyes staring me down, waiting for me to exit the SUV. I take a deep breath and paste on a blank face, not wanting anyone to see my emotions.

Opening the door, I slowly slip from the vehicle, leaving the door open as I come to stand at the hood, looking at the guy standing on the other side. His eyes are swollen, and his face red as he tries to look at me. His temples are peppered with grey hairs that run into his overgrown beard. His blue eyes look sadder than mine, and I didn't think that was possible.

Has he been crying?

Clearing his throat, he looks off into the distance. "You must be Eden. I'm, uh, Richard."

I don't know what this man is going through, but I can feel his pain from here.

"Yeah, that's me," I mumble, wringing my hands nervously in front of me. "Why am I here?" I ask, not wanting to waste time on small talk.

His deep blue eyes burn into mine as he rubs the back of his neck. "Because they deem it so. Don't let the false pretenses of this town trick you, Eden. As pretty as it may look at first glance, it's rotten to the core. We're all puppets in *their* bigger games, and they take fun in playing with our lives." Turning, he walks back to the front door, pausing just before he steps back inside.

"Make yourself at home. Your room is the third door to the right on the top floor."

With that, he's gone, and I'm left by my SUV even more confused than I already was.

Does he just expect me to go in there? He didn't even let me ask if he knew anything about my father's death. Shit. Did he have something to do with it? Fuck. I can feel a migraine coming on. I think I'm still in shock with the past week, so I don't know how to handle anything. My mind is overwhelmed and crashing at the same time.

Nausea turns my stomach as I realize how alone I really am. I can't trust anyone.

"Miss Eden?"

Whipping my head back around to the door, another man is standing politely with his hands behind his back. He looks like house staff, wearing a cream polo top and chino shorts.

"Uh, that's me," I offer, and he nods his head with a sad smile I just can't seem to place.

"Miss, I'm Stevens. If you would like to follow Mr. Richard's directions to your room, we'll have all of your things brought to you in no time."

Glancing at my belongings in the SUV, I consider my options. Where else am I supposed to go? It's not like I can go back to White River to be with my mom. I don't even know where she is.

With a resigned sigh, I grab my phone and head for the door.

Finally taking a deeper look at the house before me, its sleek lines and overall pearl white exterior walls are filled with floor-length glass windows, offering a sneak peek inside the formal house. The driveway continues to lead down to the beach. Light fixtures line the way, in between little shrubs planted all the way down the slope at the side of the house.

The sound of the waves crashing in the distance, on the other side of the house, is what draws me closer. The sea breeze ruffles my hair as I sweat beneath my hoodie. Stepping through the double-doored entry, I have to stop my jaw from hitting the floor when I see it leads straight into a huge open space.

The opposite wall is pure glass, offering the most amazing view of the ocean, with a huge pool and lawn space in between. The entire first floor is an open plan, with two sets of stairs leading both up and down to my left. The open space is broken down into a huge den, the largest sofa I have ever seen takes up most of the space, and the most amazing television to watch football hangs on the wall.

A high cabinet divides the living room from the dining area, where a twelve-seat sleek wooden dining set sits, and the high-tech kitchen is all laid out on the other side of it. Is that divider filled with bottles and bottles of alcohol? Yes, please.

This place is ultra modern, yet it almost feels like no one lives here. It's too damn clean.

"Top of the stairs, third door on your right," Stevens calls out, reminding me where I'm supposed to be going, and I offer a weak smile before following his instruction as he points in the direction I should go.

Wrapping my arms around myself, I notice Richard is nowhere to be seen, but there is a lot of noise coming from outside, yet I don't see anyone.

Taking the glass panel stairs, I reach the top and count three doors down. With slow steps, I come to a stop outside of a wooden door and push it open with the tip of my finger.

The door doesn't make a single creak as I push it wide and slowly step inside. I gulp at the room before me. A four-poster bed is centered on the wall beside me, looking straight out of another full glass wall, which leads onto a balcony with its own patio set and sun loungers.

What the fuck even is this place?

We have never lived outside of our means, even when we have lived in gated communities, but this is next-level wealthy.

Moving farther into the room, I notice the left door leads into a walk-in closet, while a door to the right leads into a bathroom. Walking out onto the balcony, I gaze out at the beach and take a deep breath. Why am I in a luxurious house, against my will, without my mom? I can't figure out what any of this means.

And why the hell do I feel so fucking numb to it all? I should be kicking and screaming, freaking out at a minimum. Not accepting my future without question, just like my parents seemed to do.

The memory of my father sends a direct shock of pain straight to my heart, and I remember what I need to do.

Laughter pulls my attention down to the beach, and I watch as a large group of people joke around, making their way up to this house. Probably fifteen or twenty of them, almost like a football team with groupies hanging off their every word.

Not wanting to draw attention to myself, I turn to head back inside, but not before freezing in place as I take in the rugged god hovering at the back of the group. His thick brown hair is swept off his face, and even with his black aviators covering his eyes, I can feel them burning my skin, scrutinizing me. In nothing but a short pair of navy swim shorts, he looks like he slays demons with his fucking tanned abs.

Shaking off the hold he has on me, I slide the glass door shut behind me. I did not come here to feel some asshole's judgment from afar.

I was forced here, and my focus has to be on finding answers.

KC KEAN

FIVE
Eden

I don't know how long I lie on the bed, staring up at the ceiling, but the sun is slowly starting to hit the horizon when I finally lift myself, mentally pulling myself together.

I haven't left the room since I arrived. Stevens had quickly brought up all the things my mother had packed for me, but it remained exactly where he left it. He offered me food too, except I can't even stomach the idea of eating right now.

Unpacking would mean giving in, and my brain just can't process the defeat just yet. Even if I want to dig through my belongings to check that my favorite photo of my dad and me is in there.

I need to get my headphones in, my sneakers on, and go for a run. It's the one thing that always helps me put things in perspective, and if there is anything I need right now, it's some damn perspective.

Since I'm already in my yoga pants, I take off my hoodie, thankful for the sports bra I'd thrown on this morning. Slipping my sneakers on, I find my purse sitting on top of my luggage. Grabbing my wireless earphones and Ray-Ban's, I head downstairs.

Nerves kick in as I step out to leave, worrying I'll bump into someone, but there isn't anyone in the wide-open space again. I can see the group from earlier relaxing by the pool area through the glass wall, so I sneak out of the front door before anyone sees me.

With "DJ Turn It Up" by Yellow Claw pounding in my ears, I take off down the path running by the side of the house, which slopes down to the beach.

As much as the water calls to me, I stick to the edge of the beach, away from the water, and start jogging alongside the houses. With the heat beating down on me and the pounding of my feet in the sand, I get lost in the rhythm.

The music is drowned out by the memory of the fear and panic in my mom's voice earlier today. How was that even today? She has always been the strongest person I know, so to see her like that devastates me. But it also puts into perspective what we are up against. Something bad.

I haven't been able to ask a single question yet, so I'm no closer to getting any answers, but my gut tells me it won't be that simple anyway. I know it's naïve of me to expect everything to happen all at once, but I don't know what else to do.

She believed me being here would keep the peace, seemingly to buy us some time to get out of this shit that I don't truly understand. But if that's what it takes, that's what I'll do. Someone has to pay for what happened to my dad.

My footsteps slow as I reach the end of the beach, my eyes fixed on the house that sits like a museum at the end. It's easily the biggest house on the row, and the way it sits on the edge of the cliff only adds to its grandeur.

It looks like the ultimate mansion you'd see in magazines. Ultra sleek and modern, with a wooden set of steps leading down to the beach, which looks almost out of place.

Turning back in the direction I just came, the house doesn't look that far away, but it's over half a mile, with the time it took me to get here with the sand under my feet. Heading back, I decide to run along the water's edge this time so that I can pick up speed with the slightly smoother surface underneath me.

Nearing the house, I think this little route will suit me well in the mornings, but I would have to do some research to find better trails and longer distances.

Fuck. That sounded a hell of a lot like me settling in.

Bracing my hands on my hips, I look out at the ocean, finally giving in to its pull. I should have brought a bottle of water with me, my mouth is bone-dry, but I didn't want to intrude. Especially when it seemed Richard was very reluctant to have me here.

Feeling the sweat trickle down my back and gather along my hairline, I turn to head back inside. Taking the slope, I slip back in the front door and instantly pause as a guy waves at me from the kitchen area.

Forcing myself to remove my earphones, I offer the smallest smile, grateful he isn't the intense Adonis from earlier.

"Hey, Eden, right?" he asks, strolling over to me casually with an easy going vibe about him.

"Right," I answer, scanning his eyes for any ulterior motive, but he seems completely relaxed and at ease.

"I'm Archie, and this is my house." Stopping in front of me, he leans on the banister.

Ah, shit. If he has an issue with me being here, then join the club.

"I didn't know that," I offer, trying to rein in my bitchiness.

His blue eyes flicker down, indicating for me to follow his gaze, and I see him holding out a bottle of ice-cold water.

"I saw you take off for a run without any liquid. It's important to stay hydrated, you know." His tone is teasing and warm all at once, and it has me a little off-kilter.

"Thanks," I finally respond, taking the drink from his outstretched hand. "Does anyone else live here?"

"Just my dad. He mentioned we were having someone stay with us. Are you excited to start school?"

Archie's attempt at polite conversation has me relaxing a

little and dropping my defensive instincts. His blond hair is messy, like he was born to surf, but his build is bigger than average, making me inclined to think he plays sports. His biceps bulge under his short-sleeved white T-shirt as he raises an eyebrow at me, waiting for a response.

Opting to ignore his question until I get an answer for myself, I try to plaster a soft smile on my face, attempting to make myself look approachable and nice, I guess.

"Uh, do you know why I'm here?" I ask, causing a crinkle to form between his eyes.

"No… Should I?" he asks, rubbing the back of his neck nervously, and I shake my head.

"I don't know anything, to be honest. My life is a little upside down right now, and I'm trying to figure out which way is up," I answer honestly, without giving him the in-depth sorrows of my life.

"You want to come and join us?" he offers, pointing over his shoulder to the group hanging by the pool, but I'm shaking my head before he's even finished his sentence.

"No, thanks. The alcohol I'd be game for, the socializing, not so much."

"I get it, new girl in a new town. It's all good. I'm about to order pizzas before the rest of the crowd gets here. I'm the party king, just FYI. You want me to order you a pizza too? I can bring it up to your room if you're going to be hiding out."

It's weird how he's simply stating facts without calling me

out or being shitty because I don't want to join him and his friends.

"That would be awesome, thanks. I'll literally go for any pizza, just no pineapple, that's weird."

Placing his hand on his heart, he acts wounded by my words. "You break my heart, Eden. Pineapple on pizza is god level." My eyes widen as I snicker at his theatrics.

"That's gross, Archie. So gross." I shiver, and he laughs wholeheartedly in response.

"Fine, no pineapple. If I was to slip you some alcohol from the infamous wall, what would you appreciate?" he asks, waving his hand to the divider behind him. "And don't break my heart again with your bad life choices." He grins, and I refrain from rolling my eyes at him.

"Literally anything as long as it comes with a sealed lid. No roofies for me," I answer, and he smiles with approval.

"Your wish is my command." Bowing before me, I shake my head at him.

"Are you always this crazy?"

"Like you wouldn't believe. Don't you worry, Eden, I've got your back." He winks, and it feels strange to be in a guy's company without him pawing at me. There is something about Archie that makes him feel like a lighthouse guiding me home as I'm lost at sea.

"Archie, let's go, man," someone calls out, interrupting our conversation, and I turn to the open glass doors to find the smoking hot broody guy from earlier. His glasses still remain in place, yet I can feel his intensity from here.

"Run before the big bad wolf gets you." Archie chuckles at me, indicating the guy who holds my attention, clearly feeling the same vibes as I am before heading in his direction. "I'll bring everything up when it gets here," he calls out over his shoulder.

Archie bypasses the guy, who remains still, staring me down without saying a word. Feeling my skin heat under his gaze, I force myself to place one foot in front of the other and march up the stairs.

I can't explain the vibes he's giving off. He's intense for sure, but there is something in me desperate to get closer, to see if the pull gets stronger.

As I get to the top, I can't stop myself from glancing over my shoulder, but he's gone. God, he's intense. He has a totally different spectrum of personality traits compared to Archie. I can feel it in the air. I mean, who stares someone down without at least offering a hello or a smile? But damn, I'm all hot and sticky for completely different reasons now.

Mystery guy can feature in my dirty imagination anytime he likes.

Stepping into my room, I shut the door behind me, eyeing the luggage that still waits for me. How likely am I to find the sex toys Lou-Lou bought me for Christmas? I mean, I don't want my mom to have seen them, but I know a good orgasm will calm me right now.

Ah, fuck it. Let's find out.

Yep.

My mom either threw my old sneaker box, containing my gizmos and gadgets, into the car without looking inside, or she knows I'm currently an underage sex-fiend for the next six weeks. I'm praying it's not the latter. There is already enough drama in our life.

Finding my happy ending didn't take long at all, and after I washed my hair, I decided to move all the luggage to the adjoining walk-in closet, which was almost the size of the damn bedroom itself.

I may have pulled out an outfit or two, some clean underwear, and my toiletries, but other than that, everything remained where it was. Except for my toys, of course, which found themselves a nice little home inside my bedside table.

Sex has always been a 'take control' kind of action for me. I can't control very much of my life, but I can control that. It's not a surprise I have trust and commitment issues, which is why I don't do repeats.

When I was fifteen, we lived much farther north, and I finally gave in to my boyfriend at the time, letting him dick me in the back of his car. After taking my virginity, he ghosted, and two days later, we were suddenly leaving for White River.

We'd met in high school and had dated for nearly ten

months, but when he turned seventeen, he suddenly changed, acting like a total asshole. I was already into partying, so with some persistent pressure, I'd given in.

He might have ruined me afterward, putting me off committing myself to one person, but I got the taste of my first orgasm, and there was no looking back. Even if it was mixed in with the pain and burn of my virginity being taken.

My badass fifteen-year-old self made a pact, and I've stuck with it ever since. Making sure I don't get hurt, which feels like the best decision, especially since I'm now dealing with the pain of my father's death. I don't need anybody else to worry about as well.

Squeals draw my attention as the partiers below have the time of their lives. If we were back in White River, I would be down there with them. Maybe I will join eventually, but today isn't that day. Getting lost in the music and a hot body, while alcohol zings through your blood, is the perfect kind of night for me.

Nursing the bottle of spiced rum that Archie brought up earlier with my pepperoni pizza, I watch as a few of the girls strip down to nothing and jump in the pool, earning themselves a round of whistles from some of the guys.

I tried playing my own music, but it was instantly drowned out by the music coming from downstairs, and I didn't want to sit with my earphones in. So instead, I'm sitting, watching life pass me by with a definite buzz from the alcohol, wishing for my mom to return one of my calls.

I glance at her last message again, trying not to get annoyed.

Mom: I'm safe, Eden. Don't worry about me. Focus on yourself. We will figure all of this out in time. I'm going to be driving for a while, so I will try and call in the morning. I love you.

I don't want to talk in the morning. I want to talk now. But screw me, right? Just force me to pack up and move to an unknown town, with nowhere near enough fucking answers, while feeding me small snippets of texts.

Sighing, I stand from the lounge chair and stretch my arms above my head. I can feel myself getting bitter and I know I shouldn't, but I'm fucking mad and I can't get over it.

Gulping down another mouthful of rum, I look out to the ocean, the moonlight bouncing off the water.

If my dad could see me—

Nope. No. I'm not going there. Why the hell isn't this rum fucking working? Growling, I take another big sip and place the bottle on the table beside me, letting it burn my throat as I strum my fingers on the railing.

I feel antsy.

Maybe I should go down to the party, find a willing guy, and fuck my night away. That might even help me sleep too.

"What has you mad?"

I startle, whirling around to find Mr. Broody himself standing in my room where my glass doors are open.

"What are you doing in my room?" I counter, but he doesn't even raise his eyebrow at me as he waits for me to answer his question.

I don't know whether the rum just kicked up a notch or if I'm intoxicated by him as well.

He's finally taken his glasses off, and his hazel eyes sparkle in the moonlight. His square jaw and chiseled cheekbones have me almost ready to cream my pants. My tongue feels glued to the roof of my mouth as I spot a scar running down the side of his right ear. I want to lick it, and every inch of his olive skin.

This guy is eye candy from a distance, but up close, he's hot as sin. In his skinny denim jeans with a black muscle fit T-shirt, he shouldn't look this good.

Finally finding my voice, I respond, "What doesn't have me mad is more the question."

I can't stop myself from instinctively trying to straighten my messy bun, like my body is trying to impress him, even when my brain doesn't want to. Clearing my throat, I straighten my shoulders and brush down the oversized T-shirt that reaches my knees, suddenly remembering I have nothing else on.

"Can I help you?"

His eyes take in every inch of me, my curves hidden by my T-shirt, but my pert nipples give me away.

"What's your name?" he asks, not answering my question again, and I shrug.

"I won't be here long enough for it to matter," I murmur,

and his eyes flicker with heat, liking my answer.

"Right answer, Nafas," he mutters, standing beside me but staring down at the party below. "Why haven't you joined the party?"

"What does that mean? Nafas?" I ask, and the smallest grin graces his lips as he keeps his eyes trained away from me.

"You won't be here long enough for it to matter."

Touché.

"What has you up here bothering me, instead of down there with a groupie hanging off your every word? Because let me tell you, I do not have the temperament to put you up on a pedestal right now." I can feel his big dick energy from here, and he needs to know I have no interest in pumping his ego.

Mirroring his stance, I lean against the railing, letting the night's air blow the wisps of hair around my face, but it's still fucking hot. The rum fizzes through my veins as I stand side by side with this stranger, no longer caring about the intrusion, letting his woodsy scent envelop me.

"Your siren skills stop working when your mouth doesn't shut up," he finally mutters, side-eyeing me, and a flicker of a smile touches my lips.

Any other time and I'd be focused on lecturing these fuckers on how I don't let any man tell me what to do, my dad would have never allowed it, but the silence beckons me more than my backbone does tonight.

"Better," he breathes, and I tilt my gaze to him.

"Don't fucking push it," I say with a pout, turning away dismissively as I head back inside, grabbing the rum off the table as I pass.

Pressing play on the movie I have paused on the television, my eyes fall back to my guest, who is watching me over his shoulder, a serious look in his eyes.

As if agreeing with himself, he nods before patting the railing and stalking towards me.

"You really don't know who I am, do you?" he asks, a hint of surprise in his deep voice as he comes to stand toe-to-toe with me.

"Should I?" I ask, lifting the rum to my lips, but he grabs my wrist, pausing my movement. His other hand comes up to my chin, holding me in place, and I have to squeeze my thighs together as the dominant move goes straight to my core.

Fucking hussy.

"Probably," he whispers, looking deep into my eyes as his own hazel eyes swirl with darkness. "But I like the pain in your eyes, and I actually like knowing I didn't cause it for a change."

His words strip me apart. I want to squeeze my eyes shut and stop him from seeing into my soul, but instead, I stand helpless as he pries the rum from my hand and places it on the table on the balcony.

Turning back to me, I watch in slow motion as he raises his hand above his head and pulls the neck of his T-shirt up, revealing his defined abs and chest, moving towards me.

Licking my lips, my skin heats at the question in his eyes. Holy fuck, this is exactly what I need right now. Him. Beneath me, above me, behind me. Wherever the fuck he wants to be. I just want to forget.

I watch as he kicks off his shoes, raising his eyebrow at me in question, and I'm pulling my T-shirt over my head without a second thought.

Standing before him, completely naked, I toss my T-shirt aside. He doesn't utter a word as he unbuttons his jeans in front of me, and my breath hitches as I realize he is commando underneath.

Fuck yes.

Discarding his jeans, he doesn't move to touch me as he surrounds my space, all my focus completely on him, but I don't miss the condom he tosses on the bed.

"You have to show me what you want, Nafas," he murmurs, his eyes searing into mine.

Glancing down at his hard length, I see a bead of pre-cum glistening, summoning me closer. Tentatively placing my hands on the perfect V at his waist, I indicate for us to turn, putting him closer to the bed.

"Sit," I whisper, and he continues to stare down at me.

"I said show me, not order me around," he responds, but there's no bite to his words.

In one swift motion, I drop straight to my knees, gripping his cock in my hand as I lick the pre-cum away. Glancing up at him, he doesn't utter a word, but his hands are fisted at his side and the cords in his neck are tight.

So Mr. Broody wants me to show him what I want but is struggling with not being in control. Noted. Not wanting to waste another second, I lean forward and wrap my lips around his dick, heading straight for gold and making it known I have no gag reflex.

With the tip of his dick at the back of my throat, I swallow, and it knocks him off balance.

"Fuck," he growls as his cock slips from my mouth and he falls to the bed.

Shuffling forward, I waste no time taking him deep in my throat again, loving the feel of his hard length pulsing in my mouth. Bracing one hand on his thigh, I bring the other to cup his balls, and his hips rise off the bed. Fucking him with my mouth, I hold still, keeping my lips locked tightly around his cock as I tug at his balls, my eyes closed as I refuse to search out his gaze.

He's intoxicating. I want more, and I want it now.

As if sensing the same thing, he threads his fingers through my hair and pulls my mouth off his cock. Instinctively, we both move for the condom, but I relent, letting him tear the wrapper and slowly roll it down his length.

His eyes bore into mine like he's contemplating where this will go next. And it surprises me when he leans back on the palm of his hands, encouraging me to take a seat.

Without pause, I turn, placing my hand on his thigh as I line him up at my entrance and slam straight down.

Fuckkk. The stretch of his cock isn't as rough as I wanted it to be. Even without him touching my pussy, I'm wet as fuck, and the grip of his fingers at my waist only adds to the heat.

Feeling his heat at my back, I look over my shoulder to see he's leaned forward, clearly surprised I opted for this position instead. His thick thighs frame mine as I roll my hips, a sweet gasp passing my lips as I do.

"What is it about you that has me out of fucking sorts, Nafas?" he growls out, not impressed with his own reaction to me.

"I have no idea what you're talking about," I murmur, rolling my hips again and lifting a hand to cup my breast as I stroke a finger across my clit, moaning as my skin tingles.

His grip on my waist tightens as he glares at me, searching my eyes for some secret I must be holding, but he won't find what he's looking for. All that lives inside of me right now is pain and desire.

His other hand grips my bun, tilting my neck back. "Fuck it," he grunts, beads of sweat gathering on his brows, and he crushes his lips to mine. Devouring my lips as I grind against him, I gasp, making his fingers tighten in my hair.

Keeping my neck twisted and his lips against mine, he thrusts his hips, making me bounce on his dick, and I match his rhythm, falling in sync all too easily.

His hand releases my hip and bats my own fingers away from my clit, instantly hitting the perfect spot. My orgasm starts at my toes, setting my skin alight as it rips through me, and he catches every one of my screams with his lips.

My vision blacks out as I come down from my high, but his constant thrusts have me filling with ecstasy all over again.

My eyes open as he suddenly lifts me off him and tosses me down on the bed effortlessly. I bounce a couple of times before he settles between my thighs and sinks straight back into my pussy, his lips capturing one of my nipples as he does.

With my head thrown back in pleasure, I brace myself on my elbows as he shows me what he can *really* do with his cock. His thrusts are brutal, hard, and fast, and I fucking love it.

Pleading and chanting for more, he gives me exactly what I want, biting down on my taut nipple as he does.

I stroke my hands over his shoulders, but he quickly grabs both my wrists in one of his hands and pins them above my head, releasing my nipple from his mouth as he does.

As he stares down at me, I feel his moves stutter, losing rhythm as he chases his orgasm. His other hand pinches my clit as he does, and I follow him off the cliff, seeing stars as my second climax hits me.

Fuck. Me.

He buries his head in my neck as we both catch our breath before he slowly pulls out and discards the condom.

Lying in complete bliss, my eyes fall closed as I bask in the tingles still coursing through my body.

It's a pity I don't double fuck because he would be worth seeking out again, I think as the world goes dark and sleep washes over me. That was just the distraction I needed.

TOXIC CREEK

SIX
Eden

Peeking my eyes open, it takes a moment for me to remember where I am, and more importantly, what state I fell asleep in. The scent of a woodsy aftershave lingers on the pillow beside me—the only indication Mr. Broody was even here last night. I sag in relief when I don't see him around, lingering for more.

I can't believe I fell asleep like that, but I can't deny the effects of an intense orgasm or two.

Stretching out, I groan in pleasure as my muscles relax before lifting onto my elbows. I have a frontline view of the ocean. Even through the balcony glass door and the balcony itself, I can see the crystal clear waters sparkling in the distance, the melodic sound of the waves crashing calming my soul.

Damn. It's just so pretty. The balcony doors are still open a little, and the bottle of spiced rum sits on the little table just as he left it. I can hear the sound of the waves in the distance, but the light is doing nothing for my headache.

Finding my phone on my nightstand, I notice it's a little after eleven in the morning. I need to get out of bed, freshen myself up, and go in search of answers. Richard seemed very distant yesterday, although the emotion in his face caught me completely off guard.

I don't think he'll give me much information, but maybe his son, Archie, will know more.

With a plan in mind, I jump in the shower, hating to see my cosmetics naturally around my en suite. I know the space is mine and I'm thankful I've not found myself in a hellhole, but it's still not where I want to be.

The ache between my legs is magic, as I remember last night in more detail. He seemed confused with his own actions, but he couldn't stop the inevitable from happening either. I'm just glad we were both on the same page, wanting nothing more than the pleasure for the night.

I pause as I reach for my coconut body wash. I'm a little obsessive with making sure my lids are closed on any products I have, and it's not sealed shut.

Glancing over my shoulder, as if someone's watching me, I shake my head. Did Mr. Broody shower before he left? Who knows? I don't need to see him again to find out.

Stepping from the shower, steam engulfs the bathroom,

making it impossible to see my reflection in the mirror. So I grab a fluffy grey towel from the rack and rub it through the ends of my hair as I step back into my room naked.

Thump.

"Ah, shit."

Startling, I quickly drop the towel, attempting to cover my body as I search for the person who just fucking said that.

My eyes fall to Archie as he fumbles to pick up my favorite dildo and put it back in my drawer.

Wait. My fucking…

"Archie, what the fuck are you doing in my room?" I squeal, pulling the towel around my chest and waist.

"I, uh." Clearing his throat, he can't reach my gaze as he slams the drawer shut on my nightstand. "Sorry, I came to see if you wanted something to eat. I called out, but you must not have heard me over the shower," he rambles, and I continue to glare at him.

"So you decided to go snooping around through my stuff?" I grumble, nowhere near as embarrassed as he is right now. His face is bright red as he rubs nervously at the back of his neck.

"Sorry about that," he murmurs, finally meeting my stare. "I'm a slightly nosey person. I won't do it again," he offers, giving me some fake as shit angelic voice, which somehow calms my annoyance.

"Fine, you're forgiven," I relent, and he instantly perks up like a little puppy. "If, and only if, you wow me with these breakfast skills. I'm starving," I admit, and his smile widens.

"Food is my specialty. Well, food, parties, and football are." Almost bouncing all on the balls of his feet, he rubs his hands together. "You get dressed, and I'll meet you downstairs. We're going to Pete's."

With that, he waltzes out of the door, shutting it gently behind him before I even have a chance to respond. Out for breakfast it is then.

Rummaging through my clothes, I pull out my favorite ripped jeans with a cropped white top and my thin beige jacket. Opting to French braid my hair down my back, I bypass my makeup and slip on my black sunglasses. Securing my black Gucci belt, I'm good to go.

Casual badass. That's the vibe I want. Hopefully, it will encourage everyone to avoid me at all costs.

Grabbing my wallet and phone, I check to see if my mom has tried to call or text, but there aren't any notifications. It's not that our relationship has ever been strained, we just haven't really had anything in common, which has impacted our dynamic.

Even when we were under the same roof, we could go days without talking to each other. Whereas my dad would call and text all the time, whether I liked it or not, making sure to insert himself in my life. It makes me wonder if I would have felt this broken if it was the other way around.

Refusing to contact her again after repeatedly doing so, I make my way downstairs to find Archie and his father murmuring to each other in the kitchen. Richard's face scrunches in pain as he catches sight of me reaching the bottom of the stairs. He instantly pushes some papers into Archie's chest and storms out of the room.

I don't think he likes me very much. Or he doesn't like me invading their space at least.

Archie gets a better grip on the papers, frowning at the spot his dad was standing moments ago before turning to me with his megawatt smile back in place. I have no idea who this guy really is, but I've never seen a forced smile quite like it. It looks genuine, but it doesn't quite meet his eyes.

"Let's go, trouble." He breezes right past me and opens the front door wide, indicating for me to lead the way. "Is this your G-Wagon?" he asks, a hint of appreciation in his tone as I nod in agreement. "Damn, nice ride. Who'd you have to convince to get you these wheels?"

He moves closer to the vehicle as I remain frozen in place, my words stuck on the tip of my tongue as emotion overwhelms me. As if sensing a shift in the air, Archie glances over his shoulder at me, a stricken look instantly on his face.

"Not a topic of conversation for today?" he asks, and I swallow hard before responding, licking my suddenly parched lips. He's either being polite or doesn't actually know about my current situation.

"It was from my dad," I mumble, and understanding washes over his features as he walks back towards me, flinging his arm around my shoulder.

Without a word, he guides me to my SUV, letting me unlock it before he opens the door. As he shuts the door and circles the front of the SUV, I realize I'm in the driver's seat, and that was the most chivalrous shit I've ever seen.

Climbing in beside me, he clips his seatbelt and stares at me expectantly, waiting for me to do the same as I force myself not to make a joke about his chivalry. I don't really know this guy enough to be myself and let my walls down.

"I thought it might be good for you to drive. Get a feel for the town. And…my dad may have taken my car away, and I don't get it back for another two months since I totaled the last one."

My eyes flash to his as I press the button to start the engine, taken aback by his admission.

"How on earth did you total it? Were you injured?" I ask, reversing out of the driveway and heading to the left as Archie directs with his hand.

"It's all good. I was just a little reckless at the time." Guilt lingers in his eyes before he blinks it away. He's a master at hiding his emotions, just like me. "My mom had just died, and I didn't really give a shit about much."

I can't stop my eyes from flickering to his, completely forgetting I'm driving. That's where his understanding comes from. He must have seen it in my eyes when he asked about the G-Wagon.

I focus back on the road, and neither of us says anything except for him offering directions. I expected us to head inland, but I'm surprised when we drive through the town of Knight's Creek and head straight back to the coast.

The local radio station plays through the speakers, the latest hot tracks playing quietly in the background as Archie points out places and hotspots that mean nothing to me. Except for the local classic record store, which also deals with retro movies too. Now *that* I'm interested in. My dad made me watch them until I loved them just as much as he did.

I instantly see Pete's up ahead, surrounded by nothing but sand, right on the water's edge, and I'm thankful to see the parking lot isn't packed.

Wordlessly, I put the G-Wagon into park and follow Archie towards the front door. The whole exterior is made up mostly of glass, offering views from all angles. The Pete's sign sits proudly in red neon lights on the light wooden roof, giving a retro vibe to the modern-looking diner.

Stepping inside, I'm surprised to see ultramodern fixtures and fittings and not some sixties diner or sea shack. It makes me wonder why the sign isn't up to date like it is in here.

Huge windows line the opposite wall, giving you the perfect view as oak tables scatter the open space, framed with cushioned grey chairs. There are even a few leather sofas and coffee tables dotted around the edge for a more relaxed atmosphere too.

"Archie darling, grab your spot. I'll be two seconds,"

a woman calls out, and Archie shouts back his thanks as he moves us towards the semi circle booth by the window. A large flatscreen television hangs on the wall with the latest sports news playing.

Taking the offered menu from Archie, I get comfortable in the booth as I browse through the food options.

"Anything you choose will be amazing, Eden. I swear they are masters at putting me in a food coma every time I come here." Archie smiles, and my lips tilt up in response.

It's weird how he has a crazy ability to make me smile so effortlessly. I've never really had a platonic guy friend before, but there's a first time for everything. It's weird to have friend-zoned him so soon, but it feels natural.

"And who might this be, Archie?" a lady sings as she steps up to our table.

She's tiny, probably five feet in height with a slim frame, and a blonde pixie cut perfectly styled frames her face, her blue eyes sparkling with mischief. Her apron and name badge are the only things giving away that she works here, since she's wearing a pair of jeans and a casual T-shirt.

"Linda, this is Eden. Eden, Linda," Archie offers, introducing us, and her face lights up with her smile. Laughter lines scatter her face, showing her age, but it melts my heart seeing her raw happiness.

"Hi," I murmur, attempting a half wave, but she instantly wraps my hand in both of hers.

"Someone got the D last night, didn't they?" she says with a chuckle, and I gape openly at her in shock.

Archie bursts out laughing, failing to smother his outburst with his hand as he gains control of himself.

"Linda, she hasn't even been here twenty-four hours. She's had no time for that yet. Unless it was the plastic variation," he adds, shooting me a wink, and I want the floor to open up beneath me. Send me to hell now.

Linda joins in with his laughter, finally releasing my hand, and I try to act unaffected. If only he knew what I'd gotten up to last night. There was definitely nothing plastic about it.

Finally managing to calm themselves, Linda pulls her little notepad and pencil from her apron and asks what we would like.

"I'll take a spicy breakfast burrito and a soda, please, Linda," Archie orders, and I can't deny that it sounds good.

"I'll take that too, please."

"Good choice, girly, you'll fit in well around here, I'm sure," she offers before hurrying back to the kitchen.

The second she is out of earshot, I fix my glare on Archie, who already has his hands raised in surrender.

"I'm nosey, and I have a big mouth. I apologize. You're finding out all of my flaws in a very short period of time. I just can't help myself, but you should have seen your face." He chuckles, and a snicker passes my lips in response.

Dammit. I need to work on my stern look around this guy. He has me losing my resting bitch face and shitty attitude.

Falling into a comfortable silence, neither of us says anything as we watch the sports news flicker across the screen. An MLB game was played last night locally, and the recaps are being run repeatedly on a decision the referee made.

I watch as they slow the clip down again when I hear Archie murmur beside me.

"Cancer." My heart almost stops as I turn to face him, seeing the pain in his eyes as he opens up to me. "My mom, she died of cancer," he clarifies, running his hand through his blond hair, and I instinctively reach out to squeeze his arm.

"I'm so sorry, Archie," I offer, knowing it does nothing to heal his pain, but it's the only words I can find.

"Thanks," he mutters as Linda drops two glasses of soda at the table, along with our breakfast burritos. She must sense the emotion at the table because she says nothing and heads straight back to the kitchen.

Deciding to spill my truth before I start eating, I take a sip of my soda, trying to relax my suddenly dry throat.

"My dad was killed, Archie. Less than a week ago. Shot between the eyes in our family home while I was at a party."

Finally, bringing my gaze to meet his, I find him staring at me with his mouth wide open. I don't think he expected me to say that.

"Eden, I—"

"It's okay," I whisper, shaking my head. "Everything is just really raw right now," I admit, and he nods in understanding.

"Of course it is, Eden. You don't need to explain yourself." He pats my hand on the table in gentle support, but it makes me feel clammy, and I pull away. "Does that link back to why you're here?" he asks, taking a bite of his burrito, and I frown at him for questioning me further when he just said I didn't need to explain myself. He really is nosey.

Although, his question does make me pause.

"Archie, why do you think I'm here?" I ask, intrigued to find out what he's been told by Richard.

"Oh, my dad just said you would be spending your senior year with us, he didn't say much more than that, and I honestly didn't question it. One thing I've learned growing up in Knight's Creek is that you don't question shit the adults say because you'll never get the truth. There's always some form of ulterior motive in play. Besides, you're a cute little cookie, and you're going to be my wing-woman this year. I've already decided."

I try to process his words as he swiftly changes the subject, and I agree, it does seem like the adults in this town are playing a real-life game of chess and we're their pawns, if what everyone has said so far is true. My mom, Richard, and the way that bitch acted with my mom solidifies it. I've lived in enough towns to see the signs.

Deciding to accept his change of subject for now, I offer him a fake glare. "I am not a cute cookie. I'm a badass bitch. You just make me nice for some reason. This is not my usual demeanor," I say with a pout, and he only smiles wider.

"Whatever you say, cookie." He grins, chowing down on his burrito, and I decide to join him.

Oh my fucking god. It's delicious. I groan as the spice explodes in my mouth, and my eyes close as I savor every bite.

"This is the best damn burrito I have *ever* had!" I exclaim, and Archie chuckles at me.

"I told you—food coma."

He's not wrong. Wasting no time talking, we demolish the food on our plates, him a lot quicker than me admittedly, but I'm still impressed I manage to eat it all. I love this place. The general vibe, people chatting, the usual sounds of plates being stacked and cutlery clattering around makes it feel homey.

"I think I need a nap," I say on a sigh, slumping back into the sofa, and Archie grins.

"Same. So are you ready for me to give you the lowdown on school starting Monday?" he asks, bursting my bubble of joy.

"Archie, you seem like an awesome guy, really, but I don't think that'll be necessary. I'm not going to be around long enough to give a shit."

"What do you mean? My dad gave me all this stuff for you." He frowns, pulling the papers from earlier from beside him in the booth. I'd totally forgotten about them.

Offering them to me, my eyes flicker over confirmed school applications that had been completed on my behalf, along with the school's welcome pack.

Asheville High?

Everything is so fucked up right now, and the only person I have to talk to is Archie. Deciding I need a sounding board for all this shit, I place the papers back on the table in front of me and clasp my hands together as I meet his gaze.

"I didn't know I was coming here until yesterday morning when I was forced into my G-Wagon by my mom at the risk of our lives. There was someone there, watching us, making sure I got in my car and headed here. I believe that same someone is linked to my dad's murder and lives in Knight's Creek. So I have no idea why I'm here, but I want answers, and I want the murderer convicted."

Relief floods my veins at being able to speak about this with someone, but it takes me a moment to realize he isn't surprised by my words. It reminds me of the ulterior motives he mentioned earlier.

"I'm here for whatever you need," he states, honesty and determination laced in his voice. "But one thing about Knight's Creek, Eden, is you have to beat them at their own game. And to do that, you have to play the game first."

Shit. I know he's right. I need to blend in, get the lay of the land, and then I can figure this shit out. I'll get no information if I just run around guns blazing, demanding answers in a town like this.

"Asheville High, here I come."

SEVEN
Eden

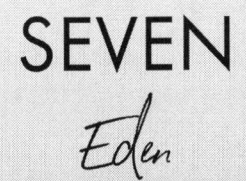

Glancing at my reflection one more time, I've kept my makeup natural today. Running my fingers through my wavy blonde hair, I decide I'm good to go.

"Eden, hurry up," Archie calls out from downstairs, and I fight back my eye roll. If we will coexist in this house and if he wants a ride, he'll damn well wait another minute.

I'm grateful Asheville High isn't so prestigious we have to wear a uniform. Instead, I get to rock my ripped skinny jeans with my long-sleeved white lace-up top. The lace ties in a bow at my breast, revealing a hint of my bra beneath.

It's hot as hell, but Archie promised the school was perfectly air conditioned, and I didn't want to show up on my first day with my ass hanging out. I'd save that for tomorrow.

Grabbing my drawstring backpack, I add another layer of my favorite lip gloss nervously when my phone vibrates on the bed. Rushing to grab it, my heart sinks a little when I see a text message from my mom and not an actual phone call.

Mom: Have an amazing first day, Eden. I love you. We will get through this. As your dad would always say, knock 'em dead.

I grip the phone tightly in my hands. I do not need her trying to channel my father, today of all days. Taking a deep breath, I quickly type out a simple thanks in response and head out to find Archie.

Waiting at the bottom of the open stairs, tapping away on his phone, Archie looks up as soon as he hears the stairs creak.

"About time, cookie, let's go." He sighs in exaggeration.

Over the past few days, I've barely left the house, except for running up and down the beach every day. Archie has been around on occasion, dressed in shorts and a tank top at all times, a total stereotypical California guy like I've seen in magazines, which is why he looks so different now in his skinny jeans and fitted black top. With his aviators perched on his nose, he looks way cooler than I give him credit for.

"Holy fuck. Who knew Archie Freemont had game?" I respond, ruffling his hair as I pass him.

"Archie Freemont always has game I'll have you know," he retorts, and I snicker as I unlock the G-Wagon.

"And does Archie Freemont always talk about himself in

the third person?" I throw back, and he gives me a pout. It's so easy to relax around him. I should definitely be more concerned than I am. I don't usually fall into sync with someone so easily.

"Just drive, cookie. You never keep the boys waiting."

Climbing in, we simultaneously fasten our seatbelts, and as I start the engine, he tries to take over the music system. Quickly smacking his hand away, I link my Spotify account up and let my new playlist filter through the speakers.

"Hey, no fair," he grumbles, and I don't even look in his direction. Instead, I focus on the road as I start moving while he inputs the school address into the GPS.

"Is this your G-Wagon?" I ask, not giving him a second to answer. "Nope, it definitely is not. You want your music on, you get your own vehicle, comprende?"

"Com-what now? You're extra sassy this morning," Archie states, and I can't even argue with that statement.

New surroundings, new school, and new people mean my defenses are on high alert. Slay them before they slay you.

Taking a deep breath, I quickly glance in his direction, and he's already grinning at me. Douchebag.

"Sorry, the whole new school vibes are rattling me," I say honestly, turning at the end of the road.

"It's all good, cookie. We just don't keep the boys waiting."

Shaking my head, I don't know what to ask first. Why the hell he keeps calling me cookie, or who the fuck are these boys? I decide on the latter since the nickname doesn't make me all that mad.

"Why should I be worried about keeping some boys waiting? I couldn't really give a shit."

Archie chuckles, wiping his hands on his jeans as he stares me down. "I forget you don't know the whole ins and outs of Knight's Creek. I'm on the football team." He leaves his sentence open, clearly waiting for me to say something, but I just shrug.

"I assumed so."

Sighing, I can feel his exaggerated glare at the side of my head. "The Asheville football team is what Knight's Creek lives for. We are motherfucking beasts on the field and pretty much have every girl dropping at our feet. Especially my friends. They practically run this town."

Run the town? How do three seniors run the town? He must see the doubt in my eyes, and his tone becomes a little more serious.

"Seriously, Eden. My friends are awesome to me. Everyone else, not so much."

"Noted."

"They were actually at my party the other night when you showed up. You would have met them if you came down. Party pooper," he says with a pout, lightening the mood again, just as we pull up outside the school parking lot.

"What the fuck?" I mumble, taking in the building before me.

I've been to enough schools to know when one screams of money. I even did a stint at a boarding school at one point, with uniforms and massive living quarters. But none of them have ever seemed this grand.

Four stories high, the ground floor is lined with archways with an undercover walkway running around the building. But it's the staircase leading you up there that holds my attention. The steps lead outwards before turning back on themselves, like a grand stately home.

Following the cars in front, I circle the parking lot.

"Head straight to the front, and you can park in my spot," Archie offers, and I frown.

"You have your own spot?" I clarify, and he nods in agreement.

"Yeah, football players get priority parking, with the cheerleaders right behind them. Then the rest is carnage." He says it so casually. It baffles me, but I don't call him out. Not yet anyway.

Pulling into his spot as he guides me, I spy the huge group of guys surrounded by girls twirling their hair, and I instantly know I located the football team and cheerleaders. I hope Archie doesn't expect me to play along with his little group.

I'm my own person, and that is most definitely *not* my group.

"I know my crew is not going to be your crew, cookie, but I have your back no matter what. Just don't do anything to piss off the three Allstars of Knight's Creek, all right? Like, they're my closest friends, but I'm not in their inner circle, so I can't do anything to protect you from them."

He clearly knows me well enough already to see I don't really give a shit about people's status, but I acknowledge his warning nonetheless.

Swinging my door open, I jump down from the G-Wagon. Using the tinted back window, I flatten the wispy pieces of hair floating around my face and slip on my sunglasses.

I meet Archie at the front of the SUV, where he has my backpack in hand. Slinging it over my shoulder, I walk alongside him since his friends are a little up the path, closer to the stairs.

"Where do I go once I get inside again?" I ask, needing to get to the office before the first bell rings.

"I can walk you if you like?" he offers for the hundredth time, but I'm already shaking my head. "Fine, Miss Independent. As soon as you get through the doors, you turn right, and it's at the end of the hall."

"Thanks," I murmur in response as he slows, his friends turning to see him, and my heart stills.

Shit.

Standing dead center of the group in front of me is Mr. Broody.

The same Mr. Broody who brought me to orgasm twice while everyone partied downstairs, too lost in our own minds to care about each other's names, wanting nothing more than to chase the ecstasy we both found.

I refuse to blush or acknowledge him as I take note of the two guys standing on either side of him, and I instantly know these are the three Archie was talking about.

"Freemont, my man, I thought you were going to be late," one of the guys chastises as he walks towards us, wrapping his arm around Archie's shoulder and standing right in front of me.

Wearing a plain black wool hat in the dead of summer, his brunette hair flicking out at the sides, I'm completely blindsided by his bright blue eyes and tanned face. Slightly taller than Archie, he smiles down at me, his teeth pearly white as he takes me in from head to toe.

"What's up, Holmes?" Archie responds, glancing at me with wide eyes, confirming this is one of the big dogs he spoke about earlier. The eyes must be a warning to make sure I don't cause a scene.

"Never mind me, Freemont. Who is this little beauty?"

With no sense of personal space, he steps closer, capturing a lock of my hair between his fingertips.

My skin prickles under his inquisitive gaze, and my eyes flicker behind him, coming straight in line with Mr. Broody, who stands stock-still, hands clenched at his side as he watches us.

Returning my stare to Holmes, who stands in front of me, I clear my throat.

"Sorry, I'm late," I murmur, feeling the eyes of everyone in the group, including the bitchy glares from the girls. Swiping my hair back out of his grip, I sidestep everyone, and my eyes are drawn to the quiet blond standing beside Mr. Broody, locking on to the tormented soul I haven't met yet.

Forcing myself to keep moving, I bypass everyone, including Archie.

"Fuck, baby, why you got to look so hot when you walk away from me?" Holmes calls out, and a smirk graces my lips.

Fucking player.

That's just my type. But I've already fucked his friend. Shame. I wonder if they've ever shared before?

Shut up, Eden.

My phone vibrates in my pocket, and I pull it out as I take the steps up to the entrance.

Archie: If you need me, just call or text. Behave!

Rolling my eyes, I refuse to glance back at them as I step inside the building, suddenly surrounded by a sea of people. Perfect. I love nothing more than slinking into the background undetected.

There'll be no reason to have to behave then.

Xavier

What the ever-loving fuck was that?

Forcing myself to unclench my hands, I swipe my hand

over my mouth, trying to count to ten in my mind to calm the stress building inside of me.

I knew I should have stayed away from her. Dammit.

Our parties are always at Archie's, since no one is allowed in our home and he only lives a little farther down the beach. The Allstars' end of summer party was just like any other, until a blonde siren snuck out of Archie's front door and took off jogging down the sand.

I was drawn to her in a way I can't even explain, which is why she is a siren, luring me out to the water's edge. I watched her jog all the way to our home, which juts out at the edge of the cliff before circling back.

I'd watched as she talked with Archie at the bottom of the stairs in his house, noticing beads of sweat trickled down the side of her face and her chest heaved rapidly with each breath she took.

Her long wavy blonde hair was pulled back from her face, which was bare of makeup, and I couldn't deny her raw beauty. The smallest sprinkling of tiny freckles were scattered across her cheeks and on her nose as her full pink lips begged to be touched. Her hourglass figure and long legs made her a hot topic for Knight's Creek for sure.

I didn't ask Archie who she was. That goes against all the codes written in hidden ink in Knight's Creek. I know everything and everyone, right down to bra size. I don't ever ask for details because I should already know the information.

So I acted completely unfazed by her presence, but when she didn't come down to party with us, my curiosity got the better of me.

I'd seen her on her balcony a few times, so I knew where to head. I was supposed to question her, find out exactly what I wanted to know, then rejoin the party. I wanted to know who the fuck she was and what the hell she was doing in Knight's Creek without me knowing. But one sultry glance from her sapphire blue eyes, and I found myself breaking all of my rules.

For one night only.

She said who she was didn't matter because she wouldn't be around long enough. Now she's showing up at my fucking school, in my fucking town, and I know little to nothing about her.

As if sensing my internal battle, Hunter raises his eyebrow at me as Tobias shouts after the girl in question.

We don't keep secrets. None. This town is already full of enough of them, so there's no room for them in our circle. But I didn't tell them about her, since I expected her to be gone.

When they questioned where'd I'd disappeared to, I murmured an excuse of a migraine, all while her coconut scent lingered all around me after showering in her en suite. I never hook up with girls I'm unfamiliar with, especially with a girl who didn't even offer her name.

She'd blown my mind, and I'd almost fallen asleep beside her—another rule broken. I can feel her getting under my skin again, and I won't fucking allow it, even if my subconscious felt safe enough around her to lull me to sleep.

"Archie, man, who is that fine specimen?" Tobias asks, still watching her as she climbs the steps, hands on his hips as he bites his lip, already picturing her beneath him.

"That's Eden. She's staying with us for the foreseeable future. My dad didn't care to tell me any more than that," Archie offers, rubbing the back of his neck as his gaze flickers between us. He's not watching her ass sway like Tobias is, so he's not hot for her. Yet I feel like a bond has already formed between them.

A light growl draws my attention to Roxy, who's pouting at not being the center of attention, and I have to physically force myself to not react to her childish shit.

"Let's go," I grunt, not waiting for any acknowledgment as I head for the steps. As expected, everyone follows suit, all while Tobias continues to pepper Archie with questions.

"You need to tell me what she's into, Arch, so I can cut the bullshit and find a connection with her."

Hunter snickers beside me, mumbling under his breath, "She's about the only girl his dick hasn't had a connection with."

He's not wrong, but that's Tobias.

"Honestly, Holmes, from what I can tell, she's going through a rough time right now," Archie answers sincerely, and I almost pause to find out what exactly is causing her pain, but I catch myself just in time.

She refused to tell me herself the other night, and when I

find out, it'll come from her lips. But I *will* find out, whether she likes it or not.

As I step inside the school doors, the sea of bodies suddenly parts as we stroll through the halls. If you see an Allstar, Hunter, Tobias, and me, you step the fuck out of the way. We are not above ruining you. Maybe someone needs to get Eden up to speed because I don't think Archie did a good enough job. I can already sense the trouble she's going to be.

Eden. It fits her. Just like the Garden of Eden, luring unsuspecting Adam in to take a bite of the forbidden fruit. Fuck.

"English first," Hunter murmurs, walking beside us as we head straight for the end of the hall.

"Xav, darling, wait up," Kate, aka KitKat, calls out, and I'm just about at my limit with fucking females today already.

I continue walking, but as I near the door for our English class, I feel her claws wrap around my bicep as she presses herself up against me.

"Darling, you didn't answer my texts last night." Glancing down at her, she flattens her vibrant pink hair down on her head. Her blue eyes filled with disappointment, already gazing up at me.

This is why you don't fuck girls without further information. You can't fucking shake them. I haven't let her wet my dick in almost a year, but since we've been in school together since kindergarten, she seems to think we're Mr. and Mrs. Knight's Creek.

Just as I'm about to throw her off me, I see Eden walking in our direction, her gaze flitting between what's in front of her and the piece of paper in her hand. She looks flustered, her eyebrows drawn together and her cheeks a little red as she flips her sunglasses up onto the top of her head.

Sidestepping us all, like we're not the fucking gods of this school, she moves effortlessly into the class. My feet move of their own accord, following after her like Tobias, just as the teacher points for her to take a seat beside Charlie James.

Tobias is instantly at her side, laying it on thick, but she barely makes eye contact as I take my assigned seat right behind her.

"What do you say, beauty? Lunch?" Tobias asks, but before she can respond, Mrs. Leach interrupts.

"Mr. Holmes, can you please give Miss Grady a little breathing space? She's barely been at Asheville High for five minutes and you're already polluting her space."

Tobias pouts as he takes the seat to my right as Hunter sits to my left, but my focus is on exactly what she called Eden.

Miss Grady.

Eden Grady.

I swallow past the lump in my throat as my mother's words play through my mind.

A blood feud against the Gradys was started long before we were born, Xavier. We ran them out of town. You come across one, you stand by the Knight name. Do you understand? If you see one, I put them there for a reason and you reign hell down on them.

I understand loud and clear. Mother may be a cunt, but she brought me a brand-new toy to play with.

TOXIC CREEK

EIGHT
Eden

The lesson seems to be a general back-to-class overview as Mrs. Leach drones on about the importance of grammar, specifically commas, those little bitches. The girl sitting to my left has smiled at me every time we've made eye contact, and I can already feel her ready to approach me when the bell rings.

Maybe that won't be so much of a bad idea if I don't want to be following Archie around like a lost puppy, especially since I want to avoid his friends at all costs.

He sat behind me throughout the class, and I've felt his eyes burning the back of my head the whole time. I can feel the tension growing between us, almost like a sixth sense washing over me. Mr. Broody is not happy, which means I need to be prepared for whatever shit he wants to say.

The bell rings, causing everyone around me to jump from their seats.

"That's it for today, class. Be prepared for the next lesson as we dig deeper into novels. The chosen title will be sent to your emails by the end of the day, and you're expected to have a copy for the next class."

Great, reading material of the variety I'm not interested in. What are the chances she'll choose smut books? Not likely.

As expected, I rise from my seat, lifting my bag off the ground as I do, and the girl beside me is waiting patiently with another smile.

"Hey, I'm Charlie. Eden, right?"

Her brown hair is pulled back in a sleek ponytail, and her big brown eyes are framed with black-rimmed glasses. She's wearing a similar outfit to me—ripped skinny jeans and a T-shirt. We're already matching.

"Right," I answer, nodding towards the door for her to follow me out of the classroom.

"First day, huh?"

"Yeah," I mutter in response, giving her a pointed look at her question, since the teacher already said I was new, but we're cut off by the guy from earlier, Holmes, I think, as he groans behind us.

"For real, X. How can someone be off-limits before I've fucking boned them?"

A quick glance over my shoulder shows Archie's friends

all staring at me. Mr. Broody wears a smug ass grin as he stares me down, sending a shiver down my spine. Why do I feel like things just went from bad to worse? Because that statement was definitely about me.

Archie steps out of the class, glancing between his friends and me, and I decide to keep walking.

Turning my back to them, Charlie suddenly links her arm through mine.

"So, you've met the three musketeers then?" she asks, and I raise my eyebrows.

"How are we defining met? One has already tried to get in my pants as soon as I parked my SUV. The other looks like he wants to bite my head off, while the blond just stares impassively at me. Yet I don't know any of their names." I sigh, frustrated by the fact that their names seem to matter to me.

She chuckles at my response, swiping a hand over her mouth. "I can meet you at lunch if you'd like, give you the lowdown. You're going to need it," she offers, and I find myself instantly nodding in agreement. "Awesome, do you have business class now?" she asks, and I groan.

"No. I showed up today and was given no say in my course schedule. So I have computer programming, which is actually awesome, but I don't understand why that is a replacement for business. Surely I should be able to do both, right?"

"Oh, Eden, this town is as backward as it is wealthy. You do as they say, not as they do. Classic cliché. Computer programming is down the hall to the right, but my business class is here," Charlie murmurs, pulling us to a stop as she points to the room at her left.

"Thanks."

"No worries, do you have gym before lunch?" she asks as we stand in the middle of the hallway, not caring about people trying to get past us. Although many of the students from our English class are now walking into the business room Charlie just pointed out.

Checking my schedule, I smile. "Yeah, it says I have track before lunch."

Why haven't I told her to get off my arm yet? So strange, but I kind of like it. She reminds me a little of Lou-Lou, bypassing my ice queen vibes and friending me anyway.

"Awesome, I'm on the cheer squad, so I have gymnastics at the same time."

My eyes widen at her statement. She is not the usual cheer squad material I would have guessed. The two girls with pink and red hair who glare at me as they pass us look more like cheerleader material, and I groan at myself for stereotyping. But those girls were hanging off the guys when I first arrived. #Cleatchasers.

"Sorry, I shouldn't—"

Charlie's chuckle stops me short as she interrupts. "Don't stress it, Eden. I like to cheer, but I don't like to be a bitch. Catch you after track."

With that, she disappears into the room beside us, leaving me to head farther down the hall. I'm surprised the hallway is suddenly empty as I make my way to the end, clearly not many people take this class, or if they do, I just spent too long talking with Charlie.

Spotting the computer programming room to my right, I pick up my pace a little when my foot catches on something, and I'm suddenly flying through the air.

Bracing my hands in front of me, my knees slam into the hardwood floor as my bag falls off my shoulder and my belongings spill out around me.

What the fuck?

Brushing my hair back off my face, I glance over my shoulder while on my hands and knees and freeze in place.

Mr. fucking Broody.

He snickers as he looks down at me, making my blood pump even faster through my body as anger fills my veins.

The blond guy walks around us, nodding to Mr. Broody as he goes, leaving me alone with this fucking lunatic.

Turning my back to him, my body is on high alert. I fucking know he tripped me, and I can feel my dismissal of him with my back turned won't make things any better for me, but I refuse to give him the satisfaction he obviously desires.

Pushing back onto my knees, I wipe my hands down my thighs before grabbing my belongings and putting them back in my bag. Thankfully, my phone doesn't look damaged and my sunglasses look unscathed, and those are the most important things. Although I make sure to grab my spare condoms and tampons as quickly as possible.

Just as I'm about to finish, I don't react quick enough as he loops his boot through the strap of my backpack and swipes it from beside me, flinging it straight into the wall.

What is this guy's fucking problem?

Standing, I whirl around to face him, but before I can give him a piece of my mind, he's stalking towards me, his shoulders back as he sneers at me, forcing me to walk backward as his hand wraps around my throat, and all too late, my back hits the wall behind me. The glare in his sinful eyes and the squeeze of his fingers has my heart pounding in my ears as I try to kick myself into action.

I'm too shocked to speak as I stare up at him, watching as he crowds my space. His nose nearly brushes mine as he lifts my chin, almost forcing me to my tiptoes, and even at five foot seven, he towers above me. He's that close, but there's no intimacy, not like that night. Is he just fucking with me because I'm the new girl?

No. His eyes are filled with something else entirely. Fury and a tinge of intrigue darken his hazel eyes as he stares me down.

"Get. Your. Fucking. Hand. Off. Me," I growl out, my throat bulging against the grip of his hand, but that only makes his fingers flex against my throat, making my pulse beat wildly as I try to push against his chest.

"Eden Grady," he murmurs, and I hate how my body reacts to hearing my name on his gruff lips. "You said your name didn't matter, siren. You said you wouldn't be around long enough for it to matter, but now I know who you are. I'm going to rip your soul to shreds and make sure no one can piece you back together again."

The dark threat laced in his words quickly dulls my body's reaction as fear coats my skin. I can tell he isn't joking, but I refuse to be pushed around by some douche who likes getting his own way, especially when I have no idea why.

"I'm not fucking Humpty Dumpty, asshole," I snap, but he doesn't respond, ignoring me just like he did the other night.

Wrapping my hand around his wrist at my throat, I try to pull his grip away, but he doesn't move an inch, his lip pulling in a sneer. Digging my nails into his skin, I'm sure there will be blood, but all he does is lean in further, bringing his mouth to my ear.

"Dig deeper, Eden. I love it rough, but you already know that, right? If that was part of some big plan to get under my skin and stop me from coming for you, you're truly mistaken. If anything, it only makes it worse for you."

"I have no idea what you're talking about, and you came to me, remember?" I purr, dragging my nails down his skin, and he jumps back like I burned him.

"Tell yourself what you want," he growls out, straightening

his jacket as I spy little drops of blood at his wrist. "But you're mine to fuck with, you better get used to that."

Turning on his heels, he marches away, entering the room for business before slamming the door shut behind him. I can feel the rattle from here, but I don't have time to compose myself.

Quickly throwing everything back into my bag for the second time, I hitch it over my shoulder and step into the classroom. I can't help but rub my neck, feeling exactly where he held me, knowing it's going to bruise. But I falter when I see everyone staring at me, including the teacher.

Clearing his throat, he refuses to make eye contact with me. Ah, so someone with authority heard but did nothing about it. Great. Dick.

"We don't accept tardiness in this classroom, Miss Grady. Take a seat beside Hunter, and let's get on with the lesson, shall we?"

Who the fuck is Hunter? Glancing around the room, the walls are lined with iMacs, and the only spare seat must be where he means, at the end of the line to the right, but I stall as I walk towards it.

Blondie. Mr. Broody's friend is the person occupying the seat beside it. Fucking great. His focus is on the screen in front of him, his shoulders relaxed like he has no cares in the world.

Dropping down into the seat, I make sure to train my eyes on the screen. I could do with a minute to understand what the fuck just happened out there, but I refuse to show any weakness in front of this guy.

"Everyone's ID and password details haven't changed from last year, so if everyone can log in, we're going to get straight to it," the teacher announces, and I start rifling through my bag, looking for the details I might need.

Pulling all the paperwork out, I search again, struggling to find any information, when my eyes snag on a small piece of paper that looks like login details.

Placing it beside the keyboard, I throw everything back in my bag, but when I turn to log in, the paper is gone. I glance at the guy beside me, and he's tapping away like nothing's going on.

Finally getting a good look at him, I notice his blond hair is styled like he spent the morning surfing or running his fingers through it, while his green eyes shine like emeralds, but not with happiness. No, there's trouble and pain shimmering beneath the surface of his calm, nonchalant façade.

Remembering what I'm supposed to be doing, I check down at my feet and under the keyboard and find nothing. It's this douche canoe, I can feel it, likely playing petty games on behalf of his friend. Classy.

"Are we going to pretend you don't have my login details for the whole lesson?" I ask, cutting the bullshit and getting straight to the point. These people have already pissed me off today.

He looks at me from the corner of his eye, his face impassive as I glare at him. Lifting his shoulder, I watch as his arms bulge in his muscle fit T-shirt. He's bigger up close than I expected.

"I don't know what you're talking about," he grumbles, his husky voice reverberating around us, and I pinch the bridge of my nose while I count to ten, trying desperately not to lean closer and smell him. Whatever aftershave he uses is intoxicating, and I'm a sucker for sandalwood.

"What is this even all about? If I'd have known who your friend was, I wouldn't have let him fuck me for god's sake," I growl out, turning my gaze to him.

His mouth is wide open as he gapes at me, clearly surprised by what I just said, and it's the most reaction I've seen him offer so far. That's when I spot the smallest piece of paper sticking out of the pocket in his jeans.

With no care while he's caught off guard, I dig my hand in his pocket and rip the piece of paper away from him. My fingers squeeze his thigh instinctively as I do, and I can't decide if it's to cause him pain or not because his thighs are thick.

Shit. Why am I constantly drawn to the hot douchebags?

Shaking my head, I focus on the login details. Giving him a pointed look as he remembers to close his mouth, I turn away from him. Fuck these assholes. Quickly typing my details in, I memorize them, so this fucker can't play me again.

"For clarification, you're saying that my friend, Xavier Knight, fucked you?" he asks, turning to meet my gaze.

Leaning back in my seat, I sigh. I probably shouldn't have

said that.

"I have no idea who Xavier Knight is, and it doesn't matter."

The deep chuckle that passes his lips causes me to still as he leans into my personal space, his breath fanning against my lips.

"Xavier Knight just had you on your hands and knees in the hallway, and it does matter. You see, we share, Xavier, Toby, and me. So, if you've had one of us..." He trails off, leaving the sentence unfinished for me to come to my own conclusions, but I say nothing.

Swallowing past the lump in my throat, I berate myself for opening my mouth, the thought of being sandwiched between the three of them playing in my mind.

What the fuck actually is this place? I need answers, yet a million more fucking questions surface as well. This place is going to chew me up and spit me out...or more specifically, they are. If I let *them*.

KC KEAN

NINE
Tobias

"Perfect play, Allstars. If we continue like this, the championship will be ours once again this year," Coach shouts as he paces in front of the team. "Let's make sure that happens. I want focus, determination, and awards." Coach Carmichael's arms are doing more talking than his mouth as he swings them around enthusiastically. "This is the final year for a lot of you. Let's make it count and go down in history for the most consecutive wins. Now, stretch it out. I'll see you boys in the morning, bright and early."

Happy with his little speech, he nods at everyone before turning on his heels and heading inside.

Thank god for that. The first day back, and he's already got my muscles screaming more than ever. Fuck. I work out every day on cardio and strength building, but he somehow seems to make me feel like a newbie.

Dropping my water bottle at my feet, I start by stretching my legs out like everyone else. Hunter and Xavier stand on either side of me, in the same position, away from the rest of the team, except Xavier isn't panting for breath like the rest of us. He takes this shit far too seriously.

I guess he thinks this might be his only outlet to step out of his parent's shadow, but we all know that's not likely. He could go pro in a heartbeat, but his parents will find a way to keep him in Knight's Creek forever.

We should just count ourselves lucky that they let us live in the beach house while they destroy the world from their fucking mansion up in the hills.

"So, X, I had a nice little chat with the new girl after you left earlier," Hunter murmurs, his face as impassive as ever.

My interest is piqued, and hearing about the sexy new blonde that graces our halls has my dick waking up too.

Scanning the area, I spot her running track with the rest of the team, and she's fucking fast. I have a feeling they'll be trying to get her to represent the school with form like that.

With her blonde wavy hair pulled back into a hair tie and her body donning the school gym uniform, I zone out as I watch her tits bounce as she runs.

Hot. As. Fuck.

"I thought we agreed to not fucking speak to her," Xavier

grumbles, leaning forward to touch his toes, but I'm more focused on the slight curl of Hunter's lips, and I instantly know that he knows something Xavier thinks he doesn't.

"Hmm, we did. You also said to fuck with her, and you know I'm not big on tripping girls in the hall, then pinning them to the wall," Hunter mumbles, and my mouth instantly feels dry. I should have known he was up to something when he didn't come to business straight away.

Licking my lips, Xavier rolls his eyes at me as he catches the movement, but there is a lot I could do with a pretty girl like that pinned up against the wall.

Xavier turns his gaze to Hunter, waiting for him to continue with whatever he's trying to say, but they already have me bored. I continue to listen, though, as I go back to tracking Eden's every move.

"So I stole her login details so she couldn't start the class, and she downright called me out. Girl's got balls, that's for sure." I don't miss the hint of genuine surprise in his voice, and if anything, that has me even more intrigued.

"Archie needs to fucking pull her in line. He clearly hasn't updated her on the rules," Xavier grunts, and speaking of the devil, he's sauntering over to her right now.

I watch as she sips her water, listening to Archie as he talks animatedly with her, and she playfully smacks him on the arm, laughing at whatever shit came out of his mouth.

I pout. If Xavier says we boycott her, then that's what we

do. But I want to see a little glimpse of her like this before I fuck her into next week.

Turning, they head inside together while I get a semi over the way her ass sways with each step.

"Well, she may have gotten angry and growled something along the lines of, 'If I'd have known who your friend was, I wouldn't have let him fuck me, for god's sake.' Care to expand on that, Xavier?"

I almost pull a muscle in my neck as I whip around to look at the two of them. The silence from Xavier only confirms exactly what Hunter just said, and I openly gape at this fucker. The smug grin on Hunter's face as Xavier frowns only confirms what he said.

"Wait, you fucked her? When? And why the fuck was this not a team effort?"

I'm not saying every time has to be a train, but damn I would have killed to have been on the end of that. For as long as I can remember, we've shared girls. That way, no bitch is going to get between us. But we fuck them once and walk away. Otherwise, you end up with girls like Roxy or KitKat who don't back off.

That's exactly why you don't go near someone twice around here.

"More importantly, did you wear a condom?"

The pair of us stare at Hunter like he grew a third head. Why would we ever *not* do that?

"Shut the fuck up, Hunter. I'm not stupid. We fucked 'with

a condom.'" Using air quotes, he frowns at Hunter, who rolls his eyes at Xavier's rare theatrics.

"Good. We don't need to give anyone any more excuses to stick our asses in juvie. You know our parents would all but die if you got some girl pregnant senior year, and they already use the prison as a warning. They'd actually fucking do that shit to us," Hunter states so matter-of-factly, and he's not fucking wrong.

"We're getting off track here," I interrupt, nodding for us to start heading inside, and they both follow. We're the last ones on the field since we're too busy gossiping. "Please explain when you got to play with the hot new girl. I'm fucking jelly." I pout again, but it never works on him.

"It doesn't matter. I did, and it won't be happening again. I made a mistake, and now I know who she is." Xavier's voice is gruffer than usual as his nose scrunches in disgust. Is someone disappointed?

"What do you mean now you know who she is?" Hunter asks as we step into the school hallway that leads to the locker room.

"I mean, we didn't exchange names, but when Mrs. Leach called out her full name in English, I remembered something my mother once said." Staring at him expectantly, he sighs. "My mother said there has always been a family feud with the Gradys, and if I ever came across one, it's because she put them there. She ran them out of town years ago, but Eden is Eden

Grady. It can't be a coincidence."

Fuck.

Xavier is Xavier Knight, as in Knight's Creek. His parents fucking run this town on a legacy. Knight's Creek has never been anything else but a toxic town run by the Knight family. Twisted fuckers. But if what he says is true, which it usually is, then his mother had something to do with her arrival, and we want nothing to do with shit his mother fucks up.

"Well, as true as all that may be, I need a loophole because she is divine," I murmur, squeezing my dick as proof, but they simply shake their heads.

"Stop pouting over lost pussy, Toby," Hunter grumbles, stepping into the locker room, and I turn my gaze to Xavier.

"Do what you want, Tobias, but it all revolves around hate. So, if you fuck her, it's a hate fuck, and I want the filthy details laundered around the school. Gradys are mine to play with, and I'm going to make her life a living hell so she gets the hell out of Knight's Creek for good. No one will want to stick around to feel the wrath of a Knight."

Well, fuck. That I can definitely work with.

Eden

Fuck, I'm starving.

I love running, and track is thankfully my go-to sport, so

I'm lucky they automatically assigned me there, I guess. But running in the midday heat only made me sweat more. So I rush a quick shower in the girls' locker room, thankful for the provided products, which actually smell of coconut and not some chemical formula.

While I was running track, Charlie was on the other side of the field practicing with the cheer squad, and now she's sitting on the bench with my things, waiting patiently for me so we can go to lunch.

Rolling my gym clothes up, I force them into my bag. I was lucky they provided the clothes onsite, since I didn't show up with any. But I did have to listen to the woman at the desk drone on about how you are only given one set. Blah. Blah. Blah.

After touching up my makeup and releasing my hair so it floats around my shoulders again, I'm good to go.

"Sorry, I'm ready," I murmur, and Charlie jumps from her seat on the bench.

I may have taken my time to avoid all the bodies in the locker room, so only a few people remain as we head for the door. I do not need to take on the rest of the cheer squad, with their glares and murmurs at the new girl stepping on their territory.

I follow Charlie's lead, desperate for food as she probes into my day so far.

"How have your classes been?"

"Shit," I answer honestly, and she grins beside me. "I actually need you to get me up to speed because I know nothing about the hierarchy here. It's not going to stop me from acting how I would, but I need to know who I'm up against."

"For sure. Let's grab our food, and I'll give you the lowdown." She nods enthusiastically as she pushes open the doors to the cafeteria.

Just like any other lunch hall I've ever been in, the huge space has the food at the far end, with open space to the left to line up, while the rest of the room is filled with long tables and benches on either side.

My eyes instantly fall to the center of the room where douchebag numbers one and two from earlier are sitting. Their friend, Holmes, with his hat firmly on his head, stares me down in return, licking his lips as he does, and I roll my eyes.

Joining the line for food, we fall into a comfortable silence between us as I eye the menu up on the wall.

We might be lining up like any other school, but damn, the food is anything but standard. Poached salmon, filet steak, even dauphinoise potatoes. It's like Gordon Ramsey's been in here and revamped the whole thing. But I won't be complaining, I need sustenance right now, and it definitely beats cardboard meatloaf I've had at other schools.

Just as we near the counter, an arm wraps around my shoulders, and the zesty smell instantly tells me it's Archie.

"How are my favorite girls?" he sings, glancing down at me before turning his gaze to Charlie, and I watch his pupils dilate in appreciation. Ahh, I see.

"We are good, and you are cramping our style," I mutter, making Charlie giggle as she glances between us.

"Wait, are you two…"

"Ew, no," we both chime in at the same time as Archie drops his arm, and we put a little distance between each other.

"No, sillies," Charlie laughs. "That is just, no. I was trying to ask if you two are related?" She finishes around her giggles, making me frown.

Slowly turning to Archie, I find him staring at me the exact same way, and we both shake our heads.

"What would make you ask that?" I ask, and she simply shrugs her shoulders.

"It's your eyes. Ignore me," she rambles before stepping up to the counter to order her food.

Glancing at Archie out of the corner of my eye, he snickers, and I roll my eyes. Charlie is officially crazy. I mean, we both have big blue eyes, but his are more of a blue-grey, while mine are like ice. Not the same.

"So, how has everything been? Are you behaving?" he asks, and I give him a pointed look.

"I have been minding my own business, but it seems like your little friend is unhappy with my arrival," I murmur in response, and he gives a heavy sigh, knowing instantly who I'm talking about, like it's a common occurrence.

I continue down the line, opting for the steak and potatoes as Archie awkwardly stumbles over how to respond, wanting to keep his friends while seemingly wanting to protect me in some strange way.

"I'll try and talk to him or something—"

"No, Archie, you won't. I don't want you to get any unnecessary backlash. You're Switzerland, okay? Their actions don't reflect on you, and as much as I think you're cool, I'm not sticking around, remember? I don't want you putting your neck on the line for nothing."

He looks like he's about to object, but I stare at him, pleading with my eyes to understand, and he relents, giving me a nod in confirmation.

There is something so pure about him that makes me want to keep him out of trouble. Maybe it's because we've both lost a parent and it connects us on another level.

The thought of my dad and his lifeless body, flashes through my mind, and I immediately feel my mood sour. As if knowing where my head just went, Archie squeezes my shoulder in silent comfort.

"Where are we sitting, Charlie?" I ask, and she indicates to follow her. Archie stays at my side, his tray loaded up with the exact same food as mine, but to serve like five people since he's stocking up on calories.

My back tenses as Charlie walks past the center table, and I know I'm not making it past without being stopped. Archie must think the same because he opts to move to my left side, putting a little space between me and the table.

"You can sit with us if you want?" Archie offers, but I just raise my eyebrows at him. That is never going to happen.

"Please stop trying to force me into some magical circle. I'm good. Please just sit down with them. It's all good," I mumble, and he does at least walk down the bench when we get to the table.

Xavier sits dead center, Hunter to his left and Holmes to his right. It annoys me that I don't know Holmes' first name, I mean unless it is his first name and I am completely out of the loop.

I can feel their eyes tracking me as I force myself to look straight ahead. The whole table seems to hang on their every word.

The second I'm almost free of walking by the table, I feel Holmes' attention zero in on me before his hand reaches out to grab my arm, and I struggle to contain the way my body flinches.

I expect the grip to be harsher, so I'm surprised when he's grinning up at me as his thumb rubs back and forth on my arm, skin on skin, leaving goosebumps in his wake.

"Are you not even going to attempt to fit in with the popular kids, new girl? You're hurting my feelings." He widens his blue eyes, giving me his puppy dog look as he rests his cheek on his other hand, and I swear under any other circumstances, it would have fucking worked too.

But I'm all too familiar with the bitter taste the people at this table can leave in your mouth.

"I'm good, but thanks," I say, glancing over to Charlie,

who is standing at the table she was walking us to, but she can't decide whether to sit down or help me out. I subtly shake my head before glancing around the table.

Archie sits facing Hunter, and a few other guys I'm assuming are on the football team sit on either side of him, while a few members of the cheer squad maul them all.

"She's not fucking worthy to sit here anyway," the girl sitting across from Xavier declares as she rises from her seat and tosses her pink hair dramatically over her shoulder.

She circles around me as Holmes keeps hold of my arm and plops down onto Xavier's lap, attempting to show a united front, but I don't miss the clouding of his eyes as she does, and I smirk.

"Isn't that right, Xavier? We were literally just saying if Archie walked her over here and she tried to take a seat, I am to knock her out. Didn't we?"

She fakes sweet and innocent as I refrain from rolling my eyes to the back of my head in irritation.

"Bitch, you can try, but don't be butt hurt when I put you on the floor," I respond casually, and if looks could kill, she might have just slain me. "So, if you're done practicing your stroking skills?" I say, glancing down at Holmes, who releases his hold on me suddenly as if only just realizing what he was doing.

"You can stay if you show us your head skills." Hunter winks, surprising me with his outburst. I thought he was the quiet, observant, and obedient one, maybe he still is. "Because

X mentioned they might have been less than par." I want to wipe the smug ass look from his face, but I refuse to act embarrassed about my sexuality.

"I'm sorry, was that before or after you gripped my waist so hard with pleasure, you left bruises?" I retort, with a sly grin of my own, staring Xavier dead in the eyes. "Maybe next time, don't shower and use the girl's products to keep the smell of her on your skin. It makes you look desperate."

Before I can see it coming, the other bitch sitting at the table with red hair hits the bottom of my tray and sends my food flying as the tray remains in my hands. A little goes on my top and pants, but not enough as I'm sure she would have liked.

It feels like the whole cafeteria is staring, laughing, even if only under their breath, and it just seems to fuel my anger.

My blood is boiling, and as much as I try to keep myself calm and collected, it's no use. "Oh no, whatever shall I do?" I ask sweetly, and without much thought, I tighten my grip on the edge of the tray in my hand and swing it at her motherfucking face.

I've learned over the years as the new kid not to give them a fucking inch and always aim for the face. It shows you mean business.

I grin like a maniac as she screams in pain, and the whole table stands in the chaos. I can feel hundreds of eyes on me, but I don't give a shit.

I have enough to deal with, and I don't need some rich,

bratty bitches in my face as well. They need to know that I'm not going to take their shit.

"Get her the fuck out of here, Archie, before I do it myself," Xavier growls out, but I see the glimmer in his eyes which tells me I caught these assholes by surprise. Especially with the way Hunter and Tobias stare around the table in slow motion.

Good.

I hear Charlie call my name, but before I can do anything else, Archie is throwing me over his shoulder and escorting me out of the hall like a ragdoll, and I let him. I don't want to be in their presence a second longer.

Fuck this town, and fuck these people.

TOXIC CREEK

TEN
Eden

One foot in front of the other, I continue in the sand up and down the beach, trying to calm the stress inside of me as the anger still burns from earlier.

Archie carried my ass out of the cafeteria and put me straight in my G-Wagon, insisting I go home and calm down.

Home. This isn't my fucking home. But he was right—staying wouldn't have helped anyone. Which is why I didn't bitch him out for manhandling me.

I wallowed in my room for a while, but my heart wouldn't calm down, the rage continuing to build inside of me. I've always had a backbone, but these douchebags just rub me the wrong way, and I can't seem to move past it.

I don't know what their problem is, and I don't know why

I let them get under my skin so much, but the three apparent rulers at Asheville High are at another level compared to other schools I've attended.

That's when I decided to slip into my black sports bra and matching running shorts and hit the sand. Taking the water's edge, I decided a couple of laps up and down the stretch of beach might help.

Since the first run, I've learned to bring two bottles of water, keeping one on the deck of Archie's house and the other on a rock at the opposite end of the beach, right where the huge house sticks out at the end.

Swiping my face on the towel, I close my eyes as "High Hopes" by Panic! At the Disco plays through my earphones. I already feel calmer, more in control of my emotions.

The music shuts off as an incoming call comes through, and I quickly pull my phone from the waterproof safety strap on my arm, dropping the towel to the sand as I do.

Mom flashes across the screen, and I quickly answer, my heart rate increasing as a sense of hope washes over me.

"Mom?"

"Eden, why am I getting calls telling me you hit someone in the face at lunchtime and then skipped school?"

I look down at the phone as her voice rings in my ears through the earphones and try to process what she just said. There's no 'Hi, Eden. How are you? Are you okay?' She's simply calling to give me shit. What the hell.

"Who called you?" I finally ask, and she scoffs down the phone.

"That's all you have to say, Eden?"

Taking a deep breath, I try to calm myself again, but she's literally making me even angrier than I was before.

"What do you have to say about the fact that I'm in a town I don't want to be in? With some guy and his son who I don't even know. While attending a school filled with some spoiled rich kids with an ego complex who try to tear me down, but the second I stand up for myself, *I'm* the problem?"

I don't hold back as I practically growl the words at her, and she remains silent for a moment before responding. Pacing in front of the water's edge, I try to let the sound of the waves calm the hurt building inside me at the fact my mom only wants to call and lecture me. Not to check how I am or make sure I'm okay, but to fucking *lecture* me.

"You can't mess with these people, Eden. They'll destroy you," she murmurs, and my hand clenches at my side, my nails biting into my skin as I let her words sink in.

"I don't know what's going on here, Mom, but Dad always told me to stand my ground and not let anyone make a fool out of me."

"Yeah, and look where that got us," she chides back, and her tone makes me freeze.

"If there is something you want to say, let me know. Otherwise, I'm finished. I don't need you to make snide remarks about my dead dad," I snap back, forcing myself to hold back the tears.

"I'm sorry, Eden. That wasn't fair of me," she soothes down the phone, but it feels like the damage has already been done.

"I've got to go, but just an FYI, I am here alone, Mom. I can already tell how these people operate, and I will *never* let them treat me the way they clearly treated you. I want answers, and I'm going to get them. Whatever it takes."

With that, I end the call. Fuck her for only calling when something happened, not when I've needed her the past few days. And fuck her for not checking to see if I'm okay.

As I place my phone in my waterproof arm strap, the music starts playing again in my ears, leaving me to take off running down the beach, trying to chase the anger away. With the heat beating down on me, I run up and down a few times before I stop at the opposite end of the beach and take a swig of my water.

Looking up to the sky as the sun beats down on me, I down the last of my drink, feeling the beads of sweat trickle down my back. My chest heaves with each breath I take, but I'm feeling much better. The combination of the music, the ocean, and the burn in my body from running is soothing me.

The music dies in my ears again, but this time, it's the batteries dying. Just as I'm pulling them out, I hear laughter, and all at once, I'm lifting off the ground, my earphones drop to the sand as I'm hoisted over someone's shoulder. Again.

I expect to have to brace myself for coming face-to-face with someone's ass, so it catches me completely off guard when I find myself staring at some guy's junk bulging behind his denim jeans.

"What the fuck! Put me down!" I shout, trying to see who the hell is touching me, but before I can look up, they're charging into the water, the sprays kicking up into my face before they drop me unceremoniously in the ocean.

Panic kicks in as I fear I'm going to drown, but whoever it is quickly pulls me from under the waves, and I find myself waist-deep in the water.

Coughing and spluttering, I swipe my hair out of my face to find Holmes staring down at me with a grin covering his face.

Motherfucking Holmes. What an absolute asshole.

But if I know anything, I know he won't likely be here alone. Those three seem to travel in a pack, and a quick glance over his shoulder proves me right as I see Hunter standing at the water's edge and Xavier halfway up the wooden steps that lead up to the massive beach house at the end.

"What the fuck, douchebag?" I finally yell as the ringing calms in my ears, and Holmes just fucking laughs at me, dripping wet from the waist down, but his beanie hat remains in place.

"You looked like you needed to cool off, so I helped you out."

"I don't fucking need your help, shithead," I grumble, starting to step around him, but with the pull of the water, I'm not moving fast enough, and he wraps his hand around my arm. Just like he did in the cafeteria earlier.

"I like you all feisty, little Eden," he murmurs, sex dripping from every word, and if he wasn't such a douche, I might have fallen for it.

"That's great, but you can let go now," I grunt, trying to pull my arm from his hold, but he only seems to draw me closer.

Bringing us chest to chest, he looks now at my cleavage showing and licks his lips. Finally meeting my gaze again, he bites his lips, and I can't help the butterflies that swarm in the pit of my stomach. Why the hell am I not pushing him away?

Fuck.

I need to get the hell away from him and his friends. They're nothing but trouble, and I really don't need any more shit on my plate right now. They're so obnoxious.

"Let me go," I whisper, and he flashes me his pearly whites, not moving an inch.

"I will if you come to my birthday party on Friday."

I almost laugh until I see he's serious. "Why would I do that?" I ask, my eyes staring at the way the wet top covering his body clings to him.

"Because I asked nicely."

"You think this is asking nicely?" I ask, waving my free hand between us, and he simply shrugs.

"Baby, I'm an Allstar, I get what I want, when I want it, and I don't usually have to ask at all."

I can see in his eyes that his statement is true, but my response is cut off by Xavier shouting down.

"Let's go, Tobias. Let the trash dry out."

I know he means me, fucker. But my focus is more on the douche before me. Tobias. Tobias Holmes.

"Nah, I like her wet," he murmurs with a wink before sinking me back into the water.

Motherfucker.

When I resurface, I find him halfway up the beach, walking side by side with Hunter as I feel Xavier's eyes burning my skin from his little pedestal.

I offer him a one-finger salute before I make my way out of the water. Luckily, my earphones are unharmed, scattered on the beach, so I grab them and make my way to Archie's house. Thank God my arm strap is waterproof, otherwise I'd be needing *another* new phone.

The salty water feels scratchy against my skin as the sun attempts to dry me, which makes me walk a little quicker so I can shower.

The second I step into the house, I spot Archie and Charlie on separate sofas to the right, and they both jump up when they see me.

"Hey, where have you been? Wait, have you been swimming in your sneakers?" Charlie makes a face as she takes me in, and I glance down at myself too. I wish that's what it was.

"No, I was running on the beach when Mr. Tobias Holmes

decided to dunk me. Twice." They both cringe, but I stop them before they can say anything. "It's fine. I'm fine. I just need a shower."

Charlie stares me down for a moment before nodding in agreement, likely seeing I'm not going to budge on this. "Awesome, I'll wait around for you. I gave Archie a ride home so we could have that conversation we were going to have at lunch."

I have to think back to what she's talking about when I remember she had planned to give me the lowdown on this stupid school, town, and the ridiculous people who live here.

"I definitely need that talk now more than ever," I mutter in response. "Give me five minutes, okay?"

Taking the stairs two at a time, I slam my door shut behind me and peel my damp clothes off my body. Pulling my phone from the waterproof holder, I toss it on the bed before I step into the shower.

Letting the cold water cool my skin, I make quick work of washing the sea salt from my skin and throwing on my favorite Jerry Rice San Francisco 49ers football jersey. It's from the 1993 season when he won NFL offensive player of the year for the second time, and it used to belong to my dad. He gave it to me when I was twelve when he had to work away for six months, and even now, it makes me feel close to him.

It falls mid-thigh, so I slip a pair of booty shorts on, pull my hair into a messy bun on top of my head and make my way back downstairs.

I see Archie and Charlie out by the pool, but I don't miss the box of donuts sitting on the kitchen island. Grabbing a honey cruller and a Boston crème, I make my way outside.

This is the first time I've really been out by the pool. Sleek parasols and cushioned sun-loungers surround a kidney-shaped pool with a jacuzzi attached. There is a lot of open space between the pool and the glass balcony that frames the whole outdoor space, with a huge barbeque set up and a covered daybed.

No wonder Archie is the party king. He has the space for it.

"You found the donuts," Archie says as I take a seat on the lounger beside Charlie. I take a giant bite out of the Boston crème and wave the other in the air at him in response, and he grins at my antics. "Are you okay?" he asks, the seriousness in his eyes catching me by surprise.

"I'm fine, Archie. Well, as fine as I can be," I answer honestly, feeling a little uncomfortable with the fact he seems to care so instantly, but he actually feels like a friend too.

"Okay, I'll give you girls some space for that gossipy shit I know you do. Yell if you need me. I'll be in the shower. Charlie, you can join me in the shower at any time." He offers her an exaggerated wink that makes her blush, and I smile at them.

I don't miss Charlie watching Archie leave before clearing her throat and tucking her hair behind her ear. The blush that colors her cheeks makes me grin, but I don't push the subject.

"So, where do we even begin with Asheville High?" I ask,

taking another bite of the delicious donut and recline on the lounger.

Sighing, Charlie turns to face me, stretching her legs out as she grips the edge of her chair.

"Well, Asheville High is as messed up as Knight's Creek as a whole. Everyone's parents are teaching their kids to act just like they did in high school, creating a never-ending cycle of torture for everyone but themselves."

"Does that include your parents?" I ask, watching for her response, but she simply huffs.

"My mom was the nerd, and my dad was a tech guy. Thankfully, they blended in under the radar mostly. If anything, they broke the mold with me because you would have never caught my mom in a cheerleading outfit. But it's my family name that gives me a shield, so to speak."

"How do you mean?" Finishing one donut, I bite straight into the next, loving the sugary goodness.

"Well, I'm Charlie James, and my great-grandparents were awesome or something, and the national park hiking spot is named Mount James, even though it is nowhere near the size of a mountain." She waves her hand around dismissively. I like that she doesn't seem to take herself too seriously.

"Noted, names get you places around here, it seems. Does anyone else have a link like that? I mean, I'm assuming they do."

"Yeah, Xavier Knight as in Knight's Creek, the founders

of the town. Hunter Asheville as in Asheville High. Archie Freemont as in Freemont Beach." She starts reeling all of these names off and landmarks around town, and my mouth falls farther open with each one.

"Holy shit," I splutter. "No wonder those assholes think they run the place, they practically do," I say, referring to Xavier and Hunter, probably Holmes too, and she nods with a grimace.

"Pretty much, the Allstars are the be-all and end-all of this whole town. They even had the school football team changed to be the Allstars instead of the Asheville Knights. "

Sitting up, I brace my arms on my thighs as I sigh. "And I somehow managed to piss them off, huh?" I roll my eyes, and she nods in agreement.

"Yeah. Roxy and KitKat, the girls from earlier, are serious bitches too. Roxy is the cheer captain, and KitKat her second-in-command. I can barely tolerate them, but like I said, my name shields me."

Swiping a hand down my face, I come to the only conclusion I can see. "I have no name to shield me, so I'm fair game then."

"It seems so. Do you have any links to the town?" she asks, leaning her face to the sun, and I consider how much I want her to know. I don't know this girl for shit, but other than Archie, I have no one else to ask.

"I think my parents were from here, but I have a feeling that'll only make things worse for me, especially if my name isn't on anything. That seems to matter around here," I admit, and she peers down at me.

"I can ask my parents if you like. They're super chill and avoid all the toxic bullshit that goes on in this town." The sincerity in her voice has me nodding before I've really considered the situation.

"Thanks. My last name is Grady."

Before she can respond, Archie is hollering down from the balcony on the opposite side of the house to mine.

"The boys are on their way over. I thought you might want a heads-up."

By boys, I know he means the Allstars, and I groan. "Really? Can't you go to their house?"

Even Charlie laughs at me as she rises from the lounger and throws her backpack over her shoulder.

"No one goes to their house, cookie," Archie shouts, and I look to Charlie for confirmation.

"Never. They live there together, alone. And if they say they're on their way over, then you fucking accommodate them. No questions asked." They live by themselves?

Dammit. I want to stomp my foot like a petulant child, but I refrain as Charlie grins. "I'm heading out. Maybe lock yourself in your room?" she offers, but Archie interrupts.

"Yeah, apparently that doesn't work either." He smirks down at me, finally bringing up the whole Xavier and me situation he found out about earlier at lunch.

Fuckity, fuck, fuck, fuck.

Standing, Archie nods in the direction of the beach, and even from here through the glass balcony, I can see them making their way along the water.

This is all part of their mind games. They know they can fuck with me however they like. But what they don't seem to realize is I'm not as fucking breakable as they might think.

ELEVEN

Hunter

The only drama that ever takes place at Asheville High is the drama we control, so color me shocked when some mysterious blonde appears, wreaking havoc in her wake.

I watched her saunter past us when she arrived at school, leaving Toby's jaw on the floor as she rejected his flirting, which was instantly something new.

Toby says drop your panties, and girls will do it, hoping for a moment with an Allstar. Because they are few and far between, and any girl around here jumps at the chance.

People in this town always want something, *always*, and she'll be no different.

Then I sat in computer programming, knowing Xavier was pulling his usual shit outside with her, but when she walked in, she was completely unfazed, continuing like she hadn't been threatened by the school's ruling Knight.

I was almost intrigued, especially when she said she'd fucked Xavier, because that shit was laughable until he outright confirmed it at practice. I would not have said no to that sharing party. I'm man enough to admit she's fucking hot, with her hourglass figure, long legs, and perky tits. But there's something beneath the surface to her that catches me off guard, I just can't put my finger on it.

But it wasn't until Roxy purposely slapped Eden's tray in her hands that I saw the real side of the new girl. The dark, broken soul, numbing all the pain twisting inside her. Unable to contain her rage any longer, she smashed it against Roxy's face, and *that* was the moment I was fascinated.

"Let's go, asshole," Xavier mutters, hitting my back a little harder than necessary, but that's probably because he was watching her ass sway as she stormed away too.

Standing at the top of the steps that lead up to our house, Toby grins, dripping wet from racing into the water with Eden. I'm not jealous, but I wish those were my hands on her body.

"Bro, she fucking sizzles against me. I'm officially addicted. No wonder you tapped that ass and kept her a secret."

Shaking my head, I tear my gaze from Eden's legs and follow Xavier into the house.

"Shut the gate behind you, Tobias," Xavier calls out over his shoulder as he deactivates the alarm with his thumbprint.

We didn't even unlock the house when Toby called out that he saw Eden on the beach, the three of us rushing to the sand to see for ourselves. I didn't expect Tobias to race off down the steps, my feet moving after him before I even really realized what I was doing, but I could only gape at him as he ran into the water with Eden in his arms.

Stepping into the open plan kitchen, I head straight to the fridge for a water. Xavier flicks his mellow music on like he always does, controlling the sound system through his phone as he takes a seat at the breakfast bar, and I sit across the marble counter from him, the bar stool raised high, but I still sit comfortably. He's obsessed with Strange Fruits on Spotify at the minute, the chilled vibes seem to make him relax a little.

"Don't even think about sitting your wet ass on a stool," Xavier threatens without raising his voice as Toby shuts the door behind him, a pout on his lips.

"Stop being all jelly because I got to have fun in the water with Eden, X. You're the one that wants to make her off-limits."

I watch as Xavier's hands fist on the table while his face remains impassive, and I have to cover my smile at seeing his reaction. If Toby sees, it'll only encourage him, but I've never seen him act like this before. Especially not over a girl.

Pleased with himself, Toby saunters off, just as the old ass house phone starts to ring. Since this is technically Xavier's house, I sit back in my seat, picturing legs for days, while he reluctantly stands to grab it. Only the school or his mother calls that line, so it would be no use me answering it anyway.

The school might be named after me, but I refuse to have anything to do with the politics, happily letting Xavier do it.

Being Hunter Asheville never offers me luxuries. Only expectation and brutality, which is why Xavier placed me under his wing when we were in kindergarten, and I haven't left since.

If it weren't for him, I'd be staring at the confines of my parent's basement instead of the glass-paneled wall that offers the most spectacular view of the infinity pool seamlessly blending into the ocean from my seat.

"Mr. Bernard, thank you for calling me first. I understand your need for our input on the matter. Let me discuss this with Tobias and Hunter, and I will call you straight back," Xavier murmurs into the phone, pulling me from my thoughts as he slams the phone down on the counter.

"Tobias," I yell, knowing he'll want him here too if his facial expression is anything to go by. I can see his brain working overtime as his eyebrows draw together. It's always easier to read people's body language than their words.

"Two minutes," he calls back, and Xavier pulls his face in disgust.

"I'm not waiting two minutes while you wank over the new girl. Get your ass in here," Xavier barks as he retakes his seat, and the stomp of Toby's feet as he approaches makes me grin. Xavier was right.

"What's so important I can't finish?" Toby moans, literally

grabbing his dick through his shorts to prove his point, and Xavier scowls. I can't stop my eye roll, these two are like oil and water on the best of days, but we're brothers no matter what.

Ignoring Toby's question, Xavier continues, tapping his fingers on the counter as he does. "That was Mr. Bernard on the phone. Apparently, Roxy and her parents are demanding that Eden be expelled, and he wants our decision on the matter." His facial expression gives nothing away as he processes it himself.

I frown in confusion and glare at Tobias. "I thought you said you took care of that?"

The second Archie got Eden out of the cafeteria, we went into damage control mode. Which meant Xavier controlled the chaos amongst the students, I dealt with the teachers, and Toby took care of Roxy. We decide what happens and when it happens, not Roxy or KitKat with their catty moves.

"I did, man. I swear." Taking the seat beside me, he looks between us with an exasperated look on his face. "I took Roxy to the nurse's office, and while she lay on the bed with an ice pack on her bloodied nose, I gave her exactly what she said would make it all go away."

"Did you fuck her?" I ask, cringing at the thought, since we'd already made that mistake before, and we didn't want her thinking there was a chance again.

"No, I'm not stupid," Toby answers quickly, throwing his arms out wide. "But I did agree to take her to the fall dance," he admits, and that almost makes me cringe more. Nobody needs to spend unwanted time with that girl. "Don't even say it, man. I took one for the team."

Xavier and I glance at each other, neither of us voicing the fact that he took one for the team for no reason now, apparently. But I'm not going to be the one to mention she broke the agreement, I like watching him stew.

"So why do you think she's suddenly in school with her parents right now demanding Eden's expulsion?" I ask, trying to figure out what could have changed. Toby rubs the back of his neck, coming up as blank as I do.

We run the school. Nothing goes to the teachers unless we want it to, and surprisingly, Xavier hadn't wanted anything to come of Eden's outburst at lunch.

"Honestly, there was no issue when I left her. Everything was cool." Toby sighs, running his fingers through his damp hair, and we both turn to Xavier for guidance like always.

Bracing his elbows on the table, his fingers laced together, he leans his forehead on his knuckles as he zones out. When it almost feels like an eternity has passed, he stands tall, straightening his spine and huffs.

"It's probably my mother," he finally murmurs, and I continue to stare at him, waiting for him to continue. "During one of her many lectures, she mentioned that I would only ever see a Grady if she put them there, and I should always stand by the Knight name. I should have probably asked why, but it never really mattered until now."

Nodding, I instantly understand. His mother would make the devil himself run and hide with all her sly, manipulating games. She's worse than my parents as a whole, but at least she leaves us here alone.

"So it's a test," I say, and Xavier hums.

"Like she's trying to see your move. How you'll handle a blonde-haired, blue-eyed, beautiful ragdoll she's laid at your feet," Toby chimes in, and it definitely makes sense.

"But why? What's the motive, and why now? I've tried calling her four times since lunch, and she hasn't answered a single call," Xavier says, thinking out loud.

"She's probably waiting to see how you handle the situation first," I offer, and his jaw tightens, knowing my words are likely true.

"Which means someone in that school informed her of what happened, or Roxy's mom went running straight to her," Xavier adds, and I'm already bored of the mind fuck. His mother probably has a mole somewhere planted in the school, it wouldn't surprise me. "We all know her mom will kiss my mother's ass any chance she gets, be it out of fear or appreciation, and she'll have seen Roxy's face because there was no way of hiding the swelling."

"What do we do then?" Toby asks, and I find myself answering before my brain can even catch up.

"She stays."

Xavier stares me down for a moment, not saying a word,

but eventually nods. "Agreed, but she needs to learn the fucking rules. I mean, she's still a Grady, so we fuck with her either way, but rules are rules, and we can't sway from the path this close to graduation. So I say we have her suspended for a few days."

"Is that really a punishment for her? She didn't look all that impressed with being there to begin with," Toby mutters, and I can't say he's wrong.

"True, but it will still teach her who is in charge here," Xavier throws back, and we nod in agreement.

"I still need to convince her to come to my birthday party, though, so maybe suspend her until Friday?" Toby offers, and Xavier sighs.

"Fine, but I need you to fuck her real quick so we can destroy her. It's clear what my mother wants us to do, and we need her off our backs for the rest of the year if we want to get out of here. She'll likely be watching us, and we have to play our roles."

"Agreed." Standing from the table, I pull out my phone. "How about you call Bernard back, and I'll call Archie. We can head over, force her to spend the evening in her room. She'll see we rule over everything, even in her own home," I offer, and they both grin in agreement.

"Let's go, boys," Toby hollers, heading for the door without a backward glance, but Xavier calls his name and makes him pause.

"We don't speak to her, not a word. Not until Friday at

least."

Fuck. Sometimes I pity the person on the receiving end of his wrath. He definitely gets his mean streak from his mother, even if I would never admit that to him.

Raised by a monster, become a monster.

TWELVE
Eden

Three days. Three fucking days I've been holed up in this house alone, no closer to any answers. The distance of my daily runs increases to get me out of the same four walls.

Richard doesn't seem to give a shit. He hasn't made eye contact with me once the whole time, not even when he advised me of the principal's decision. While my mom has done nothing but berate me, so I've stopped answering her calls.

Whenever Archie tried to bring up what happened, I shut him down. I can tell he isn't happy with the situation, but it's not something he needs to get in the middle of. All my lessons were sent electronically, so at least I didn't fall behind.

Every night after school, Archie has come home with his fucking boys and their cleat chasers in tow, and I've made sure to stay out of their sight. So I've retreated to my room before they even make it through the front door, making sure my door is locked before I put my earphones in and turn the music up high.

I'm going to be deaf before I'm thirty, but at least I haven't had to listen to them laughing and joking out by the pool.

I haven't seen Richard once either, not since he dropped the news about my suspension and hurried back off to his room. Someone is clearly succeeding at hide and seek, which leads me to be in the exact same position as I was when I first arrived. In the dark. I'm ready to start snooping if I have to.

My phone vibrates beside me on the bathroom vanity as I apply my coat of mascara, and I already know it's Charlie. That girl has made sure to reach out to me every day. She even gave me the heads-up that some rumors have started since Monday's incident, which even Archie hadn't wanted to tell me about.

Girl's got my back, it seems. I still feel very wary, wondering if there's more to the situation than meets the eye, but deep down, she seems genuine. It's just this town is already doing a number on me. I've never felt paranoia like this. Even in the place I'm supposed to call home, I feel unease, distrusting of this whole fucking town.

I'm expected back at school today. A part of me wanted to flash a big fuck you to them all and not show up, but I know it'll piss them off to see me show up on top of my game, completely unaffected by their shit, and looking hot as hell.

So, that's why I've opted for heavier makeup today, with some bright red lipstick and my two-piece top and shorts set. It's black with dusty pink and white flowers scattered across it. The Bardot top makes it playful as the shorts sit just under my ass. I love putting effort into my outfits, and the confidence boost is appreciated.

Please send me home, I beg you. Especially since the girl I smacked in the face with my tray had much less material covering her body on Monday.

Checking the message that flashes across my screen, I was right to guess it was Charlie.

Charlie: Girl, I'm heading out now. You better be there when I arrive, or I'm coming to get you!

She's bossier than Archie. But I'm not ashamed to admit I'd feel better walking in with her than alone.

"Cookie, let's go!" Archie shouts as he bangs on my door, and I quickly spray my favorite coconut passion scented perfume before heading toward all the noise he's making.

Swinging the door open, I glare at him. "I'm ready. Stop making so much noise," I grouch, but he just grins.

"Oh, they're so screwed," he mutters to himself with a shake of his head before turning. "We're both only children, but you definitely suffer from the only child syndrome much more than I do," he states with a smile as he takes the stairs first, and I get the craziest feeling of déjà vu with him.

The banter and easiness feels just like it did on Monday, and

I'm really glad he took my word when I said I wanted him to be Switzerland. I already know I'm going to get shit today, but he's still here for me, and I'm happy for him to go be the cool football player when we get to school.

I seem to care enough not to want to ruin his life and reputation while I'm here, and that honestly feels strange.

Archie locks up as I climb into the G-Wagon. As he climbs in beside me, I notice another gym bag in his hand, and he gives me a pointed look.

"You have track again today, remember?"

"Thanks," I mumble, not admitting that I'd forgotten to look at my schedule. But he doesn't pry, and when he goes to touch the music system, I don't even complain, letting the indie rock band filter through the speakers.

My body is starting to thrum with nervous anticipation as I put the SUV in drive and head toward the school. I'm a little sad that I already know my way a little around town without the GPS.

Giving Archie free rein of the music seems to occupy him for a while, giving me the peace I'd hoped for, but I know it's too good to last when he clears his throat.

"Spit it out, Arch," I murmur, and he instantly lowers the volume of the Livingstone song blaring through the speakers.

"Do you need a pep talk?" he asks tentatively, and I try not to sigh.

"Archie, I already told you, I don't regret what I did. That bitch started it. They're like fucking vultures, circling me like prey, and I'm not just going to stand there and let them bully me. That isn't who I am. So if someone does or says anything today, I'm going to stand my ground."

He doesn't respond for a moment, likely trying to come up with an argument that I can't push back on, but he must see the look of determination on my face because he just chuckles instead.

"Your dad made you a badass bitch, huh?"

It catches me by surprise, and when I turn to look at him, there's only kindness and appreciation in his gaze.

"A badass *boss* bitch, actually," I throw back, and he laughs while nodding agreement.

"Well, good. We don't have too many of those around here, cookie."

"Why do you call me that?" I finally ask, my palms starting to sweat as we pull into the school parking lot, and he snickers in response.

"Because if I looked in a dictionary, it would be your face next to the description of one. Hard on the outside, but a softy on the inside," he admits, instantly continuing and changing the subject as he points towards his parking space again. "Park in my spot."

"Are you sure that's a good idea?" I ask, and he just rolls his eyes at me, pointing for me to do it. I relent since the parking lot is already nearly full, and pull into his space. I give him my best glare as I put the SUV in park. "And for the record, I am *not* a cookie," I grumble, which he ignores as he steps out.

"If you need me, and I mean it, you call, text, whatever. I can drop the Switzerland act in a second if you need me to," he offers, again, the softness in his eyes showing me how serious he is, and it only adds to my confusion with him.

"Why? Why would you do that?" I ask, unable to just leave it be, and he glances over his shoulder at his friends before responding.

"Because your soul is a little bit broken, like mine. But theirs—theirs are already shattered into a million pieces, and there's no coming back from that. I don't want that for you."

Without waiting for a response, he shuts the door and heads for the group of football players waiting at the edge of the path.

I finally let my eyes drift over to them fully, and I'm not really surprised to see the three Allstar dicks staring straight at me.

A knock on my window catches me by surprise and I about jump out of my skin as I whirl around to find Charlie smiling through the glass and waving at me like a maniac. Her brown hair is pulled back in a ponytail, thick black rim glasses sit on her nose, and a light touch of makeup. I love the cute dress she's wearing, covered in little sunflowers, falling to mid-thigh.

My hand falls to my chest as I try to calm my racing heart and take a deep breath.

Charlie opens the door before I even get a chance, her smile widening as she sees my outfit. "Girl, you are trouble on legs, you know that?"

"And you almost gave me a heart attack," I say with a pout, but she only grins wider.

"No more hovering, let's get this over with, shall we," she states, not really asking me a question at all, and I try not to grimace.

Making sure to grab my gym bag along with my purse, I climb down from the G-Wagon and brush off my shorts as Charlie shuts the door for me, already feeling the heat of the day on my back.

She takes off for the long path, lined with perfectly manicured lawns on either side, leading up to the stairs, and I fall into step beside her.

Instantly, I feel eyes on me from all directions, whispers and snickers picking up as we near the walkway, but I place my sunglasses on my nose, covering my eyes from view as my wavy blonde hair floats around my face.

With each step we take, we get closer to the douches, but I lift my chin up, straighten my spine, and continue walking.

Thankfully, they are standing more on the grass to the left of the path, so we have a clear walking area to the steps. There must be another six guys standing along with Archie and the Allstars, in addition to the two bitches from Friday, and a handful of more girls rubbing themselves up against any guy they can.

I hate that my eyes take in every inch of Xavier, Hunter,

and Tobias, committing their muscular frames, messy hair, and piercing eyes to memory. Especially since they're bound to open their mouths and ruin everything anyway.

Just when I think I've managed to get by the group, I hear someone clap their hands in slow motion, and I force myself to keep on walking.

"The whore has arrived ladies and gentlemen," a girl sings out, and I hear laughter burst from a few people, but I don't stop putting one foot in front of another. I hear a deep voice grunt something, and everyone in the group falls silent, but I don't dare look back to see who. I just hope it wasn't Archie.

"It's all good, girl. We made it through arrival, just the next six hours to go," Charlie offers, bumping her shoulder against mine, and I shake my head at her.

"Charlie, where are your friends? Aren't some of those girls on the cheer squad?" I ask, unable to stop myself, and she scoffs in response.

"Eden, I said I was shielded, not popular." I have no idea how that worked, but she seemed okay either way. "Have you got calculus first?" she asks, moving the conversation, and I pull my phone out to check.

"Yeah, sadly."

"Good, me too. The teacher is super chill, so I should be able to get you up to speed on everything that has happened since Monday," she offers, and I smile appreciatively.

I hate gossip, but fuck, I'm pretty sure ninety-nine percent of it was about me, and I'd rather be in the know than shove my head in the sand.

I follow Charlie blindly to her locker, then she shows me where my own is, across from her, and my heart pounds when she murmurs that Hunter's is beside mine. I make quick work of dropping my gym bag inside and hightailing it to class with her.

I should have visited here on my first day, but there was no time in the morning, and by the end of lunch, I wasn't even here.

Taking the seat beside her when we arrive, no one really pays us any mind until Xavier walks in with Tobias and Hunter hot on his toes.

My skin prickles as Xavier stops just inside of the door, the other two douches flanking his sides as he glares at me, stopping anyone else from stepping through the doors.

Xavier's chiseled jaw is set tight as he stares me down, his biceps bulging under his black muscle fit T-shirt as his fists clench at his side. Looking to his right, I almost grin at seeing Tobias wearing his beanie in this heat, but I can't deny the fact that it suits him. In his white tee and grey joggers, he is way more casual than Xavier. While Hunter is rocking jeans and a checkered shirt with a tank underneath, his blond hair swept to the side in disarray.

God, I'm always a sucker for the villains in the movies, it makes sense I think they're hot here too. The Allstars scream town bad boys.

"Price," he calls, not taking his eyes off me, and the teacher quickly stands from his desk, his sole attention on Xavier as he swipes his comb-over down on his head. Fucking suck-up.

"Yes, Mr. Knight?" Even I almost laugh at how much of an ass-kisser he sounds like right now, but Tobias does, patting him on the shoulder as he walks away from them and straight towards me, but my brain is too focused on what Xavier will say next.

"I think it would be best for the new girl to sit in the back row with me. We don't want her up front distracted by her friends, do we?" He says it like he's a fucking angel of god, not a disciple of the devil. My hands instantly clench, my nails digging into my palms once again, and I hate that he gains any kind of response from me. Asshole.

"Uh, yes. Yes, I agree." The teacher turns to face me, guilt in his eyes as he tries to find the words to follow through on what Xavier just said. But there's no need when Tobias is standing by my desk, my purse in one hand as he uses the other to grab my arm and pull me from my seat.

I try to shove him off, but he just grins down at me, licking his lips. "Fight me, you know I'll love it." He grins, and I stop.

"I don't know you for shit," I grind out, letting him pull me through the aisle of desks, and stopping at the one at the end. He dumps my purse beside it but doesn't release his hold.

"We can rectify that whenever you like," he whispers, his lips brushing against the shell of my ear, and a shiver ripples through me. Fuck. "Especially in this little sexy outfit."

Pushing at his chest again, he releases me, and gives me no space but to sit down. Glancing around the classroom, I find everyone staring. I can either put up a fight, giving everyone what they want, or succumb to their little power play.

Taking a deep breath, I brush my hair behind my ear and fall into the seat, turning to face the front, and I don't miss the smug grin on Xavier's face as I do so.

I give him the middle finger, which makes Hunter grin and Tobias clap his hands with glee. They either like my sass or the challenge I seem to offer.

Training my gaze at the board, I attempt to ignore them as Tobias takes the seat to my right and Xavier takes the spot to my left, leaving Hunter to sink down in the seat in front of me.

Great. Fucking great.

"You're ours, Nafas, and you'll do well to remember we own everyone."

With that, Xavier turns to face the front, ignoring me, and the others do as well, all while I sit waiting for them to pounce. I barely catch a word the teacher says, I feel so off-kilter. Every breath they take, the slightest movement, I feel it, spending the whole time forcing myself not to flinch.

And when the bell rings, drawing the damn lesson to an end, I realize that was their plan along.

Narcissistic, manipulating motherfuckers.

THIRTEEN
Eden

Every. Fucking. Lesson. Is. The. Same.

As soon as the bell rings, I stand, grabbing my oversized purse and hightail it out of the classroom, and every time, they let me.

Fuck. They don't let me. I don't let them let me. Shit. They're messing with my brain.

I can't catch a break. They're in every class except track, but they're still out on the field at the same time.

I get up and leave like I have control, then the second we step into the next class, one or all of them make a show in front of everyone, clearly reminding them and *me* who's in charge here.

Arrogant motherfucking assholes.

I've officially got today's schedule memorized, I've stared at it so much. Track, followed by lunch, and then homeroom. Perfect. I can run off some steam, eat, then ditch for the last hour. Give myself some breathing space.

Maybe I could convince Charlie to go get lunch off-campus with me and drag it out over homeroom.

She doesn't seem as surprised with the Allstars' actions as I am, neither does Archie, who has sent me four text messages asking if I want him to pull me out of the middle of them, but I keep refusing. Let them make a show, it'll only make bringing them to their knees all the sweeter.

Because I've decided that's my new fucking challenge, alongside finding answers to my life that is nothing but a mess. I'm going to prove to these douches that I'm not their little ragdoll to play with. They don't deserve my revenge or rage, not yet at least, but I will stand taller and reign higher than them so they can't break me like they want to.

Stepping into the changing rooms, I follow Charlie to the far-left corner of the white tiled space and drop my gym bag beside hers.

"Are you sure you're okay?" Charlie asks again, concern in her eyes as she pulls her cheer outfit from her gym bag. I don't think I've ever been to a school where you don't have to do any other sports if you're on the cheer squad.

"I'm fine, Charlie, honestly. I'm not going to let them intimidate me," I answer, not even truly believing my own words as I say them, but she lets it settle.

Quickly changing into my track shorts and tank top, I slip my phone in my pocket. I don't have a sports bra with me, I guess that's my fault for forgetting and letting Archie pick up the slack.

I'm lacing my sneakers up when the chatter around me quietens, and the hairs on my arms stand on end, my gut telling me the sudden silence has something to do with me.

Since my back is to everyone as I have my foot up on the bench, I force myself to finish what I'm doing and look unaffected as I slowly turn around to find the bitch I smacked in the face, standing before me.

Seeing her for the first time today, I have to force the smile off my lips as I take in her bruised nose. No amount of makeup seems to be able to cover the purple coloring on her face, and I'm not even sorry about it.

With her hands on her hips, her perfectly pressed cheerleading outfit in place, and red hair pulled back off her face, she stares me down like I'm shit beneath her shoe.

Rolling my shoulders, I raise my eyebrow, refusing to voice any acknowledgment of her presence, but letting her know I see, I just don't really care.

"You think you're something special because you managed to convince Xavier to fuck you. You are nothing but a fucking whore, and I want you gone." I refrain from rolling my eyes and shrug my shoulders instead.

"Sweetheart, is it because my notch is higher on his bedpost than yours? 'Cause let me tell you, I won't be going back for a repeat, so I'm sure you will be able to convince him to slip inside your loose pussy again without any problem." My voice is sickeningly sweet as I widen my eyes and stick out my bottom lip like a child, and she practically growls as she fists her hands at her side.

Not waiting for a response, I head for the gym door, swinging it open without a backwards glance and making my way to the field.

Charlie is at my side in an instant, a grin on her face as she tightens her ponytail. "You're fucking fire," she says with a chuckle, and I can't stop my grin in response as we step onto the grass, my eyes automatically searching out the football team.

Standing in the center of the field in a team huddle, my heart rate increases as the three assholes feel me on their radar, their eyes tracking my every move.

The football jerseys' colors are green and white. No one should look that good in green and white. Standing side by side with their white helmets in hand, they look every inch of the rugged football players I could only dream about.

Forcing myself to look away, I glance at Charlie.

"Stop, I—"

Something smacks the back of my head, not hitting me hard enough to knock me to the ground thankfully, but as I turn around instantly, I see the same bitch wanting more attention from me.

Refusing to rub my head, I glance down at my feet to see a football. This bitch threw a fucking inflated oval at the back of my head.

A *fucking* brand-new, hard as shit football. At. My. Head.

Yet she still couldn't knock me down.

Oh. She's fucking dead. Has she suddenly forgotten how I responded last time?

"Bitch!" she screeches at me, and if I wasn't so angry, I'd laugh.

Marching towards her, I wave my finger in the air like an idiot. This girl gets under my fucking skin. I can deal with mind games. I can deal with massive catcalling and rumors, but *don't* fucking hit me when my back is turned.

She's a coward. Coming at me while my back is turned is the pussy way.

"You are so fucking stupid. I'm—"

Suddenly lifted off my feet and thrown over someone's shoulder, my threat cut off. I don't say a word, not a fucking peep. I don't even try to shake out of their hold or hit out because I fucking know that's what he would want—a scene.

There's no need because I already know how this narcissistic fucker works, and nobody has ever had a woodsy scent like his.

Xavier.

He says nothing as he takes long strides separating me from everyone else, but I don't miss the sound of Hunter's voice as Xavier carries me away, his uncomfortable shoulder pads digging into my stomach like a bitch.

"Nobody fucks with her except us. Understand?"

"Fuck you, Hunter," the girl spits out in response, and I rack my brain to try and remember her fucking name, but my body is taking over as all my focus is on Xavier.

His strong arm is braced against the back of my legs as his fingers dig into my thigh, and I'm embarrassingly close to squirming.

Just as I try to lift my head up to see where we are, Xavier slowly lowers me to the ground, dragging my body down every inch of his, and I fucking hate how my body reacts.

My feet must be barely six inches off the ground when he pauses, pinning me to him with his arm now firmly around my waist and my face perfectly in line with his.

His hazel eyes pierce mine as his brown hair falls over his forehead. With his shoulder pads on, he looks even bigger than usual, and I can feel myself almost melting against him, but I refuse.

I push off his chest, but he doesn't budge as he continues to hold me firmly in place, clearly not impressed with my efforts.

"Put me down," I bite out, continuing to push on his chest with my fists as he literally does nothing. "Put. Me. Down."

"Have you not been paying attention, Eden? You don't get a say in what happens here at Asheville High, or in Knight's Creek in general. No. Fucking. Say," he adds, repeating my same tone from only a moment earlier.

Glancing around, I ignore him as I realize we are on the complete opposite end of the field by the bleachers.

"Why did you stop me? That bitch keeps pushing me, and I deserve to push back. Why are you smiling? Stop fucking smiling," I growl out, watching as the menacing smile only makes him look even crazier.

"You don't get a say. Remember? Now do as you're told. If someone pushes you, you fucking take it. No pushing back, no violent little tantrums from you, Nafas. Do you understand?"

"Quit calling me that!" I yell, my heart pounding in my chest as frustration pumps through my body. "I'm fucking sick to death of everyone thinking good old Eden will do as she's fucking told, because let me tell you—I won't."

"Put her down, man," Archie interrupts, and my head quickly whips around to see him standing beside us, his helmet tucked under his arm as his eyes flicker between us.

"It's fine, Arch—"

"Fuck off, Archie," Xavier interrupts, not moving his gaze from me as I shake my head at Archie, pleading with him not to get involved.

"I can't, Xavier. I told you guys she's going through a lot right now, and I know what that feels like. There is enough going on in her mind with her dad being murdered to have to deal with you guys too. Not on top of the girls as well." His words are firmer than I've ever heard from him, and I appreciate his protective nature, but I did *not* need him telling them my private fucking business.

"Archie, that was not your fucking shit to tell," I spit out, my heart beating wildly in my chest as I try to push out of Xavier's hold, but if anything, he manages to grip me tighter. How is he not fucking bored of gripping me like this yet?

I watch as the color drains from Archie's face as he realizes what he just did, and he scrambles to apologize. "Fuck, cookie. I'm so, so sorry. I didn't think, I just—"

"Fuck. Off. Archie. I won't say it again," Xavier growls out, finally turning to look at him, but surprisingly, Archie stares me down, waiting for me to decide what to do.

"Archie, it's fine. Give me a minute, okay?" I murmur, forcing myself to calm down, otherwise I know he won't go, and the quicker he goes, the quicker Xavier will put me down. I'll deal with his stupid mouth later.

With a sigh, he nods, communicating he's just a shout away before he turns on his heels and stalks off.

Turning back to Xavier, he's already staring me down. He searches my eyes, I don't know what for, and I don't care anymore. I'm bored of his shit. It makes me feel uncomfortable, like he's trying to see what is written on my soul so he can tear it apart easier.

"Put me down now, Xavier," I say calmly, my hands resting against his chest as I prepare to push him away again.

"Dead dad, huh? Is that what has you all twisted up inside?"

"*Murdered* dad, and that's none of your damn business," I argue, swinging my leg back and kicking him in the shin, but he still doesn't fucking budge. I hate to admit that I could be putting up more of a fight, but as much of a douche that he is, my body remembers how we collided.

"Why are you here, Eden?" he asks, his voice a lot quieter and more curious than demanding compared to usual, and it almost breaks down my defenses.

I focus my eyes on his chest as I push against him once again, but he cups my chin with his hand and forces me to look at him as he keeps me pinned against him with only one arm.

"I'm not telling you shit."

"I'll make you, whether you like it or not," he murmurs, his eyes flickering to my lips before he remembers himself and drops me to my feet. Finally.

"Suck my dick," I grind out, beyond done with his alpha tendencies, and he just snickers at me.

Before I can even respond, his hand is cupping my pussy, his palm pressing against my sensitive clit as he growls in my ear, and I hum under my breath, hating how turned on I am by the whole thing.

"I don't remember you fucking having one."

I gasp in response, my body electric right now before I push his hand away, and he doesn't put up a fight this time.

"What I mean is, I'll buy one, wear it, and make you fucking choke on it," I retort, and he throws his head back as a laugh bursts out of him.

I'm left stunned as I watch him actually laugh. Not forced, not a part of some controlling mastermind, but a wholehearted belly laugh. I don't move an inch, absorbing the smallest bit of light from him.

"Let's go, Xav. We have our first game tonight!" Tobias shouts, pulling our attention to the rest of the people out here, who are all staring at us.

Have they been watching us the whole fucking time? Hunter and Tobias stand in front of everyone as if they're trying to keep us separated, and I hate that I forgot where we even were.

I search the group for the bitch from earlier, but my anger is not thrumming through my body for her now. I'm more stressed with Xavier and the fact Archie spilled my truth without thought. The moment has gone, and maybe that was Xavier's intention all along, but why?

Hearing Tobias' voice kicks Xavier's dickish attitude back into play, and his eyebrows knit together as he frowns down at me. Swiping his hand over his mouth he looks away, dismissing me.

Without a word, he turns and joins the football team as the coach stands by waiting patiently, and I can't help but watch every step he takes.

Fuck. What am I even going to do here?

TOXIC CREEK

FOURTEEN
Eden

My mind is still reeling as track comes to an end. Everybody kept their distance from me, as if the whole scene with Xavier made me a bad omen or something. It's obvious Xavier is the king around here, and what happened earlier has them confused so they're avoiding me like the plague.

I could feel Archie and Charlie both looking at me constantly, likely worrying, but my focus was to run my problems away.

I just crossed the finish line when the coach blows the whistle, calling time, and everyone literally bolts for the locker rooms, but I just need another minute.

Keeping my pace, I continue around the now empty track, pushing myself harder, and I love the burn in my calves as my heart beats rapidly in my chest.

Rounding back to the finish line marker, I slow, bracing my hands on my knees as I catch my breath, feeling my top stick to my back with sweat. The extra lap gave me a minute to try and process everything with Xavier and the 'bitchleader.' Trying being the keyword because I'm no wiser, but I'm at least a little quieter.

"Nice ass. I shall name you bubble butt." Glancing over my shoulder, I find Tobias biting his bottom lip while he stares at me, or more specifically, my ass. I'm not even going to take him on. They've gotten under my skin enough today, and I'm at my limit. Even if he does look good with dirt on his arms and sweat dripping down his face.

Standing tall, I keep my back to him as I head for the locker room, I don't even turn to see if he's alone or not, but I feel his gaze on my ass the whole fucking way.

I slip into the locker room, closing the door as quickly as I can behind me, and prepare for another onslaught of shit from little miss bitch face. Roxy. That's her name. It's embarrassing how long it took me to remember that.

To my surprise, no one says a word, no one even looks at me either, except Charlie, who cringes as she glances up at me from her phone, fully dressed and ready to go.

"I'm so sorry, are you going to be okay here? I've had a notification to go to the principal's office, and if I don't go as soon as possible, I won't get any lunch and I am starving."

"Of course, don't stress," I murmur in response as she flashes the text message in my face. Huh. Well, I guess it's better than calling you out of the school sound system. "I need to shower anyway," I add when she doesn't instantly move.

"Meet you in the cafeteria then?" she clarifies as she throws her bag over her shoulder, and I nod in agreement.

Stripping out of my gym clothes, I step into a free shower cubicle, throwing my towel over the door before I step under the spray. The cool temperature relaxes my body since it's so damn hot today. The body wash dispenser on the wall smells like strawberries, which isn't my usual go-to, but it will do for now. I'll just need to remember to pack my own in future.

Shutting off the water, I reach for my towel over the door but come up empty. Fuck's sake, has it fallen down?

Opening the door slightly, I don't find it on the floor, and my dirty gym clothes aren't there either. Heaving a sigh, I already know in my gut I've been fucking played. Déjà vu all over again. I'm not oblivious to how some people treat the new girl at school.

Silence is all that greets me when I strain my ears, and that only adds to my suspicion. Refusing to be ashamed of my naked body, I walk into the main area of the locker room to find it empty. Completely fucking empty.

Literally not a soul. Not even my motherfucking bag and all of my other belongings. All I'm greeted with is my fucking car keys and a handwritten note sticky taped to the wall.

IF YOU WANT TO ACT LIKE A WHORE AND DRESS

LIKE A WHORE, THEN FIND SOMEWHERE ELSE TO FUCKING DO IT. YOU AREN'T WANTED HERE.

I can't help but grin at their shitty little speech as I pull the paper off the wall. I mean, they could have at least made me fucking tremble with fear or something. But this, this is just an *inconvenience.* I'm slightly more pissed that they've taken my bag with my phone in it.

How do I always find myself on the end of the school bitches' wrath? It's boring. They clearly don't know how many times I've been the new girl, and sadly, this isn't my first walk of shame. At least this time I have this scrappy piece of paper to cover myself with. This isn't my first bullying rodeo, and every time, I get stronger.

Sticking the tape just below my belly button, the text facing out, I look ridiculous, but the paper covers my vajayjay at least. Everyone will hopefully be too busy reading the fucking note to look at my ass and tits. Not likely, but there's always hope.

Grabbing my car keys, I pull my hair from the messy bun on top of my head and let the waves cascade over my chest. I hate that I don't feel any anxiety, no feelings at all, just total numbness.

I'm accustomed to being dragged through the dirt, but I will always come out stronger. Always.

Steeling my spine, I grab my keys, taking a deep breath as I relax my shoulders, and lift my chin. These bitches don't know who they're fucking with. I won't bow down to them, and I sure as hell won't follow their rules.

Swinging the door open wide, I instantly expect onlookers, but thankfully, the hallway is actually empty. The only way I know where to find my G-Wagon is through the main corridor past the cafeteria, so I know my peace and quiet will be short-lived.

The slightest breeze pebbles my nipples, fluttering the loose tendrils of hair around my face as I ready to turn down the busier hallway, my feet desperate to get on the hardwood floor instead of the concrete beneath me right now.

The second I push open the door, linking the sports area to the main core of the school, I hear chatter in the distance, there are a few people in the hall, but I refuse to see who exactly as I keep my focus trained ahead.

My skin prickles as I hear the chatter turn into murmurs, whispers, and giggles as people see me. A few guys whistle in appreciation, but I offer no reaction.

Just as I near the cafeteria to my left, someone rushes past me and hollers into the room.

"Have you seen these tits, man? Fucking fire."

I can't help it, I glance his way, and it's a guy I've never even seen before. He's looking back at me over his shoulder, a leering grin on his lips as he takes me in. His greasy hair is brushed back off his face, and his eyes are bloodshot. Stoner.

Fucking asshole. I did not need more attention right now.

"Oh my god, is she seriously naked?"

The screeching of chairs and feet pounding on the floor tells me everyone's coming to see what he's talking about me. Me. A naked me. Fuck. I refuse to glance over at them properly, knowing at least someone has their phone out.

Giving him the finger, I turn my gaze away from him and try to pick up my speed without downright running, because I won't be seen as weak.

"Show us your tits, honey!" someone calls out, making everyone laugh louder, and I force myself not to roll my eyes. Why doesn't it surprise me that this place doesn't have any staff members on hand?

We always come out stronger. We always come out stronger.

My dad's go to mantra bounces around in my head, guiding me towards the end of the corridor, which feels like a hundred miles away, and my eyes prickle, the instant reminder of my loss trying to consume me. But not right now, it can't right now.

"Who the fuck did this?" A growl so sinister reverberates around the corridor, and even my steps falter as the sound of Xavier's anger meets my ears, but I do manage to continue placing one foot in front of the other.

I hear footsteps near me, but I refuse to turn around, I'm only twenty feet from stepping outside, and away from these assholes. But an arm suddenly comes around my front, pinning me to a hard chest at my back as the person moves me to the side of the hall, my front facing the nearby lockers.

I almost swing around to punch the fucker in the face, but

they whisper in my ear just in time.

"Don't hit me, I'm shielding you."

Hunter?

Tilting my head back, I look up to see his attention focused over his own shoulder.

"I'm fine, I don't need shielding," I murmur, making no attempt to actually step out of his hold, and he completely ignores me.

"Don't make me fucking repeat myself," Xavier shouts again, and I really don't want to stay around for this.

"Fine, if you're going to shield me, could you just help me get to my SUV? Then I can be out of your hair," I offer, and his green eyes instantly find mine.

His blond hair is brushed over to the side, a natural wave trying to take over his attempt at a clean look, and I feel my fingers itching to run through it. With a simple nod, his fingers tighten on my waist as he glances over his shoulder again.

"Tobias, jacket," he mutters, and before I can protest, Tobias magically appears at our side, his lightweight black jacket in hand.

He grins down at me as he holds the jacket out for me to slot my arms in, but Hunter still hasn't let go of my waist.

I'm surprised to see such anger in Tobias' blue eyes, but in a flash, it's gone as he plants a huge grin on his face and trails his gaze over my body.

"Are you done?" I hiss, and he continues to take in the

display before him.

"There's nothing else for me to do until Hunter releases you so I can *assist*," he mutters with a waggle of his eyebrows, and I want to kick him in the dick, but thankfully, Hunter gets the message and slowly releases his hold on me.

I feel every inch of his fingerprints as he skims his fingers across my stomach until his hand falls away altogether, but he doesn't move from my back, continuing to block me from everyone else.

I step forward a little, and Tobias envelops me in his jacket, and I push my arms into the sleeves, appreciating the fact it sits just above my knee.

"We won't be needing this now, will we?" Tobias murmurs, pulling the sticky tape from my skin, his touch sending a shiver down my spine, but I'm more surprised to find his eyes on mine the whole time, not attempting to catch a glimpse of me.

Wordlessly, he zips up the jacket, completely distracting me from the arguing going on behind us as some high-pitched scream bounces off the walls.

"I've got it from here, Hunter," Tobias mutters before lifting me off my feet and pinning my chest to his.

Before I can say anything, he's spinning us around and walking towards the exit. I don't miss the way Hunter stares after us, or the fact that Xavier has Roxy pinned to the wall beside the cafeteria.

This is a surprising turn of events. A part of me expected

them to have something to do with it, and I don't know how to feel about them seemingly protecting me.

The door swings shut behind us as Tobias marches towards the main doors leading outside, and I'm annoyed with myself for not putting up more of a fight.

"Do you guys always have to manhandle me?" I finally grouch, finding my voice.

"Shut the fuck up, bubble butt, you love it."

I feel the blush attempting to take over my cheeks, and I glance away. "I don't love it. I didn't ask for you guys to help. I was perfectly fine walking back to my SUV on my own." I pout as we step outside into the heat, and Tobias jogs down the steps effortlessly with me in his arms.

"Tell yourself what you want, we both know the truth." I hate how fucking smug he sounds, but I still don't put up a fight as he carries me toward my G-Wagon, my arms pinned under his.

Getting to the bottom of the steps, I try to glance over my shoulder to point out my SUV, but I come face-to-face with him. Without warning, he fucking licks my nose. Licks. My. Nose. Who the fuck is this guy?

"What the fuck?" I scrunch my face up in disgust, but he just laughs at me. "That's gross, dude," I gripe, wiping my nose on his T-shirt, and I'm instantly hit with his citrusy scent. Holy fuck, he smells good. My body moves closer to his on instinct. He doesn't respond as he continues towards the parking lot, and

I sigh. "Why are you guys helping me anyway?"

"Who said we are helping you?" he throws back immediately, and I glare at the side of his head. "We gave an order, we're protecting that. You just happen to reap a few benefits for a minute, that's all."

Well, that definitely makes more sense than them looking out for me, but it still has me confused, especially with earlier, and my mind's a mess.

"Do you want to continue reaping the benefits?" he asks, and before I can ask what he means, my back is slammed into the side of my G-Wagon and he's lifted my thighs up so my legs are at his waist. "I could fuck you up against the side of your fancy car, make you scream my name for everyone to hear. Would you like that?"

Our lips are so close together, his nose brushes against mine as our breaths mingle between us. He grinds his hard cock against my core, and my heart about stops as heat spreads through my body.

"I—"

"I told you, you want me, bubble, everyone does, but I like a little delayed gratification. Especially when we have a game tonight, it only adds to the fire between us. You'll get to sit on my dick soon, I promise, but I'm good with teasing you for now." His hand comes up to cup my chin, stroking his thumb against my bottom lip. I'm stunned.

Without warning, I bite down on his thumb, hard, and he

quickly pulls it from my grasp, laughter bursting from his lips as he throws his head back.

"Hmm, feisty, I like it." Stepping back, he lowers me to the ground, and the gravel instantly feels rough beneath my feet. "Don't forget about my birthday party tonight," he says with a wink and takes off back towards the school.

What in the ever-loving fuck just happened to me?

FIFTEEN

Xavier

I fucking knew Roxy wouldn't do as she was told. Clearly, someone must be intimidated by the new girl, because she never lays it on this thick so soon. Usually, she's obedient, doing whatever I ask, hoping I will slip back into bed with her. I don't mind playing on her wants if it gets me what I need, but this time, her jealousy seems to have gotten the better of her.

We told her repeatedly to keep the fuck away from Eden, that we would handle her since she was ours to play with, but Roxy seems to have forgotten how to fall in line.

I'll come up with a plan for her, I always do, but tonight is Tobias' birthday, and I promised I would *try* and have a good time. Which is why I'm sitting around the bonfire on the beach, down the steps from Archie's house.

We won the game tonight by a long shot as always. A solid 42-3, even though my mind was distracted with all this shit. I need to try and relax, find a distraction to settle my mind, or more specifically, get Eden off it.

It might be Tobias' birthday, but parties take place as they usually do. I can hear people splashing around in the ocean to my left, while others dance to my right. The rest of the crowd is split off into groups around the fire. Unless they've found a hidden spot to fuck.

Ninety percent of people are dressed in their swimwear since it's so warm still, but not a single girl takes my fancy. All these people here, who only know the person I portray myself as, bore me. None of them know anything more than what I want them to see.

That thought alone pulls my gaze back to the balcony that taunts me. I can barely see her from here, but I know she's there, my body sensing hers. Eden.

I fucking hate it.

The way she felt in my arms when I pulled her away this morning before practice only caused me more confusion. I want to toy with her, pull her apart piece by piece, and see if she knows how to mend herself. While another part of me wants to drape every inch of her skin with mine.

Raking my fingers through my hair, I lean back in my deck chair, trying to rid her from my mind. Or maybe it's time to have a little play instead.

As if sensing my train of thought, Hunter glances in my direction from across the fire, and I signal for him to join me.

Searching out Tobias, he's being blocked from the party by the one and only Roxy and KitKat duo, one on each side. I'm sure he's enjoying the little strokes up his bare chest, but most definitely not from those two. Their asses are barely covered and their tits are close to hanging out, but we aren't fools enough to ever go there again.

He can't even seem to smile as he keeps his hands behind his back, looking around like a deer caught in the headlights. His eyes find mine, and I wave for him to come over, but he simply looks at me with pleading eyes.

Why can't he just tell them to fuck off? I'm confused.

"Hey, KitKat, Roxy!" I shout over the music, making them whip their heads around.

I watch as KitKat actually lowers the neckline of her strapless dress, offering me a peek of the areolas surrounding her fucking nipples. How ridiculous. No class at all. She takes one step forward, and I raise my hand to pause her.

Like a damn puppet she does, and Roxy turns to stand beside her, offering Tobias the opportunity to slip from behind them.

"Fuck off," I call out dismissively, turning away from them before they can even respond.

Bitches are lucky they are even here tonight. I'd have had them on house arrest for the rest of the month for that shit earlier today, but my mother apparently overruled me, so here they are.

She runs the town of course, she oversees everyone's fucking movements.

Taking a sip of my beer, I swallow down the bitter taste, along with my analytical brain over my mother's interference.

So, here we are, laughing and joking on the beach late at night, with a fire roaring in the middle of us all. And out of all of the faces here, I only care to be around two of them—Hunter and Tobias. Archie too, just not on the same level.

That guy always has our back, even though we don't let him into our little circle, but he never argues or complains and that's what makes me like him more. But his sudden need to protect Eden from us, going as far as to make a scene earlier at practice when I carried Eden away from the girls, has surprised me. He's not a yes-man, but he's usually too nonchalant to give a shit, especially since his mom died.

"What's on your mind, meathead?" Hunter asks, taking the seat beside me and pulling me from my thoughts.

I want to say the difference between having my hand wrapped around Eden's throat and Roxy's throat. One practically purred while the other cried like a little bitch, but I refuse to admit that shit.

Instead, I wait for Tobias to fall down in the seat to my right before answering.

"I think it's time to play a game with our little Eden, don't you? This party is questionable as shit with the same old boring people. Let's spice it up."

"Yes, yes, yes." Tobias claps his hands instantly, while Hunter simply shakes his head. "But first, you have to let me try and hit that because you know she won't want to fuck me after you've thought up one of your stupid games."

He's not wrong. "Convince her to come down with you, and Hunter and I will brainstorm."

"Do I tell her about the phone?"

"No," I respond instantly, and he's up and on his feet in seconds, running straight past KitKat and Roxy as they try to single him out again, but Tobias doesn't even offer them a backwards glance.

My gaze flickers back to the balcony, but she's nowhere to be seen. My hands clench. For some reason, I like having her in my sight.

I can't help but remember what Archie said about her dad being murdered, and that's why she's here. *If you come across a Grady, it's because I put them there.* My mother's words repeat in my mind, and I can't stop the frown from marking my forehead as I contemplate her involvement in the matter.

"Fuck, Hunter. Entertain me, I'm fucking drowning in my mind," I admit under my breath, and he's quick to jump to his feet.

"Let's go, asshole. Archie and a few of the others from the team are a little farther down the beach with a football. Let's go play catch." His words are sarcastic, but he knows the throw of the ball will bring me back to the here and now.

It's exactly what I need. Then I can focus on the fun we can have with Eden.

The perfect distraction.

Eden

"This is my favorite part of the movie," I murmur, face resting in my palms as I lie flat on my stomach across my bed with Charlie at my side.

"Your favorite part of the movie is when the Joker blows up the hospital?" she confirms, and I grin.

"Look how happy he is, though. And his little jump when the explosion actually goes off. It gets me every time."

Shaking her head at me, she scoops more popcorn into her mouth as we continue to block out the party downstairs. Their taste in music is pretty decent, but the people down there are all pretty much assholes, except Archie of course.

Poor guy keeps texting Charlie and checking in on us like we're children. It's almost sweet, but I'm pretty sure it's because he is interested in getting to know Charlie a little more. I've told her to go down and join him, but she refuses.

So here we are instead, relaxing with snacks, movies, and wine like pro teenagers in our tank tops and shorts since it's so warm.

"Oh, I forgot to mention, I'm going to see my grandmother

on Sunday, and if there is anything to know about in this town, Granny James knows it. So if I can pull any Grady name details out of her, I'll be straight over." She nods enthusiastically at her own words, and a slight tinge of hope warms me.

I need something, anything really, because right now, I have nothing at all to go on. I'll never get answers and get out of this town at this rate.

"Thanks, Charlie," I murmur in response, taking a bite out of my apple Laffy Taffy.

"Hmm, no problem. So are we going to talk about earlier?"

Scoffing, I shake my head, not pulling my gaze from the television. "Which part? Today has just been another shit show."

"Roxy and KitKat are bitches. I can't believe they took all of your belongings, what are you going to do without your phone?"

"I'll get my phone back, whatever it takes. I have pictures of my dad on there." My heart aches, but I refuse to let them tear me down. "Archie said he would ask around at the party, see if anyone knows what they did with it."

"Fingers crossed," she murmurs in response. "What's going on with you and the Allstars?" she adds, catching me by surprise, and I finally turn to frown at her.

"The Allstars? You're fucking with me, right? I show up here, and all they're doing is causing shit for me."

She tucks her hair behind her ear nervously as she pulls herself to a sitting position, crossing her legs as she stares me down.

"Yeah, but KitKat's pulled that trick before, and no one stopped her. If anything, the last time someone was forced to walk naked through the halls, the Allstars encouraged all the verbal abuse thrown their way." I don't miss the surprise on her face at that statement too.

"Wait, what?" I ask, standing from the bed with my hands planted on my hips. Why would they have shielded me then?

"Honestly, everyone is way more shocked with how they protected you from view in comparison to you actually being naked."

Pacing at the bottom of the bed, I try to let her words process in my mind, but I'm at a complete loss. It makes no sense.

Stopping to face her, I'm about to ask a question when a voice behind me makes me jump out of my skin.

"What are you girls up here talking about?"

Whirling around, I come face-to-face with Tobias as Charlie screams, followed by a thud as she falls off the bed.

"What the fuck, Tobias Holmes! You scared me half to death," Charlie cries, coming to stand beside me with her hand on her chest. My heart is pounding wildly in my chest, but he simply grins at us.

"How the hell did you get in here?" I ask, moving past him out onto the balcony, since that must have been his only point of entry.

"I climbed up like a big boy, Eden."

I turn to glare at him, stalling at the sight of his beanie in place and his chest on display, and even though my name on his lips sounds like a wet dream, I point over the side of the balcony.

"Well, you can fuck right off back where you came from, thank you very much." My little outburst only makes him laugh, while Charlie continues to stare between us.

"Charlotte, give us a few minutes, will you?" Tobias says, glancing at Charlie with a gentle smile, but she gives him a pointed stare and looks back to me for guidance.

Walking back inside, I sigh. "It's all right, Charlie. Why don't you get us some fresh drinks and hunt down Archie for a few minutes? I won't be long."

"If you're sure," she mumbles, waiting for me to reconfirm as she glares at Tobias behind me.

"I am, honestly."

"Okay, well, I know Tobias thinks he's cool and all that, and he probably is, but I just want you to know that in second grade, I saw him pick his nose. It was completely gross, and I've never been able to unsee it." She pokes out her tongue and is out of my room in a flash.

I glance at Tobias with raised eyebrows, and he shrugs. "I do not still do that." He pouts with a wrinkle of his nose, and I can't stop the snicker from passing my lips.

I have never *ever* seen a guy pout before, but why the hell does it make his lips look so good?

With a shake of my head, I fold my arms, covering my

chest. "Are you going to explain why you climbed up the side of my balcony?"

Taking a step closer to me, I hold my ground, but his closeness only serves as a reminder of how he made me feel earlier pinned against the side of my G-Wagon.

"It's my party, and you aren't there." He states it so matter-of-factly I don't know how to respond. He arranges his beanie on his head like it isn't hot as shit, while wearing a pair of swim shorts and nothing else.

The guy is a complete walking contrast.

"I never said I would be," I finally answer, and he tsks me instantly.

"That's not how this works around here. I say jump, and you ask how high." He points a finger to himself before poking my chest, letting his finger linger against my bare skin, and that's when I remember what I'm wearing.

It's too fucking warm, even with the central air conditioning on, so I threw on a tiny, thin, white strappy crop top with a pair of gym shorts. I may not be dressed all pretty, but there's a lot of skin on show right now.

His finger slowly creeps down my chest, but I smack his hand away before he can get to the swell of my breasts.

"What do you want, Tobias?"

"You."

With that, he lifts me off the ground, pulling my thighs to his waist, and turns to march back towards the balcony.

"Tobias, put me down. I swear to god, put me down. What did we say about manhandling?" I yell, but I can feel his body shake with laughter.

"You, Eden Grady, are being a spoiled brat. Celebrate the team win with me," he mutters as he balances my ass on the rim of the balcony.

My arms tighten around his neck as my legs squeeze his hips. I'm not afraid of heights, but I don't trust him enough near the edge of the balcony with such a drop beneath us.

"Is this where you push me off? Murder me just like my dad?" I ask, my heart in my throat as the reality of those words play on my mind.

"What?" His brows knit together as he stares me down, shaking his head. "Not today, Xavier said I get to have you first." He waggles his eyebrows, losing the confusion that was previously etched all over his face, but his words piss me off just as much.

"Oh, he did, huh? Screw you." I push against his chest, but he doesn't budge.

"That's exactly what I'm talking about, bubble. You must have some magic pussy if Xavier didn't even mention your little fuck session to us." His crude words make me cringe, but it's his nickname that has me intrigued.

"Why do you keep calling me that?"

"What, bubble?" When I nod, his grin is full of sex, and I already regret asking. "Because you have the finest bubble butt

I ever did see. I did tell you that." As if to drive his message home, he squeezes my ass, pulling me in closer to his body and bringing our faces within an inch of each other.

Locked in a stare off, I can hear my heart pounding in my ears as I find myself lost in his gaze. I remember him saying it, I just didn't expect it to stick.

"Let me taste your sweet lips, Eden," he breathes out, and like a magnet, my mouth slowly begins to move towards his. My eyes are fixed on his, his blue eyes holding my captive.

Just as my lips are about to touch his, a deep voice interrupts us.

"Let's fucking go, Tobias," Xavier growls out, his voice coming from below with what almost sounds like a hint of jealousy in his words, making Tobias sigh but hold me against his body even tighter.

"Come on, bubble. Time to go. I'll even let you walk down the stairs like a normal person," he offers as he lowers me to the ground, but I just roll my eyes.

"I'm not going anywhere with you," I throw back, brushing my hands down my top, and he huffs.

"Fine, Xavier isn't going to be happy that I told you this, but he managed to get your phone off Roxy before they destroyed it. Come have fun with us, and I'll give it back to you."

Fuck. The glimmer in his eyes tells me he already knows he has me backed into a corner. I need my phone, for the pictures if nothing else. Which is why I find myself nodding in agreement.

"Fine, let me just get changed," I grumble, but he wraps his hand around mine and starts pulling me towards the door.

"No need, you look good as you are," he states over his shoulder, and I try to dig my heels in.

"This top is made of nothing, Tobias, and my ass is close to hanging out of these shorts."

"Exactly." He winks, continuing towards the door, but I pull back.

"I am not—"

"Fine," he says with a sigh. "Where is my jacket from earlier? You can throw that over." Standing to search my room, he spots his jacket on the chaise lounge and releases his hold on me to run and grab it.

"That's not what I was talking about," I grumble, but it's like he doesn't hear me as he holds out his jacket for me to slip my arms in. "You're an asshole, you know that?"

"It's my middle name, bubble, now let's fucking go already."

Following his lead, I can feel myself stepping towards hell, but I promised myself I would do anything to get my phone back. Let's just hope I survive the night to get it.

KC KEAN

SIXTEEN
Tobias

I can feel every step she takes as she follows behind me. The sight of her in my jacket does more to me than I care to admit, but this is nothing more than a little fun. Once I get a taste of the new girl, I'll get her out of my system and I'll move on to the next.

We made a pact when we were fourteen, Xavier, Hunter, and me. No commitments and no ties to this place. Ever. Then the day we graduate, we give a huge fuck you to this town, leaving nothing but dust in our wake as we never look back.

Deep down, I think we know we'll never be able to step out of the shadows of our parents, but nothing else forcing us to remain in this town will make our attempts easier at least.

Shaking away the darkness that always hangs over my head,

I open the front door to Archie's house wide, hinting for Eden to step through first, and with a wary look on her face, she does.

Shutting the door behind me, I instantly regret giving her my jacket. Now I can't see her bubble butt sway as she walks in front of me.

"Where are we going?" she asks, peeking over her shoulder at me as she nibbles her bottom lip, and I have to refrain from squeezing my dick. So. Fucking. Hot.

"Does it really matter?" I counter, and she rolls her eyes. Walking side by side, we pass a few drunken couples and groups. They're all having the time of their life in their own way. Some are stoned beyond repair, while others are drunk on the atmosphere alone, laughing and talking animatedly like they have no care in the world.

This is why Archie is the party king. I don't know what he does exactly, but everyone always has a good time. The only time things get out of hand or fights start is if we start them.

My hand itches at my side, wanting to reach out and take Eden's. Her gaze is focused straight ahead, paying no attention to me or the people around us, like she's lost in her own mind.

Poking her side, she jumps back and glares at me. "What was that for?"

"Just bringing you back to the present." I grin, but it only makes her squint at me even more. Someone doesn't like the truth.

"You guys took your time," Xavier grumbles, his presence

catching me by surprise since all my focus has been on Eden.

Turning to face him, I don't miss the frown on his face as his gaze flickers between us.

"I'm here for my phone," Eden states casually, and Xavier gives me a pointed look as his fists clench at his side.

Asshole hates it when I go against what he says. "She wouldn't have come otherwise," I state, and he looks at me like I'm stupid.

"You don't give her a choice, asswipe." With that, he turns on his heels in the sand and starts walking down to the beach, the people in his path automatically stepping out of his way.

Eden instantly falls into step with him, and I'm quick to place myself on her other side.

"No can do, Xavier. We're working on our manhandling, aren't we, bubble?" I glance down at her. She's only about three or four inches shorter than me, but it's enough for me to feel like the alpha.

"Stop calling me that," she mumbles under her breath, not looking at me as she pulls my jacket tighter around herself, and I can't help but enjoy getting under her skin.

"Where's Hunter?" I ask, giving Eden a break for just a second as I look to Xavier.

"Already back at the house pulling Eden's phone from the safe because I thought of a fun game."

I rub my hands together in excitement, the devilish glint in his eyes tells me this is going to be fun. Eden pauses her movements, and I stop to glance at her, surprised that Xavier stops to do the same.

"What do you mean you thought of a game? Tobias just said I had to come and I'd get my phone back." She stares Xavier down like he isn't the damn prince of Knight's Creek, and if anything, it only makes my dick harder.

"Rules, Eden Grady. We make them, you follow them. It's up to you, but it's the only way you'll get it back," Xavier calls out as he continues to walk away from the crowd.

With a heavy sigh, Eden continues, and her determination is inspiring, even if it is going to be the death of her. I like it. I think.

We walk in silence, the anticipation building with each step we take as it seems only Xavier holds all the cards, but I like it. The surprise sends a buzz through my veins and has me excited to get our little party started.

As Xavier starts to climb the wooden steps to our home, it dawns on me that he's allowing Eden to come on to our property. Something we never do. Ever. It's on the tip of my tongue to ask why, but I don't want to put a stop to the night.

Swinging my arm up in the direction of the steps, I encourage Eden to follow after Xavier, but she gapes at me for a moment, her eyes glancing between me and the back of Xavier's retreating shadow.

"I thought you don't let people in here?" she asks quietly, directing her question at me instead of Xavier, and I simply shrug my shoulders.

I don't lie, so if I don't have an answer, I don't offer one.

With another sigh, she brushes past me, stomping up each step. Her blonde hair shines in the moonlight, like a beacon beckoning me closer.

Shaking my head, I take the steps two at a time to catch up to her. When I reach the top, I find the gate shut. It seems Xavier showed no manners in holding it open for her. Typical.

Reaching around her, my chest brushing against her back, I lift my hand to the scanner, the sound of the lock clicks, and the gate creaks open.

"After you," I murmur against her ear. I don't miss the sudden intake of breath at my close proximity, but we'll have plenty of time to play those games later. I want to know what Xavier has cooked up for us.

Standing taller, she lifts her head high and steps through the gate. She glances around slightly but keeps her focus on the kitchen door open ahead.

I try to picture the house from her view, but the grand features don't really impress me anymore. Not when I know the people who own it and how they get the things that they want.

Eden doesn't pause at the backdoor like she did at the bottom of the stairs, instead stepping straight in like she lives here, and her confidence blows me away. I could get down with this. With her. Even if it confuses the hell out of me because we are supposed to be destroying her.

Kicking the door shut behind me, I stop right behind Eden as Xavier and Hunter sit at the breakfast bar, staring at Eden like she's their prey.

"What's the game then?" I ask, not wanting to waste a single second of fun time, and Xavier waves his hand for us to take a seat.

Placing my hand at the bottom of Eden's spine, I force myself to not grope her ass, even if it calls to me, I don't want to piss her off. Yet.

She pulls the bar stool out, facing Hunter, and I slip into the seat to her right, facing Xavier. Smart move. They both look like dangerous motherfuckers, but Hunter is definitely a little softer than Xavier overall, depending how I look at it.

"Where's my phone?" Eden asks, glancing between them, and it's Hunter who responds.

"You finding your phone is the game."

"What?" Her nose scrunches as she frowns at him, and Xavier taps his fingers on the counter as he stares her down.

"We are going to play a game of tag. If you can make it to your phone without being tagged, you get your phone back without question," Xavier states, his gaze not faltering from hers.

"And if someone tags me?" Eden murmurs, and excitement fizzles in my veins. Fuck, we haven't played around like this with someone in what feels like forever. Everyone is too scared to find themselves in this kind of situation with us anymore.

"Then that person gets what they want."

"You have got to be joking with me," Eden states, but the way Xavier looks at her makes it clear he isn't. "So you think if you tag me, like we're fucking children I might add, you get to do whatever you want and I have no say in the matter? Yeah, no thanks."

Planting her hands on the table, her stool starts to scrape across the tiled floor when Xavier responds. "We aren't going to pin you down and rape you, Eden. We agree on stakes before we begin," he states simply, and Eden stops moving.

"Is everything always a game around here?"

"Pretty much," I answer, leaning forward on my elbows to get a better look at her face. "So, you in?" My hands clasp together as I wait for her to answer, praying she doesn't chicken out yet.

Slowly, one by one, she stares us down, and I can almost feel her brain ticking overtime as she weighs up her options. How important is her phone? That's the question, ultimately.

"Fine, what are the terms?" she finally asks with a huff, swiping a lock of hair from her face, and my pulse picks up with excitement.

"If I tag you, I get seven minutes in heaven with you, bubble," I blurt out, a grin playing on my lips as she scoffs in response.

"That's childish."

"She's not wrong, man," Hunter chimes in, and I send him

a glare.

"Screw you. I want some private time with bubble here, and I'm not going to force myself on her. So, seven minutes in heaven. Nothing scary about it, right?"

Turning my gaze back to hers, she looks at me like I'm crazy but nods reluctantly.

"Fine, what else?" she questions, looking to the others, waiting to see what they say.

"If I tag you, we go skinny dipping," Hunter says, surprising me, and Eden raises her eyebrow at him. The challenge in both of their eyes is unmistakable, and just as I hope, she doesn't relent.

"Fine, and you?" she asks, turning her attention to Xavier, and he frowns.

"Is that how you address everyone you've fucked?"

"I don't usually speak to them again, to be honest. You want a medal?" she sasses back, and Xavier doesn't take the bait, even though I can see he's affected by the way his eyes round a little.

"If I tag you, you answer some questions I have." As simple as that, and of course, she eagerly nods in agreement.

"I also want something other than my phone back if no one gets me," Eden states, pulling the cuffs of my jacket over her hands nervously.

"What?" I ask, quite eager to give her anything right now for the chance of a little cat and mouse chasing.

"I want to ask some questions of my own."

"Done," I answer before Xavier can shut her down, and he grumbles under his breath in annoyance like I knew he would.

"Perfect, so where do I have to go for my phone?" Eden asks, rising from her stool.

"My room," Hunter answers. "We'll even give you a five second head start."

"Wait, I don't know where your room is."

"Not my problem. Five…four…"

Panicked eyes look at mine, but if she thinks I'm going to help her, she's rudely mistaken. I'm probably the most excited here.

"Three…two…"

"Fuck," she curses, taking off through the door that leads to the hallway, and seconds later, I hear her feet pounding up the stairs.

"One. Ready or not, here we come."

SEVENTEEN
Eden

Adrenaline courses through my veins as my feet carry me up the stairs on autopilot.

What the fuck are we even playing right now? And why the hell am I even playing along? I can't deny the fact that excitement tingles across my skin, though.

My phone. I need my phone. Every picture or memory I have with my dad is on there, and if I have to outrun these assholes to get it back, then I will.

Quickly unzipping Tobias' jacket so it doesn't restrict my movement as it gathers around my thighs, I reach the top of the stairs, panicking for a moment as I try to decide which direction to go. Rooms lead off in both directions, the hallway lit, doors everywhere, and I have no fucking clue which way to take.

The sound of chairs scraping across the tiled kitchen floor kick me into action, and I opt to go to the right, paying little attention as I swing each door open carelessly. A closet, a bathroom, and finally what looks to be someone's room, but other than a bed and a chest of drawers, there is nothing personal in there.

I hear them creeping up the stairs, not chasing after me like I expected them to, but it doesn't calm the spike of nervousness that beats through my body. If they know which direction I turned, then they'll know if I'm close or not.

Swinging open the next door, I instantly know I'm in one of their rooms. The man cave vibes overwhelm me immediately. A guitar sits on a stand perfectly in the corner, while paper is scattered across the desk beside the huge bed in here.

I don't see my phone on the bed, and the whole room strangely screams Tobias, so I leave the door open and move on to the next one.

Bathroom. Fuck.

Glancing over my shoulder, I see all three of them standing at the top of the stairs, smirks marking their faces as Xavier makes a show of lifting his phone in the air and pressing a button. I frown in confusion, but mere seconds later, the whole house goes black.

I try to blink through the darkness as I realize he just turned off the fucking lights and stumble to try the next door.

"No fair, you cheating motherfucking bitch faces," I yell,

finding the doorknob for the next room, but it's pitch black when I swing the door open wide.

Nothing. Fuck.

Stumbling in the dark, I rush for the next door, hearing their footsteps near, and my heart is in my throat.

"Turn the fucking lights back on," I growl out, but all I hear is a snicker in response. Swinging the next door open, I pause as I realize it's a bedroom.

Squinting as my heart pounds in my chest, I try to make out the room. I can see the outline of furniture, but I don't think I see a bed. As I go to step back, I move straight into someone's chest, and before I can surge forward out of their reach, arms band around my waist, holding me close.

"Put me the fuck down. You turned the lights off and that was no way near a fucking decent head start. You don't play fair," I grind out as I swing my legs and arms about, trying to wrestle out of their hold.

Whoever holds me captive chuckles in my ear, but it's so low, I can't place which douchebag it is. It sends a shiver down my spine as I feel their hands hold me tighter.

"I said. Put. Me. Down," I growl out, holding still against them as they say nothing in response. Wait, did he— "Did you just fucking sniff my hair? Creep, get off."

Throwing my elbow back, I get him in the stomach, making him grunt. "Fuck, bubble, I was starting to think I was your favorite," Tobias murmurs, his lips brushing the shell of my ear, and I freeze.

A dim light suddenly comes on from across the room as an alarm sounds from Xavier's phone, and I see Xavier raise his finger to his lip, telling me to be quiet.

What the fuck is going on?

"What the hell is your mom doing here, X?" Hunter mutters quietly, glancing down at his phone too as he comes to stand to the side of us, and I realize I'm still letting Tobias hold me.

"Put me down," I whisper, but even that seems like too much noise for Xavier as he storms towards me, sandwiching me in between him and Tobias.

"If you value anything about your life, you'll shut the fuck up." His words are laced with venom, and I can't tell if the tone is aimed at me or the situation, but for once, I listen and keep my mouth shut.

The sound of a door slamming shut in the distance is followed by heels clicking on the ground floor.

"Why the fuck aren't the lights coming on?" A woman's husky voice complains, and Xavier quickly pulls his phone from his pocket and presses a few buttons, not moving from where he stands before me, and in the next moment, the lights outside of the room flicker on. She sounds familiar, but I can't place it.

"Xavier must have been playing around with the security again, don't stress so much, *mi amor*," a man responds to her as I strain to hear them coming up the stairs.

"He shouldn't be messing with anything, Reza. We give

him too much fucking freedom as it is."

"Let's just get what you wanted to grab, and then we can go home, okay?" the man soothes, and they sound much closer now.

Xavier mouths for Hunter to shut the door, and he's stealthy for the bulky size of him because I don't hear a single sound.

The couple continues to mumble, but with the door closed, I can no longer hear what they're saying. My eyes finally take in the room around me as I try to remain quiet.

A navy bedspread lies perfectly on the huge Alaskan-sized bed, a walk-in closet and access to a bathroom are just off to the right, while very little of anything else is in here. If there weren't pictures on the wall to my left, I wouldn't have believed someone slept in here.

That's when I spot my phone sitting centered on the bed. This is Hunter's room?

"I want my phone," I murmur, nodding towards the bed, but Tobias doesn't release me, and Xavier continues to stare at his phone. I spot Hunter over by the window ignoring us all, and my blood starts to boil. "Somebody passes me my phone right now, or I start fucking screaming," I snap, and that finally makes Xavier lift his head from his phone.

Lifting his hand to my chin, he holds me in place as he leans in. Whatever he is about to say is cut off by Tobias planting his palm on Xavier's face. The strength he has surprises me as he continues to hold me with just one arm around me.

"I caught her, I get my seven minutes in heaven," Tobias mutters before dropping his hand back to my waist. His fingers skim across my tummy, and the feel of his skin on mine reminds me I undid his jacket earlier, leaving my tiny tank top and short shorts on display.

Trying to pull the jacket closed, Xavier's hands stop me, holding the jacket out wide as he looks me over. I feel his eyes graze every inch of my skin, just like they did that night, and I refuse to be embarrassed about my body.

"Nobody gets anything if I don't get my phone," I repeat, and Xavier's hand on my chin tightens, almost to the point of pain.

"What did I tell you about your mouth ruining shit?" he rumbles, finally bringing his eyes to mine, and I give him a pointed look.

"Tobias, please put me down," I whisper sweetly, and to my surprise, he does, although he makes sure to drag my ass across his hard length beneath his shorts. Once I'm comfortable on the floor, I wrap my hand around Xavier's wrist and try to pull him off me, but he doesn't move.

He must sense my mind going into overdrive, thinking up all the ways I can hurt him, because he, too, releases me, and I rush for my phone.

Pressing the button, the screen comes to life, the photo of my father and me filling the screen, and I hold it to my chest. Thanking my lucky stars those bitches didn't do anything crazy with it.

"They're leaving," Hunter murmurs from beside the window, and I can't help but step towards him so I can look down at the people he's talking about.

It sounded like they were Xavier's parents, but then why would they not all live together? Why would they come to get something and then leave just as quickly?

The second I stand beside Hunter at the huge open window, he pulls me back.

"We're snooping, Eden. Don't stand so openly while you do it. Ilana has eyes like a hawk. She'll fucking sense a small thing like you from a mile away," he mutters, and just as he says that, the woman looks over her shoulder directly at the window, and my heart stops.

My legs go weak, and if Hunter didn't have hold of me, I'd be flat on my face. I can't pull my gaze from her, but eventually, she climbs into the back of the waiting SUV.

It feels like a million needles are pricking my skin as I hear the guys talking around me, but I can't pick out their words as tears well in my eyes. I grip my phone even tighter in my hand as Tobias comes to stand in front of me, but I jolt back as he tries to reach his hand out.

My world feels upside down, but I push back on Hunter until he releases me, and I brush past Tobias, racing for the door.

I'm not safe here. Not with their games or their strange embraces that are meant to shield me yet burn me all the same.

"We're not fucking done here." Xavier's voice finally filters through my clouded brain as he wraps his hand around my arm, and I scream like my life depends on it. I can't breathe, fear tearing at my insides.

"What the fuck is going on?" Tobias growls out as Xavier releases his hold on me, and I back away towards the door.

"Stay the fuck away from me. All of you. No games, no seven minutes in heaven, you get fucking nothing at all. Do you hear me?" I'm shaking from head to toe as I continue to walk backwards, and the guys stare at me like I've grown a second head. "And you tell Ilana, or whoever the fuck she is, I'm going to find a way to prove she killed my father. Whatever it takes, she'll pay."

"Wait, what?" Hunter murmurs, glancing at me, then the others.

"Like you don't fucking know. She's the whole reason I'm here, without my mom, and why my dad is dead."

Lingering on the edge of having what I believe to be a panic attack, I can barely breathe, my world spinning, and I can't calm my pounding heart or overactive mind.

They all stand in shock, Tobias and Hunter more than Xavier, as I turn around and run, thankful with every ounce of my being that they don't chase me.

TOXIC CREEK

EIGHTEEN
Eden

Coffee in hand, I find myself out by the pool the following morning, relaxing back on a sun lounger in my bathrobe, and if I hadn't been here last night, seeing the party with my own eyes, I would never have believed there had even been one.

Not an ounce of litter or empty bottles to be seen. Either these kids are clean as fuck, or someone has an awesome cleanup crew in place. Not even a sleeping body or two.

I've barely slept a wink, if at all, after racing from Xavier's house last night. Instead, I lay on my bed, looking up at the ceiling helplessly, until the sun came up and I could no longer stay inside my room when it felt like the walls were caving in.

I'm running with the fact that this Ilana woman is Xavier's mom, and deep down, I know it shouldn't surprise me that he's related to the bitch that has me here. Xavier Knight, son of the bitch, Ilana Knight. All I can think about now, since I've calmed a little, is how I'm going to convince Xavier to share information with me.

Surely he must know something about his mom, anything at all. You can't have what seems to be a powerful woman as your parent without knowing even just a tad of information.

Last night was just… Fuck. Swiping my hair back off my face, I tilt my head up to the sky, feeling the sun beat down on me. Last night was not how I planned to relax at all. I went from hanging out with Charlie to being chased around a damn mansion by the Allstars.

I hate how my heart beats rapidly for a totally different reason when I think about it. I hate them, all three of them. They literally are the biggest assholes I've ever met. They don't play fair, and it seems they always get what they want. But not from me. I refuse. They can have my anger and rage instead.

Walking away from that house last night, I left with them firmly as my sworn enemies, which doesn't help my cause right now or offer me answers to my dad's death, but I hate how they fuck with my mind with the games they play.

With a heavy sigh, I stand from the lounger, forcing myself to stop getting lost in my mind again, but it's difficult without a distraction.

Walking towards the balcony edge, I stare out at the water, letting the sound of the waves crashing wash over me.

I would usually go for a run at times like this, but I'm not going back down to that end of the beach right now, and there isn't much beach in the opposite direction. Besides, I'm so exhausted, I feel like death warmed over.

My phone vibrates in the pocket of my bathrobe, and guilt hits my gut as I see Charlie's name flash across the screen with an incoming message. I'd left her last night, not intentionally, but I did manage to send her a message when I got back, and she'd instantly responded that Archie had taken her home in her car.

I needed to thank him for that today. Charlie is nothing like Lou-Lou from back home. Lou-Lou could handle herself better than a forty-year-old bodybuilder, whereas Charlie has completely different vibes. I know she isn't my responsibility, but I left her in the lurch last night so I could get my phone back.

Charlie: Hey girl, you sleep yet?

Me: It doesn't feel like I have.

Charlie: It's almost ten, Eden. Let me know if you need to chat or eat. I'm free all day.

Me: Thanks.

"Good morning."

I turn quickly, to see Richard standing just outside the open patio doors. His eyes are trained at the floor as he runs his fingers through his already messy hair.

"Morning," I murmur after checking to make sure he was actually talking to me, but there isn't anyone else around.

He slowly walks around the pool before leaning against the balcony beside me, and I turn to take up the position I was in moments ago, mirroring him.

Nobody speaks for a moment as we both look out to the ocean. I don't know what I'm supposed to say to this man who seems to be forced to home me, but thankfully, he speaks first.

"Is everything okay? I saw you race in last night and you looked a little panicked, but I didn't want to disturb you after you locked yourself in your room."

I watch out of the corner of my eye as he frowns, almost disappointed that he didn't stop me last night, but if he'd have tried, I wouldn't have listened anyways.

"I'm okay, I just learned some things about Knight's Creek is all." I don't trust this guy enough to be more specific, unless he's going to offer to help.

"Ahh, and there is never anything good to learn about this place," he responds, and he's not wrong. I haven't learned anything decent since I came here, but I guess I'm also not looking for happy information either.

"That is a very true statement."

Turning to look at me head-on, my heart pounds a little in my chest as I watch his eyes swirl with pain. It reminds me that he lost his wife, and he must have loved her very much. He looks a little more put together than the first time we met, but there is still a lot going on under the surface with him.

Before I can say anything else, he pats my shoulder and

stalks off without a backwards glance.

Okay, then. Great talk.

"Morning, Dad. Hey, Eden, come be my friend." Archie appears in the open doorway, his arms out wide as he grins at me.

"You have way too much fucking energy for me right now," I grumble, but he continues to rush over to me.

"Be my friend, Eden," he repeats, giving me puppy dog eyes like a child as he stops just before knocking me over, and I'm too damn soft on him.

"What did you want to do?"

"It's Saturday, and we won yesterday. I'm hungover from celebrating, so I want video games, then food. I'll let you chill beside me while I shoot my shit on *Apex*, a battle royale shooting game, but I just want some company," he admits, his voice getting quieter towards the end, and I can already feel myself relenting.

His blond hair is stuck up in all directions, his eyes tired as he offers me a soft smile.

Pulling my bathrobe tighter, I huff at him as I brush past and head towards the house. I don't even bother to look back at him as I holler over my shoulder.

"Archie Freemont, if you think I'm going to sit by and watch you play, you have another thing coming. *Lifeline* is my favorite."

It takes him longer than I expect to catch on to what I'm

saying, but I'm pretty sure he squeals like a girl before chasing me down. Suddenly lifted off my feet, Archie does some crazy kung fu shit, and I'm suddenly on his back getting a piggyback ride as he carries me into the house and down the stairs.

"You are my new best friend," Archie states, and I grin.

"Whatever you say, bestie," I joke back, and he purposely bounces so I hold on tighter, panicked I'm going to fall.

I've never been down here, especially since I always see Richard head this way and I've wanted to keep out of his path. The mini landing we come to is neutral tones with cream carpet lining the floor, and there are five or six doors leading off, but Archie takes the second to the right.

Swinging the door open, my jaw drops as I take in the room. There are no windows in here, and when Archie flicks the light switch, LED lights come to life around the edge of the room, offering the perfect glow for the gaming setup of all gaming setups as they come into view.

Oh my fucking god. Six gaming monitors line the far wall, each hooked up to a PC and Xbox, with a headset and controller at each station. Top of the range gaming chairs sit in front of each. All from the same company, but in different colors.

"Holy fucking shit. I feel like I just walked into the Power Rangers' headquarters or something." Archie barks with laughter as he places me back on my feet, and I straighten my robe. "This place is awesome as shit, Arch. My dad would have fucking loved it in here."

The smile drops from my face as a surge of guilt shoots through my body, any inch of excitement or joy instantly gone. I don't want to feel any of that, not without my dad.

"Hey. Hey, Eden. Where did you just go?" I can see the sadness in his eyes, as if he knows exactly where I just went, and I can bet everything I have that he does the same when he thinks of his mom. "Now, I'm not going to pretend that I know who your dad was because I didn't. But if your dad would have loved something like this, would he have wanted you to pass up on such a good time?"

Archie's words make me pause and practically rewire my brain, if only for a moment, because he's right—my dad would be furious, in the best way possible.

With a deep breath, I stand tall and shake my hands out. "You're right, but if you think I'm carrying you, you are truly mistaken, understand?" I'm bragging, but I *am* good at this game.

With a huge grin on his face, he leads me to the purple chair, and I turn everything on as he grabs two bottles of water from the small fridge in the corner of the room. There is a huge stack of candy beside it too.

Ultimate fucking setup.

Taking the seat to my left, he quietly gets ready too, and I actually feel excited.

"Champion squad or nothing. Agreed?" I ask, and Archie nods repeatedly.

"Always, cookie."

This one's for you, Dad.

"Yes! Fuck yes!" Archie yells, rising from his chair and punching the air ecstatically again. I laugh along with him, feeling the endorphins boost my mentality as we win another game. "Where have you been all my life, Eden? That was fire."

Shaking my head at him, I focus on the screen, readying up for another game as he finally takes his seat.

"You aren't as bad as I worried you would be, Archie," I say with a grin, and he just laughs louder.

"You are queen at this, I swear. We have to make a commitment to the game now, Eden. The battle pass only has another four weeks left, and I need to get to tier one hundred."

Laughing at his enthusiasm, I nod. "We'll figure it out."

"You'll figure what out?" a deep voice interrupts us from behind, and I already know who it is, and I find myself losing all the happiness I had just moments ago, a stark reminder of who he is repeating in my mind.

I turn my eyes to my lap as Archie greets Xavier, Hunter, and Tobias, and they all talk football for a minute.

I feel the seat to my right pull out, and moments later, Hunter sits down.

"You play video games, huh?" I hum in agreement but don't lift my gaze from my twiddling fingers in my lap.

"Play video games? Man, she just got kill leader four games in a row," Archie boasts, and I feel a little embarrassed under their watchful gaze. "You want to join us? There are too many of us for—"

"Actually, we stopped by to talk to Eden about last night," Xavier says, cutting Archie off, and my hands instantly fist in my lap at his arrogance to do so.

"There's nothing to talk about. Let's ready up, Arch," I murmur, meeting his gaze as he sinks back into the chair beside me.

"It wasn't a request," Hunter adds, and the telltale sound of my Xbox being shut down sounds out around the room, and I instantly throw him a glare as I refrain from throwing my controller at his head.

His smug ass face grins at me as he purposely holds his finger against the console, driving home that he did indeed switch it off.

"What's going on?" Archie asks, his voice laced with concern, and I sigh.

Just as I open my mouth to answer him, a hand is clamped over my mouth and an angry Xavier is leaning over the chair glaring down at me.

"It's a private matter," he barks, but Archie instantly stands and crowds in over me.

"Xavier, I respect you man, a lot, but you better take your fucking hand off her. Right now." He's rigid from head to toe, his eyes searching mine as he stands his ground.

Tobias chuckles from somewhere behind me as my hands dig into the armrest, refusing to show weakness and try to fight him off. It's useless right now.

"Do you really want to make threats, Archie? Throw everything away for a girl who just showed up? Where's your loyalty?" Hunter asks, and Archie wastes no time responding.

"With her. My loyalty is with her. She has no one. Fucking no one, and I refuse to let her get lost to this sick and twisted town."

His words lie heavy on my chest as they wash over me. He isn't wrong. The one person I always had, no matter what, is gone, but I hate that Archie's putting everything on the line for me. I'm not worth it. Meeting my gaze, I plead at him to stop, but all he does is roll his eyes.

"Even now, she's trying to tell me to shut the fuck up so nothing happens to me, trying to protect me from the moment she arrived. Well she deserves that in return too. So like I said, take your fucking hand off her."

Silence fills the room, no one utters a single word, until Xavier suddenly releases his hand from my mouth. I watch as Archie swallows past the lump in his throat as he stares the Allstars down, but it's Tobias who finally speaks first.

"Nice speech, Archie," he mutters before my chair is suddenly spun around and I come face-to-face with Tobias. My hands cover the armrests, so he places his hands over mine as he looks down at me. "Eden, we need to talk."

His words are sincere, but his facial expression is much harsher, and as much as I fucking hate these assholes right now, if they're willing to talk, I might be able to get some answers for myself.

Wetting my lips, I keep my eyes trained on him, not looking to the others. "I can talk, but I have questions too." He nods in agreement, and I take a deep breath, trying to calm myself. I don't think I can take any of these guys at their word, but I have to try if I want answers. My body hums with trepidation. I can't tell if it's from the adrenaline of Archie's little showdown or from Tobias' touch, but I refuse to focus on it. "I would rather talk somewhere neutral, preferably with food, and with Archie present too."

Tobias stands back, and I miss the warmth of his touch instantly, but to my surprise, the others all move back too, looking at Xavier for the final answer.

Sighing, he rubs the back of his neck, and I notice it's the first time he's ever shown an inch of uncertainty. He doesn't like my mouth, we all know that, but he must want to talk enough to consider my demands.

"Deal. Get dressed. We're going to Pete's."

KC KEAN

NINETEEN

Xavier

Pulling into the parking lot at Pete's, my fingers wrap tightly around the steering wheel of my Jaguar F-Pace. I'd offered to drive everyone, but Eden refused. Some shit about not choking on our toxic air.

She gets under my fucking skin, and I seem to just let her. But what stuns me most is Archie finally finding a reason to stand up for something, or *someone* in this case. The determination in his gaze as he tracked his eyes from where I held Eden to mine left me speechless for a moment.

I don't know how I feel about it, but for now, I guess he can pretend to be the hero in Eden's story.

Looking in the rearview mirror, I watch as the two of them jump down from Eden's SUV, laughing and joking like we aren't trying to find out some important information.

"Stop gripping the wheel like it's treating you badly, X," Hunter mumbles from beside me, and I frown at him as I release my grip on the wheel. We drove in silence, as they likely felt the stress written all over my face and the tension from my body.

"Let's just get this over with. I have better shit to be doing."

Jumping down from my SUV, I slam my door shut behind me, and even I can admit that was more than necessary. I've been antsy as hell since Eden left our home in a blind panic last night. I don't like her knowing things I don't.

Hunter had been the first to jump into action and at least made sure she got to Archie's unscathed. We didn't need her running out into the ocean in her state, since a dead body wouldn't go down well for the Allstars.

We then spent the rest of the night trying to figure out how she thinks my mother had something to do with her father's death, and it wasn't until Tobias suggested just actually asking her that I considered it. I was all out of options myself.

So here I am, being forced to fucking socialize with the enemy.

Pushing through the doors of Pete's, I don't bother holding it open for anyone as I head straight to my usual table. It's not overly crowded in here, but there are a few tables filled with couples and families, all of whom make sure not to meet my gaze. They all know who I am, or my mother at least. The power I seem to wield almost feels fake, but I'll take anything as a barrier between us and this town, my mother included.

Dropping down into the booth by the floor-length windows overlooking the ocean, Linda is at my side instantly.

"What has my Xavier all in a twist, huh?" she asks, fluffing her hair as she meets my eyes, and I give her a pointed look.

"Linda, when am I ever in a twist?"

"You tell me, Xavier. I was about to charge you for a new door since you almost shattered the glass in that one." She points over her shoulder and rolls her eyes at me. She always has the ability to ground me.

"I'm sorry," I mumble, and she grins, letting me know I've been played. "Yeah, yeah. Look at me being all humble."

She steps to the side as Hunter and Tobias slip into the booth on either side of me, both greeting her with a kiss to the cheek before taking a seat. Linda is the closest the three of us have to a true maternal woman in our life, and she fucking knows it.

"What am I getting my boys today?"

"And me," Archie adds, squeezing her shoulder as he passes, with Eden right behind him.

I watch as Archie sits beside Tobias to my left, leaving Eden to slip in beside Hunter to my right.

"Oh, you brought this little cutie back again, Archie. Nice." Eden smiles politely at her, and it winds me the fuck up. We're wasting time here. "Are we eating or just drinking?" Linda asks, scanning her eyes across us all as we answer.

Hunter, Tobias, and Archie call out for food as Eden and I

murmur 'drinks' in unison, making Linda shake her head at us.

"How about I go and get you guys some drinks, and you can decide if you want to eat when I get back." She doesn't wait for an answer, retreating to the diner countertop area before we can even utter what we want.

Silence surrounds us as I watch Eden glance down at her phone for the third time since she sat down.

"If we're keeping you from something, just say the word," I bite out, and she rolls her eyes, like I'm not a fucking Allstar and the Knight's prince of this town.

"My mom is supposed to call me today. Is that an issue?" Her sapphire blue eyes sparkle with challenge.

"If I had a good side, this wouldn't be the way to get on it," I respond, sitting back in my seat and stretching my arms out wide on the back of the booth.

"Oh, Xavier. I've had what I wanted from you, there is no need for anything else. Besides, we both know you are rotten to the core. I wouldn't even attempt to go looking for your good side." Her words strike hard, but I just grin at her with malice in my eyes as my words hang on the tip of my tongue, but Hunter interrupts.

"How about you explain why you aren't with your mom?"

Her eyes remain on mine for a moment, waiting to see if I will respond, but my friend, *my brother*, has overridden my bullshit and gotten us back on track, so I won't derail us again.

She glances to Archie, who offers a subtle nod, and with a

heavy sigh, she finally answers. "She said they wouldn't allow it."

There is more to the story, I can feel it, the whos, the whys, the everything, but it looks like she's keeping her cards close to her chest.

"Who wouldn't allow it?" I ask, and she doesn't meet my gaze as she answers.

"I'm assuming the woman from last night."

"That would be Ilana Knight, Xavier's mom," Tobias offers, and I want to tell him to shut up, but I know deep down if we offer her a little of the information she wants, we will get everything we need too.

Her eyes flicker to mine for the briefest second before Linda arrives with a tray full of iced teas. Placing them down on the table, her eyes find Eden's, and the knowing smirk that takes over her face has me on edge for what her mouth is about to say next.

"Eden, you do not look as happy as you did last time you were here. If these boys are giving you any trouble, you just let me know." She glares at us all quickly before looking back to Eden. "You're missing your afterglow from last time too. Is Archie not putting out?"

She winks at Eden as Archie spits out his iced tea in a coughing fit of laughter, but all my focus is on staying calm because I feel like my head is about to explode.

She fucked him. She fucked Archie? They didn't seem to

have that kind of vibe going on, but I guess she fucked me and look at us now. Tobias has a napkin scrunched up in his fist as he glares at the side of Archie's head, and Hunter rubs the back of his neck, confused with the turn of events and how they make him feel.

"Linda!" Eden laughs as Archie waves his hand in front of his face.

"Oh my god, Linda, it wasn't me. Turns out it wasn't the collection of toys in her drawer either. It was Xavier."

All eyes fall to me, except Eden, who places her head in her hands, and it takes me a second to catch up. Her shoulders shake with laughter as her blonde, wavy hair frames her face.

Why does my body suddenly relax at the knowledge that she didn't sleep with him? I feel my chest puff out as the sticky feeling of jealousy washes away.

"Ah, well then. Maybe dick her again, Xavier, she was practically glowing. It does wonders to a woman. Am I right?" She rubs Eden's arm, and she reluctantly nods with her head still in her hands. "I'll give you a few minutes to decide on food." With a wink, she floats over to the next table, continuing with her job.

I hate that I feel a smile wanting to stretch across my lips. Knowing she was so noticeably fucked the day after is a massive fucking ego boost.

"I want my seven minutes in heaven now," Tobias says, and Eden chuckles as she pulls her hands from her face. She looks anywhere but at me as she takes a sip of her drink, her cheeks stained red with embarrassment.

"Your mouth is annoying as shit," she mumbles to Archie, but he just wiggles his eyebrows at her in response. "And you are getting way off topic. Plus, you guys cheated, so no rules stand," she states giving a pointed look to Tobias, who pouts like he always does when he doesn't get his own way.

"Where did you see Ilana before?" Hunter finally asks, but I don't miss him readjusting himself as he does. Eden is fucking bewitching them all, and it's ridiculous.

"After my dad's funeral, she showed up at the house and was talking to my mom outside." Biting her lip nervously she looks to Hunter at her side.

His arm rests on the back of the booth, his fingers close to her shoulder, and I wonder if he's contemplating touching the bare skin on display. That pisses me off. It's my need for control because I refuse to feel any jealousy, ever. It's on the tip of my tongue to tell him to switch places, but he cuts off my train of thought as he asks her another question.

"Did she say anything to you?" he asks, holding her attention, while the three of us stare on.

"Not to me specifically, but she was warning my mom. I didn't understand at the time, but when I woke up the next morning, all my belongings had been packed into my G-Wagon and my mom was hysterically crying for me to get in and drive, while an SUV was parked across the street watching us. The

GPS led me here."

I'm too focused on the brush of his fingers against her fucking tanned skin to fully process what she's saying. I can literally see her leaning closer into him, letting him pull her story from her lips so willingly. Hunter's sense of stability does that to people. Makes them feel like they can tell him anything in the world, and it's always for our own gain. He spits them out easier than I do, and it causes me no stress.

"Did your mom say what they were threatening her with?" Hunter asks, not taking his eyes from hers, and she nods in response.

"She said if I didn't do as they say, they would kill us both, just like they killed my dad."

The pain of her statement darkens her blue eyes, reminding me of the soul that drew me in that first night I saw her.

"And what do they want you to do here?"

"Go to school and graduate while living with Archie and his dad, other than that, I have no clue. My mom has said nothing too. But I want answers. None of this makes sense to me at all." Her eyes fall to Hunter's fingertips stroking her shoulder, and she suddenly moves back as if remembering herself and focuses on the drink in front of her.

"Hey, at least you have an awesome roommate now," Archie interjects, trying to boost her spirits, and the softest smile graces her lips, and she looks like a completely different person.

"I need to know—"

"Hey, boys." Whatever Eden was about to say is cut off by the arrival of Roxy and KitKat in their matching miniskirts and cropped tops. "We aren't interrupting anything, are we?" Roxy asks, running her tongue over her bottom lip as she looks at us. Until she sees Eden at the end, and her facial expression morphs into utter disgust.

"Actually—"

"We were done here. Eden was just leaving," I interrupt, cutting her off again, but as annoying as they are, Roxy and KitKat have created the perfect distraction. There is nothing else Eden knows that she hasn't already told us, and I need space from her because the longer she sits there, the more she gets under my skin, and it's a foreign feeling I have no interest in.

"No, I need to know—"

"Don't be silly, Nafas. This was for our personal gain, not yours. You've told us all we needed to know."

The hurt that crosses her face as she realizes I won't be telling her shit has me wavering for a moment, but this is who I am, and it's one of the many lessons she needs to learn.

I hear Tobias mumble something about never getting his fucking seven minutes in heaven at this rate as Eden stands from the table, Archie following behind her.

Neither of the girls move back to give her space, but Eden remains unfazed as she stares them down. "I'm not in the mood for your little fucking whores right now, Xavier. Move your bitches."

"And if I don't?"

"I'm walking away nicely. I can change that," she states, her hands fisted at her sides, and a part of me wants to see what she would do. That's probably why she's leaving without a battle, because she knows I love it when she puts up a fight.

"KitKat, come climb in my lap." With that one line, both girls jump out of Eden's way, scooting along the bench that Archie just vacated.

Without a backwards glance, Eden storms from the diner, my eyes following her every move, even when KitKat does as I asked and grinds down on my dick. My hard dick. But it's not for her.

It's for the forbidden fruit that dismisses me so easily. I want to make her jealous, I want to cause her pain, just like she seems to ignite in me. But she'd have to care for that, I guess. Not that I do.

Not. At. All.

TOXIC CREEK

TWENTY
Eden

After spending the rest of the weekend holed up in Archie's game room, the contrast of the English classroom is completely dulling. Surrounded by a room full of stereotypical teenagers, all sitting in their cliques, while I'm sandwiched between the Allstars once again.

I decided to avoid a show, taking the seat I knew they'd force me into anyway, and they thankfully fell into their seats around me without uttering a word in my direction.

It's like Saturday never happened. Like I didn't give them the information they wanted, while they left me hanging by a thread, inevitably offering me nothing in response.

I could see the moment Xavier shut down, and the challenge in his eyes, begging me to push for more details, but I refused to give him what he wanted. Motherfucker.

Archie had driven home with me, not uttering a word, and proceeded to spend the weekend distracting me with video games, pizza, football games on the television, and ice cream. My mom had given me some lame excuse in a text, explaining why she couldn't call, and I was getting angrier with her every day.

Other than her, it was perfect. It was exactly what I needed without even asking, and it feels strange having someone so close all the time, like a brother and a friend all wrapped into one.

I'd waited by the phone all day on Sunday, hoping to hear details from Charlie and her grandmother, but I got nothing. I can't help feeling a little deflated. I had hoped to gain just a speckle of information of any kind.

This morning was the first time I stepped onto school grounds without the football players and cheer squad as an audience. Thank God practice was in full swing, even if it did mean driving in on my own since Archie left early with the other players.

Taking my seat, there are a few people in here already, and as I pull my laptop out of my bag, Archie walks in. He immediately notices where I'm sitting, and I see the question in his eyes, so I smile and offer a small nod which seems to appease him.

I'm sitting exactly where the Allstars placed me all day on Friday. Because I'm going to pretend to follow their rules silently. I want answers. I saw how they all softened a little at Pete's, and I need to get to that stage again if I ever want more information.

Just as Archie takes a seat, the Allstars step in, surrounded by girls, and I don't miss how their eyes search for me, even as they're being drenched in attention already.

Xavier looks as sharp as ever, in a crisp plain black T-shirt and fitted denim jeans, his veins bulging in his arms as he carries his bag. While Hunter runs his fingers through his hair, his long-sleeved polo top lifting at the waist, revealing a toned bronze stomach as he does. Tobias looks the most casual in his jersey shorts and muscle fit white top, his black hat in place like always.

Xavier shakes off Roxy, who hangs on his arm, and strolls straight to the seat beside me, not saying a word as he drops down. I don't watch him. My eyes are too busy glaring daggers at KitKat as she practically froths at the mouth because of where I'm sitting. Boohoo. I offer the bitch a wink, forcing the anger from my features before I turn to the front.

Hunter slips into the seat in front of me, his blond hair still slightly damp, and my fingers itch to touch it. I can't help but remember the slight touch of his fingers stroking my arm back at Pete's, each swipe causing goosebumps to spread all over my body.

"Good morning, bubble. Want to get out of here? We could extend our seven minutes in heaven to a whole hour if you like."

Tobias wiggles his eyebrows as he leans over my desk, mischief twinkling in his eyes as he smiles down at me.

It's tempting, oh so fucking tempting. Especially when he looks at me like that, undressing me with his eyes. It feels like too long ago since I was able to relieve some tension in that way, and it just so happens to have been with his friend.

My response is on the tip of my tongue when Xavier interrupts us. "Sit the fuck down, Tobias."

With a pout and a roll of his eyes, Tobias does as he says. Do these guys do everything Xavier asks? Turning to glance at Xavier, he's already staring with a smug ass grin on his face like he knows exactly what he just did.

Douchebag.

"You just let me know when, Holmes," I purr, smirking back at Xavier as I say it before going back to ignoring them.

Mrs. Leach starts the lesson, drawing my attention back to the front of the class as she drones on about the latest media she wants us to dissect. It's all about the English language and different ways of getting your message across. I feel my eyes getting tired. I've barely slept since seeing Ilana. Raiding Archie's natural energy drink stash has become my new pastime.

"Jeremy, can you shut off the lights, and I'll bring the video up for you all to watch. Take notes, people, you're going to need them."

With a heavy sigh, I sit a little straighter, wiggling my fingers before opening my laptop. I can feel Tobias staring at me from my right, some lewd comment likely on his lips, but my attention is drawn to the front of the class as the lights go down and the projector screen comes to life.

Not with the reel Mrs. Leach just mentioned. No. No, it's a front-row seat to my naked walk through school from last Friday. The room bursts into laughter as every inch of my body comes into view, the feed cutting off just as Xavier stepped into the hallway and growled.

KitKat claps loudly, standing from her seat as she encourages the room to mock me.

I sit ramrod straight in my seat, not even a blush tinging my cheeks as I watch with a neutral expression as the recording loops and starts again.

Mrs. Leach fumbles around, trying to turn the screen off as Archie rushes to help her, but the Allstars remain in place, and that's my answer. This is their doing.

I refuse to look at either side of me, but when Hunter looks back over his shoulder at me, I blow him a kiss, adding a wink for good measure, causing him to frown in confusion.

These douches want to offer me a little reminder of who's in charge here, and they're probably hoping for a little breakdown in the process. But I think this is more about them feeling in control than my emotions.

"Such a fucking slut," KitKat calls out, resting her cheek on her fist as she sneers at me, the whole room quietening, waiting for my reaction, but I just grin wider.

"I hate it when people don't like a confident woman. I shouldn't have to rein myself in just to ease your insecurities." I can feel eyes flicking between the two of us, people likely still waiting for me to attack like last time. I refuse to look at the Allstars, who are also watching us go back and forth.

I love my body. Would I change parts if I had a magic wand? For sure, but this is me, flaws and all, and I won't be slut-shamed for it. Especially not when this bitch played such a big part in the reason this video was fucking taken.

"Do you know who you are talking to?" Roxy adds, standing as she points her finger at me, hatred fresh in her eyes as she glares daggers at me.

Scoffing, I pinch the bridge of my nose, hoping for a moment's peace in a sea full of playground drama, when the video finally shuts off and Archie whirls around to face me before glaring at the guys surrounding me.

They still haven't said a word, and I can't stop myself from glancing at Xavier, who is looking straight ahead with his hands fisted on the table in front of him, and his jaw is tight.

Ahh. This must have been his master plan, to fuck with me. But the state of him makes it seem like it didn't go to plan. Did he not get the reaction he wanted?

Looking over my shoulder, I find Tobias looking right at me, guilt swirling in his blue eyes, and I feel my anger rising.

Rising from my seat, I close my laptop and slip it under my arm, grabbing my bag as I do.

"Well, it seems I love to share, huh?" I joke, glancing around at everyone in the class before settling my eyes on Roxy, referring to my naked body on display just moments ago. "I'm talking to everyone, sweetheart, neither of you are important enough for me to talk to directly."

Turning, I dismiss her without a backward glance, stepping forward and stopping by Hunter. Planting my hand on his desk, Hunter leans back in his seat to look up at me, searching my eyes like he's trying to get a read on me.

Tilting my head down, I move into his space, keeping my voice loud enough for everyone to hear.

"Hunter, maybe next time your knight gives an order, you should all have a better execution plan and at least believe in your attempt at bullying, because that was poor. Like, my feelings are not hurt that I got to flash my body to all the available guys in here. Again."

He grinds his teeth, eyes squinting in discomfort as I throw him a wink, the sound of a few whistles and catcalls filling the room.

With that, I spin on my heels and slip through the door before anything else can be said or done. Not even Mrs. Leach stops me. Screw them all. They aren't worth my time. They're simply an unnecessary distraction. I guess I'll have to figure out another way to dig deeper into this town and my father's death.

I should have just gone home, but instead, I'd gone to the library to have some peace and quiet. When the bell rang again, I took a deep breath and rejoined my classes. I refuse to be seen as weak, and I won't let them scare me away with some stupid video.

Every lesson that followed consisted of no one actually speaking to me. Instead, they were all whispering and murmuring about me to each other in front of me. A guy or two tried to approach me, but I gave them the finger before they could get too close.

Archie and Charlie tried to tell people to shut the fuck up, but it was no use, especially if Xavier has told them to do it. It's like everyone here is compelled to do exactly as he says. Fucking boring and fucking predictable.

When it came time for track, I was surprised no one uttered a word to me in the changing room except Charlie, who promised an explanation at lunch to explain why she hadn't reached out yesterday.

I also made the conscious decision to take it easy during track. No streneous exercise for me. Nothing that would require a shower afterward anyway. I didn't fancy another walk of shame again today.

The sound of the football coach blowing the whistle has a domino effect on all the other coaches drawing their classes to an end. I don't pay full attention to a word Coach Worth says as she explains an upcoming track meet.

My focus is on the football team. I love sports in general,

but the sight of a man in his full gear, mud on his jersey as he pulls his helmet off, is nothing short of amazing. I watch as one of them does it, almost like it's in slow motion, and the second his helmet is off, he's lifting the hem of his jersey to wipe the sweat from his face. Number twenty-one has me close to catching fire.

Holy mother of God, that's hot. I can feel myself practically drooling at the sight before me until he drops the jersey, and I catch a glimpse of Tobias with no hat on for a split second. He grins, watching me devouring him as he runs his fingers through his damp, wavy brown hair and slips his beanie on.

Motherfucker's hot, and he knows it. I can still feel the hard press of his cock as he pinned me to my G-Wagon the other day. So good. It's difficult to remember I hate him in moments like that. Maybe we could hate fuck and get over it?

"Miss Grady, are you even listening to me?"

"Oh, uh, sorry." I stumble over my words, spinning my attention to the coach, who just rolls her eyes at me.

"Track meet. Two weeks. Be ready. No slacking like you did today." Biting my lip, I nod in response as I try not to glance back at Tobias. "Dismissed."

Thank God.

Eyes fixed on the tunnel leading to the locker room, I ignore my name being called by some of the football players, upping my pace and slipping into the room quickly.

Roxy and KitKat glare at me the second the door shuts

behind me, but surprisingly, they keep their mouths shut. Their eyes, however, could kill me on the spot with the daggers they're throwing my way.

The chatter in the room quiets, a heavy sign I was the topic of conversation, and I refrain from rolling my eyes at their shit. Walking over to the corner I changed in earlier, I'm impressed to find everything untouched.

"Don't worry, I made sure everyone kept away from your things," Charlie says as she slips her tank top over her head.

"Thanks." I offer a soft smile before stepping into my leggings and switching out my sports bra for my lacy number. Throwing on my loose purple tank top, I run my hands over my French braids that fall down my back, making sure they haven't come loose and step into my sandals.

"You ready to eat?" Glancing to Charlie, I see she's ready too, in her skinny jeans and floral blouse. I nod in agreement, ready to understand why she hasn't mentioned her grandmother yet.

"I'm ready for pizza. Does the cafeteria even offer that here?" I ask, throwing my bags over my shoulder and slipping my sunglasses onto the hem of my top.

Heading for the door, I feel Charlie follow me, a sigh playing on my lips when I step out, and everyone leaves us alone, not uttering a word. Falling into step beside me, Charlie nervously swipes her hair behind her ear, and I can tell she has something to say.

"Whatever's on your mind, Charlie, just spit it out."

"My grandmother nearly lost her teeth when I asked her about the Grady name."

What the... A bubble of laughter bursts from my lips as we stop beside my locker, and I glance over at her.

"I have no idea where you fucking get the things that leave your mouth," I say with a chuckle, and she nudges her shoulder against mine.

"Well, I had no update for you yesterday because she kind of locked down, refusing to discuss anything at all." My heart sinks. Wetting my lips, I nod. It's not her fault. She was trying to help me out, it just didn't go to plan.

"No stress," I mutter, opening my locker and throwing my gym bag inside. I'm caught off guard when I slam it shut and find Hunter right beside me.

My hand is frozen against the metal of my locker as I stare into his green eyes. My head is tilted back as I stand face-to-face with him in complete silence, feeling lost in his trance. Until a slow grin starts to morph his face, and I remember what he was a part of earlier.

"Hey, Eden." Turning to my left, I find a guy I've seen before but know nothing about. "I was wondering if you were busy on Friday night? We have a game, but I'd love to meet up afterward. You could even come watch me play. I'll even save a spot for you at the pep rally."

Licking his bottom lip, his eyes trail over my body from

head to toe, making me cringe, but the anger I can feel radiating off Hunter encourages me in the other direction, considering this guy's offer because I do love a good pep rally.

He's easily six and a half feet, his hair trimmed super short, with deep brown eyes and broad shoulders.

Stepping forward, I place my hand on his chest, looking up at him through my lashes, and he smirks down at me. He's like putty in my hands.

"What position do you play? Football is my favorite." Biting my lip, I walk my fingers up his chest, and his eyes light up like it's Christmas.

Before he can respond, an arm stretches across my chest and pushes me back into the locker behind me. I gape in shock as I look to see it's Hunter, but he isn't looking at me. His deadly glare is aimed at the new guy.

Remembering myself, I push his arm away, and he moves to stand between the new guy and me. Everyone in the hall is staring as I find myself the center of Asheville High drama. Again.

"Eden Grady is off-limits in all capacities," Hunter growls out, and I frown. What the fuck? "She belongs to the Allstars. Now back off, Billy."

The guy, Billy, holds his hands up in surrender and slowly steps away as everyone murmurs at Hunter's statement.

"Are you fucking joking me!" Fury boils in my veins. Who do these guys even think they are? "I can do whatever the hell

I want, fuck whoever I please. That is no one else's decision to make." Pulling on his shoulder, I force him to face me, but he barely raises his eyebrow in response.

"That sounds exactly how it's going to go," Xavier murmurs, appearing out of nowhere and standing beside Hunter.

"Screw you," I grind out, my nails digging into my palms as I feel everyone's eyes flickering between us.

"You already did. You said no repeats, though, right?" He thinks he's so fucking funny, with his perfectly fucking styled hair, chiseled jaw, smart mouth, and devilish mind. Fuck him.

Tobias slides into my view, his usually pearly grin in place. "You heard Hunter—Eden is off-limits. If she's going to the pep rally with anyone, it'll be us. Now fuck off."

Over my dead fucking body. My love for pep rallies has suddenly vanished.

Simultaneously, everyone moves, putting distance between them and us, except Archie and Charlie. I immediately shake my head as Archie goes to step forward. Arguing with our eyes alone, I beg for him to listen, and with a heavy sigh and a wave of his hands, he steps back.

Looking back to the Allstars as they all stand before me, a challenge in their eyes as they wait for me to respond, and I have to force myself to calm down, not wanting to give them the fire they're wanting.

"Your obsession with me is flattering, really. But I have an itch that needs scratching from time to time, and I'll find someone to do it."

"Not here you won't," Xavier throws back, and I snicker.

"I can go looking." Turning away from him, I give him my back, dismissing him as I smile at Charlie. "Can we grab pizza off-campus?"

"For sure," she answers instantly, not looking to see how the guys react, and I like that she isn't afraid of them.

"I'll come with," Archie adds, and I nod in agreement.

"Perfect."

I put one foot in front of the other and stalk away from the assholes intent on ruining my life, surprised when no one tries to stop me. When I'm far enough away, I glance over my shoulder at them, mischief fluttering in my eyes as I talk loud enough for the Allstars to hear.

"Can we go to the next town over? It seems I need some fresh spots to go looking for dick."

TOXIC CREEK

KC KEAN

TWENTY ONE
Hunter

She's ours. Whether she likes it or not, that's how it's going to be.

We spent the whole weekend practically obsessing over her and what she said at Pete's. It is very likely Ilana had something to do with her father's death, and Xavier needs to figure out a way to approach his mother for more details. Not in a sense of helping her, but more to do with the fact we need every piece of information we can get if we plan to try and get out of here and live our own lives. If she can give us any information regarding Ilana, it will work in our favor.

A hiccup like this, less than twelve months before we graduate, does not make it easy for us.

Any and all leverage or information we can get over Ilana,

the better. She's as devious and cunning as they come. It'll make trying to leave this damn town a little easier if we can. This isn't the first time she's been linked to a murder.

Even with all this in mind, little Miss Eden Grady intrigues me. A complete enigma compared to all the other girls at Asheville High.

She owns her body, her confidence, and her strength, refusing to falter or bend at will, and when I would usually hold her at arm's length, I want to pull her closer, have her nearer.

I saw the green-eyed monster shining in Xavier's eyes this weekend when I coaxed Eden's story from her own lips, a look I've *never* seen on his face before. Not even when we were younger and were all fighting over the same girl, who suddenly upped and left with her family. We were ten, and she was our childhood crush, but I still remember the black eye Xavier gave Tobias.

From that day on, we promised not to let a girl get between us ever again, which is how we found ourselves sharing. A girl won't be able to get between us if we place her there on purpose.

"Are you ready to tell me what the fuck that was before?"

Xavier's words breaks through my thoughts as I refocus on the television playing in the den. Sitting back into the cushions on the sofa, I swipe a hand down my face, pausing the *Italian Job* before they get to the big climax.

I knew it wouldn't take long for him to start asking questions when we got home from school, but I did manage to watch most of the movie at least.

"What was what about?" I ask, fucking with him as he stands before me, arms folded across his chest as he glares down at me, and Tobias dives on the sofa beside me.

"Warning everyone off Eden and claiming her as ours? That wasn't part of the plan." His words are nowhere near as harsh as he thinks they are as he flickers his gaze between the two of us.

"If you were that mad about it, why did you go along with what I said?" Clasping my hands together behind my head, I hold his stare, feeling Tobias wriggling beside me, but I don't react to it.

"Because we're brothers, we stand together first before everything else, and I wasn't about to go toe-to-toe with you in front of the damn school, Hunter." Turning his back to me, he rubs the back of his neck.

Wetting my dry lips, I glance at Tobias, who only offers a shrug, no help at all.

"I hated that video, Xavier. Hated it." I sigh. "I get it, needing to show power, restore the hierarchy, and show your mother we are doing what she expects us to do. But the video exposed her, when we worked so quickly to shield her when it actually happened."

My blood boils again, hating the whole situation but remembering how she stood tall and floored us all, not giving in to embarrassment like others would. And the balls she had to stand over my desk and basically call me a sheep gave me a fucking semi.

"That still doesn't explain why you said all that," he states, falling into the chair to my right.

"Because I hated someone else hitting on her in front of me even more."

I let my words hang between us all as Xavier searches my eyes, but he'll only see the truth. Billy was trying to touch what doesn't belong to him. I saw the moment Eden decided to encourage him just to piss me off, and I couldn't control what followed, my body taking over and claiming exactly what it wanted.

Her.

Eden.

"Well I, for one, am down with this," Tobias adds. "I need to woo her for my seven minutes in heaven. But at this rate, I won't need more than thirty fucking seconds, she is lickable, and my wet dreams aren't doing her justice."

Squeezing my temple, I try to block his shit out. There aren't any words to describe him and what goes on in his mind. He's going to say whatever he wants without any care.

I can see Xavier's mind working overtime as he considers my words, but there's no surprise on his face, which tells me he knew I was being sucked in by her. I've barely spent any time with her, but when I sat beside her at Pete's, the feel of her skin beneath my touch set me alight. But how do we show that? By causing a scene once again, and I just let it happen anyway.

"We should go talk to her. Archie didn't show for practice, and she hinted at going on a 'dick hunt' at lunch and didn't come back, and that, honestly, makes me worried," Tobias admits, bouncing his leg nervously, his worry definitely for Eden's virtue.

"Over my dead fucking body," Xavier grinds out, making me raise my eyebrows in surprise at the raw emotion vibrating from him. "She needs to learn that when we say she's off-limits and belongs to the Allstars, that's *exactly* what it means."

"Do any of us truly understand what that means?" I ask, and silence surrounds us. I'll take that as a no, but in my gut, I know that the closer we are to her, the closer we are to removing the noose this town has placed around our necks. I don't know why or how, but my gut is pulling me to her for a reason.

Tobias

Convincing the guys to go to Archie's surprisingly took little to no effort at all. I expect to see the other players laughing and joking around the pool with a couple of chicks hanging off of them. So I'm completely surprised to find Archie swimming laps in the pool while Eden lies on her front on a nearby lounger in the sun.

Her blonde hair is still in braids, desperate for me to tug on them like I've longed to all day, and her skin looks golden.

Especially with the little white bikini she's wearing, enhancing her tan. She looks like an angel, and we're the devils, tempting her to fall from grace. Or could she be our undoing instead?

Before I can take another step in her direction, Archie is climbing out of the pool and holding his finger to his lips, making me pause.

"Hey, sorry, I sent a message to the football group chat telling them not to come," he whispers, glancing over his shoulder at Eden as she remains in place, and that's when I realize she must be sleeping.

"She's sleeping," I blurt out, unable to take my eyes off her, and he nods in agreement.

"Yeah. We came back here after lunch since she kept yawning. I knew she hadn't been sleeping well, and she wouldn't go for an actual nap in her bedroom, but the second she lay down on the lounger, she fell asleep."

"So you didn't come to practice this afternoon because you were here with Eden?" Xavier asks, and I can feel the annoyance radiating off him.

"Not like that, X." Archie sighs with a roll of his eyes.

"You sure?" Hunter murmurs, coming to stand beside me, and Archie waves his hand dismissively.

"I'm *sure* that I've seen the three of you drilling holes into her with your eyes, trying to decide if you want to tear her apart or piece her back together again. But we're men, so we don't talk about that shit, right?" The humor in his eyes makes me scoff, and Xavier barely grunts a response, refusing to admit to anything as Hunter heads straight for the girl in question.

"Don't wake—"

Hunter cuts Archie off with a one-finger salute behind his back, and we instantly trail after him in silence. Coming to a stop at her side, Archie walks around to her left as Xavier stands by her head, and I crouch down beside Hunter.

She looks so peaceful in comparison to every other time I've seen her.

"Does she have sunblock on?" Hunter asks, glancing at Archie, who shrugs in response. "Don't just fucking shrug, Archie. Skin cancer is a real thing, you know." The bark in his voice causes Eden to stir, while the four of us look down at her like circling vultures.

"Shut up, man, you'll wake her," I grumble, rising on my feet as I glare at him, but the look on his face tells me he doesn't give a shit if it means she's safe.

"My skin will burn from the four of you staring at me while I sleep, you fucking creeps." Eden's blue eyes peek open, and she instantly finds Hunter before glancing at me and rolling over onto her back.

I can't help but bite my knuckles as her perky tits are revealed, hidden beneath small white triangles of material. Her nipples are pebbled, begging to be touched as she casually wipes the sleep from her eyes.

"You want a water, cookie?" Archie asks, stepping back,

and she hums in response as he heads inside.

"Cookie? What the fuck does that mean?" Xavier grinds out, and Eden just snickers in response.

"It doesn't matter to you, asshole. Do you all want to give me some space to wake up?"

"No, not really," I answer before my brain can even catch up, dropping my hands to my sides, and her gaze flickers to mine in surprise as Hunter and Xavier take a seat at the nearby table under the umbrella.

"You going to stand there staring at me all day, Holmes?" she asks, and the use of my last name on her lips feels like she's making sure to put distance between us because there was nothing personal about it. Challenge accepted. I'm not against chasing what I want.

"I mean, I could, or you could let me lie down on top of you. You could maybe even come swimming with me, but realistically, I just want you involved."

"I'm not awake enough for your shit right now. You already fucked with me twice in school today. I don't really care for it here as well." She slowly rises, stretching her arms above her head as she stands. "Holmes, my eyes are up here." Pulling my eyes from her body, I meet her gaze. She grins knowingly at me as I ignore her remarks on what went down earlier.

"I'm very aware." I fix my beanie as I bite down on my bottom lip, loving how her blue eyes track the movement, dilating with arousal as I step in closer.

"You still owe me seven minutes in heaven, bubble," I murmur, stroking a loose tendril behind her ear. "Or have you forgotten?"

The way she holds my attention makes it feel like we're the only two people in the world, never mind here in this moment too. I like having her undivided attention as well. The way she looks over every inch of me feels like magic.

"You bitches cheated. I owe you nothing," she murmurs, and my hands fall to her waist, loving the feel of her skin under my fingertips, all soft and delicate against my touch.

"I could definitely make it worth your while if you let me." Excitement zips through my body. Having her this close alone has my dick begging to be touched.

Eden looks over her shoulder, her grin not wavering as she turns back to face me and places her palms on my bare chest. Thank god I changed into a pair of shorts when we got home and boycotted a T-shirt. Now I get to feel her hands on me.

I hear one of the guys grumble from behind her, but I don't let them distract me from the attention I'm finally getting from Eden.

"Oh yeah, and how might you do that?" she asks, turning us and slowly walking us towards the house. I can't see where we're going, but right now, I'd let her lead my ass anywhere.

"Well, it depends on how strict we are with the seven minutes because I can do this thing with my tongue—"

My arms flail at my side, trying to keep my balance, but it's no use as I feel myself falling, a snicker on Eden's lips the last thing I see.

One second, I'm talking a big game to the hot blonde who has taken over my wet dreams, and the next…I'm wet. Literally dripping fucking wet because she shoved me hard in the chest, pushing me into the pool. I should have noticed the switch in her eyes, but I was too late, the devilish glimmer the only hint before I was toppling into the water.

Emerging from the pool, I pull my hat from my head as I swipe the water from my eyes, and all I can hear is laughter.

"And the crowd goes wild as Eden Grady makes the tackle of the season," Eden cheers, hands waving enthusiastically in the air.

Archie is laughing at the table with Hunter and Xavier as they clap and cheer at her efforts, while she stands at the side of the pool, hands on her hips as she grins down at me. I can't help but laugh along with the rest of them, even if I am the reason for the joke.

Crouching down at the edge, she gives me a pointed look. "I deserved that," I murmur, moving closer to where she is, and she nods.

"You *really* fucking did, and much more if I'm honest, especially with all the shit you guys have done to me."

I don't deny it. I can't.

"Come swim with me."

"Nah, I've given you enough of my time already." She

grins, offering me a wink before grabbing the bottle of water from Archie's outstretched hand and heading for the house.

Her ass sways like a pendulum, and I watch every step she takes as she disappears inside.

Finally looking at the others, I notice Hunter and Xavier are still watching where she just left, while Archie taps away on his phone. There is no way in hell he is into her because it would have been impossible to pull your gaze away from her bubble butt.

TWENTY TWO
Eden

Wednesdays are starting to be one of my favorite days at Asheville High. One hour's worth of homeroom before lunch has me chilled out, and I suddenly can survive hump day.

Taking a seat with Charlie at the round table by the window, I drop my bag at my feet and pull my laptop out. I'm as up to date as I can be on homework, so I don't need to work on anything except the work given to me in marketing today. I might have missed a shit ton of work so far, but I take it seriously, learning without really trying.

It's probably one of the only lessons I enjoy. If I have a future past this town, I think I could consider that career path.

The whispers and rumors about me are in full swing, especially since Hunter's public show on Monday. Even though they actually left me alone yesterday, everyone is questioning what level of a whore I am. Apparently, being publicly claimed by the Allstars means I spend every minute of the day with my legs open. *I wish.*

The sneers and dirty looks from the girls don't bother me, nor do the leery eyes from some of the guys. Each of them suddenly gives me a wide-berth now, but I can hold my own. I've been through the gossip mill enough to let it all just fly over my head. But I know Roxy and KitKat are not just going to let me be.

"Have you seen the state of my face?" Charlie groans, pointing to the thick orange makeup lines around her face, and I bite my lip, stifling my smile. "It's not funny. Connie doesn't know what she's fucking doing in cosmetology. You should see how pretty I made her, and I end up with this."

Her bright blue eyeshadow isn't blended in. None of it is, really. I can see the highlighter and contouring from a mile away like a beacon, but I don't want to make her feel any worse.

Opening her laptop, she switches the camera on, pulling a pack of wet wipes from her bag and rubbing vigorously at her face.

"I'm just glad I had no choice and got put in marketing," I offer in response, laughing as the wet wipe is covered in makeup in seconds, barely taking any of the product off her face. "It's a good job you've got a full pack of wet wipes there." I chuckle, making her glare at me.

"Hey, hey, cookie," Archie hollers, dropping into the chair in between us, and I groan at how loud he's being.

"Can you shush your musher?" I grumble, and they both look at me like I've grown a second head. "Can you shush your musher?" I repeat, leaning forward and flicking his lips, and they both chuckle at me. "Don't you laugh, Oompa Loompa," I say, pointing a finger at Charlie, who gestures for me to fuck off, but we all laugh together.

"So I keep forgetting to ask, but you're coming to the game on Friday night, right?" Archie asks, folding his arms on the table as he leans forward, and I grin slightly as I watch Charlie drool at his bulging biceps.

Since they're hitting football practice morning, noon, and night, we're like passing ships at the moment, and he's getting a ride to school from someone on the team as well. It's crazy how much I miss our morning drive to school together. Listening to my own music in my own sanctuary doesn't feel as good as it used to.

"What? And have her sit in those shitty seats at the back?" Charlie asks with a frown, pulling her gaze from Archie to look at me. "Girl, it's not even worth it. Honestly."

"I—"

"Of course not in those seats. You can take my family spot close to the field, Eden," Archie says, cutting me off as he shakes his head at Charlie, who ignores us as she continues wiping her face.

"Wait, it's high school. Why do they even have family spots?" I ask, fanning the neckline of my T-shirt to cool my body since it seems the air conditioning isn't working today.

"Because they think they're way more badass than they are," Charlie chimes in, winking at me as Archie rolls his eyes.

"Well, I can't accept an invitation until you tell me which football team you're actually a fan of. It's important information. Our whole friendship hangs in the balance," I say with a straight face as I stare Archie down, and he sits tall in his seat, the challenge in his eyes.

"We both say which team at the same time," Archie throws back, and I nod in agreement.

"Three... Two... One..." Charlie says, counting us in.

"San Fran 49ers," we both call out at the same time, and the surprise has me throwing my head back with laughter.

"Jinx!" Archie shouts, and I offer him my middle finger.

"Fuck off, Arch, we're not in grade school now," I say with a chuckle, pulling my phone from my bag, but still no call or text from my mom.

"You're only saying that because I said it first."

"I mean, we can argue about it, or I can accept your invite to the game and we can carry on as adults?" I offer, and it's Charlie who scoffs this time.

"Adults? Archibald Freemont? Never."

Clamping a hand over my mouth, I gape at Archie as he blushes at the full use of his name. God, I've not laughed this much in forever.

There's a reason for that, I remind myself, and sadness seeps into me. Not as much as usual, but enough to remind me why I'm here.

"Hey, don't do that," Archie murmurs, rubbing my arm supportively, and I offer him a soft smile.

"So, what are we talking about, people, bubble?" Tobias asks as he takes the seat to my right, and I welcome the distraction.

Turning my attention to him, he smiles wide at me, his whole face lighting up as he does. He adjusts his beanie, his brown hair flicking out at the back as he relaxes back into his seat, dropping his arm on the back of mine, and butterflies instantly start in my stomach.

"Eden was just telling me how she's a 49ers fan, and she's going to take my family spot for the game on Friday," Archie offers as Hunter and Xavier join the table too, dropping down into their seats like they've never sat anywhere else.

The three of them together, at my table, fills me with suspicion. Nothing good comes out of situations like this when they're involved, and I'm enjoying today. I don't actually want any trouble.

Charlie exchanges a glance with me, feeling the same as I do, and I lean back from Tobias.

"The 49ers used to be okay. They're not the New England Patriots though," Hunter states casually, his eyes on mine.

"Have you ever even been to New England?" I ask, and he

offers the smallest grin that doesn't meet his eyes.

"That's where his first boarding school was," Xavier states as he scrolls through his phone, not even looking at anyone, and the table falls into silence. I instantly get the vibe that we don't discuss that period of time in Hunter's life.

"So, you're coming to the game on Friday, Eden?" Tobias asks, scraping my chair closer to his, a grin on his lips as he patiently waits for me to answer.

Their calm demeanor has me relaxing back into my chair a little as I nod in response to Tobias' question.

"The view from the top is shit. I wouldn't waste your time," Xavier throws in, still not looking up from his phone, and Archie clears his throat.

"Actually, she's going to take my family spot." Xavier finally glances up, his eyes finding mine immediately as he says nothing, keeping his facial expression neutral.

"What position do you think I play?" Tobias asks, distracting the conversation again, and I tap my finger against my lip as I stare at the four of them.

"Archie already told me he was running back, which makes sense with why you trust him," I state, and none of them argue in response. "Which tells me Xavier is the QB because he also seems like the least trusting and does most of the shouting when we're all out on the field at the same time during gym class."

"None of that means I'm the QB, Nafas," Xavier grunts with a roll of his stormy eyes, but that only makes me believe it more.

"Tobias looks like he would fit the role of a wide receiver with his speed and agility, while Hunter looks like he could handle tight end like nobody's business."

Tobias grins wide as Hunter's eyes crinkle in surprise.

"How did you guess that? Or who told you?" Xavier asks, and I sigh.

"I like football, almost obsessively. I can just tell these things," I say with a shrug, making Charlie giggle.

"You are too damn pretty to be a tomboy." She laughs with a shake of her head.

"No stereotyping, Miss 'looks like a pretty valedictorian while also being on the cheer squad,'" I throw back, and she holds her hands up in surrender with a smile.

"It'll be awesome, Eden. We always have a party down on the beach afterward. Even Charlie might show this time, since she never usually joins the cheer squad at the others," Archie continues, making Charlie sigh at him.

A hand on my thigh makes me still until I turn and see the challenge in Tobias' eyes as he leans forward.

"They are good parties. You should come to this one. Or we could have a party for two in your room," he murmurs against my ear, and I shiver with desire. Fuck, why am I so drawn to him? "You know you want to," he adds, dipping his head to graze his lips against my collarbone, and I about die from sexual tension.

Holy. Fuck.

His lips are so soft against my skin, but he's pulling back all too quickly.

"Hmm, you might be onto something there," I murmur in response as he lifts his gaze to mine, heat in his eyes just like I expect there to be in mine. He glances between my eyes and my mouth, freezing me in place, and I think he's about to touch his lips to mine when Xavier interrupts us.

"Tobias doesn't know his way around a woman's body like I do, so don't be disappointed when you have to finish yourself off in the bathroom when you're done."

Hunter bursts out with laughter as Tobias growls, turning a dark glare on his friend while I try to calm my racing heart. I had been seconds away from practically jumping him in the damn homeroom.

"TMI, man," Archie grumbles as my phone vibrates on the table, *Mom* flashing across the screen.

Standing, I grab my phone, "I need to take this," I murmur, moving around the table to take it outside when Xavier grabs my arm.

"Take the call here," he orders, clearly expecting my mom to have some information that might be of interest to him, and I frown down at him.

"Are you going to clue me in on Ilana?" I ask as my phone stops vibrating in my hand, and frustration bubbles through my veins.

"No."

"Then it's going to be a hard no from me too," I bite back, snatching my arm from his grip and rushing from the room.

I hit redial as soon as I step out into the hall, but it instantly connects to her voicemail. Fuck. Trying a few more times, I get nothing.

Pinching the bridge of my nose, I sigh with irritation, opting to leave her a voicemail.

"Hey, Mom. It's me. You literally rang seconds ago, and now I can't get through. What's going on? Call me back. I love you," I add at the end, worry settling in the pit of my stomach as I glance back inside the classroom to feel the Allstars staring at me, while Roxy has suddenly found herself in Hunter's lap and KitKat has taken my seat.

I can see Charlie heading towards me with my things, but I don't care. I'm more bothered about Roxy cupping Hunter's chin and turning him away from me.

No way. No fucking way. I am *not* jealous, not of her or for him.

Right?

"Want to head for lunch early?" Charlie offers as she comes to stand in front of me, and I nod in agreement.

"Yeah, pull me away from their crazy before I do something stupid."

KC KEAN

TWENTY THREE

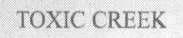

Xavier

"You ready for the game tonight, X?"

I glance over my shoulder as I grab my bag to see Billy rubbing his hands together. He's the captain of our defense, a good player, but a real fucking pain in my ass.

If I offered to let him suck my dick, he would, just to get closer to us. It's embarrassing.

"We're always ready, Billy. Let's hope you've got the boys tight and ready to go, huh," Hunter says, knowing I won't respond when I'm trying to get into the zone, and we head to the door, leaving him rambling to himself near my locker.

Tobias is already waiting outside of the door, Archie by his side as a flash of blonde catches my attention.

Eden.

Tobias grins, biting his lips as he watches her leave, and I can't deny that she holds my attention just like she did the first time I saw her. The pain in her eyes still swirls, intoxicating me. But I have restraint, most of the time, unlike Tobias and now even Hunter, which is a huge surprise.

He doesn't like anyone all that much, but his eyes are watching her ass sway as she gives us her back. Again. I feel like she's always walking away.

"What did you say to her?" Hunter asks, looking straight at Tobias, who shrugs playfully.

"Me? I would never." He gapes between us, acting innocent, which makes Archie scoff.

"Someone, aka Tobias, stole my phone and Eden's number along with it. She left, grumbling something about getting a new sim card."

Her number? I like the sound of that. It makes her even more available to me. To us. Which means she cannot be allowed to change it. Hunter stares at me, his eyes flickering to my hands now fisted at my side, and he reads me like a book. I can't believe we didn't *already* have her details.

"If she changes her number, we'll just get that one too," he states, and Archie shakes his head at us.

"I do not hear any of this. Nope. I'm going to go and find Eden and Charlie for lunch. Are you guys all coming too?"

"Hell yeah, or I hope to be tonight at least," Tobias says, wiggling his eyebrows, and Archie cringes at his joke while

Hunter and I say nothing. Although, my dick definitely heard his statement.

It reminds me how close Tobias had been to getting Eden the other day. The way she reacted to him kissing her collarbone had made me as hard as a rock in an instant. Her eyelashes fluttered against her cheeks as her neck instantly flushed, and I couldn't stop myself from interrupting, cockblocking the hell out of him.

I wanted her to remember how I had made her feel, how she had whimpered and moaned under my touch.

Heading down the hall towards the cafeteria, I feel much more at ease than I did earlier in the week. The only thing knocking me off balance is Eden. Everyone else is remembering their place and falling in line, and that includes Roxy and KitKat.

My phone vibrates in my jeans pocket, and when I pull it out, I'm surprised to see my mother's name flashing across the screen.

"You guys go on ahead," I murmur, flashing the guys my screen, and they nod in understanding.

Slipping into the closest empty classroom, I shut the door behind me as I answer, not breathing a word as I wait for her to speak.

"Xavier, are you there?" I can hear the annoyance and irritation in her voice, the only emotions she ever really offers. Unless she's going hardcore with hatred and anger, so this is practically her being mellow.

"Who else do you think is going to answer my phone?" I answer back, bored with her already as I take a seat on the edge of the teacher's desk.

"Need I remind you who you are speaking to?" she bites out, needing to try and pull me in line like she does everyone else, when it really should be the other way around. Just a little longer, then we can make a play to get out of here. Tension vibrates through my body as I force myself to remain calm.

"What did you call for?" I ask, ignoring her question with one of my own, and her sigh is heavy down the line.

"We won't be coming to your game tonight, I'm afraid."

I frown down at my phone before bringing it back to my ear. "You never come to my games anyway."

"Well, that's because it's a fucking ridiculous sport that takes you away from your responsibilities. I told you, once you finish school at Asheville High, you'll have no time for such useless shit. Your money stops unless you join the family business."

I roll my eyes at her usual lecture. It's bullshit. *She's* bullshit. She also has no clue that I have every intention to get the fuck out of here the second we throw our graduation caps in the air, if I even stick around that long.

I don't need her or her money.

I've already had an early acceptance scholarship for football at Ohio State, and even without that, she has no clue we set up our own company. She would have to jump through a lot of hoops to find it. With all our offshore accounts, it bounces around all the time, never linking to any of our names. Just how we like it.

Hunter is a fucking tech genius. Coding should be his middle name.

"I'm very aware, Mother," I finally respond, not reacting to her usual outbursts.

"I was going to come to your game this evening, your father and I have some important news to share with you and the town."

Ah, so there's the hidden agenda.

"And what might that news be?" Swiping a hand down my face, I glance at the clock on the wall, willing her to get a move on so I can eat.

"I'm running for mayor." She says the words so sweetly and almost joyfully that I replay the words to make sure she really is my mother. "Aren't you going to congratulate me?" She tsks, confirming she is the one and only Ilana Knight.

"I thought Montgomery was the mayor?" Roxy's father has been the mayor of the town for as long as I can remember, running to the beat of my mother's drum the whole time.

"We have come to a disagreement, which is none of your concern, and I always say, if you want a job done properly, do it yourself."

I'm intrigued to know why this is suddenly happening, but I know she'll never say a word. Roxy might, though. Maybe. She's closer with her family than I am anyway.

"I'll congratulate you when you win."

"Like that wouldn't happen," she says with a scoff. "So, have you been having fun?"

"With what?" I play dumb, knowing full well the conversation has turned to Eden.

"Don't play coy, Xavier. It doesn't suit you."

Pacing in front of the desk, I rub the back of my neck, needing to play this exactly as she expects me to.

"Oh, you mean the Grady? Yeah, what's that about?"

"Honestly, Xavier, you should have seen the fear in Jennifer Grady's eyes when I forced her to pack Eden up in her fancy SUV and send her to Knight's Creek." The laughter in her voice would usually resonate inside of me, but I only feel a chill down my spine as my protective instincts try to kick in. "She cried, pleaded, and screamed for nothing."

"Why is she even here? She's a pariah." I have to force myself to remain neutral, dismissive, but the words burn my throat. She's not, but if I can get some kind of explanation, maybe it'll help us. Help Eden.

"That's not information you're required to know just yet. But let's just say it's an old feud I decided to cash in on. Make her pay, my prince."

With that, the call goes dead, and I'm left no wiser than I was earlier. Fuck. Her crazy is off the scales at the minute. She's always been unpredictable, but knowing she's targeted Eden puts me at a disadvantage.

Anger slowly starts to simmer at my core. I hate the dirty

games my mother plays when I don't get the insight. If I knew what was happening, I would feel differently, but she always leaves me feeling under *her control* instead of in control.

I want to drive my fist into the wooden desk at my side in anger, but that'll only pull me off the field tonight and I can't let that happen. Not when I know she'll benefit from the situation overall. I know this is an intentional attempt at trying to see if I'll react to her talking about Eden, and I won't rise to the bait.

Grabbing my bag, I storm from the classroom, striding confidently into the cafeteria to find the guys sitting at our usual table, and Eden to the far right with Charlie like she always is.

I can never decide if I'm checking her out or deciding what would be the best way to kill her. Either way, I can't keep my eyes off her. Whatever she brings out in me, I don't like it. It makes me feel even less in control than my mother does, and I won't allow it.

KC KEAN

TWENTY FOUR
Eden

I can hear the chants and cheers from the gates of Knight's Creek's very own fully equipped football stadium. I had to use my GPS to get here, heading away from the ocean, taking about twenty minutes.

I'm excited for the game. The buzz of the crowd, and the chance to finally see the Allstars in action.

Charlie had messaged me to make sure I was still coming, and there was no way I could say no. Not when Archie had left my entry ticket on my bed with an Asheville Knight's Allstars jersey beside it. *Freemont* was printed on the back, so it was either his or he had it made, but either way, it was awesome.

He's my rock in this toxic, fucked-up town, never questioning or judging me and always offering support and friendship. The first platonic relationship I've ever had with a guy, and as much as I won't admit it to him, I can't picture him not in my life.

Handing over my ticket, the lady directs me to take the stairs straight ahead, which will lead me to the family seating. I can hear the music thumping through the stadium as the crowd cheers, and the upbeat tune makes me believe the cheer squad is already dancing.

It's still so warm, especially since there's no sea breeze this far inland, so I'm glad I paired my newly acquired jersey with a pair of denim shorts and my black Converse. My hair is piled on top of my head in a messy bun, and my makeup is at a minimum with my sunglasses perfectly in place.

I promised Charlie I would go to the after-party and even make an effort, so I'll do all that after the game. I'm horny and sexually frustrated beyond belief, so the effort will be worth it if it attracts the attention I want. I just need to decide who to set my sights on.

Taking the steps two at a time, I brush past all the bodies standing around the food stand, the smell of hot dogs and popcorn polluting the space. Making my way to the steps on the other side, I stop to take in the view.

Holy shit, do they take this sport seriously. Glancing around at the field and capacity, it's easily college-sized. I remember going to the Notre Dame Stadium when we lived in Indiana, and this is probably the same size. The capacity easily holds over seventy-thousand people, a lot of the seats built up high, and

Charlie's comments about the tower seats suddenly make sense.

It's like a sea of green and white surrounding me as everyone soaks in the team colors, and it only adds to the energy and excitement in here.

What surprises me even more is how many people are actually here. It looks as though the seats are three-quarters full, and that's not taking into consideration all the people that are still lingering around the stadium.

Quickly checking my ticket, I search the rows and slowly start making my way down. I'm right where the team huddles are, only two rows back, with the most amazing view of the field and the tunnel right in front of me. The family seating is just like general seating, just with a better view, and close to all the action.

Excitement bubbles inside of me. It's been far too long since I've been to a game instead of catching the latest NFL mash-up on the big screen.

The bottom four rows are cornered off for the family zone, and I slip past the few members already seated, dropping down into a padded seat. My butt appreciates the little family luxuries in comparison to the usual hard plastic.

I feel a few side glances from other members of the crowd, likely gossiping about the new girl in the hot seats, but no one speaks to me directly.

The cheerleaders and mascot are dancing a little farther to my left, and it looks like their seats are near to where they are, and I'm glad they aren't too close to the family seating.

Charlie spots me and smiles wide before being spun up in the air, and my stomach takes a dip. Nope. Not for me.

I relax back into my seat, silently excited to see the Allstars in all of their hot football glory, when a small hand is placed on my leg, pulling my gaze from the field. The cutest little boy I ever did see stares back at me, with messy blond curls and big grey eyes.

He can't be more than two, three at the most, smiling from ear to ear as he pats my knee.

"Oh my gosh, I'm so sorry, he has no social boundaries yet," a woman murmurs, coming to stand behind him before flopping down into a seat, leaving one free between us and pulling the little boy onto her lap.

He fusses in her arms, reaching his hands out to try and grab me as she continues to apologize.

Her blonde wavy hair is pulled back with a hair tie, her blue eyes filled with a mixture of exhaustion and love.

"It's no stress at all, honestly." I offer her a genuine smile, and her face relaxes with relief as I glance back at the man of the hour. "Hello, little man, what's your name?" I ask, letting him grab my finger, and he calms instantly.

"Cody, Cody, Cody," he chants, waving my hand around as he does, making me smile.

"Are you a good boy for your mama, Cody?" I ask, and he nods eagerly.

"He's a liar," the woman mutters, and I snicker along with her. "I'm Bethany, Hunter Asheville's older sister. You know him?" she asks, and I just raise my eyebrow at her, which is all the answer she needs. "Right. Of course. He's a d-i-c-k head. I apologize for him too. No manners at all."

"Do I really have to spend the rest of my life apologizing for the men around me? I do not have time for that." I scoff, letting Cody continue to swing my finger playfully. "I'm Eden. A friend of Archie Freemont."

She nods in understanding, and I can see the sparkle in her eyes as she's about to question what I mean by a friend, but the intro music starts up and the whole stadium begins to cheer.

The banging of drums from the school band begins to play, and green balloons suddenly start drifting into the air on the other end of the fifty-yard line, and the reaction from the crowd is wild.

I instinctively glance at little Cody, worried about all the noise, but Bethany has placed some noise defenders over his ears. Standing, they do the same, but Cody won't release my finger. If anything, he pulls me closer.

Offering my hands out, Bethany gives me a look to make sure I know what I'm getting myself into, but I just can't bring myself to say no to him, especially with his little puppy dog eyes pleading with me.

The second she hands him off to me, he wraps his arms around my neck and legs around my waist, squeezing me tight.

Holding him close, my eyes fall shut on their own accord. My heart swells with love. Damn, do I need this.

I don't think anyone has held me so tightly since my dad was taken from me, and it's in the arms of a two-year-old. I feel calmer than I ever have since I arrived here. The feel of a hand squeezing my arm in comfort forces me to open my eyes, and a sympathetic Bethany smiles at me.

Not liking the attention, I look out to the field just as the team lines up, helmets at their feet as they hold their position for the national anthem to play.

Archie spots me immediately, waving before placing his hand on his chest. I don't see Richard anywhere, and it makes me even more glad that I came to support him. He deserves it.

Moving my eyes down the line, I don't have to go far to find three sets of eyes staring back at me. Tobias is grinning wide as he trails his eyes over my bare legs, while Xavier stares at me with surprise. It's not until I look closer at a frowning Hunter do I understand why.

Cody.

Bethany leans in, pointing out Hunter to Cody, and he releases an arm from around my neck to wave manically at Hunter, who stuns me when he waves back, wiping the frown from his face as he does.

Forcing myself to look away from them, I fuss over Cody, who loves the attention as they get ready to start the game. The second the referee blows the whistle, we retake our seats, and

Bethany magically pulls snacks out of thin air to keep Cody happy.

I watch as the Allstars start the game off, the atmosphere is electric as Xavier steps back onto his right foot, crouching ever so slightly, before launching the ball forward, and the whole field lights up. Tobias catches the ball with ease, his pace powerful as he easily makes it twenty yards before he's wiped off his feet.

My heart lurches in my chest, but he's quick to bounce back up again. The team huddles around, and they go again, but this time Hunter has the ball and covers a huge distance in the middle of the field. I can't pull my eyes from him, watching every move he makes as he practically rolls into the end zone, and just like that, the points roll in.

This whole team is a power drive. The defense is solid, the opposition lucky to cover anything more than ten yards, while the offense is an absolute force to be reckoned with. Xavier is probably the best QB I have ever seen live, with the potential to make history. I can feel it in my soul.

I watch as Xavier, Tobias, Hunter, and Archie work in sync, encouraging the rest of the team to feel their energy, and it really is electric.

Completely lost to the pure magic taking place before me, with a happy Cody clapping along with the rest of the crowd, the game goes all too quickly. The referee signals for the fourth quarter as the score sits at 31-6 to the Allstars.

"I'm going to take Cody for a diaper change while everyone

has retaken their seats. Do you want me to grab you anything on the way back?" Bethany asks, and I hand the little man over.

"I'm good, thanks."

"Are you sure? I feel like I owe you or something for entertaining him so much." Her smile is appreciative, and I shake my head.

"It was no trouble at all."

She mouths her thanks before grabbing the bag at her feet and heading for the bathroom.

The other team has the ball, so I pull my phone from my bag and frown when I see a message from an unknown number waiting for me.

Glancing around like someone will wave to say it was them, I roll my eyes at myself before clicking the message open. My heart stills as I read the words over and over again.

Unknown: YOU'RE GOING TO END UP JUST AS HE DID—SIX FEET UNDER AND ALL ALONE. YOU MAY JUST STILL BE ALIVE WHEN WE DO IT.

Who the fuck would send that? I can only assume they're referencing my dad, but why?

My fingers tremble with nerves as I hit dial on the number, refusing to let these people get the better of me, but the call goes straight to voicemail.

Is this Tobias?

He stole my fucking number earlier today from Archie, but this shit's just not funny. Wetting my suddenly dry lips, I glance in their direction on the edge of the field to find Archie already frowning up at me.

My confusion and concern must show on my face as he asks if I'm okay, and I wave my hand dismissively, not wanting to distract him from the game.

"Oh my god, I'm nosey as hell, but who on earth has sent you that?" Bethany gasps, snatching my phone from my hand as she balances Cody on her hip, her face a picture of genuine horror.

"I don't know. I don't recognize the number, and I tried to call them back, but there was no answer," I admit, slightly taken back by her intrusion, but I can feel that she means well.

She hits the number again, holding the phone to her ear to double-check, but it goes to voicemail again.

"Why would someone even send something like that? It's so typical of this stupid town." She sighs, looking out to the field as I slip my phone back in my pocket when she suddenly waves for someone to come to her.

Following her line of sight, I find Hunter taking the steps two at a time to get to her. The crowds around us look on in confusion as he leaves his helmet in place and walks off the fucking field while they're in the middle of the game.

My eyes flicker to the coach, who doesn't even offer him a backward glance, and mere seconds later, Hunter is standing in front of us.

"What's wrong? What's going on?" he barks, glancing between the two of us, and I shake my head, murmuring nothing, but Bethany has an entirely different idea.

"Someone is sending Eden threatening messages. I'm not fucking happy about it. If I find out it was one of you guys, I'll gut you. Do you understand?"

"What are you even talking about, and language, Beth. Cody can hear you, you know," he grumbles, reaching his hand out to softly stroke Cody's cheek as he does, a complete contrast to his harsh tone.

"Don't play dumb. You boys know everything that goes on in this town. Someone's threatening to bury Eden alive. If it wasn't one of you three, you better find out who."

"Show me," he grinds out, his eyes burning into mine, but I shake my head.

"Can we *not* do this while we're in the middle of a game? I'm fine, and I'll figure it out. *Alone.*" I cross my hands over my chest defensively, but Hunter continues to stare me down.

"What's going on?" Tobias calls out, drawing even more attention our way as he saddles up beside Hunter.

"Oh my god, nothing. Please, just please go back to the game."

"Someone's threatening to bury her alive," Bethany repeats, and I stare at her with wide eyes. Who is this woman, and why doesn't she shut up? "Don't look at me like that. I'm doing this for your own good," she states, and I bury my head in my hands, too afraid to look and see how many people are looking.

"Hunter, T," Xavier calls out from the bottom of the steps,

causing an eerie silence to fall over the people surrounding us, and I groan.

"Please," I whisper, and Hunter must see the pleading in my eyes because he nods once in understanding and pats Tobias on the shoulder to go.

"Do not leave this spot without someone, understood? We'll look at the message after the game." I nod reluctantly, but that doesn't seem to be enough. "Understood?" he repeats, and I sigh.

"Understood, now please, p-i-double-s off," I say, covering my lips from Cody, even though I spelled it out, and he's got noise defenders over his ears.

With that, he finally descends back down the stairs, but everyone is still looking, including the cheer squad. Charlie offers a reassuring smile while Roxy and KitKat stare at me like I just kicked their dog or something.

For fucks sake.

I don't need to deal with them on top of all this, unless it was them?

Shaking my head, I focus back on the game, needing the distraction. I've not heard from my mom since I tried to call her back the other day, and now I'm getting messages like this. I hope she is okay. What if she called with a warning or because she was in danger and I didn't answer?

Fuck this town, and its mind fuck abilities.

I need to party, drink, and forget all about this shit.

KC KEAN

TWENTY FIVE
Tobias

As we make our way down the beach, the sun has set and the party is in full swing at Archie's. I can see the campfire roaring from here as people fill the space in groups, dancing, singing, drinking. The atmosphere continues from the win earlier, and it's a high I never want to come down from.

"Can anyone see her?" Hunter asks, talking about Eden, but I don't see her pretty blonde hair in the crowd.

"Maybe she's still inside," I offer, but he doesn't relax, and neither does Xavier.

We have never rushed to someone's aid before, not mid-game and definitely not for a girl. But the fear written in Eden's eyes, along with Bethany's, had Hunter off the grass and climbing the stairs as quickly as he could. I have no idea who he was rushing to get to first, but the two of them together had him acting without thought.

The dark words of the threatening message linger in my mind. Threatening to bury someone alive is deep, even for us, and what's worse is we have no idea who it came from.

Bethany made Eden pass all the information on, and she sent the details to Hunter, who has left the computer scanning for information on the number. Hopefully, we'll get something, but so far, it's just dead end after dead end.

Eden pacified Bethany, letting her walk her to her SUV with Charlie, and as much as she said she was okay, concern had washed over her.

"I need to see with my own eyes that she's here," Hunter mutters, stressed out more than I actually expected him to be.

"Fuck me, is this you pussy-whipped?" Xavier murmurs, and Hunter shoves him, not offering a response, and the slight grin on Xavier's face surprises me. "What? Don't be so sensitive, Hunter."

"Shut up, Xavier," I grumble, fixing my favorite black hat in place. "You're showing your little green-eyed monster again." He grunts in response, biting his tongue on whatever he wants to say as Roxy stops in front of him. "I'll leave you with that," I murmur, indicating the disaster that is Roxy Montgomery, and continue heading for the house.

He told us earlier how he wants to dig into some information with the Montgomerys, and sadly, the best way to do that is with that bitch.

"Fuck. You find Eden, bring her down so I can see she's safe, and I'll hold KitKat off so X can try and get details on what the disagreement was between the Montgomerys and his mother," Hunter says, glancing over his shoulder, and he's right. KitKat is all up between them, which means he'll be there forever if someone doesn't distract her.

Patting him on the shoulder, I take the slope up the side of Archie's house, smiling at everyone calling my name as I enter through the front door and come to a complete stop at the bottom of the stairs.

Holy mother of sweet baby Jesus. Is this what it looks like, standing at the gates of heaven, staring up at an angel?

Eden stands at the top of the stairs, her long blonde hair is straight and slick down her back. Her bright blue eyes look even bigger with her fancy makeup shit, and her bright red lips are begging to be smeared.

Letting my gaze drop, I take in her outfit. In a khaki green lace bodice, her tits are perfectly on display. The sexy look is finished off with a pair of jeans and a thick black belt, and her pretty red toenails peeking out of her sandals.

I have never paid attention to a woman's outfit so much in my life, but her presence demands it, forcing me to burn every inch of her to memory. But my concern is it's going to have the same effect on all the guys here tonight.

"Stop fucking staring at me," she grumbles, breaking my

trance, and I grin as she approaches me.

"I just can't seem to stop myself." Biting my lip, I don't move, letting her come to a stop right in front of me.

"You're not even trying." The pointed look she gives me only makes my dick harder as I mindlessly stroke a finger down her arm, watching as she shivers at my touch.

"But I don't want anyone to take you. You're mine." My eyes are locked on hers as the words slip from my mouth, her lips parted with a gasp as her coconut scent wraps around me, pulling me in deeper.

The moment is broken as Charlie clears her throat, coming to stand behind Eden. As if remembering herself, Eden steps by me and out of my reach.

"Where are you going?"

"Wherever you aren't," she throws back at me, not even looking over her shoulder as she walks away.

Charlie smothers her grin as she follows after her, clearly enjoying this little game of cat and mouse Eden is playing with me. I watch every step Eden takes, heading outside to the pool area, and I don't miss all the guys checking her out as well.

Following behind her, the pathway clears as people move out of my way. The frown on my face is likely encouraging them not to approach me.

Eden stops beside Archie, whose eyes are fixed on little Charlie James in her denim fitted dress. Interesting. As long as his attention isn't on Eden, I don't care. Watching as they head down to the beach with a few of the other guys on the football team, I pick up my pace, not liking her closeness to Billy. His bulky shoulder brushes up against hers, and I'm close to losing my cool.

"I didn't think you were the type to lose your sanity for a girl." Xavier is walking towards me, four drinks in his hands as he stares me down.

"I didn't either," I admit, walking beside him as we near the bonfire. Eden sits to the left with Archie and the others, while Hunter is on the right with KitKat and Roxy.

The bonfire is massive tonight, the crackling sound settling my soul. The relaxing atmosphere, with the ocean off to our right, is what I enjoy about these parties.

"We never differ from the plan, though, Tobias. Not even for golden pussy, you remember that." Taking off to join Hunter, he drops down into a deckchair, and Roxy instantly climbs in his lap. I can see the cringe in his eyes as he encourages her, but she's not paying enough attention to notice.

With a deep breath, I head towards Eden, watching as she glares across the roaring flames at Hunter and Xavier. My brothers are doing what is necessary to get answers, but I like the hint of jealousy in Eden's eyes.

Drink in hand, she looks away from them, sipping the fruity alcohol with a straw. Her lips wrap around the tip, her cheeks hollowing ever so slightly as she drinks, and my mind instantly pictures her down on her knees before me. My cock in her hands instead, and her big blue eyes peering up at me as she takes my length.

"You're staring again," Eden calls out, looking at me with a grin on her lips, and I take that as my cue to join her.

Charlie sits to her left, while Billy leans in on her right. Standing in front of him, I give him my most bored expression.

"Thanks, Billy, but I've got it from here," I state, pointing over my shoulder for him to get the fuck up and go.

"But we were just talking about Eden's football knowledge," he argues back, not moving, and that's his biggest mistake.

I can feel Eden's eyes on me, watching to see what my reaction will be, and I can't help but grin at her. The challenge in her eyes, daring me to push back and fight for her attention, has me shrugging.

"No stress, man, you stay where you are." Spying an empty deck chair out on its own a little farther around the fire, looking out to sea, I fix my eyes back on Eden's. "Please, may I manhandle you for just a moment?" I ask, and I think the fact that I asked and didn't just haul her away catches Eden by surprise.

"Since you asked so nicely," she murmurs back, her voice huskier than usual, and I scoop her up into my arms before she can change her mind.

She wraps her legs around my waist, and her eyes don't leave mine as she places her hands on my shoulders.

"Billy, get the shots, will you," I say over my shoulder,

watching as he sags in disappointment as I carry her away.

Dropping down into the chair, I'm thankful there are no arms on it so Eden can keep straddling me, her legs draped over mine as she gets comfortable in my lap. Stroking her hair behind her ear, I grin at the sparkle of mischief in her eyes, rubbing my other hand up the outside of her thigh.

"You had to pick somewhere with only one chair, huh?" She doesn't try to move away. If anything, I feel her move closer, her eyes widening as she brushes against my hard cock in my jeans beneath her.

"Are you not comfortable or something?" I murmur, a challenge in my eyes this time, and she doesn't disappoint. Not backing down, she inches closer, her tits close to grazing against my chest as her fingers stroke the back of my neck.

"I can make do." She smirks.

Just as I'm about to lean in closer, a bottle of tequila is placed between us, with an angry Billy holding it out. Taking it from his outstretched hand, I meet his gaze, letting my anger at his approach shine through in my eyes.

"Billy, it'll serve you well to remember who the fuck I am and what I'm capable of. Do I also have to remind you that Hunter marked Eden as off-limits?" His eyes widen as his lips pop like a fish, trying to find a reason for the shit he's pulling, but I cut him off before he can. "Fuck. Off. Billy."

I roll my eyes at the quick change in his demeanor as he scurries away. Eden raises her eyebrows at me, and I scoff. "Please, he didn't put up much of a fight, now did he? Besides, you want me. Otherwise, you'd have said no to the manhandling."

Without saying a word, she takes the fresh bottle of tequila from my hands, unscrewing the cap and bringing it to her lips in one swift move. I watch her throat as she swallows the liquid down before she holds it out for me to take.

Repeating her same motion, I take a shot of tequila straight from the bottle before placing it in the sand beside us. I want a buzz, not complete intoxication. There is something much sweeter I'd like to be drunk on right now.

"So, Billy says you know football, huh? What else do you like?"

"Does it really matter?" she murmurs, subtly grinding down against me again, and I bite back a moan. It feels like we're the only two people in the world right now, and I'm all for voyeurism, but I need this girl alone first.

"Amuse me." Rubbing my hands on her thighs, I squeeze as I near her apex, watching as she arches her back ever so slightly. She's so responsive, and I haven't even started.

"I like video games and old movies. Music, any music at all, really. The ocean," she adds, glancing over her shoulder. "Sex." Turning back to me, her eyes hold me captive, "Lots and lots of sex. Orgasms. Cock." Her face moves closer to mine with each word that leaves her mouth, and my grip on her tightens, loving her confidence and where her mind is heading.

"I can get behind all of those things, bubble," I murmur in her ear, dragging my lips against her jaw, and she whimpers. "I could make you scream with two fingers, baby."

Leaning back ever so slightly, a grin on her lips, she stares me down. "Why, what are you going to do? Jab me in the eyes?"

A burst of laughter rises from my belly as I pull her closer, loving her quick-witted sass. "Kiss me, bubble." I don't care who's watching, especially Hunter and Xavier. Eden is mine tonight.

Her lips are barely a breath away from mine as she continues to stare deeply into my eyes. "I don't make the first move."

"And I don't let consent be a question. I've asked you to kiss me, you know I want you too. So if—"

My words are cut off by the softness of her bright red lips meeting mine. Tantalizingly slow, her mouth takes mine as her fingers cup the back of my head, stroking my hair under my hat as I squeeze her waist.

Fuck.

She tastes so sweet, like honey, and smells like coconuts, completely intoxicating me. Keeping my hands on her waist, I stroke my thumbs against the lace material of her bodice, letting her set the pace. Fuck, she knows what she's doing. Her back arches as she grinds down against my throbbing cock, biting my bottom lip as she does, pulling a throaty groan from my lips.

"Let me take you somewhere private, Eden. Ease some of this sexual tension from your hot body," I whisper, slowly raising my hand to cup under her breast, desperate to drag my thumb across her peaked nipple. But I won't until she says so.

Her eyes flicker to where my hand is, and as she bites her lip, she looks back up to me and nods, hissing as I circle her nipple.

"I'm not a rehab center for badly raised boys, you know," she murmurs, making me grin.

"There is no fixing me, bubble. I'm like an addict. I'll take what I want, when I want, without a care for the consequences. The question is, do you want to join me?" I ask, waiting with bated breath for her response.

"Take me to my room, and prove Xavier wrong, Tobias," she whispers seductively, moving to jump off my lap, but I pull her closer and stand with her still in my arms.

"Bubble, you're not even going to remember his name by the time I'm done with you."

Blindly heading for the house, I carry her through the crowds of people surrounding us, happy to leave the party far too early. I don't pay attention to anyone, as my mind is focused on one thing and one thing only.

Eden Grady is mine tonight.

TOXIC CREEK

KC KEAN

TWENTY SIX
Eden

I can't even complain at the manhandling from Tobias right now. Not when I'm this turned on and ready to combust.

Holding on tight as he leads us towards the house, Charlie wiggles her eyebrows at me as Tobias walks around the fire.

I feel their stares before they even come into view, but Tobias doesn't pay them any mind. Xavier and Hunter watch us leave the beach, KitKat and Roxy in their laps, but I don't let them sour my mood, my focus strictly on the hot, beanie wearing, wide smiling wide receiver that's held my attention since the first day on school grounds.

I need the distraction, and I need it from him. His touch drives me wild, and his lips... Fuck, his lips are perfect.

Maybe we can fuck the sexual tension out of each other,

then continue on our separate paths. Either way, I'm ready to give in to my desires.

"Even though you have such a bubble butt, you're as light as a feather," he murmurs in my ear as we reach the bottom of the stairs leading up to my room.

"I'm already a sure thing. You don't need to keep buttering me up," I say with a chuckle in response, and he squeezes me tighter against his chest.

"I'm just stating facts, bubble. Which is your room? I'm not sure from this side, since I came in through the balcony last time." I grin at the memory, the excitement I'd felt until Ilana made an appearance.

Shaking my head, I point at my door and wrap a hand tight around his neck as I use the other to dig into my jeans pocket for my key. I was not leaving my room unlocked when there were so many people hovering around tonight.

Dangling the key between us, Tobias pins me to my door, his lips finally finding mine again as he fumbles around, trying to open it. I can feel his cock pressing up against my core as he holds me in place, making me shiver with anticipation.

The second the lock clicks, he's stepping inside, spinning us around to slam the door shut and pinning me against it once again. All while his lips remain on mine, and I grip his shirt, holding him as close as I can.

We're a complete mess of hands and lips, grabbing at each other as our lips crash together, desperate and wanting. It's not enough. I need more. I need *everything*.

Pulling my lips from his, he moves his lips to my neck, dotting kisses against my skin, and I feel like I'm on fire. My head falls back, hitting the door as I let him explore, his lips descending until he reaches the swell of my breasts, and my back arches as a moan escapes my mouth when he bites down hard, the sting making me groan louder.

Pain mixed with pleasure floods my body as he sucks on my skin, marking me. A typical alpha male, primal move I would usually hate, but I hold his head against me, silently begging for more, and he doesn't disappoint.

My head drops forward, watching as he trails his lips to my other breast, biting down on my nipple through the flimsy lace covering it.

"Fuck," I hiss, my hips taking on a mind of their own as they grind towards him, searching for the friction. "Tobias, I need more. Fuck. More, please."

Looking up at me through his long lashes, he grins a knowing smile. "I want to fuck you under the stars, Eden," he murmurs, slowly dropping my legs, sliding me down his body. My hard nipples graze against his chest, and I shiver again as I process what he said.

Looking past him to the balcony, I frown. "The balcony isn't private. The glass will give everyone down at the beach a view."

"Well, you better find some blankets and sheets to throw over the glass then, shouldn't you?"

I pause for a moment, deciding whether it'll be worth it or not, but I know it will. I'm too pent-up to stop now.

"You better know what you're doing with that dick of yours, Tobias Holmes," I grumble, brushing past him to rush into the walk-in closet. Grabbing every piece of bedding off the shelf, I rush back into my room to find him in my top drawer, tossing my toys onto the bed.

"What the fuck are you doing?"

He doesn't even bother to look at me as he twirls my favorite purple vibrator in his hand before adding it to the pile on the bed. "Eden, we're going to be here for a long time. I was looking for extra condoms. It's not my fault I also stumbled on your collection of peens." I'm stunned, speechless. But I can't argue, not when his words only make me hotter. "Shield the balcony, Eden," he adds, finally glancing over at me, his eyes burning with desire, and I nod like an idiot, racing outside to do so.

This almost feels like far too much preparation to be fucked. To be fair, it doesn't usually happen in such a personal space. It's usually at a party, in someone else's house. But the anticipation builds inside me with every sheet I put in place, blocking us from view from those below.

Throwing the sheets over the railing, I make quick work of making sure there aren't any gaps. Looking down at everyone, a sparkle of excitement courses through me as the idea of screaming out here with everyone below, unable to see, but with the possibility that they might hear me.

Placing the last sheet, my eyes zone in on the fire. Hunter and Xavier glance up at me, the fire burning beside them, lighting up their faces as Tobias comes to stand beside me.

Brushing my hair over my left shoulder, he slowly peppers kisses down the right side of my neck, making my mouth fall open as I gasp, gripping the railing like my life depends on it.

His arm wraps around my waist as his hand slowly teases up the lace of my bodice, cupping my breasts as the other Allstars hold my gaze.

"Look at them."

Kiss.

"Looking at you."

Kiss.

"Wanting you."

Kiss.

"Desperate for you."

I push my ass back into him, loving his touch as he teases me with his words too.

"They're going to be down there, wondering what we're doing, where I'm touching you, how loud you'll scream. But it's all mine tonight. Isn't it, Eden?" he whispers, bringing his lips to my ear so I can hear him perfectly over the music below.

I don't answer straight away, and he quickly turns me to face him, my back now to the party below as he holds my attention.

"Isn't it, Eden?" he repeats, slowly sinking to his knees

before me, heat in his blue eyes, and I almost crumble along with him.

"Yes."

One simple word, offering my consent, and it flips a switch within him. Unbuckling the belt at my waist, he pulls it slowly through the loops of jeans and drops it beside him.

Hands braced on the railing behind me, I'm entranced, watching every move he makes, and the glint in his eyes tells me he knows *exactly* what he's doing to me.

Unbuttoning my jeans, he pulls them down my legs, grinning when he finds the bodice fastened between my legs and nothing else in his way. Popping the buttons, he makes sure not to touch me, which only increases my desperate need to feel him.

Standing back up to full height, his fingers tease against the hem of the bodice, the question clear in his eyes as he waits to see if he can remove it. We are revealed from the waist up, but my hair will still cover my body from view. I hope. So I nod, wetting my lips as his devilish smile takes over his face.

"You're lucky they're so far away. Otherwise, I would make a point of throwing this in their direction," he mutters against my lips as I hold my hands above my head, feeling eyes on my back from the other Allstars as he removes my bodice. Stepping in closer, he drops the scrap of material to the floor near my jeans and belt and places his hands on either side of my body, shielding me from anyone trying to look up at a different angle.

I don't know if we have anyone else's attention, and I don't want to. All I want is to feel him. My heart is pounding in my chest, desperate for his touch, and I refuse to let anything stop us now. Not when the buildup has me so hot, so excited, so desperate.

Stroking his hand up my back, tangling his fingers in my hair, he tilts my head back as his mouth devours mine. His other hand teases down my stomach, grazing his fingertips on my clit.

I moan against his lips, my hands grabbing at his waist under his T-shirt before he drops back down to his knees again.

"Tobias, they'll—"

My words turn into another moan as he strokes his tongue against my clit, circling and teasing me slowly as I steady myself against the balcony.

I force myself to look down at him instead of throwing my head back in ecstasy. Watching him on his knees before me makes me feel powerful beyond words. It feels like they're always trying to make me feel powerless, but right now, I feel like a fucking queen.

Still fully dressed, he glides his hand up my thigh, and I can feel how wet I am as he reaches my entrance, slowly circling in time with his tongue.

He wastes no time, thrusting first one, then two fingers inside of me, and I cry out with pleasure as my walls stretch against his digits, which rub perfectly against my G-spot with precision, over and over again.

"Fuck yes," I cry as he bites down on my clit, and lightning fast, my orgasm rips from my toes, setting every nerve alight as he twirls his fingers inside of me.

Buckling under his touch as ecstasy lingers, he catches my fall, lowering me onto the lounger beside us.

"You taste like heaven," he states, pulling his T-shirt over his head as I try to catch my breath. His jeans follow a moment later, revealing his thick hard length pulsing in his hand. The deep V at his waist frames the most delectable abs, his defined tanned body every woman's wet dream.

My mouth waters, wanting to return the favor, but Tobias has other ideas.

Grabbing my belt off the floor, he signals for me to hold my hands out, and like a vixen desperate for another orgasm, I do. Tightening the strap, he wraps the other end of the belt around the pole at the back of the lounger, forcing my hands above my head, but there's no discomfort. It would be easy enough for me to release my hands. It's an illusion more than anything.

My chest juts out, my back arches, and my legs fall open, encouraging him closer.

"Almost," he murmurs, stepping inside my bedroom, and I panic for a moment until he comes back out with my purple vibrator in his hand. Sitting at the bottom of the lounger, I drape my legs over his.

I want to beg and plead for him to fill me up, but I'm intrigued to see what he wants, so I say nothing, biting on my bottom lip so hard, I'm close to drawing blood.

Palming his cock, the tip bulges, begging to be licked, but he holds the vibrator towards my lips instead,

"Suck."

The one-word demand has my lips parting instantly, and he tentatively strokes it across my bottom lip.

"You're a fucking tease, Tobias," I moan before wrapping my lips around the purple device and sucking down to where his fingers grip it. His eyes widen in surprise as I release it from my lips and do it again. "Now, you either fuck me with it or use your cock, but if you don't, I'm about to take over."

He chuckles at my little growl as he glides the vibrator from my clit to my entrance, turning it on to the first setting as he pushes it inside me.

My mouth falls open as my core clenches around it, and Tobias squeezes his cock in a death grip. My arms pull on the belt as my hips move with his thrusts, desperate for more.

I don't need to say a word, my eyes doing all the pleading for me as he turns the setting up. I want him, and his thick rigid cock stretching me out, but the pleasure in his eyes adds to my own as the vibrations increase.

"You look so pretty in pink, Eden. Imagine how flushed your skin would be if I was to spank your ass." He licks his lips, burning my skin with his gaze as he winks at me.

"More," I groan out, and he leans forward, adding the perfect friction to my clit as he sucks my nipple into his mouth. "Yes. God, yes," I pant, my hips rising to meet the motion of the vibrator, and just as I start to feel my orgasm, the device is tossed aside and I whine with need.

My disappointment is short-lived as Tobias lifts my legs over his shoulders, thrusting his cock deep inside me in one swift motion, his thumb adding pressure to my clit as I hold on to the belt for dear life.

Sweat mingles between us as he tosses his hat to the side, revealing his chocolate brown wavy hair. His biceps bulge as he drops my legs to his waist and balances himself over me, fucking me into the lounger.

My whole body zings with ecstasy as a second orgasm rips through my body, tearing me apart as an endless scream of pleasure vibrates in my throat. My heart pounds in my ears as Tobias fucks me hard and fast, all the pent-up teasing catching up to him as his pace falters, and he groans against my lips, finding his own climax.

Slowly riding out the waves together, I wiggle my wrists, releasing them from the belt strap, and run my fingers through his hair.

Holy fuck. What is it with the guys of Knight's Creek fucking me into a sex coma? I could nap all weekend long right now, but the twitch of Tobias' cock inside of me tells me he's nowhere near done.

"Oh shit," he mutters, shock laced in his voice as his eyebrows knit together, his eyes widening.

"I know, you have a magic di—"

"No. No. Well, I do, but I... Fuck, I didn't use a condom." We both still at his words. Is that why it felt so electric? The skin on skin connection without a layer of rubber between us?

He slowly pulls out of my body, confirming what he just said, and we both stare in disbelief.

"I have the implant, but I've never not used a condom before," I admit, watching as his shoulders sag with relief. "You don't have any gross diseases or something I should be aware of, right?"

"What? No, of course not," he answers quickly, swiping his hand through his hair as he stands. "I've just had a physical for football too."

"Good. I did too, just before I came here," I offer, feeling the need to confirm, and he nods. How did we get carried away like that? He'd literally pulled them out, but the heat of the moment overruled everything.

"Good."

Neither of us moves, staring at each other as we let the stress from moments earlier drift away.

"Well then," Tobias murmurs, his gaze traveling down to my pussy and his eyes lighting up with desire again. "I'm not going to lie. Watching my cum drip from your pussy is hot as fuck." I stare at him in surprise, watching his cock harden before my eyes, still not actually moving until his gaze meets mine again. "I think we should go again, and again, and again, Eden. Just with condoms now."

My brain says to sleep, but my body tingles with his offer, on the same wavelength as him.

"Let's move inside where the condoms are then," I purr, letting him pull me to his naked chest and quickly move us inside, throwing me down on the bed.

"I knew I liked you for a reason, bubble."

TOXIC CREEK

KC KEAN

TWENTY SEVEN

Xavier

This whole fucking night has been stupid. Absolutely fucking ridiculous.

I had the best game tonight, but it's done nothing to improve my mood. Not even a 45-6 win can pull me out of this shit mood.

I had to endure Roxy Montgomery all night, for her to have no information at all. Or if she did, she was more than tight-lipped about it, even if she was drinking herself into the gutter. That's when I knew I had to cut my losses, nobody needs to deal with a drunk Roxy.

Hunter stormed off hours ago, leaving me to put Roxy and KitKat in an Uber by myself. I feel like my skin is covered with a rash after all the groping Roxy did. I need to wash her touch off me. The ocean beckons me to do it, but I've had too much to drink to trust myself out there right now.

Glancing over my shoulder, I notice Archie's house and pool behind me remain lit. There are still a few people here, the music quieter in the background as the fire still burns on the beach. It's just past three in the morning, so I should go home, but I know exactly why I haven't gone yet.

They're up there still. *She* is up there, and I'm down here.

Tobias is going to pay for that little stunt he played. He knew we were watching every move they made, our gazes transfixed on them as he stripped her bare.

She looked sinful in her outfit, but I know what she looks like naked, and I can admit there is no better sight.

I was angry that he was putting her on display, but no one else was paying any attention, except Hunter, of course. Everyone else was enjoying the party. Then, I was even angrier when they slipped from view.

We share everything all the time, and it's never an issue. I think that's because I'm happy fucking them once and stepping away, but with her, with Eden, I want to feel her one more time.

Looking up at her balcony, the sheets still perfectly in place from earlier, I can't see or hear anything. My mind is at war with itself, but fuck it, I'm done hanging around down here, not getting what I want.

Stalking around the pool, I can thankfully still walk in a straight line, but I know I shoulder check a few people when I can't step to the side. I never usually drink this much, and really,

I'm just tipsy, but tipsy is more than I would usually get to when at a public party. But seeing Tobias with her earlier only got Eden under my skin even more.

"Hey, X, where are you going, man?" Archie calls out as I step inside. He's sprawled out on the huge sofa, Charlie's head resting in his lap as she giggles.

"Fuck off, Archie," I grumble back, cutting through the house to the stairs, racing up them to get to the door I remember.

Trying the handle, not caring for privacy, I find it locked, which only adds to my frustration. So many barriers continue to stand between us.

Raising my fist, I knock on the door loud enough to wake the dead, bouncing on the balls of my feet as I impatiently wait. Why the fuck is no one answering?

Just as I go to rap my knuckles against the door again, it swings open, revealing Eden in a tiny white bathrobe.

Her blonde hair is wild compared to the slick straight style earlier, her red lipstick long gone and her mascara slightly smudged around her shimmering blue eyes. Yet she still looks divine.

"What the fuck, Xavier?" she whisper-shouts, holding the bathrobe closed with one hand as she keeps the other on the door handle, and glances over her shoulder.

Ah, so he's still here then.

Her eyes fall back to mine, waiting for an answer, but I don't offer one as I push against the door, and she lets it fall open. Walking around her, I spot Tobias passed out in her bed, a fucking teasing smile on his lips as he sleeps.

The door clicks shut before a hand wraps around my arm, turning me to face a frowning Eden.

"Xavier, what are you doing here?"

Turning to face her fully, I cup her chin softly. "I'm mad."

Her frown deepens as she stares me down, waiting for more of an explanation, but I already feel like I said too much.

"Xavier, are you drunk?" she asks, crossing her arms over her chest, and the material of her robe falls open a little, offering me a glimpse of the marks Tobias has left.

Jealousy floods my veins as I release her chin, stroking my finger over the top mark on her breast, the skin a mixture of red and purple already. She doesn't push me away or try to cover her skin. Instead, she squeezes my shoulder.

"Xavier, go home. You're drunk."

Moving to step back, I grab her hand before she gets too far, pulling her back into me. Her chest hits mine as I stare down at her, and she looks up at me with wide eyes, the sleep that was there moments ago long gone.

Wrapping my other arm around her chest, I say nothing at all as I just take her in.

"You are so annoying when you say nothing at all, keeping your face neutral so I don't know what you're thinking. I'm too tired for your shit right now, Xav—"

I press my lips to hers gently, letting them mold together as

I inhale her. The second I feel her kiss me back, I increase my pressure, swiping my tongue against her delectable lips as she moans into my mouth.

Her free hand wraps around my neck, deepening the kiss, when movement from the bed makes her pause. Pulling her lips from mine, she glances over her shoulder, and I look over her head to see Tobias getting comfortable in his sleep.

Turning to face me again, I lower my lips to hers, but she presses her fingers against my mouth.

"Xavier, what are we doing here?"

"I mean, do you not know what kissing is? Because I thought you did, but if you need a training plan, I'm feeling generous enough to help out." I grin down at her, but my smile only seems to make her more confused.

"Did you bump your head or something? Like, you know I'm Eden Grady, right? We hate each other. We've established that." She searches my gaze, likely looking for the usual anger that simmers beneath the surface.

"I never said I hated you, Nafas," I murmur against her fingers. "Do you hate me, Eden?"

"You're an asshole, Xavier. A complete douche who manhandles me and pushes me around to do exactly what you want."

"But do you hate me?" I repeat, stroking a finger down the side of her face, and her eyes almost close.

"You played the video of me walking through school naked

in class to fuck with me," she states, her voice barely above a murmur.

"I'm not hearing an answer to my question."

Her eyes pop back open, meeting my gaze head-on. "You won't tell me more about Ilana." I don't repeat myself. Instead, I stare her down, waiting for her to fill the silence with her answer, and she sighs. "But no. No, I can't seem to bring myself to hate you."

Moving her hand from my mouth, I drop my lips back to hers, feeling the urgency in every fiber of my body, but she pushes back all too soon.

"But Tobias is in my bed, Xavier." There's no guilt in her eyes, and I don't expect there to be.

"I know that Hunter told you we share, and he wasn't joking." Resting my hands on her waist, I don't want her to step out of my reach. Uncertainty flashes in her eyes a little. "I can't stop thinking about the night I first came up here, intrigued by the blonde with pain in her eyes. It's like I was compelled, but so were you, the way you dropped to your knees…" My voice trails off as lust fills each word, heat filling her gaze as she looks me over.

Stroking her hands up to my neck, I squeeze her waist, silently begging for something, anything from her as my cock burns to be touched.

Slowly, she trails her hands from my neck, down my chest and abs, to the waist of my jeans, looping her fingers through the belt loops at the front and pulling me in even closer.

That move alone has me close to bursting, but the way she looks up at me as she drops to her knees is my undoing. She doesn't take her eyes off me as she pops the button of my jeans and lowers my zipper, my cock instantly jutting out in desperation, and her eyes widen, clearly liking me commando again.

Wrapping her fingers around my length, my cock humming with pleasure at the familiar touch of her delicate hands, she leans forward and strokes her tongue from the base of my dick all the way to the tip.

Hissing with pleasure, my chin rests against my chest as I watch her every move. Squeezing my cock, she wraps her lips around my bulging end and slowly swallows me down, her eyes fixed on mine as my mouth falls open. Hitting the back of her throat, I use all my willpower not to inch forward, fucking her face, but a second later, her other hand squeezes my thigh, encouraging me to do just that.

Releasing her hand from my cock, she strokes my balls, keeping the pressure on the back of my thigh for me to thrust into her mouth, moaning with pleasure as I do.

Testing her nonexistent gag reflex again and again, I watch as her eyes water, her plump lips wrapped perfectly around my cock as she digs her nails into my ass, encouraging me. Her robe falls open, revealing her perfect tits as they bounce with each thrust.

"Holy fuck," I bite out, raking my fingers through her hair, wrapping it around my wrist at the back of her head.

"Stop going easy on me. I want it all," she murmurs, catching her breath for a second before sucking on the tip hard.

Fuck. She asked for it.

Holding her head in place, I fuck her mouth harder, faster as she tugs on my sac and squeezes my ass, urging me forward.

I start to stutter, my mouth falling open as pleasure rushes through my body, and just as my orgasm starts, she holds me at the back of her throat, swallowing around my cock, enhancing my climax to another level.

"Fuck. Holy fuck. Shit," I ramble as I feel my skin flush with heat as she swallows my cum.

How the fuck did she have me fuck her mouth, yet she was practically the one in control the whole time? There are no words. No words.

Standing before me, the grin on her face tells me just how pleased she is with herself. I stroke a hand down the opening of her robe, wanting to bring her the same pleasure as she just gave me, but she pauses my movement.

"I'm sure," she whispers, and it takes me a moment to understand what she's saying.

"But I want to give you an orgasm."

"You did. I just swallowed it." She grins, making me shake my head as I pull her in close, and we stand staring at each other.

"Can you guys get in bed now? I'm trying to fucking sleep,"

Tobias grouses, making Eden startle, but the grin on his lips as he settles in with his eyes closed proves my point on sharing.

"Oh good, I'm fucking exhausted. Hot show, though." My gaze flickers to the door, where Hunter leans against the doorframe before stepping farther into the room and shutting the door behind him.

Without a word, he falls onto her bed with a stumble, blindly kicking his shoes off as he rolls onto his side next to Tobias.

"What the fuck is happening right now?" Eden mutters under her breath, and I grin.

"We're sleeping, Nafas." Tucking myself back in my pants, I lift her off her feet, placing her down on the bed beside Hunter as I climb on beside her.

Her California king is nowhere near big enough for the four of us, but it'll do for the night.

Not bothering with the blankets since there is enough body heat between us, I close my eyes, but I feel her watching me.

"Don't think, just sleep, Eden," I whisper, falling too easily into my own slumber, my mind at peace, even if just for a moment, my arm wrapped tight around her waist.

KC KEAN

TWENTY EIGHT
Eden

The heat of the sun through my balcony doors beats down on me, the brightness burning my eyelids, forcing me awake. It feels like a damn heat box in here.

Prying my eyes open, I find wavy blond hair in my face, my fingers laced through it from when I was sleeping. My robe has fallen open, my bare chest pressed up against Hunter. As I extract my hand, Hunter doesn't stir when I try to move, but a leg thrown over mine and an arm banded tight around my waist doesn't let me go far.

Peering over my shoulder, I'm surprised to find Xavier clinging to me so tightly, reminding me of what happened in the middle of the night. I should feel guilty about tasting Xavier's cock after all the sex I'd had with Tobias, but I don't. I can't help but question his motives, since nothing is ever straightforward with him, but I feel liberated and fucking starving.

Slipping my legs from under Xavier's, it takes a minute to extract myself from under his arm, since he tightens it every time I move. This guy confuses me, holding me close yet at arm's length all at the same time. Nothing good will come from this.

Crawling down the bed, I tiptoe to the bathroom, shutting the door quietly behind myself before I drop my robe to the floor.

While the shower warms up, I catch a glimpse of myself in the mirror and gape at the marks on my chest. Dragging my finger over the bruises on the swell of both my breasts, I move closer to the mirror.

Tiny blue fingerprint bruises mark my hips, and I can't lie, my core is sensitive in the most blissful way possible.

Damn Tobias and his fucking cock. I feel lighter almost. Spending the night fucking all my problems away had the perfect impact on me. Now it's back to reality, but I need a shower first.

Quickly showering, I drench myself in coconut body wash, using the same scent on my hair, and I feel fresh. With a towel around my body and another around my hair, I sneak back into my room to where the guys are still sleeping and slip into the closet.

Throwing on a pair of denim shorts and my favorite Machine Gun Kelly tee, I French braid my wet hair down my back as my stomach grumbles for food. A quick glance at my phone tells me it's just past eleven in the morning, no wonder I'm hungry.

Stepping back into my room, the three of them don't stir at all, so I make my way downstairs, the smell of bacon filling the air as I do. I don't expect it to be Richard, since Archie said he was away for the weekend on business. Rounding the stairs, I freeze in place as I spy Charlie sitting on the countertop, with Archie between her legs, peppering kisses all over her face.

Well then.

"I want to say it's about time, but I'm not the cheesy type to really say I told you so, and it feels the same," I say, making them jump apart as I approach them. Charlie's cheeks redden, but Archie grins as he shakes his head.

"Oh my god, Eden, I am so sorry," she gushes, pushing Archie back so she can drop down, and I can't help but laugh at the panic in her eyes.

"Why are you saying sorry?" I whisper-shout, stopping in front of her as I place my hands on her shoulders in support.

"Because...... Is this weird for you?" she whispers back, glancing over her shoulder to see if Archie can hear her, and the innocent look in his eyes tells me he can.

"Why would it be weird for me? You two have been giving each other the googly eyes since I got here. I can't imagine what you were like before I arrived. As long as you don't like, get married and expect to split me in the divorce, then I'm all good," I say with a smile, hip checking her as I pass to grab the freshly brewed coffee from the machine.

"See, I told you Eden is as cool as a cucumber. It's why we're her friends, remember?" Archie mutters, cupping her cheek, and the sight of them is almost sickly sweet, especially seeing Charlie swoon over Archie's touch.

I can already see the wedding, the children, and fur babies. Their whole life is mapped out before them. The epic kind of high school sweetheart love you dream of. Basically, everything I am against.

"Do either of you two want a cup of coffee?" I ask, adding the sugar and creamer to my own mug, but they both point to the mugs on the counter beside them.

"So did someone have fun last night with a certain Allstar?" Charlie asks, linking her arm through mine before I can take a sip of my coffee, pulling me towards the huge sofa area, and I refrain from rolling my eyes at her.

"You say a certain *Allstar* like you saw the other two actually leave last night, Charlie," Archie teases, giving me a smirk as he throws himself down on the sofa, patting the seat beside him for Charlie to take, but she gives him the middle finger and sits next to me.

Sticking my tongue out at him, I glance at Charlie, who finally catches on to what Archie just said and gapes at me.

"Wait, how many Allstars are up in your room right now?" Charlie shouts in surprise.

Taking a huge gulp of my coffee, the liquid burning my

tongue a little, I look at everything around the room before finally looking back at her. I don't need her judgment, and it's not all as it seems, but I'm not embarrassed.

"Three."

"Three! Holy shit, Eden. Did you..." She wiggles her eyebrows suggestively as I take a sip of my coffee and almost spit it out as her question catches me off guard, and I cough as it goes down the wrong hole.

"What the fuck, Charlie. Are we at the stage of our friendship where we discuss this?" I ask sarcastically, but she nods eagerly. "No, no, I did not," I grumble, answering her question, but I don't add that I would not have said no to that scenario either.

"Are they still up there now?" She leans back on the sofa, her arm stretching out on the back, desperate for the gossip, and her face lights up when I nod. "So what are you guys then?"

"What are you two?" I throw back, and she balks, blushing again as she refuses to glance in Archie's direction. "Don't ask me questions you're too afraid to answer yourself, Charlie James."

"What questions might they be?"

I almost get whiplash turning in the direction of Xavier's voice as he walks down the stairs like he owns the joint. He's still in his clothes from yesterday, yet he looks ready to walk a runway. His clothes don't look rumpled, his eyes are wide and alert, and his hair is swept back into place. Unbelievable.

"Ignore the gossiping girls, X. You want coffee or a

smoothie?" Archie responds, jumping to his feet and heading back to the open kitchen as Xavier continues towards me.

When he drops down beside me, I can feel the heat radiating off him, even without his touch, as my body seems to become more accustomed to his.

"The other two will be down in a minute as well, so smoothies, please, man," Xavier calls over his shoulder before turning to face me.

Up close, I notice his five o'clock shadow and the little bags under his eyes as he searches my face. I assume he's looking for embarrassment or regret, but he won't find it. That's not how I operate.

"So while you were becoming more acquainted with Tobias and his body, did you guys happen to discuss the threatening message you received yesterday?" Xavier asks, his facial expression remaining neutral with his usual asshole attitude back in place, and I lean towards him, a sly grin on my face, wanting to get a rise out of him.

"We were a little too busy for that. And if I'm being truly honest, we didn't do all that much talking in general."

I hear Charlie giggle behind me as Xavier quirks his eyebrow, licking his lips as he remains in place.

"Hmm, true. I know what it's like to have you naked and pleading for more. I couldn't get a word in when you were begging me either." I can't tell if he was talking about last night or the first night, but either way, he's not that wrong.

Charlie's giggles turn into all-out laughter, making Xavier grin, pleased with himself as I glare at him. I hear Archie laughing from the kitchen too, so I stick my middle finger up in his direction, then in Charlie's as my eyes stay fixed on Xavier.

"You think you're so high and mighty, but you fucking love my mouth. So much so that you came knocking on my door last night while you were drunk because you felt left out. Isn't that right, snoockums?" I goad, my face mere inches from his as we stare each other down.

"Okay, children, settle down." Hunter's voice breaks through the moment, but before I pull away, Xavier leans forward, touching his lips to mine ever so slightly, leaving me stunned as he relaxes back onto the sofa.

Hunter rounds the sofa, a soft smile on his lips as he takes a seat on the other side of Xavier. How is it Hunter makes me feel more nervous than Xavier or Tobias, but he hasn't seen me fully naked? I think it's because I know where I stand with the other two, at least a little bit, while Hunter is an enigma.

At a glance, he looks like some surfer dude who's the life of the party, but actually, he's so closed off, I'm surprised he is even friends with the other two.

I don't know what's developing here at all, with any of them, they're so confusing.

"Heyyyy," Tobias shouts moments before throwing himself over the back of the sofa, almost knocking the coffee from my hands as he lands upside down in between Xavier and me, his legs up in the air and his hat firmly back in place as he grins up at me.

"You're acting ridiculous, Toby," Hunter mutters as he silently accepts a smoothie from Archie, who proceeds to hand the others out to Xavier and Tobias as well. "I'm still coming up with nothing from the message you received yesterday. Which tells me whoever sent it had the phone signal set up to bounce around the damn world to make it untraceable," Hunter admits, and I sigh, annoyed that I seem to get outsmarted at every turn.

"Don't worry about it, it really isn't your problem," I murmur, smiling in thanks, but nobody agrees with me.

"We'll find out who sent it," Xavier bites out, and when I meet his gaze, I know he means it. If there is anything I have learned about Xavier Knight, it's that he too doesn't like to be outsmarted, and that's what will be causing him more concern than anything. *Not* the actual threat against me. But I appreciate any help they're willing to offer.

"So, bubble, we have a free day today. Want to spend the day around the pool relaxing together?" Tobias asks, changing the topic as he palms my thigh, leaving a trail of goosebumps in his track.

Glancing to Charlie, she nods excitedly, likely wanting to do the same with Archie, and I shrug.

"Sure. Are you guys going to tell me anything else about Ilana while you're here?" I ask, meeting Xavier's gaze as I push for details, and he sighs as he rises to his feet.

"Don't push it, Eden," he mutters, giving me his back as he heads for the door, and I sigh. Simultaneously, Hunter and Tobias stand, the latter offering me a playful wink as they follow after him, leaving their empty smoothie glasses behind.

"Twenty minutes, bubble, and I'll be back," Tobias calls out over his shoulder, and I'm left to stare after them like a fool.

The front door slams shut behind them, and silence falls over the house.

"I think you just might have your hands full there, Eden," Charlie murmurs, and I slowly nod in agreement.

I am so fucking screwed.

Lying side by side with Charlie on the loungers, the sun beating down on us, I feel like I'm in an alternate universe. The Allstars were back within twenty minutes, just like they said they would be, and that was almost four hours ago. Only Tobias mentioned actually coming back, so it surprised me when they were all here in their swim shorts, relaxed and completely out of character.

Xavier is standing in the same navy swim shorts I saw him in the first day I arrived, his aviator sunglasses in place as he shows off his physique. Hunter is shirtless too, his striped board shorts tight around his thighs as he relaxes in his chair. Tobias, on the other hand, is wearing orange swim shorts. Bright, bold, and totally him. I want to lick my way up all of their abs, preferably one after the other, but I won't tell them that.

The strangest part is they're actually being...nice? Not douches is probably the better way to describe it. There's been no harsh words or anger towards me, they've simply laughed and joked without a care in the world.

"I have honestly never seen them so chill, Eden. It's almost weird. I think Xavier was born with a stick up his ass." Charlie chuckles, straightening the strap on the bikini I loaned her. The deep red takes her from the quiet girl next door to sexy vixen, and she fucking knows it. Archie hasn't taken his eyes off her all day.

"I fucking heard that," Xavier grumbles from the patio table where the guys are playing poker. I have no idea who's winning, but they're playing with chips, jibing each other, and relaxing, so I guess it doesn't really matter.

"I'm not sorry that you did," Charlie throws back, and I grin, looking past her to see Xavier scowling, but the smallest lilt of his lips tells me it's not serious.

"So, you and Archie, huh?" I whisper, doing a better job of keeping the conversation between the two of us, and she blushes, swiping her wispy hair from her face, her body tensing for a moment before she releases a breath.

"Is it embarrassing to admit I've crushed on him so hard since we were twelve?" She cringes, and I just smile.

"No way. You guys are cute, and you've never acted as the cleat chasers do." Her face scrunches in disapproval, knowing who and what I'm talking about, since we all watch them hang all over the players.

"I just don't want to get my hopes up. He's a football player with plenty of options. I don't want to get screwed over or fuck it up myself."

"You are totally playing it cool, no stress, Charlie. But if you're really worried, you should do that hangman thing I saw on social media the other day," I murmur with a grin before taking a sip of my water.

"What hangman thing?"

"You know, where you put their name in your phone, and every time they fuck up, you delete a letter. Fuck up enough to lose all their letters, and they're gone."

Charlie practically cackles beside me as my words sink in, making the guys pause their game as they stare over at us. Turning my head away, I chuckle as I look out to sea.

"That is some next-level shit, Eden."

"Right? Lou-Lou used to do it all the time too." The mention of my friend from White River feels almost nostalgic, but the reminder that I still haven't heard from my mom plays havoc on my mind. I need to call Lou-Lou soon.

I have to stay strong and hope everything is okay because there is no one I can turn to who will know where to look or what to do. Well, no one who is willing to help at least, I think, glancing over at the guys again with a heavy sigh.

"Turn that frown upside down, bubble," Tobias calls out, fixing his hat like he always does as he grins from ear to ear at me. I give him the two-finger salute, which was apparently the wrong thing to do when he jumps out of his chair instantly.

"I think Eden looks a little hot, Toby. She probably needs to cool off," Hunter murmurs, a sly grin on his face as he brushes his blond hair back, and I gape at him in surprise, knowing exactly what he's insinuating.

Tobias stalks towards me, and I quickly stand, my arms outstretched as he nears.

"I swear to God, Tobias, don't even think about it."

His grin only widens as he nears, and I start to back away. The damn pool takes up far too much space out here, there isn't nearly enough room for me to run, but the second I get to the bottom end of the pool, I take off to the left, running around it as I feel heavy footsteps close behind me.

"Why are you always fucking chasing me?" I grumble, stopping beside a sun lounger and using it as a shield between us.

"Because, bubble butt." He says it so casually, I frown, making him chuckle. "Your ass when you run makes it totally fucking worth it, bubble, especially in your little two-piece," he states, pointing his finger at my black bikini.

"You're an asshole."

"You fucking love it. Now come here," he murmurs, trying to lure me in with a cheeky grin on his face, and I falter for too long, watching as Tobias strokes a hand over his abs, giving him the opportunity to wrap his arms around me.

Spinning me so my back is to his chest, my arms pinned at my side, I'm lifted off the ground as he takes off running, straight for the pool.

"Tobias, don't you—"

My words are cut off as we both plunge into the cool water, fully submerging as I barely manage to hold my breath, but he quickly pulls me back to the surface, his arms around my waist as he turns me to face him.

With my eyes still closed, I swipe the loose bits of hair from my face, thankful I braided it back this morning and opted against wearing makeup, hearing the others laughing in the distance.

"You are so dead," I murmur, finally wiping my eyes so I can open them, but when I do, I'm not impressed with the wide smile on Tobias' face. "So dead," I repeat.

He doesn't say anything as he pulls me in against his chest, lifting his hand to stroke his thumb under my eye before tilting my chin up. His blue eyes sparkle as he lowers his lips to mine, and my body instantly heats.

I shouldn't let him kiss me. We fucked last night, but that's supposed to be where it ends. I just can't bring myself to pull away. Instead, my hands wrap around his neck as I hold him closer, deepening the kiss.

A sudden splash disturbs us, pulling our lips apart as we turn to see what's going on. Hunter is in the pool across from us with a frown on his face as he glares at Xavier, who stands on the side. But Xavier's eyes are transfixed on Tobias and me.

Someone is chucking their toys out of the crib again, or more specifically, pushing Hunter in the pool because he feels left out.

A part of me wants to beckon Xavier over, give in to his little tantrum, and satisfy myself at the same time, but I can't help but enjoy riling him up, which is why I give him my back and bring my lips to Tobias' once more. I feel him grin against my lips, enjoying the path I chose as he wraps my legs around his waist and squeezes my ass cheeks under water, likely for Xavier's benefit.

"This is absolutely fucking riveting. Like we can't see the hickeys all over her body, now we get to actually *watch* you mark her skin with your hands. Excellent. I can't breathe with how much joy I feel," Xavier scolds, and a sudden splash follows his little speech.

"You should cool off. You were turning green, hulk man," Charlie sings. I pull my lips from Tobias' to glance over my shoulder, and sure enough, Xavier is in the water beside a laughing Hunter, swiping his hair back off his face as he glares at her.

"I'm hardcore, call me Kraken," Archie cries, scooping Charlie up into his arms and jumping into the water, splashing Xavier as he does, which only makes me laugh harder.

"This isn't over, bubble," Tobias murmurs in my ear seductively before lifting me in the air and throwing me into the water closer to the group, my scream barely leaving my lips before I sink underwater again.

I let myself sink to the bottom a minute in an attempt to cool off, but I also need a moment to gather myself. It feels like forever since I had a day like today, and I don't see many of them in my future in this toxic town of Knight's Creek, but it's given me the chance to relax.

Now I'm fully charged and ready to figure my shit out.

TWENTY NINE
Eden

Sitting on my bed as I tie my running shoes, I can't decide how I feel, my mind going round and round in an endless circle of confusion.

School today was...fine. There was the odd rumor and whisper from people who saw me on Tobias' lap down at the water's edge, but I can deal with rumors because I don't care.

I'm a whore. Washed-up trash. A master at threesomes. I like women.

You name it, they've said it. KitKat and Roxy have been encouraging the sneers and harsh words, as always.

I mean, someone actually sang Meatloaf's "Two out of Three Ain't Bad," and I struggled to keep myself from laughing, while another part of me wanted to jump Hunter here and now, make it a full house.

But really, there was no actual drama all day.

There was also nothing from the Allstars. Not a single word. I sat where they had expected me to be, and they swarmed me like usual, but there were no jibes, no death glares, not even a hello.

It's so nice when toxic people stop talking to you. It's like the trash took itself out.

I should be glad. One and done is my own fucking motto. So why do I feel so deflated?

Bracing my hands on my knees, I sigh. Get your shit together, Eden. They're a distraction anyway. Saturday was fun, definitely different, but it was a one-off rarity. No one had mentioned anything from the night before. Tobias kissed me a few times, and I let him, unable to stop myself, but otherwise, we were just six high school seniors enjoying a school-free day.

Archie and Charlie, on the other hand, are besotted with each other, which is why I declined to go to Pete's with them after school. I needed a break from all their sweetness.

Standing, I link my earphones to my phone and find my favorite Lofi Fruits playlist which always helps relax me. Just as I slip my wireless earphones in my ears, my phone lights with an incoming call. *Mom*. The shrill ringtone blasts in my ears.

Hitting the accept button as quickly as I can, I drop back down to my bed.

"Mom? Mom." My heart pounds in my chest, desperate to

hear her voice.

"Hey, Eden," she murmurs, her voice sounding tired, offering more relief than I care to admit. She's fine. My mom is fine. "Is everything okay there?"

"I'm fine, Mom. Everything here is how a new school would be anywhere else, except it's full of secrets, and the Grady name is apparently full of them. I have no way of digging further into anything it seems," I admit, and she hums in response. "Although, my mother did go off the radar for days, leaving me to worry like crazy," I add, and silence greets me.

It pisses me off that she doesn't jump to fill me in on all the secrets swarming this town. Not even my own mother wants to help me it seems.

"I'm sorry, Eden," she finally whispers. "I'm safe, there's just been an issue with my cell service the past couple of days is all."

Bad service? Her answer is bad fucking service. I want to yell and scream at her, but I feel like that's all we fucking do when she eventually calls, and I don't have the energy for it again today.

"When can I see you, Mom?" I ask, my chest aching with loss. It almost feels like they're both gone since my mom is suddenly not in my life at the minute.

I'm having to wade through troubled waters alone and hearing her voice only seems to make me feel more helpless.

"Soon, Eden. I hope," she mutters in the end, not filling

me with much confidence. I consider telling her about the threatening message I got at the game on Friday but think better of it. She's not going to be able to help or do anything about it, so what's the point? Besides, I've hinted at the Grady name, and I can't see her even caring that I'm being threatened right now.

"I miss him, Mom," I whisper, rubbing where the ache in my chest is, holding my tears at bay as I hear her sniffle down the line.

"Me too, sweetie. Me too."

My eyes fall closed as I flop back on the bed, neither of us speaking for what feels like hours, just sitting with our thoughts and memories of my dad.

"I have to go, Eden," my mom finally says, and I take a deep breath. I've had my weak and vulnerable moment, and now it's time to lock it all back up.

"Okay. Please be safe, Mom. I know there are things you aren't telling me, I can feel it, but please just be safe."

"You too, Eden. I love you."

The call ends before I can respond, and she doesn't deny that she's keeping things from me. It should annoy me more than it does, but I seem to be getting used to being left in the dark about everything. She's spent my whole life keeping things from me, I shouldn't expect her to stop now.

I need to run, clear my mind. Now.

Slipping my phone into the arm strap, I tighten my ponytail before heading downstairs. Reaching the bottom step, I find no one down here, which isn't a surprise, as I grab two bottles of water.

Taking the steps that lead off the back deck down to the beach, I can already feel the afternoon heat. Which is why I'm in running shorts that barely cover my ass cheeks and a sports bra. It's too hot for anything else.

Dropping a bottle of water in the usual spot at Archie's, I take off down the beach, pressing play on my playlist as I take the path closer to the water so I don't have to deal with the dry sand.

Letting the music wash over me, my Lofi Fruits playlist seeping into my soul, I make it to the end of the beach in no time, dropping my other bottle of water in the sand as I do, before heading right back where I came from.

My mind is like a whirlwind. There seems to be so much going on, pulling me in different directions, yet somehow, it all feels interlinked.

The Allstars, Ilana, school, Archie…even Richard. My brain is fried.

Repeating the motion over and over again, with the occasional water stop, I force myself not to look at the house at the end. Even catching a glimpse of it makes me think of the Allstars, and they're already consuming my headspace enough as it is. Between wanting to know the answers to my questions and the sexual tension, I can't take much more.

As the songs continue to play in my ear, my muscles start to ache, but my mind feels much clearer, calmer.

Stopping at the end of the beach, gulping down my water before I dehydrate, I look out to sea, loving how the sun sparkles off the water, the blues and greens of the ocean reaching as far as my eyes can see, the white waves crashing before me. It's so lulling, so peaceful.

A hand on my stomach is followed quickly by a solid body behind me as I scream in shock, my water bottle dropping to the sand.

Whipping my head around, ready to fight off whomever the fuck it is, I gape when I see Tobias grinning down at me. His lips are moving, but I can't hear him over the music.

I quickly tap my earphone, and the music pauses. "Tobias, you scared the shit out of me! Why would you fucking do that?"

"Oh hi, Tobias, how are you? I've missed you and your blessed peen so much. Let me just drop my sassy attitude so I can stick it in my mouth."

"What?" I stare at him in confusion, and he pouts at me like a child. No man should look that hot with pouty lips. His full lips pucker in my direction as his eyes drop. I can't deal with his puppy dog eyes too.

"Why are you out here alone, Eden?" he asks, his face surprisingly serious, and the fact he said my actual name tells me he means business.

I turn to face him fully, his hand remaining in place, his fingers splaying out against the base of my back, and I shiver at our closeness.

"I'm running."

"I don't mean state the obvious, Eden. I mean, have you forgotten the threatening message you got the other day? You shouldn't be alone. It's not safe. Especially when even *we* don't know who sent it."

His eyes drop to my heaving chest as I try to catch my breath from the shock, but I don't really know what to say to him.

"I—"

"Don't give me some shit excuse, Eden. Let's go. Do I still need to ask if I can manhandle you?"

"Wait, what? Tobias, I'm running. I'm not going anywhere."

His lip tilts in a half-smile as he meets my eyes.

"Between me and you, Xavier is the one who saw you running alone. I came down because we both know I have the softer approach, but it's up to you. I can give you a piggyback ride up to our house, or Xavier can enjoy exerting his control over you. Your choice."

Glancing over his shoulder, I find Xavier standing at the top of the wooden steps leading up to their house. His arms are folded over his chest as he stares down at us, every inch of the hot intimidating douchebag that he is.

His brown hair blows in the wind as his muscles bulge beneath his black tee. Holy fuck. I can see the outline of his cock through his grey sweats from here.

"Fine." I sigh, twirling my finger for him to turn around,

and he grins as he does, dropping to the sand so I can climb on.

Effortlessly, he rises, his hands under my thighs as he takes off towards the steps, and I wrap my arms around his neck gently, my head falling close to his as we move in silence.

I feel his thumb stroke the bare skin of my thigh, sending little shockwaves to my core as I try not to squirm against his back.

He climbs the steps with no effort, but Xavier and Hunter are nowhere to be found when we get to the top.

"You want a fresh drink?" Tobias asks, turning his face to glance at me as he continues to carry me.

"Well, since you made me drop my water—"

"Yeah, yeah. Imagine if I was the person who sent the message instead. You'd have lost your water and potentially your life, so I'll take my losses."

I frown at him, confused with their sudden concern for my well-being. They didn't behave like this at school today, but I guess I was always with Archie or Charlie. Come to think of it, I wasn't alone at any point. I don't like the thought of them intentionally planning this when it's not required.

"It was one message. I've had nothing since," I murmur, trying to downplay the situation, but he simply scoffs as he scans his hand to unlock the door that leads into the house, carrying me into the kitchen.

As we head straight for the fridge in the open kitchen, I can hear the strumming of a guitar in the distance, a relaxing tune filtering through the house, and I pull my earphones out to listen better.

"Do you want another water or a Gatorade?"

"Oh, a blue Gatorade if you have one," I answer, distracted by the music. "You can put me down you know," I add, and he squeezes my thighs tighter.

"I know I can, doesn't mean I want to," he responds, pulling two drinks from the fridge. I take them from him as he heads straight outside to the pool area.

This place really is grand. Modern, slick, and everything you would expect from them. Although it feels like there is nothing personal on display. Nothing laying claim that this is their home, and that makes me a little sad for them, because no matter where I lived, we always personalized it to us. Which makes me feel a little sad for me too, living in a home where nothing is mine at all.

The view over the ocean takes my breath away as I gape at the beauty before me. I can see a few boats out at sea, the crystal-clear blue water stretching for miles. Looking to my left, I see Archie's house, and the others along the front, and as beautiful as they look, they look like ant houses from up here.

The Allstars of Knight's Creek looking down over their peasants.

"Under the umbrella or on a lounger, m'lady?" Tobias asks, putting on a fake British accent as he fucking gallops, bouncing me around on his back and making me laugh.

"Umbrella." That is all I can get out as he continues to kick his legs around as he takes me past the infinity pool. God, being in there, the water feeling like you were deep in the ocean almost makes me drool in appreciation.

The table under the umbrella could easily sit twelve, the glossy black glass finish looking like something from a magazine. Standing in front of a chair, Tobias leans backward, placing my ass on the glass table as he releases me, and quickly drops into the chair, his eyes aligning with my core perfectly.

The grin on his lips tells me he's pleased with himself as I hand him a drink, and I don't bother to pretend I'm coy, leaving my legs spread as they are. Slouching back in his seat, his fingers tap on his thigh as he runs his tongue along his teeth.

"So fucking hot," he whispers, almost to himself, but I don't respond as I tilt my head back, guzzling the blue goodness as sweat trickles down my back.

My ears perk up at the sound of the guitar from earlier, and I look back at the house to my right, trying to figure out where it's coming from. It doesn't take me long to find Hunter through a floor-length glass mirror strumming on an actual guitar. Shirtless and in a pair of boxer shorts, his blond hair messy and covering his eyes as he bites his lip in concentration. He looks like a fucking rockstar.

I instantly remember the night they chased me, and I stumbled into Hunter's room looking for my phone, spotting a guitar propped up in the corner, but I know for sure that isn't the room it was in.

Staring in awe, I struggle to tear my eyes away from him, the music playing beautifully.

"Holy shit. He's amazing," I murmur, glancing at Tobias, who's staring at my pussy, and I roll my eyes. "I didn't know he could play the guitar." I tap my foot against his thigh, drawing his attention to my face, and he shrugs his shoulders.

"Nobody does," he states simply, flickering his eyes quickly in Hunter's direction before looking back at me.

"Well they should, there are no words for how good he is." Taking another sip of my drink, I glance back to the window to find him glancing in our direction, and I quickly cast my eyes away, the music stopping.

"Don't look back at him," Tobias says with a grin, moving in closer so he can rest his arms on my legs, and I frown. "There is a secret about that window that is too damn funny for you to give away, okay?" His hands slide up my legs until they reach the hem of my shorts.

"I'd have to know what the secret was for that to happen," I murmur, my breaths becoming a little quicker under his touch. I should tell him to stop. Tell him I don't ever go back for seconds, but he's intoxicating, leaving goosebumps in his wake as he slowly caresses the inside of my thigh.

"You have to promise not to tell," he repeats, and I bite down on my lip, nodding in agreement as he strokes his thumb so fucking close to my core, I want to cry. "That's his little music room. The window is tinted from the inside, so the sunlight doesn't cause him any discomfort when he's in the zone."

"Okaaay," I drag out, confused with where he's going with this.

"But it obviously doesn't have the same protective coating on the outside, right? Otherwise, you wouldn't see him."

"I'm still really confused," I admit, and Tobias tilts his gaze so he can glance in Hunter's direction, a huge grin splitting across his face as he looks back at me.

"So, Hunter hasn't realized that we can see what he's doing."

"But he's just playing the—"

"He *was* playing the guitar. Now he's playing with something else," he says with a chuckle, his fingers digging into my thighs as he smirks down at me.

As I go to turn in Hunter's direction, Tobias captures my chin, stopping me from looking as his other hand moves to my waist, holding me in place.

"Discreetly, bubble. Lie back on the table," Tobias whispers, slowly lowering me back, coming to stand above me as he does. "Now I'm going to kiss your neck so you can turn in his direction, okay?'

I nod eagerly, my body acutely aware of every brush of his body against mine, my nipples pebbling under his gaze.

Just like he said, he lowers his lips to my neck, a moan bursting from my lips as I bring my feet up onto the table, bending my legs as I automatically squeeze him with my thighs.

"Eden, you're supposed to be looking at Hunter." Tobias grins against my skin, desire tingling through my body as I remember the whole point of this.

"You're too good with your—" My response is cut off as I see Hunter.

His eyes are half-mast, his boxers long forgotten as his palm is wrapped tightly around his cock, slowly dragging up and down his hard length.

"He's watching you, bubble. He stopped strumming his guitar to start strumming his *own* guitar at the sight of you," Tobias whispers in my ear, my heartbeat pounding in my chest, the combination of Tobias' words and touch and the view of Hunter making me needy.

I can't respond, words have completely left my brain. My body takes over, consumed by the need to come.

"Let him watch me make you feel good," Tobias breathes out against my neck, and I shiver at the thought, my hand cupping the back of his head as the other grips his arm. "You like that, don't you?" he asks, stroking his fingers against the material of my shorts, making me squirm, and I groan in frustration.

"Please," I whisper, praying he doesn't make me beg any more as I watch Hunter stand, still tugging on his cock as he moves closer to the window.

Slipping his fingers under the hem of my shorts, he instantly teases my core, feeling how wet and ready I am, and he groans against my skin.

"Fuck."

Without sparing a second, Tobias thrusts two fingers deep in my pussy, a throaty groan passing my lips as Hunter leans his palm against the glass window, his eyes definitely on us now as he fucks his fist.

"Holy shit," I mumble as Tobias pulls the zipper down on the front of my sports bra, my breasts spilling from the top.

Fucking me with his fingers, he palms my clit through my shorts, adding the perfect amount of friction as he leans back, squeezing my breast in his hand, and I can see Hunter's eyes widen from here, his hand moving faster between his legs. Squeezing Tobias' shoulders, desperate for more, I can't stop my nails from digging into his skin.

Leaning forward again, Tobias takes my nipple in his mouth, biting down, and my back arches as I turn to face him, my hips grinding against his hand in time with his movement as my orgasm hits me.

Tobias keeps his pace, dragging out every last drop of my climax as I dig my fingers into his neck, ecstasy flooding my veins.

Coming down from my high, I turn to the window, but Hunter is nowhere to be seen. Although the white marks smeared across the window tell me exactly how things went in there, and I shiver again, another wave of pleasure rushing through me.

Pulling his head back, Tobias looks down at me, a pleased grin on his face as I turn to look at him.

"You make the sweetest fucking noises, bubble." Slipping his fingers from my core, I watch in slow motion as he lifts them to his lips, tasting what he just did to me. "You taste just as sweet too."

Propping myself up on my elbows, I reach my hand out to grab his waistband, but someone clears their throat, pulling my attention away from Tobias' stiff outline in his shorts.

"I didn't realize reminding her of the rules also involved orgasms," Xavier grumbles, standing at the other end of the table, his eyes glancing between the two of us, but I don't miss the way they linger on my breasts too. He stands stiff, his fists clenched at his side as he tries to keep his tone bored, but I see him. He's either jealous or pissed, maybe even a mixture of both.

"What rules?" I ask, sitting up fully as Tobias grins down at me, making a show of slowly zipping up my sports bra.

"You can't be alone until we know who sent the messages. So if you aren't with Archie or Charlie, then you come here."

"Why do you even care?" I ask, my eyebrows knitting together as I try to understand.

"I don't. But there is far too much going on right now that I know nothing about, and until that's resolved, you'll do as I say."

He goes to leave, but I shout his name as Tobias remains standing between my legs, not getting involved in the conversation.

"You expect me to tell you everything and go along with your rules, but you won't tell me anything about Ilana that will help me out. The sooner I have information, the sooner I'll be out of your hair," I state. Tobias' hands resting on my thighs squeeze, but I keep my gaze focused on Xavier.

"I don't trust you," he answers, barely glancing over his shoulder as he does.

"I'm not asking you to trust me. I'm asking you to tell me something, anything," I snap, my voice getting louder as I do.

"No."

"Fuck you and your stupid fucking no. Don't you want me gone?" I sneer, my hands fisting at my side as he whirls around to face me again.

"You don't know shit, Eden."

"Exactly!" I yell. "That's my fucking point." Is this guy deluded?

"No, you don't know shit about me or what I want."

"Then fucking tell me. Tell me something, anything." Placing my palms on Tobias' chest, I push him back a little so I can stand, and he moves reluctantly. Xavier doesn't move as I storm towards him, my heart pounding in my chest as my emotions bubble at the surface. "Please." I add, desperate for anything.

His hazel eyes sparkle with flecks of gold, emotion swirling before me as he grinds his jaw. Toe-to-toe, our chests almost touching, I wait.

"You don't deserve answers," he finally murmurs, and any hope I had is gone.

"You're an asshole. The biggest fucking self-centered douche I've *ever* met."

Stepping back, I swipe my hands down my face. I'm done. I'm so fucking done with them and the constant back and forth.

D.O.N.E.

"We know nothing," Tobias blurts out, causing Xavier to turn his way, giving Tobias a death glare.

"Shut the fuck up, Tobias," he growls out.

"We don't know what Ilana is doing, we're as much in the dark as you are," Tobias says to me, but his gaze is on Xavier as my breath catches. They know nothing?

He obviously doesn't like admitting he's out of the loop as much as I am, but he must be digging for answers if he likes to be aware of everything. He's coming up blank, clearly.

Straightening my spine, I move away from both of them, needing to put as much space between us as possible.

"I need help finding answers. You are either on my side, by my side, or in my fucking way. I'll let you decide. But fuck your rules. I'll do whatever I have to do to be safe."

With that, I turn, walking as fast as I can to the kitchen door, bumping straight into Hunter as I do. Fuck, I don't need the memory of him on my mind right now, I'm mad. I need to stay mad.

Brushing past him, I say nothing as I slip through the door

Tobias carried me in, and head for the steps. I'm halfway down the beach when I realize I left my damn earphones.

Glancing over my shoulder, I stall when I see the three of them standing side by side as they watch me walk back to Archie's. A part of me wants to flip them off, scream for them to shove it, but I force myself to ignore them. Give them a taste of their own medicine.

So much for a run to clear my mind. My head feels more screwed than ever.

TOXIC CREEK

KC KEAN

THIRTY
Eden

"Are you sure you don't want to come downstairs? Or I can stay with you, I don't mind," Charlie repeats for the hundredth time, and I'm already shaking my head before she finishes.

"Honestly, Charlie. I'm on my period. Eden Grady, on her period, is the worst person in the world to be around. I'm doing you a favor because I'm genuinely a raging bitch," I respond, snuggling further under the covers as I wait for the Midol to kick in. She looks all cute in a blue gypsy top with a pair of denim shorts and her hair curly.

I didn't go to the game tonight, my cramps have me ready to pass out, so I'm definitely not going down there and surrounding myself with all the people I don't like. Not when I'm grouchy.

Heads will literally roll.

"Okay, but if you change your mind or need anything, just say, all right? I'll be straight up here."

"Go have fun," I murmur, forcing a smile as I shoo her out of the door, sighing with relief as the door clicks shut behind her, turning the light off as she does.

Friday night, and there's obviously another party. I love parties, I really do, but they have never really been at my home or where I'm staying before. I'm PMS-ing like a bitch, and I just want everyone to shut the fuck up and go home.

Propping myself up on my elbow, I punch my pillows, trying to fluff them up, but I just can't get comfortable. My cramps are literally fucking slaying me. So I give up and flop back down on the mattress, trying to get comfortable.

I probably should have said I wanted some pizza and chocolate to make me feel better, but I don't want to bother Charlie. She should enjoy having fun with Archie tonight.

I wonder if the Allstars are down there yet?

I haven't spoken a word to them since Monday, and they haven't interacted with me either. We've sat in our seats, ignoring each other like we've never done more than that. And as much as I've tried to say a big fuck you to their rules, Archie or Charlie have been with me everywhere I've gone, until now. Finally.

They're not suffocating me. If anything, it's nice, but I hate knowing that Xavier is getting what he wants. Asshole. I feel a little calmer, knowing I have friends, the feeling of loss and being alone not as strong.

As I slap my hand around, searching for the remote, a knock sounds at the door before it swings open and Hunter strides in, his eyes glancing around the room before settling on me.

I knew I should have gotten up and locked it when Charlie left.

"Hunter, I am not in the mood for anyone's shit, I just—"

"What's wrong with you?" he asks, his face filled with concern as he looks me over. I frown at him, and he takes that as an indication to take a seat beside me on my bed. "Charlie said you aren't coming down because you don't feel well. What's wrong?" he repeats, causing me to sigh.

My fingers itch to ruffle his blond hair as he sits beside me in denim shorts, a white T-shirt, and a red checkered shirt, unbuttoned with the sleeves rolled up. So hot. But I'm in too much pain to care enough about looking just as pretty right now.

"Go away, Hunter," I grumble, cringing as I try to roll over, my stomach feeling like it's being stabbed with a thousand knives.

"I'm not going to go away when you're rolling around in pain like this," he throws back instantly, and I roll my eyes.

"I'm on my fucking period, Hunter. I'll be fine. I'm just cranky as fuck for the first two days when the cramps are unbearable. So, can you fuck off now, please?" I grouse, expecting him to go running with his tail between his legs, but instead, he leans forward, stroking his fingers down my arm.

"Oh, okay. Give me ten minutes," he murmurs, rising from the bed. He freezes above me, an awkwardness growing between us before he suddenly remembers himself and leaves. At least he closed the door again, but that felt like he was almost going to lean down and kiss me. The thought of it alone has my heartbeat spiking.

But he won't be coming back, the thought of period and blood likely frightening him away.

Grabbing the remote, I press play, letting my movie continue. Batman always makes me feel better, and since I watched the *Dark Knight* the other week with Charlie, it's only fitting to watch the third movie in the trilogy—*The Dark Knight Rises*.

I'm not sure how much time passes when my bedroom door suddenly swings open again, and I growl. I need to lock the fucking door. Throwing the blanket off me, I turn my glare to the door, only to find Hunter kicking it shut behind him, turning the lock as he does.

My glare morphs into surprise as he holds a bag in one hand and two pizza boxes in the other.

Wordlessly, he drops the things onto the bed and closes the curtain lining the balcony doors as I continue to gape at him.

Coming to stand beside the bed, he looks down at me expectantly.

"What are you doing back here?" I finally ask, picking my jaw up off the bed, and he shrugs his shoulders at me before kicking his shoes off and taking the seat beside me again.

"Scooch over. The period peaceworker is here."

"You have jokes?" I murmur, doing as he says like an idiot, and he sits back against my headboard before pulling the covers over himself and moving the bag and pizza boxes closer.

"So, I've got chocolate, candy, Dr. Pepper, extra painkillers, some heat pads," he rambles, pulling items out of the bag as he says them. "Oh, and this St. John's Worts stuff, someone recommended it. Apparently, it's good for boosting your mood and anxiety or something."

He shakes the bottle as I try to read the label, but my brain is completely fried with confusion.

"Hunter, what is all this?" I ask slowly, turning to meet his gaze, and he blushes a little as I wait for him to answer.

"Uh, you met my sister, Bethany. She didn't do too well with her period cramps, and this stuff used to make her feel better," he answers, raw honesty on his face. He must have been young when she was dealing with periods in his vicinity, maybe twelve, I'm not sure, but it stuns me how he remembered.

"And why are you doing this...for me?" I ask, wetting my dry lips as he relaxes more into the pillows like he belongs here or something.

"Because I will never forget the time she said, 'You will never understand the true differences between boys and girls, Hunter. With your little wiener, you don't have to worry about mother nature. I feel like someone is squeezing my motherfucking organs, and I just want chocolate!'" His high-pitched whine should be an insult, but I can't help but grin as I gingerly sit beside him, leaning back against the headboard.

"But I thought we were back to not speaking to each other again," I state, giving him a pointed look, but he doesn't respond. Instead, he opens the pizza boxes, putting a freshly baked pepperoni pizza in front of me.

"Are you always this grumpy when someone wants to take care of you, or is this the hormones speaking?" he asks, shaking the mood boosters at me, and I snatch them out of his hand, grabbing the Dr. Pepper as well.

Swallowing a pill quickly, I give Hunter a wide fake smile, flashing him my 'boosted spirits,' but he just smiles softly at me.

I press play on the remote, and the movie continues, and I watch as he takes a bite of his pizza, grinning along at the joke on the screen. None of this feels real. I haven't spoken two words to this guy since I saw him tugging on his cock as Tobias laid me out on the patio table earlier in the week.

But he doesn't know that I know that he did that. Yet this isn't awkward at all.

Eating in silence, Hunter clears the empty pizza boxes away and unwraps a heat patch for me, but I take it off him before he tries to put it on me himself.

"Feeling any better?" he murmurs, clearing the bed and lying down, his arm reaching out in offer to…cuddle?

I'm feeling so sorry for myself that I don't turn him down,

sinking into him and resting my head on his shoulder as his arm wraps around me.

"A little," I admit, my palm resting on his chest, feeling his heart beat beneath my palm. "Thank you."

"You're welcome," he whispers back, stroking his fingers through my hair.

"I guess I should say good game earlier too. I heard it was 42-3, and you played amazing."

"Eden, I always play amazing."

Curled up together in our little bubble with a party going on around us, I feel so close to him, yet I know little to nothing about him.

"How are the three of you so close?" I ask, not needing to specify who I'm talking about as I keep my eyes trained on the television.

"Because Xavier deemed us to be worth saving," he murmurs in response, his words making me glance at him. There is obviously more to that story—more than I think he'll offer me right now.

"So who is Hunter Asheville? Beyond bringing me my very own blood bag of goodies and causing trouble at school, of course."

Glancing down at me, a soft sigh leaves his lips as he considers my question. "I am a music loving brother, uncle, and friend, willing to blindly follow my heart, hoping it will lead to freedom."

He said a big handful of words, but what I really heard was Hunter Asheville is deep as hell.

Turning on his side, he brushes the loose wisps of hair off my face as he searches my eyes. "And who might Eden Grady be?"

It feels like forever as I try to find the right answer when I eventually go with the truth. "I have no idea who she is. I don't think I ever really have, but especially not since my dad died."

"You'll find her again, whomever you're meant to be, you're some badass goddess. You won't go down without a fight."

His green eyes hold me captive as his words hit deeper than anything else I've heard lately.

Lifting my hand to cup his cheek, I drag my thumb across his bottom lip, inching closer as I do. My eyes drift closed as our lips join, soft and delicate. He kisses me with such tenderness, I almost melt into a puddle.

Slowly pulling apart, I bite my bottom lip as he smiles back at me, his fingers tangled in my hair.

"Now, I love this movie, not as much as the second one, but enough to hold you against me for some strange reason while we watch it. If you want to bump and grind, you're going to need to join the party for that, otherwise, eyes on the TV," he says, a smirk lighting his face.

"I will ask no more questions, but only because the second one is my favorite too."

Focusing back on the television, butterflies consume my

stomach. I have no idea what the hell is happening here. Why do I seem to let the Allstars in so easily, giving them more fuel to burn me later? But for tonight—tonight, I won't question it.

THIRTY ONE
Eden

Watching the waves crash at the water's edge from my balcony, a towel wrapped around my body as the sea breeze plays havoc with my hair, I take a deep breath, inhaling the salty sea air. Last night—last night was a whole different dimension for me.

I have never lain in bed snuggled up with a guy while watching a movie. Ever. Never mind while I was on my period, and never in my wildest dreams would it finally happen with an Allstar.

The last thing I remember was being curled up on my side, my head on Hunter's chest, with the rise and fall of his breathing lulling me to sleep. But when I woke this morning, he was gone. My stomach cramps were feeling much better, and my mood last night had been surprisingly relaxed compared to usual, so I swallowed down another of those mood booster pills Hunter brought over, along with his painkillers.

The Allstars should be called 'the mind fuckers' because that's literally what they do. They're up and down like a yo-yo, and I don't know where I stand with them, which is why I've decided to give them a taste of their own medicine.

No more letting them in. No more letting them refuse to answer my questions. But most of all, no more letting them use my body. No more sex.

It's my coping mechanism, but with them, it's just making me more confused. My emotions are screaming just under the surface as I hold them at bay, and I need to shut them down, this entire situation is just too much. Allowing them to get under my skin like this is only making things harder for me.

If I ever want the answers I need, I'm going to have to make a plan. I have limited resources, but there is one person in this house whom I need to push a little harder instead of avoiding.

Stepping back inside, I twist my hair into a messy pile on top of my head and slip into a pair of black cycle shorts, a vivid pink sports bra, and a loose white tank top.

I promised to go hiking later with Charlie and Archie so I could finally see Mount James, which was named after Charlie's family. She keeps telling me it really shouldn't be a mount since it's barely a molehill, but I'm more excited about a change of scenery than the correct term of the town's landmarks. Plus, they promised me food at Pete's afterward.

Tying my running shoes, I slip my phone into the waistline pocket of my shorts and head for the stairs in search of answers.

I really haven't snooped around this place, nowhere near enough as I should have been doing, but it kind of felt disrespectful. As much as I don't want to be here, I could have been forced to live under worse conditions.

But today, I'm going to knock on every door to find Richard. But I'm going to start at the bottom floor because I really feel like I would know if he slept across the hall from me or farther down like Archie does.

Hitting the bottom of the stairs, I falter when I see him on the large sofa, staring up at the big screen as the sports news plays with the sound down low.

That was easier than I planned for.

Taking small, measured steps in his direction, my nerves kick in. I force my hands to my side, and my nails bite into my palms.

He doesn't notice me until I take a seat to his right on the sofa, my eyes also falling to the television as the commentator rips apart some of the latest sporting scandal.

"Hey, sorry. I thought you guys would all be sleeping in since you partied last night," Richard murmurs, and I cut my gaze to his.

"I didn't join them last night." His eyes widen a little in surprise like I would be crazy not to, but I don't need to explain myself to this guy. I need him to explain something to me. Taking a deep breath I continue, "I actually came down to look for you, I was hoping I could ask you a few questions."

The half-smile on his tired face instantly drops, and I feel him slowly starting to sink into his cave. "I'm sorry, Eden, I'm not sure what—"

"Did you know my parents?" I blurt out, refusing to take no for an answer, and I watch as he swallows hard before dragging his hand down his face in discomfort. "You did, didn't you?" I murmur, I can see it written all over his face.

"I'm sorry—"

"Would you please stop apologizing, it's embarrassing. What I need you to do is be honest with me for like five minutes. I don't know where my mom is or if she's even safe. With all due respect, I'm eighteen in a couple of weeks and living in a complete stranger's home because someone seems to have control over everyone."

My heart pounds in my chest as anger starts to boil under the surface. My fingers dig into my palms as I try to contain my rage.

"I don't know what you want me to say, Eden," he whispers, pain in his eyes, pleading with me to stop.

"My dad is dead, Richard. Dead. I deserve answers." His head drops into his hands as he battles with himself. I can feel him ready to tell me things, it's on the tip of his tongue, I just need to push on. "Do you know why they were run out of town?"

"Enough, Eden!" he yells, jumping to his feet as he turns to face me, forcing me to lean back in surprise as he squeezes the back of his neck. His face is bright red, emotion swimming in his eyes.

"Now, I'm sorry, Eden. Truly, I am. But I suggest you keep your head down, stop asking questions, and get through school. From there, you just have to hope you get to leave this town, and when you do, I recommend leaving the country entirely, because you know they will chase you from state to state." Without another word, he turns on his heels and storms from the room, heading downstairs while I'm left with nothing.

"What the hell is going on?" Archie shouts, rushing down the stairs. "Was my dad just yelling at you? I'll—"

"No. No, it's fine, Arch," I murmur, rubbing my chest, wishing the pain away as he stands before me, practically shaking with his hair sticking up in all directions.

"You don't look fine," he grumbles, and I can't deny that I'm shaking a little. Not from his outburst, that doesn't faze me, but from the realization that I'm never going to know the truth. This toxic town is already wrapping its chains and barbed wire around me, holding me in place so I'll fall in line, and I hate it.

Before I can say anything in response, Archie steps right up to me, his big arms wrapping around me as he pulls me into a bear hug. I freeze for a moment, surprised by his actions, but I slowly bring my arms around his waist, hugging him back.

He makes me feel safe, protected, and cared for. Three

things I rarely feel from anyone other than my dad, who can't offer me anything from the grave.

"I've got you, Eden."

"I've got you too," I whisper back, not knowing how he needs me but meaning every ounce of the words.

Charlie was right—Mount James is way grander in name than size. In this case, size really does matter. It's pretty, but more of a river walk with a couple of inclines reaching no more than three hundred feet. Although the waterfalls we've passed were nothing short of mesmerizing.

It's surprising to see so many people taking the trail, some with cute fluffy dogs, while others just enjoy the great outdoors. At least it's paved throughout, and there seem to be different access points so you could come to just see the falls if you wanted.

I'm walking slightly behind the love birds, who are all kissy, giggly, and holding hands, their cuteness making me want to gag. Although I will be taking full credit for their new-found love blossoming. I don't care if they might have had eyes for each other since they were babies, nothing happened until I arrived. Therefore, all credit goes to me.

I expected to feel like the third wheel out here, but it feels completely natural.

Neither of them has mentioned anything to do with Richard

since we left, but I can feel the questions hanging in the air. I just don't know what I'm supposed to say or do. It's not in me to be submissive or follow someone else's rules simply because they say so.

I want to know the ifs, the whats, and the whys. But how do I get them? What am I not asking? Because there is a hell of a lot that I don't know.

Lost in my own mind, I walk straight into the back of Archie, not realizing they've stopped, and Charlie throws her head back with laughter.

"Sorry," I mumble as Archie turns to check on me. "I wasn't paying enough attention."

"Well, duh. That's why we stopped. I thought you would appreciate this waterfall the most," Charlie responds, nudging me with her shoulder before linking her arm through mine and encouraging Archie to step to the side.

As he does, the waterfall comes into view. It's long, water running over rocks on the way down as it cascades powerfully into the plunge pool below.

"Apparently, there is a cave behind it, but I've never tried to find it," Archie points out as we all take in the peaceful and serene setting.

With a heavy sigh, I keep my focus on the water as I finally voice what happened earlier. "I asked Richard if he knew my parents, and the look on his face told me he did. But when I asked if he knew why they were forced to run, he clammed up, and that's when the yelling started."

"I'm sorry, Eden. My dad's a dick, especially since my mom died. But heartbreak doesn't mean he gets to treat you like that. I'll speak to him," Archie says, squeezing my shoulder in comfort, but I shake my head.

"Don't. Whatever's going on causes him pain too, Arch, I could see it in his eyes. I just don't know which way to turn. Tobias admitted they know nothing about what Ilana wants with me here, and if that's true, I don't know who else I'm supposed to convince to help me."

Swiping my hair back off my face, I lace my fingers together on top of my head, willing myself to think of another direction.

"Maybe I could talk to my grandmother again. She obviously knew something, but she shut down too, with fear, I think," Charlie offers, and I smile in appreciation.

"I don't want you to strain your relationship with your family because of me though, that's not my intention. She said no once before, I don't want you to push."

"Or my birthday is in four weeks' time and my parents always throw a family barbeque. You and Archie should come," she states, blushing a little as she extends the invite to Archie too, but he grins down at her.

"Count me in." He steps beside me, kissing her forehead, which only deepens her blush, and I grin.

"Thanks, Charlie," I add as she playfully shoves Archie back a step. "Is there anyone else who might know anything?" I ask, and Charlie huffs.

"Eden, everyone is someone in this town. You don't get to be a wallflower here. I'm sure plenty of people know, but are either too scared to rock the boat, or have something being held over their head which forces them to follow the rules," Charlie mutters, placing her hands on her hips as she looks up at the waterfall.

I'm obviously missing something. Well, a lot of somethings, but Ilana brought me here for a reason. There are too many people in this town for her to be able to control them all, right?

Looking around at the wildflowers dotted around the ground, I try to think long and hard about how else we could approach all of this.

"Does anyone go to Asheville High that isn't from Knight's Creek?" I ask, hoping that might be a lead, but Archie and Charlie simply scoff at me.

"Asheville High is way too exclusive for that," Archie says with a laugh, and I frown.

"Really though? I've been to other schools where we've had to wear a uniform, and they were some snobby-ass bitches," I grumble, and Charlie shakes her head.

"If you don't have the right zip code, you're not getting into Asheville High. It's as simple as that. It's like *90210*, have you ever watched that television show? Except there is probably more drama here, and it's not choreographed for people's entertainment."

I can't help but snicker at the truth of Charlie's statement. This town, from the outside looking in, makes you think it's safe, quaint, and wholesome. But in reality, it seeps into your soul and tears you apart.

"Maybe we could come up with a list of classmates that might have the kind of connections you might need."

"Please, I have to try and do something. Richard said I should lay low, make it through school, and hope I can get out of here."

"Maybe you should consider his advice. I know you want answers, Eden, and I'll do anything to help you, but I can't help but worry about your safety overall," Archie interjects, and admittedly, it warms my soul that he wants to keep me safe, but the easy road has never been my chosen path.

"I refuse to let them break me in any way, shape, or form, and that includes molding me into a box that they deem fit. If Ilana Knight wants me here, she should have done her research first, because I don't back down. Not now, not ever."

TOXIC CREEK

KC KEAN

THIRTY TWO

Xavier

"Fast feet! Fast feet! Let's go," Coach yells, clapping us through the last set of drills as my jersey sticks to my back with sweat.

I push harder, but my gaze flickers to Eden running track in the distance, and I lose my rhythm, slowing down. Fuck. I thought I'd gotten her out of my system. I even made sure not to go knocking on her door over the weekend.

Leaving Hunter to play Florence Nightingale was absolutely fine by me, especially when I had planned to find someone else to occupy my time. But nobody smelled like coconuts, and their hair was either too blonde or not blonde enough. Ultimately, they weren't her, and that made me madder than anything else.

I wanted her long tanned legs, soft smile, and, in Tobias'

words, her bubble butt. Fuck.

I have never been controlled by my dick, but even this feels like more than that. Like it's my fucking soul swirling inside of me, yearning to be near her.

"Okay, time. Go eat. Same again after classes. If we want to keep on top form, we'll go into Friday's game with our asses on fire. Scouts will be there. You know the drill."

Heading for the tunnel, Coach doesn't say anything else as he leaves us standing in place. Pulling my helmet off, I drop it at my feet as I swipe my hand through my damp hair.

"You're distracted," Tobias says with a grin, coming to stand in my line of sight, and I sigh at him. "Oh, don't be grumpy, X. Just say the word, and we can get on her good side again."

I scoff at Tobias as I push him back a step. Such a fucker.

"Are you forgetting the part where she said all that shit about standing with her, beside her, or against her? Because I sure as shit didn't, and I don't need anyone else trying to tell me what to do," I grumble as Hunter comes to stand beside me, patting my shoulder harder than is necessary as the rest of the team heads for the tunnel, except Archie. He hangs back on the field but remains out of ear shot.

"Do you even hear yourself, Xavier? We're brothers, which is why Tobias and I are standing here with you instead of hovering near Eden's finish line. And it's exactly why we've kept away."

"You didn't on Saturday," I throw out, interrupting him, but he frowns at me, dropping his helmet beside mine.

"She was in pain, asshole. Like physical pain, and I chose to be there for her. Get over yourself. Or do you want me to complain about the fact you fucked her without even knowing her name?" Hunter grumbles as Tobias frowns at something behind me.

"What the fuck is she doing talking to Billy again?"

In sync, Hunter and I spin around to find her smiling up at Billy. Her blonde hair is tied back off her face as she stands with her hands on her hips, laughing at whatever shit he's saying.

"He needs to remember she's off-limits," I growl out, stepping towards them, but Archie suddenly stands before me, blocking my path.

"No can do, X. Eden is trying to find answers. Her father is dead, murdered, and since no one else is offering any answers, she's hunting for some. Billy's dad is the town's corrupt sheriff, surely he might know something, right?"

Archie gives me a pointed look, rubbing the back of his neck as the three of us stare at him like he has a third head.

"*We* should be trying to help her. Hunter and I voted to do just that, but you're the one putting blockers in the way, man," Tobias murmurs, looking at me out of the corner of his eyes as he straightens his hat into place.

"Listen, I'm not getting involved with you guys. The other week, you were all laughing and joking around my pool without a care in the world. I don't know what changed, but please don't fuck with her. I can deal with you ignoring her, even if I can see how much it annoyed her. It sure as hell beats you bullying her. We all know how sharp your mother's claws can be."

Archie glances in her direction too, his words hanging heavily in the air as Tobias and Hunter stare me down.

"You'll do well to remember that you're talking about Ilana Knight, my fucking mother, Archie," I spit out. He doesn't know the relationship I have with my mother, and he doesn't *need* to know either.

"What I do remember, Xavier, is my mom always opening the door to you. Whenever she saw you down on the beach, throwing rocks in the sea, too afraid to go home, you would wind up at my house and we'd get ice cream. As we got older, we changed, you never took her hand anymore to let her lead you to safety. So she told me I should throw parties instead, give people a safe place to be," Archie states.

His eyes hold mine as he mutters a truth from long ago, although I didn't know the last part. I'm stunned. He's hit a nerve, and he knows it. If anyone else was around right now, I'd knock him to the ground, but he's lucky it's only Tobias and Hunter, and they both know the pain of my childhood. *All* of our childhoods.

Before any of us can respond, Archie takes a backwards step in Eden's direction as she walks towards the tunnel with Billy, his parting words fresh on his lips.

"We always have a choice, Xavier."

Eden

I'm so ready for this school day to be done with. I've heard nothing from the Allstars at all, even though I can feel them staring at me when they think I don't notice.

I'm so over the silent treatment. It's just a pity KitKat and Roxy aren't willing to offer me the silent treatment as well. I'd be happy with the peace and quiet. The rumors and murmurs have suddenly switched from me being a whore to a nobody.

I wish they'd make their minds up, it's giving me fucking whiplash.

"Oh my gosh, I'm starving," Charlie grumbles, rubbing her stomach for added effect, and I roll my eyes. "Come on. Let's go eat. You can tell me what Billy had to say on the way," she adds, linking her arm through mine and pulling me along, giving me no say in the matter. Not that I'd turn her down, I'm starving as well.

Stepping out of the locker room, we follow the crowd to the cafeteria.

"He didn't really have much to say, Charlie," I murmur, not wanting everyone to overhear our conversation. "He's not just going to spill any secrets he knows completely out of the blue to a total stranger, that's not how this works."

We sidestep some stoners, who are pushing and shoving

each other in the middle of the hallway, arguing over who actually bought the ounce they just smoked, but no one pays them any mind, clearly used to their bullshit, and I follow suit. I have way too much shit to be worrying about to add anyone else's problem to the list.

"Oh, did you ask him anything at all?"

"For sure, Charlie. I said, 'hey, Billy, I heard your dad's a corrupt cop, and I was wondering what it would take to dig up some dirt.'" I give her a pointed look, and she at least has the decency to blush a little. "Of course, I didn't. The last time I spoke with him, Hunter soon put an end to it. I have to butter him up a little first, make him feel safe and comfortable knowing the Allstars won't go after him," I add quietly, and she nods in understanding.

"Sorry, I just wish you could have the answers to all of your problems right now." She sweeps her hair behind her ear, offering me a soft smile, and I relax beside her.

"I know, and I appreciate it. I wish that was the case, but nothing is ever that easy, so it definitely won't be any easier in Knight's Creek and you know it."

She hums in agreement as we step into the cafeteria, heading straight for the food. The second I spot tacos on the menu board, I know what I'm having. All the food here has been amazing so far, so I hope they are too. Fish tacos with all the works are my favorite.

We make our way down the line wordlessly, each in our own

thoughts. I feel the eyes from the middle of the room watching my every movement, the Allstars tracking me like predators but too afraid to pounce.

As we get to the end of the line, Archie steps up to join us, offering me a quick smile once he's kissed Charlie good and well, and I love how open and raw they are. Archie isn't afraid to let everyone see how he feels, even if it is about a girl, and Charlie doesn't seem to play any games, revelling in his attention.

"Am I okay to sit with my two favorite ladies for lunch today?" he asks, a wide grin on his face as he strokes his finger down Charlie's face, and I stick my fingers down my throat, faking a gag at them, and they both roll their eyes.

"That depends, is your bold move to lay claim to our girl?" I ask, a hint of teasing in my voice, but I also want to help Charlie understand what they are. She'd voiced her concerns to me the other day, wanting to play it cool, and I agreed to help.

"Our girl? You mean *my* girl, right?" he hollers back instantly, a sparkle in his eyes telling me he knew exactly what he just did, and Charlie rises up on her tiptoes to kiss him.

Well, my work here is done apparently.

Heading for our usual table, I purposely take the longer route so I don't have to directly walk by the Allstars. They're not giving me any attention, good or bad, and I should be glad. God, back at White River, I wouldn't have even offered Xavier and Tobias a second glance after we fucked, and I sure as shit wouldn't have cuddled with Hunter while I was PMS-ing like a bitch. So why am I so riled up by the fact they don't care anymore?

I gave them my whole speech, practically begging them for help, and instead, it pushed them away.

It's fine. It is absolutely fine. At least I know where their loyalties lie—exactly where they've been this whole time.

Dropping my tray to the table, I take my seat, making sure to tuck my miniskirt in so my ass isn't on show. I thought it would have started to cool down by now, but it feels even hotter than it did when I first arrived. Which is why I opted for my black and white striped miniskirt, along with my off the shoulder black ribbed top and sandals.

Charlie drops down into the seat across from me as Archie takes the seat beside her, and I watch for a moment as Archie tries to communicate something, using only his eyes, to someone over my shoulder. My back stiffens, knowing he's broken away from the player's little pack in the center of the room.

I swap glances with Charlie, but Archie must feel our anticipation and focuses on us instead of them, relaxing into his seat as if he's sat there every day.

"It's all good, ladies," he says before taking a giant bite out of one of his burgers, smiling with his mouth full of food.

"You're so gross, Archie," Charlie says with a giggle, and I relax. We really don't need any more drama.

"Aww, look at you. The new girl is officially back to being

a nobody. Did you think you were special? Because you really fucking aren't," Roxy singsongs in a sickly-sweet tone as she takes the seat to my left, and KitKat stands over me to my right. Both are still in their cheerleading outfits, the skirts high up their thighs with no shorts on underneath.

I always speak too soon. That, or drama always has a way of finding me.

"Thank you so much. The level of supportive girl power you give off is totally overwhelming," I say, unable to hold my sarcasm at bay, but Roxy just sneers at me.

"They're mine, they'll always be mine, so back the fuck off."

Rising, Roxy slams her fist into the table, causing everyone's trays to shake. As I turn to look at her, a hand tightens in my hair, pulling my head back sharply, and my gaze snaps up to meet KitKat's, right as she spits in my face.

Spits. In. My. Face.

This bitch. I'm done. Literally fucking done.

I can hear Charlie shouting and screaming at KitKat as Roxy laughs like a hyena beside me.

Before she can do anything else, I pull my arm back and swing my fist straight at her tit, making her grip on me loosen. But before I can swing at her again, she's pulled away from me, my head sagging forward as I catch my breath, the yank on my hair catching me by surprise more than I want to admit.

"Are you okay?" Charlie shouts over all the noise in the

room. Everyone is watching and waiting for more drama to unfold, but I refuse to give it to them.

"I'm fine."

Glancing to my left, I watch Tobias pin Roxy against his chest, holding her away from me as Xavier does the same with KitKat. His eyes are dark as he growls in her ear, and I sigh.

Roxy and KitKat aren't sad or angry that they're being manhandled and treated badly. They're getting the attention they wanted from the Allstars just like they've been craving, completely pliant in their arms. It's embarrassing.

A hand on my shoulder pulls my gaze behind me to find Hunter staring down at me with concern in his eyes. I do *not* need his fucking sympathy. Screw all this bullshit.

"Let me help you—"

"I don't need your help, Hunter. Give the little princesses the attention they so desire, it's wasted on me," I snap, feeling the saliva starting to trail down my face, and I cringe. Scraping my chair back, pushing it into Hunter's legs unapologetically, I grab my bag, watching as Archie and Charlie stare helplessly at me.

Taking slow measured steps, I keep my head held high as I feel everyone in the cafeteria stare at me, a few even have the fucking phones out again. I should start my own YouTube channel for everything that seems to happen to me, at least I'd get the royalties off the views.

The second I'm out in the hallway, I pick up my pace,

refusing to lift a hand to my chin, but not wanting her spit to drop onto my clothes.

Thankfully, the girls' bathroom is only at the end of the hall, and I step inside, slamming the door shut behind me, sighing in relief when I realize no one is in here.

Grabbing a handful of paper towels, I quickly clean my face, wiping the spit repeatedly to make sure it's really gone, glad I didn't put very much makeup on this morning. Tossing the papers in the trash, I brace my hands on the basin, hovering over it as I try to calm my breathing.

I feel like a raging bull. How dare she? How *fucking* dare she? My blood is boiling, my fingers trembling as I try to take deep breaths.

My phone vibrates in my bag at my feet, the sound of a text message coming through following shortly behind it, and I groan. I really don't need someone sending me footage of the damn thing, I only just lived it.

The door swinging open pulls my attention away from going to grab my phone, but the sight of Hunter does little to ease my stress.

"How did you fucking find me?" I grind out, glaring at him as I keep my grip on the basin.

"Eden, you're the new girl. You may as well be walking around with a Google Maps dot above your head. I didn't have to ask very many people to find you." He sighs, his gaze flickering over me, checking I'm okay.

"I'm fine, Hunter. You can leave now."

Turning my back to him, I reach down to grab my phone from my bag, willing to deal with whatever text message came through rather than him right now. But I freeze in place as the words fill my screen.

Unknown: HAVE YOU CONSIDERED WHICH SONGS WILL BE PLAYED AT YOUR WAKE YET? WHATEVER I BURY YOU IN IS WHAT YOU'LL SPEND THE REST OF ETERNITY WEARING. PICK YOUR FUTURE OUTFITS WISELY. THIS ONE'S FOR YOU.

CLICK THE LINK BELOW.

EDEN GRADY'S OBITUARY.

What the hell? I don't need to see anything more right now.

I've had nothing, not a single message, since the football game, so why now all of a sudden? Why moments after I was just attacked again by KitKat and Roxy? Does this lead back to them?

I don't hear Hunter step up behind me, and before I can hide my phone, he's pulling it from my hands. He doesn't move from behind me, pulling my back to his chest as his eyes scan over the screen.

Within seconds, he's putting his own phone to his ear, his arm locking around my waist as he does.

"Yeah. No. No. Just… Just shut the fuck up for a second, X," he growls out, his temper catching me by surprise in comparison to the soft strokes against my stomach at the same time. "She just got another message. A threatening one again. No. We lock this shit down right now, Xavier... I don't give a fuck. Give the vote, Xavier... I said give the fucking vote, Xavier."

I have no idea what's going on between them, but the tension radiating off of Hunter is on another level. Especially when I thought he was the quiet and collected one of the group. Clearly, I was wrong.

"What's going—"

My question is cut off as Hunter shushes me, and my mouth falls open. Who does this man think he is? Some whore just spat in my fucking face, and he has the audacity to shush me when I just got a threatening text message too.

No. No way.

"Fine, I'm in," I hear Xavier growl down the line, and I frown in confusion.

"Good because we need a plan, and we need it now." Without another word, Hunter ends the call, pocketing his phone along with mine as he remains at my back, turning us to face the mirror.

My heart rate picks up, this time from his intoxicating gaze as I watch him watch me through the mirror. His green eyes brighten as he gives off a protective vibe.

"I feel like something important just happened, and I have no idea what," I whisper, holding his gaze through the glass.

"We'll help you."

"You'll what?" His words catch me by surprise, making me

frown at him as he slowly brings his other hand to my chin, tilting my head a little higher.

"All votes have to be unanimous. They weren't before, they are now," he states simply, brushing his lips against my cheek so sweetly that I almost forget the shit show happening around me right now.

I have no idea what that means, but if it keeps him this close to me, I don't really care, even though I know I should.

TOXIC CREEK

KC KEAN

THIRTY THREE
Eden

The waves crash against the rocks, soothing my mind as I stare out of the huge window at Pete's. I'm back in the booth with the Allstars, while Archie and Charlie are sitting a couple of tables away. I don't want these three in my space at Archie's right now, and they refused to let Archie and Charlie come with me to their home, so here we are.

Tobias is sitting to my left, while Xavier and Hunter sit to my right. Thankfully, it's not too busy in here, but there are a few tables filled with couples and families since school has just finished.

Xavier grumbled about not agreeing to discuss things freely with them present, but they didn't want to leave me alone and this was our compromise.

I'm still reeling from the fact that bitch spat in my face, never mind the threatening text message. I'm over this town and all its toxicity, maybe I should just cut my losses and run. They might chase, they might not, but at least things would be on *my* terms.

"What's up, honey?" Linda asks as she brings our tray of drinks over, pulling my gaze from the window as I offer her a soft smile.

"I'm fine, Linda," I murmur, taking the iced tea from her as she gives me a pointed look.

"And how many times have you said that today, hmm?" Too many times to remember, I think. Both to myself and out loud, I have repeated those two words over and over since getting here in general. "This is always a safe place for you, Eden. Understand?"

Linda keeps her eyes on mine, swiping her hands down her apron as she does, and I nod in agreement.

"Thank you."

"You're welcome. If you guys need anything else, you let me know, okay?"

I watch as she walks away, smiling and talking to all the customers as she does. I'm glad we agreed to come here. It literally is safe territory.

"We need a plan," Hunter finally says when no one is around us. "I've run checks on the number again, and the message was definitely from a different number, but they didn't seem to have set up the same defense system because I was at least able to trace it to the school."

"It's a student, it has to be," Tobias mutters, leaning forward, folding his arms on the table, and I nod in agreement.

"Tobias, it could be anyone. The janitor, a teacher, hell, it could be Mr. Bernard. If this somehow links back to Ilana, then she could be having someone do her dirty work," Xavier admits, and my eyes widen in surprise.

I still didn't believe Hunter when he said they would help, but Xavier seems to be much more open about discussing his mother in comparison to usual. He sees the expression on my face and rolls his eyes, fully aware I'm seeing the change in him.

"I can stop offering to help if you're going to stare at me like that," he grumbles, taking a drink of his soda as he hunches forward.

"Suit yourself, Xavier. I've had enough whiplash from your hot and cold behavior, I really do have enough on my plate already. So just leave if you wish." I stare him down, my fingers tapping on the table as I do, and he sneers.

"You think because I fucked you and your mouth that counts as hot and cold behavior? Nafas, honestly, we're good at hating each other. There's nothing more to it. You're just getting all prissy because I'm not stumbling over my own feet to get to you like these two."

"Fuck you!" I growl back, my hands clenching on the table,

my nails biting into my skin.

"Nah, fuck me," Tobias jumps in, catching me by surprise and cooling the moment as a bubble of laughter escapes my lips at his outburst.

Tilting my face to the ceiling, I take a deep breath before looking at Hunter, who seems to be the only sane one at the table right now.

"So we need a plan to figure out if it is a student or not."

Hunter hums his agreement, his gaze focused on his phone as he taps away. "Agreed," he mutters, placing his phone down on the table as he leans back in his seat, glancing at me.

"If it was a student, it would never just be a solo act. No one in this town has enough backbone for that. It would likely be a few people, especially if they're going against what we said," Xavier chimes in, looking anywhere but at me as he voices his opinion.

"Which means they'd obviously talk about it," Hunter responds, and I sit back watching with slight awe at the way they naturally bounce off each other.

"Every time Eden has received a text, it's been when she's been alone in a public place. At the game, and in the bathroom," Tobias adds, pointing the times out on his fingers as he goes. "Maybe we should recreate some sort of scenario like that again, but this time, we would maybe have more control over the whole situation."

"You mean at a game again?" I ask, resting my chin on my

hand as I think.

"Maybe, I don't know. But Hunter could slip in early, set up some of his listening devices and cameras, or whatever. We would just have to have someone not on the team who we trust to have your back in case something does happen." Tobias looks to Hunter and Xavier, confirming what he's saying, and I have to admit, I'm impressed.

Them stepping up and offering to help has instantly changed where I stand. If we can get past this, then it may lead to more answers regarding my family as a whole. I don't want to push for clarification on what they're willing to help me with in fear they'll go back to running for the hills.

"I could ask Bethany to get a sitter and maybe bring Ryan with her," Hunter offers, and I stare at him in confusion. "Ryan is Bethany's husband. He runs a security business two towns over."

"He's literally a beast," Tobias adds, and I nod as I take another deep breath.

"What would I need to do?" I ask, willing to do just about anything at this stage to pull myself out of this stagnant water I'm in.

"Just be your annoying self, Eden. That seems to work already," Xavier grumbles, and I bite my cheek to hold my words, not wanting to ruin the progress I feel like we're making.

"Oh my god, you look like you want to punch him in the dick," Tobias says with a chuckle beside me, always trying to diffuse the situation, and I grin.

"I want to R.K.O him Randy Orton style so bad," I mumble, widening my eyes, and Hunter laughs just as loud as Tobias, causing a few tables around us to glance our way.

"You three are all ridiculous," Xavier grouses, but the harshness in his tone has lowered.

My phone suddenly starts to vibrate on the table, *Mom* flashing across the screen, and I quickly answer.

"Hey, Mom," I murmur, holding my breath as I wait for her voice to filter through the line.

"Hey, I wasn't sure if I'd catch you or not since it's still school hours," she says, sounding tired as she sighs.

"Yeah, some stuff happened, and I'm just at Pete's now."

"Wait, Pete's as in Pete's diner on the water's edge?" she asks, her voice brightening, and I smile.

"Yeah, you've been here?"

"Eden, we practically lived there as kids. Linda took no shit, while Pete hid in the back, cooking the whole time. I think I may have seen him once, maybe twice in all the years I went in." I can sense her taking a trip down memory lane, and I hate being so close to her past, and being unable to learn more.

"I haven't met Pete yet, but Linda seems like the exact same person. She has no filter," I say with a smile, and I hear my mom chuckle in agreement.

"So what happened? Why aren't you at school?"

"Oh, uh, it was nothing," I ramble, my eyes flickering to the guys, and Tobias mouths for me to tell her. Squeezing my eyes shut, I take a leap of faith, and do as he says. "Someone has sent me two strange messages, and I'm just with some friends trying to see if we can get to the bottom of it."

"What messages?" she shouts down the phone, and I cringe, keeping my eyes closed as I sink back into my seat.

"Mom, it's nothing to—"

"Tell me. Now."

Swiping a hand down my face, I jolt in surprise as a hand wraps around mine, and I turn to find Tobias lacing his fingers through mine, squeezing them in support. I don't dwell on his comforting actions as I take a deep breath and repeat the text messages to my mom.

"Oh, Eden. I feel like history is literally repeating itself."

My blood stills at her words, my eyes flashing open to stare at the others around the table, who instantly pick up on my change in demeanour.

"What do you mean by that?"

It feels like an eternity before she responds, leaving me hanging with bated breath as I try to figure out what she means.

"There isn't very much I can say, Eden. But when I was your age, I found myself trapped in a coffin and buried in the sand as some joke gone wrong. Fuck. Eden, it was Ilana. I never knew for sure, but no one else could have been behind it."

"Wait, what? What do you mean someone actually did that to you?" Tobias squeezes my hand as my fingers tremble, the threats feeling much heavier than they did moments ago.

"Has Ilana shown her face yet? I know she was pregnant around the same time as us leaving, so her child won't be much different in age to you. Have you met them?"

My eyes fall to Xavier's, watching as he grinds his jaw, somehow hearing my mother's words through the phone, and I panic.

"No, no I haven't met them," I lie, surprise morphing Xavier's face as much as my own as I sigh.

"Good. Don't ever trust a Knight. They're liars, full of half-truths and filled with snake venom. They'll bite you, gut you, and toss you aside without a backwards glance, all for their own personal gain."

"I have to go, Mom," I whisper, my heart pounding in my ear as I keep my eyes fixed on Xavier, anger darkening his eyes as he turns away, looking out of the window.

"Remember what I said, Eden. I love you."

Nobody says a word as I place my phone on the table, my goodbye stuck on the end of my tongue since she ended the call before I could respond.

Swallowing past the lump in my throat, I release Tobias' hand as I sit taller.

"So, this plan," I say, my voice filled with determination as I act like my mother didn't just warn me against Xavier, and sigh.

"We'll set up the game on Friday, Nafas," he murmurs before climbing over Hunter and storming from the diner without a backwards glance, his change in mood surprising me.

Well at least my mom had that part right. He never looks back. Ever. But maybe he isn't as diabolical as his mother.

KC KEAN

THIRTY FOUR
Eden

The smell of sweat, and year-old socks fills the air as I try not to breathe in the stench that is the football players' locker room.

It's hot as hell outside, so I'm wearing my very own Asheville Allstars jersey, no name on the back, with a pair of denim shorts and sandals. But I can almost feel the germs sticking to my legs, just like my sandals feel glued to the floor.

They're all totally gross. Hot or not, I don't want to touch a single thing they have.

"Tell me the plan again, Eden," Hunter says, pulling his own jersey on as my eyes fixate on his bare abs. "Eyes, Eden."

Quickly pulling my gaze to his, he grins at me, expecting me to blush, but that's not my style.

"The plan is to watch the game from Archie's family spot again. Stay close to Bethany or Ryan at all times. Ryan is going to have the feed access for the cameras and audio pieces. Hopefully, someone tries to make a move, and we'll be able to catch them with the few members of Ryan's security team that are stationed around the stadium."

"Good. Now get out of the locker room," Tobias murmurs with a wink, and I roll my eyes.

"It'll be my pleasure, I'd quite happily never come in here *ever* again."

Heading straight for the door, the other players ignore me, except Billy, who smiles at me, biting his lip as he watches me walk away. I try to keep my facial expression neutral, not wanting to lead him on anymore than I have to.

But the backup plan is to hopefully catch someone out at the after-party. Unless Billy knows some of his daddy's secrets, then I might get answers that way. I'm beyond caring how I get the information anymore, I just want it.

Stepping out into the tunnel, I'm surprised to find no one here. The cheer squad is on the field, entertaining the crowd, so it makes sense.

Fixing my sunglasses in place, I pause when a hand wraps around my arm, and I almost squeal when they spin me. My back hits the concrete wall as I come face-to-face with Xavier.

"Xavier, don't do that," I mutter, my hand on my chest as he stares me down, my heart beating in my chest.

We've said very little over the few days since everything kind of exploded and he agreed to help. My mother's words seemed to cut him a little deeper than I expected, but ultimately, my guess was he didn't like being categorized with his mother.

I don't want to press anything with him. Realistically, my mom's words will continue to hover at the back of my mind, but I have zero expectations of the guy standing in front of me. Offering him even an inch would end in heartache. He's already shown how little he cares.

Chest to chest, I have to tilt my head back to meet his gaze. Raising his hands, he plants them firmly on either side of me, caging me in, and my heart stutters for a completely different reason.

"Why is there no name on your jersey?" he asks, searching my eyes for his answer, and I frown.

"Because wearing Archie's isn't the right thing to do now that he's all official with Charlie," I state. As girl code, Archie may be my friend, and Charlie hasn't mentioned a word, but it's the right thing to do. Period.

Dropping his arms to his side, he doesn't move out of my personal space as he slowly grabs the back of his jersey and pulls it over his head.

My mouth goes dry as he stands before me in his pants and pads, his gaze burning mine as he holds his jersey between us. Seemingly unable to find his words, he nods down at the jersey in his hands, indicating for me to take it from him, and my hand wraps around the material before I can even process what I'm doing.

"Put it on now," he whispers, his voice thick and husky, making my thighs rub together.

He's much too close, in my face with no apologies as he attempts to keep his emotions under control, when really, he's staking his claim without uttering a single word.

Releasing the jersey into my hands, his fingers go to the hem of the jersey I'm already wearing, and my hands lift over my head as he strips it from my skin. Not caring if anyone is around, in just my black lace bra, I keep my eyes on him.

The coil of the muscles in his arms, the clenching of his jaw, and the burning in his hazel eyes as he looks me over. He isn't as unaffected as he acts, and admittedly, neither am I.

There is just something about these Allstars that continuously has me coming back for more.

Discarding the other jersey, he makes quick work of taking the jersey from my hands and slipping it over my head, his fingers grazing my sides as he pulls it down, leaving me utterly speechless.

Leaning in, his nose brushing mine, he places a kiss to the corner of my lips, stealing my breath, before he's gone again.

"What was that for?" I manage to ask, my fingers touching where he just pressed his lips, but he shrugs his shoulders.

"I don't know, Nafas. For not letting your mom's words tarnish me with the same brush, I guess." With a deep sigh, he steps farther back. "Remember the rules, Eden," he mutters before heading back inside the locker room.

Who the fuck was that? And what did they do with the douchebag asshole that is usually Xavier Knight? And why can't I seem to keep any distance between us?

Shaking my head, I take a deep breath before grabbing the perfectly fine jersey off the ground and turning to head towards the stands, only to find Ryan waiting casually at the end of the hallway.

He doesn't say a word, so I choose to keep my mouth shut too, quickly following after him to find Bethany waiting in the same seat as last time. My fingers mindlessly stroke over the jersey, trying to understand why he gave me his, but I never want to guess with Xavier because nothing ever actually makes sense with him.

"Hey, girl. How are you doing?" she asks as soon as I take my seat, and I relax beside her.

She's openly calm and caring. I don't know if it has something to do with the fact she's a mom and it's just her maternal side kicking in, but either way, I feel like I could tell her anything. She has that way about her, just like Hunter did when I told him my story.

"I'm fine. I just want shit to be over with," I answer honestly, and she sighs, likely feeling the pressure this town puts on everyone.

"We'll figure it out. Especially Hunter. Once he puts his

mind to something, there's no stopping him until he has the answers." She turns her gaze to the field, watching as the music changes and the players start to come out.

"That's what I'm hoping for to be honest."

Charlie catches my eye, smiling and waving up at me as she joins the rest of the cheerleaders on the front row, making sure to sit as far away as possible from Roxy and KitKat. I worry that I've made her life harder with all the shit going on, but these bitches were going to act like this to someone, she just happens to be my friend. I don't get to control their behavior.

As the referee blows the whistle, the first quarter starts, and I relax into my seat, enjoying the view of the field. All those muscled thighs and bulging arms offer the perfect amount of eye candy to go along with the sport.

"Does anyone want a drink?" Ryan asks in his gruff voice, and I shake my head. Bethany is all small and petite, while Ryan looks like a bodybuilder, but the way he looks at her is next level breathtaking. Their love for each other written all over their faces.

"I'm good, thank you," I answer, offering a quick smile before turning back to the game.

Within minutes of him being gone, I feel the hairs on the back of my neck stand on end. There's someone here, I can feel it in my bones.

Glancing over my shoulder, I try to get a good look at the people surrounding me. With all the cheering and chatter going on, it's hard to pick out anyone acting suspicious. Everything looks exactly as it should, yet I don't feel any better at all.

"I'm going to quickly go to the bathroom," I murmur, smiling at Bethany, who instantly stands, ready to come with me, but I wave her off. "Honestly, don't worry. I know Ryan is up there, I'll let him know what I'm doing when I get up there."

Staring me down for a moment, she finally relents, letting me pass so I can get to the steps. I just need a minute. All the noise is playing fucking tricks on me.

Trying to get through the crowd at the top of the stairs is a nightmare, everyone standing in line for the concessions stand, a few rowdier than others as I try to get past, and someone barges past me, shoving me into a group of guys at my side.

Managing to remain on my feet, my hands outstretched in front of me as I grab on to one of the men, I try to regain my balance.

"Oh my god, I'm so sorry, I—"

"Don't worry, miss," he responds, cutting off my apology, and I smile in thanks.

The cheering outside kicks up, meaning more points for the Allstars, as someone wraps their arm around my shoulder, pulling me into their chest.

"Eden, you need to be more careful," they mutter, making me frown in confusion.

Glancing to my left, I see a guy I don't recognize, possibly a few years older than me, his face long and gaunt, his eyes almost black as he attempts to plaster a smile on his face.

"Sorry, my girl is a little worse for wear, day drinking really isn't for her," the guy says, laughing with the guy I just stumbled into, and I frown up at him.

My attempt to push him off is weak as his arm pins me in a vice-like grip.

"I...I..."

"Don't worry, I've got you. Let's get out of here, okay?"

"No. Let's not go anywhere. Who the—"

My words are cut off as he slams his fist into my stomach where no one can actually see, and I lean forward, pain ripping through my body as he mutters another apology and pulls me away.

My feet drag along the floor as I try to catch a breath. This motherfucker winded me.

"Get the fuck off me," I growl out, my voice hoarse as I push against him, but he just grins.

"I wouldn't fight me, Eden. It won't end well for dear old mommy if you do." His words have me freezing in my fight against him, my legs moving in step with his willingly as fear starts to seep in. "That's it. If you can keep quiet like this, maybe at least one of you will survive the night, huh?"

The stench of cigarettes wafts over my face as he grins down at me, his yellow crooked teeth on full display as I recoil.

Heading for the steps that lead to the parking lot, my feet stumble over a few steps, my eyes flickering around for any of Ryan's men as I scramble to think of a safe way out of this situation. But my mom's safety plays heavily on my mind.

"Who is making you do this?" I ask, praying for any sort of information and hoping we're close to one of the audio systems that are set up, but in all honesty, I have no idea how this shit works.

"That's information I'm sure you'll find out sooner or later," he mutters, pushing me through the open doors into the open space outside.

Without his arm banded tight around me, I put one foot in front of the other and start to run, my fear taking over as my sandals instantly flick off my feet, but I don't care. I refuse to let this guy get the better of me. We were supposed to have the upper hand, but this greasy fucker just appeared out of nowhere. It doesn't make sense.

The wind whips through my hair as my heart pounds out of my chest, my pulse screaming in my ears as a sharp tug at my scalp stops my movement. Pulling me back by my hair, the greaseball growls down at me as I swing my arms around.

A bang sounds from behind me, and I fall, tumbling backwards, my head hitting the concrete ground.

Groaning, I roll to my side, nausea rising to the back of my throat as I reel in agony, my vision turning to black as I bite back my sobs as my skull burns with pain.

"It's okay, Eden. I've got you."

Who? Who's got me?

They smell like sweat and sex, and as I snuggle into their chest, I feel like I'm floating. My problems drifting away as I let sleep consume me.

TOXIC CREEK

THIRTY FIVE

Xavier

As soon as the ball leaves my hands, flying through the air in Hunter's direction, I know he's going to make it. The ball slips into his hands perfectly as he takes off down the field. The play goes perfectly before my eyes, the crowd cheering as he makes it to the end zone.

Pride washes over me, my love for the game and the execution of my skill getting us the points fills me with hope for a future. A future where I get to play the game I love and be the person I want to be. Although I'm not too sure who that is anymore because of a pretty blonde siren.

Tobias pats my helmet as Hunter charges towards us, almost knocking me clean off my feet as he wraps his arm around my shoulder, an extra bounce in his step as we make it off the field, letting the defense take over.

Trying to discreetly look up at the crowd, searching out Eden, I come up empty. My pace slows as I scan my eyes across rows, stalling when I see Bethany on the phone, concern on her face as she frantically searches around her.

Something isn't right. I can feel it.

"What's wrong with Bethany?" Tobias asks, stopping beside me too as Hunter follows our gaze.

"Let me check," Hunter murmurs, crouching down beside the bench where he had placed his phone. We don't usually allow ourselves any distractions during a game, but today is a little different.

Wordlessly pulling my helmet off, I watch as Hunter does the same, bringing his phone to his ear as he does.

"What's going on?" he asks, bypassing the usual pleasantries as he freezes. Dropping my helmet to the grass, I instantly grow impatient as Tobias does the same, rubbing the back of his neck.

"They can't find her. She's not on the cameras or coming through on the audio," he mutters, and my heart pounds in my chest.

She couldn't have gone far, I saw her minutes ago, I know I did. I've been checking repeatedly.

"What's going on?" Archie asks, coming to join us, and I know I need to act fast, act *now* before something else goes wrong.

"They can't find Eden," Tobias answers, and my feet are

moving me toward the tunnel before my brain even catches up.

Rushing to the locker room, I grab my phone and pull up the app I'm looking for.

"What are you doing?" Hunter asks, and I sigh in relief, the little red dot flashing on the screen like a beacon.

"We need to move, now," I order, looking up to see Archie, Hunter, and Tobias before me. "I gave her a jersey, my jersey, with a pin on the neckline. It had a tracker fitted in the pin, just in case," I say, heading for the door and racing through the hall to get to the parking lot.

"Holy fuck," Tobias shouts in surprise, chasing after me, with Hunter and Archie behind him.

Nobody says any more, the sound of our cleats pounding on the ground the only noise surrounding us except the call from the coach, likely wondering what the fuck we're doing, but I don't have time to answer.

Spotting a fire exit door, I push through, pausing as I step out into the packed parking lot, just as a whip of blonde hair catches my attention in the distance.

"There. Over there," Hunter growls out, and we set off together, rushing through the cars as a guy wraps his hand in her blonde hair and yanks her back into him.

Motherfucker.

Tobias rushes towards him, aiming straight for the guy's legs as he charges, knocking him off his feet. The guy cries out in pain, but my focus is on Eden.

In slow motion, she falls backwards, and my heart stops as I try to rush to her as quickly as possible, but her head cracks off the gravel just as my fingers touch her hair.

"No. No, no, no, no, no!" Archie cries, dropping down beside me as I pull her away from Tobias as he lays punch after punch into the guy as he cries out in pain.

I watch as she rolls on her side, her face distorting in pain as she whimpers. Cradling her head in my lap, I pull her close, trying to be as gentle as I can.

"It's okay, Eden. I've got you," I whisper, my own panicked eyes searching for Hunter, who pulls Tobias off the fucker lying flat out on the ground beside us.

Is that Graham Brummer? Billy's older brother? Billy's disowned junkie brother?

Someone's using him. We just squashed their attempts, but my gut tells me this was a test to see if we would react.

"What the fuck is going on?" Hunter asks, his eyes flicking from mine to Graham as he releases Tobias, who drops down beside me, stroking his fingers through her hair.

"I don't know, Hunter. But am I stupid to think this was a game? A trial run to see if or how I or we would react to something happening to Eden?" I ask, holding her a little tighter as I do, watching as Hunter shakes his head.

"Boys, what the hell are you doing?" Coach Carmichael growls out, standing off to the side, and I dread to think what is happening on the field right now.

Fuck the game, fuck all of this shit.

I think we've just been played.

"Where the fuck am I?" Eden groans, dragging a hand down her face as I sit back in my chair, putting my phone away as I meet her gaze.

"Oh good, Princess Eden is awake. You snore by the way," I mumble, and she frowns at me like I'm speaking another language.

"Is this your room?" she asks, glancing around the space, and I try to see it through her eyes. Compared to the rest of the house, which offers little more than a showroom home, there is a lot of me in this space.

All the different jerseys I've ever worn are pinned to the wall next to the door, my trophies sitting perfectly organized below them on shelves. My closet is off to the right, while my bathroom is on our left, but I think it's the wall above my desk by the window that will hold her attention the most.

Photos on photos line the wall. Full print colors, black and whites, landscapes, portraits, everything. I love the muted beauty a photo offers, speaking a thousand words without noise. This damn town is filled with so much toxic noise, it ruins the scenery.

Flicking my eyes in her direction, I watch as she sees my newest obsession, my hands squeezing the wooden arms of my chair as her mouth falls open in surprise.

The doctor promised she was fine and we just had to keep an eye on her. I was unsure, worrying there was more to her fall than he was letting on, but the way she jumps out of my bed and races to the door tells me he was right.

"Xavier, this is—"

"Not really for your eyes," I say, cutting her off, not needing her judgement, and her gaze snaps to mine before she raises her hand to her head, moving too quickly, and I jump from my seat. "Sit down, Eden," I murmur, grabbing her arm to walk her to the bed, but she simply raises her eyebrow at me. "Please," I add with a sigh, and she relents.

Dropping down onto my bed, her eyes go back to the wall, and I take a seat beside her, my heart pounding in my chest. I knew she'd see, but I couldn't bear to let her rest anywhere else. I refuse to overanalyze it right now.

A few hours ago, I was cradling her on the concrete ground outside of the stadium, knowing in my gut my mother was behind all of this yet unable to put any distance between us.

"Xavier," she whispers, pulling her gaze to mine. "When... H-how... I..."

"You know, you're always walking away from me, Nafas, and somehow, I just seem to keep chasing," I murmur, speaking my truth for the first time as her gaze slips back to the section of the wall which is covered in photos of her.

There are pictures of her from the day she first showed

up. I was down at the party while she leaned over her balcony, watching the ocean. Her first day of school, at Pete's, and a few of her running on the beach. Ninety percent of them are of her walking away, turning her back on me like she always does. It's the only opportunity I have, and I can't pass them up.

The girl who confuses my brain, fucks with my control, and leaves me wanting more. She's intoxicating—to all of us. Whether I like it or not, she's under my skin.

"I can't decide if I'm flattered or in need of a restraining order," she murmurs, a grin on her lips as she rests her head on my shoulder, and I release a sigh, her body saying more than her words. "You continue to surprise me, Xavier. I guess Tobias isn't the only one interested in my bubble butt."

Sitting side by side, her head on my shoulder, I wrap my arm around her waist and take a moment to sit in peace, like our lives aren't totally fucked up.

"Thank you for saving me," she says, looking up at me, and I wipe a hand over my mouth.

"Hmm, you're welcome, but our troubles aren't over," I admit, and she nods in understanding.

"Tell me."

"The guy that grabbed you was Graham Brummer, Billy's older brother. He's a nobody, and a tool in a grander scheme I'm sure. But Archie is still going to throw a party tonight so we can try and get Billy alone, see what he knows."

Sitting up straight, she brushes her hair from her face and

looks me dead in the eyes. "I want to be there. I deserve to—"

"I had a feeling you would. We all know you're stubborn, you don't need to sell it to us," I say as she clears her throat, nodding in agreement.

"Hopefully, whoever is behind this will get desperate." Standing, she stretches her arms above her head. "I just need some painkillers, maybe a couple of those mood boosters too if I plan to get through the night."

"Tobias will take you home and stay with you while you get ready. Hunter and I will try to form a loose plan and meet you over there in a little while." Rising beside her, she offers me a small smile as a knock sounds at the door, and Tobias pops his head around the door.

"How's our damsel in distress?" he asks, making Eden roll her eyes.

"I'm fine. I've had worse headaches putting up with you guys. This is nothing," she says with a smirk as she walks over to him.

Wrapping his arm around her shoulder, he leads her from the room without a backward glance. The second they're out of sight, I send the message that's been prepared and waiting on my phone.

The only way we're going to start getting any kind of answers is if I confront my mother.

The quicker I get this over with, the sooner I can join everyone else at the party. I already sent Hunter over to set up a few audio recorders so we can have ears everywhere tonight. I needed something to get him out of the house, and that worked. He doesn't need to be here for this.

I'm fastening the last button on my shirt as I head down the stairs when the front door swings open, and the sound of her heels click on the marble floor.

"Mother," I say in a way of greeting as she props her sunglasses on top of her head, raising her eyebrow at me in question. There's never any pleasantries with her. Ever. Today won't be any different. She's in her usual tailored suit, her long-sleeved sheer shirt a desperate attempt at staying young.

"What's so urgent you invited me over here, Xavier?" she asks, turning her back to me as she heads into the lounge, and I try to not roll my eyes as I follow after her. I leave the front door open, she'll be heading out soon enough. Although, I'm a little surprised my father isn't with her. He does well at being her lap dog. It's embarrassing.

"I just wondered when you were going to catch me up to speed on everything you have going on around town at the moment," I answer, watching as she heads straight for the liquor cabinet as always, and I sigh.

Remaining on my feet, she takes her time getting comfortable in the chair by the open fireplace, straightening her outfit as she stares me down.

"I have no idea what you're talking about, Xavier."

"Don't play coy, Mother. It doesn't suit you," I say,

throwing her own words back at her, and she smirks. "What games are going on that I don't know about?" I repeat, watching the challenge shimmer in her eyes as she sips her favorite brand of bourbon.

"Xavier, I don't—"

"Don't fucking lie, *Mom*," I bite out, clenching my jaw as my hands fist at my side. "What's with the new girl? The mind games? You expect me to step into the family business, but you tell me nothing."

My mother is a saint by day and devil by night, running legitimate businesses through multiple companies in the day, laundering her dirty money from her insider trading and corrupt under-the-table business deals that take place once the sun has gone down.

Knight's Casino is the biggest front, allowing her to do whatever she wishes and letting others pay her to do the same. It welcomes criminals and two-faced politicians in, promising them anonymity, only to exploit them for her own gain later.

Ilana Knight is the queen on the chessboard, the rest of us her pawns to do with as she wishes.

"Feisty, Xavier," she says with a grin, never allowing herself to act surprised by my outbursts, but her white knuckles wrapped around her glass tell me I'm walking a thin line. "It's simple really, I don't trust you."

I frown at her words, confused why she would say that as I pace back and forth on her favorite Persian red rug. "What have

I done to make you not trust me?"

Placing her glass on the coaster on the small wooden side table beside her, she clasps her hands together in her lap.

"She is a test. Eden Grady is a test, and you're failing."

"What?" I fake surprise, but I had a feeling back at the stadium, and my gut isn't usually wrong.

"Jennifer Grady was everything I despised, making Eden Grady the exact same by association. I sent her family away because I fucking could. Nobody hurts me without feeling the consequences. I set out the rules, and they chose not to follow them. Which meant I had to make an example out of the Grady family."

She's crazy, my mother is officially batshit crazy. Shaking my head, I try to understand what Eden's parents must have done to begin with.

"What—"

"I know about Ohio State," she says, taking another sip of bourbon and licking her lips as she watches my reaction. My pulse picks up, my heartbeat pounding in my ears, but I force myself to just stare her down, giving nothing away as I freeze in place.

It's like a staring contest, each of us waiting for the other to break. I bite my tongue. Of course she fucking knows. It was naïve of me to believe she didn't, but I won't utter a word until she continues. In some instances, like now, we're too alike.

"I'll let you go, but it comes at a price," she finally adds with a sigh, tapping her fingernails against her glass.

Of course there's a price. There is *always* a price with this woman, but I really want to play football. I want out of this town, and Ohio State has always been the dream.

"Eden is the price," I murmur, gulping down the bile slowly rising, and she smiles wide.

"Yes. Her family broke me, and I'll break her, just like I did her parents. I want her spiralling further into chaos than she already is."

"Why?" I ask, my mind filled with my own brand of chaos as I try to play this cool.

Is Ohio State worth giving up Eden before I've even really had her? I haven't even given into how I feel about her, not really. Could I slip back into the careless Xavier I usually am, or am I too far gone on her?

"The why isn't for you to know, maybe not just yet at least. Not without proving yourself. So what do you say?"

"What is it you expect me to do?" I ask, and her eyes light up, loving that I'm willing to listen and bend to her will.

"Like I said, break her. I know you saved her from the Brummer boy. Does she think you love her? Does she love you?" She cackles, throwing her head back in delight as I remain still, staring her down as I wait for her to continue. Rising from the chair, she stops right in front of me, the devil burning in her eyes.

"How am I supposed to do that?"

"I'm going to tell you something about little Eden, and you're going to help shatter any last strands of hope she has left. I recall her mother telling her not to trust anyone, and she didn't listen. Tell her. That's how I'll know where you stand, agreed?"

Eden

My head doesn't hurt as much now, but I definitely won't be drinking, that's for sure. The back of my head is super sensitive and likely covered in bruises, but I refuse to look. Instead, I take some of Hunter's little magic pills. All natural herbal mood boosters are my current go to. The world doesn't seem so dark after one of these.

"You ready, gorgeous?" Tobias asks from his spot on my bed as I finish off my look in my walk-in closet.

Opting for my favorite long-sleeved, black cropped top that has a deep V and cutouts on the side with a matching black miniskirt, I'm good to go. Sticking to simple sandals and an ankle bracelet, the rest of my jewelry is minimal, and my hair is framing my face in beach waves.

Stepping back into my room, I feel Tobias' gaze heat my skin instantly.

"You are something else, bubble," he murmurs, standing from my bed as he slowly prowls towards me.

"Flattery will get you everywhere right now while I feel

sorry for myself," I admit, and he grins, wrapping his arms around me as he places a gentle kiss to my forehead, and I can't help but hum at the delicate touch.

"Hmm, I'll remember that. Hunter just messaged to say Xavier is here now too, and all his tech shit is organized."

"Good, hopefully we can get Billy to talk," I mutter in response as Tobias steps back and opens my door for me, and I lock it shut behind us.

Lacing his fingers through mine, Tobias guides me down the stairs, and I let him, allowing myself a moment to lean on somebody else, even if it is just for a night. I'm a little banged up, and admittedly, I was scared earlier. But being with him makes me feel a little safer.

Cutting through the groups of people on the ground floor, we step outside, and Charlie spots me immediately, releasing Archie's hand to come barreling towards me.

"Hey, girl. How are you feeling?" she asks, linking her arm through mine as Tobias refuses to release my hand, and she grins.

"I'm okay, thanks," I answer, having to shout a little over the music from here, and she smiles.

"Listen, do you guys want to stay and hang up here for a bit? I don't think you want to go down by the fire right now," she says, leaning in to whisper in my ear, and I frown. Why would she say that?

"What the fuck?" Tobias mutters, looking down at the

beach, but I can't really see from here.

Moving towards the steps, Charlie lets go of my arm as Tobias squeezes my fingers.

There, sitting by the fire in a deck chair, is Xavier with Roxy on his lap. His hand is on her bare thigh as she nips at his chin, giggling as he laughs with some guys from the football team.

"What the fuck is he doing?" Hunter growls out, coming to stand in front of me, and my eyebrows knit together as I stare at him. I don't have the answer, and it seems these two don't either.

"I don't know, but we won't find out standing here," Tobias says, glancing down at me with an apologetic look.

Why is everyone worried about my reaction? First Charlie, now Tobias. I want to rip her goddamn hands off him, but he's a grown ass man who can make his own life choices. He just has to fucking stand by them.

As I move toward Xavier, Tobias still holding my hand as Hunter places the palm of his hand on my lower back, he finally looks our way. His eyes are a black void of any emotion, and I know instantly that the guy from earlier is gone. Any inkling of emotion that had simmered in his eyes is gone. His body language closed off.

"Tobias, man, get the shots in, yeah?" he says with a laugh, and Roxy giggles like it's the best joke she's heard all year.

"No, no, Xavier. Tell them what you just told us. It's brilliant. Eden, will *definitely* want to hear this one," she says with a smirk on her lips as she strokes her fingers through his hair.

Archie and Charlie move to our right. Charlie looks like she's ready to rip her apart, while Archie stands stock-still, looking between Xavier and Roxy.

"I can get rid of her if you want?" Archie asks, turning to look at me, but she interrupts before I can respond.

"No way, Archie, you'll want to hear this too. Won't he Xavier, baby?" she teases. "As a matter of fact, Archie, when's your birthday again?" she asks, and he frowns.

"September twenty-first," he answers, bored with her games already, and my eyes widen in surprise.

That's my birthday too.

"That's right, and does anyone else here have the same birthday?" she calls out, looking around at everyone standing nearby before her eyes settle on mine. "Xavier knows, don't you, baby? Tell them."

I look to Xavier, but he refuses to meet my gaze, his eyes fixed on the fire as my skin prickles.

"That's enough, Roxy," Archie growls out, but she just laughs louder.

"Oh my gosh, it's like *Parent Trap* or something."

"What the fuck are you going on about, Roxy?" I shout, fed up with her talking in circles instead of getting straight to the point she's clearly trying to make.

"This is fucking brilliant, you really don't know, do you?" She stands from Xavier's lap, who continues to look anywhere but at me as Tobias grips my fingers in a deathly hold and Hunter trembles with anger beside me.

"Know what?" I ask as she comes to stand right in front of me.

"That Archie is your twin."

My what?

She laughs as she spins in a circle, loving the whispers that follow from bystanders.

My eyes burn into the side of Xavier's head, waiting for him to look at me. Who told him that bullshit? Glancing at Archie, I stall as his blue eyes meet mine, filled with guilt.

Wrenching my hand from Tobias', I step from between them and move to stand before Archie.

"You knew," I state as he swipes a hand over his face, offering me nothing. Blood burns in my veins, anger boiling beneath the surface as tears prick my eyes."You fucking knew," I cry, pushing at his chest, but he doesn't move.

"Cookie, I…"

"Don't fucking call me that. Don't you dare. How could you?" I push against his chest, panting with each ragged breath I take, and he does nothing. "Say it. Fucking. Say. It," I growl out as arms wrap around me from behind, stopping me from taking my anger and frustration out on him.

"I knew."

Of course he did. I fucking… God, I can't deal with this shit. My mind is swirling with so much, I want to curl up in a ball and cry, but not here. They've seen enough of my emotion.

"Let go of me," I say calmly, and Hunter turns me to face him, concern and surprise etched across his face, and I scoff. If Xavier fucking told Roxy, then he obviously told his brothers, their act won't work on me. "Get your filthy, lying ass hands off me."

Moving to the side, I find everyone watching me, waiting for me to break down, but I won't. Xavier finally meets my gaze, no emotion on his face, and I'm desperate to know what changed in the hours since I last saw him. But none of it matters now, not anymore.

Moving towards Xavier before I can overthink it, I shoulder past Roxy, stopping in front of him.

"You're fucking dead to me," I growl out, staring him down as I lean into his space, my hands braced on the chair as I do.

"Welcome to Knight's Creek, Eden Freemont."

EPILOGUE

Fuck these assholes. Fuck them all.

Trust no one. Trusting fucking no one.

My mom was right—Xavier Knight is as vile as his mother, tearing everyone down without a care in the world.

Grabbing a bottle of vodka from the liquor wall, I rush to my room, the sound of someone calling my name from behind me doing nothing to stop my feet from covering as much ground as possible.

Unlocking my bedroom door, I slam it shut behind me,

turning the lock quickly before I make sure the balcony doors are locked and draw the curtains.

I don't want to see anyone. Not a fucking soul right now. I want to be left alone.

Stepping into my bathroom, I make sure to lock that door too.

Climbing into the empty tub, my phone in one hand and the vodka in the other, I finally let the tears fall. My heart tears in two, and so many unanswered questions swirl in my mind. How many more secrets are there?

Who the fuck are my mom and dad? *Who the hell am I?*

Swiping at my cheeks, the tears continue to fall, and I scream, letting my lungs burn as I try to get out all my anger.

I don't know how long I sit there for, fully clothed in an empty bath, screaming like my life depends on it, but the taste of vodka makes it all better.

Unlocking my phone, I'm not surprised that no one has attempted to call or text. The damage has been done. I'm all alone. Again.

As if clicking my own self-destruct button, my fingers swipe across the screen of my phone, pulling up the link I've refused to look at, until now.

EDEN GRADY'S OBITUARY

Eden Grady, officially born as Eden Freemont, seventeen, of Knight's Creek, California, unexpectedly passed away on September 3rd as a result of suffocation after being buried alive.

She was predeceased by her parents, Carl Grady and Anabel Freemont, and is survived by her twin brother, Archie Freemont, also of Knight's Creek.

She should never have been more than a cum shot to the back of the throat. May you rot in hell, along with your father. Jennifer Grady shall be right behind you.

TOXIC CREEK

AFTERWORDS

I motherfucking did it!

I wrote another damn book! Woohoo!

You know I love to leave us wanting more, and here's hoping I did just that. Don't be mad. LOL

This story was supposed to have a different ending, and a different under theme for Eden, yet they chose to tell their own story, allowing me to join the ride. But I love it. Every inch of this book, even as a writer, had me on the edge of my seat wondering what on earth was going to come next!

So, the real question is; Xavier, Hunter, Tobias, or why choose?

The balls in your court. Come tell me in my readers group!

Roll on July 9th

THANK YOU

My partner and children have been my rocks as always. In between moving, getting a new puppy, and just about rearranging our whole lives they have supported me as always. Thank you for being my awesome nerds.

Valerie Swope. My other half, partner in crime, and biggest cheerleader! Thank you for helping me through the whole process. You're there from start to finish every time, and I couldn't do it without you! Ride or die for life!

My fabulous Beta reader's <3 Hope, Monica, Catherine, Amy, and Jessi <3 I love you all so much. I appreciate how you offer your time to make my books extra awesome, and the input you give is always next level. Thank you for being the coolest of cool.

Cassie, you got me on the co-dependent sprinting scene, and I can't ever leave. I hope you enjoy my needy ass for all eternity!

Thank you to Bellaluna Designs for the most stunning cover!

Laura, thank you for convincing her I was nice enough to snatch such a beautiful model LOL

Meredith, thank you for being hot as hell, you are fabulous!

ABOUT KC KEAN

KC Kean is the sassy half of a match made in heaven. Mummy to two beautiful children, Pokemon Master and Apex Legend world saving gamer.

Starting her adventure in the RH romance world after falling in love with it as a reader, who knows where this crazy train is heading. As long as there is plenty of steam she'll be there.

ALSO BY KC KEAN

Featherstone Academy

(Reverse Harem Contemporary Romance)

My Bloodline

Your Bloodline

Our Bloodline

Red

Freedom

All-Star Series

(Reverse Harem Contemporary Romance)

Toxic Creek

Tainted Creek

Twisted Creek

ations.

TOXIC CREEK